The Angel Maker

MARCIA CLAYTON

ISBN: 978-1-8383259-5-4

Published by Sunhillow Publishing

All characters and events in this publication, other than those clearly in the public domain, are fictitious, and any resemblance to real persons, living or dead, is purely coincidental. Any herbal remedies described in this publication are fictitious and should not be used under any circumstances.

For Bryan, Stuart and David,
and, of course, in memory of Paul Michael Clayton

Also by Marcia Clayton

The Hartford Manor Series

Betsey: The Prequel

The Mazzard Tree

The Angel Maker

The Rabbit's Foot

Millie's Escape

A Woman Scorned

ACKNOWLEDGEMENTS

Thank you to my husband, Bryan, for his patience and encouragement and also my sons Stuart, Paul and David for their help along the way.

To Bryan, my sister, Gill, and my niece, Sharon, for being the first people to read my book and provide constructive criticism and support.

To my talented daughter-in-law, Laura, for producing a fantastic cover for the book, and to Stuart for helping me to publish this book on Amazon.

Last, but not least, the biggest thank you goes to my readers. I have received some wonderful messages from readers who have told me how much they have enjoyed my books. Each and every review and message encourage me to continue writing. A simple message, particularly from a stranger, saying they loved my story helps to dispel my doubts over my ability as an author. I can't tell you how much those lovely messages mean to me.

Thank you.

The Main Characters of Hartford

The Carter Family

EDWARD CARTER (b1812)
Married **BETSEY LOVERING** (b1814)

Their children:

1. **EVELINE CARTER** (b1837)

2. **GEORGE CARTER** (b1840)
   Married Alice Brown (1840 - 1880)
   Their children:
- Harriet (b1860)
- Francis (b1862)
- Alfred (1865 – 1869)
- Theresa (b1868)
  Married (2) Mary Ann Brown (b1848)
  Their child:
- Nellie (b1883)

3. **FREDERICK CARTER** (b1841)
   Married **LUCY FULLER** (1843 - 1881)
   Their children:
- Llewellyn (b1872)
- Rosella (b1876)
- Alfie (1877 – 1877)
- Grace (1879 – 1879)
- Eddie (b1880)

4. **TOM CARTER** (1841 - 1880)
   Married **SABINA BAILEY** (b1846)
   Their children:
- **ANNIE** (b1864) married Harry Rudd (1851 – 1881)
- Mabel (1866 – 1866)
- Willie (b1869)
- Mary (b1871)
- John (b1872 - 1880)
- Emma (b1874 - 1880)
- Edward (b1876)
- Stephen (b1878)

- Helen (b1880)
- Danny (b1880) Foundling (Son of Charles and Eleanor Fellwood)

5. **WILLIAM CARTER** (1845 - 1881)
   Married Lottie Chang (1850 – 1880)
   Their children:
- Identical twins Joseph (b1875) Matthew (b1875)
- Amelia (b1876)
  Married (2) **SARAH MARTIN** (b1845)
  Their son:
- Bentley (b1882)

The Fellwood Family of Hartford Manor

LORD CHARLES FELLWOOD (b1825)
Married: **ELEANOR CHICHESTER** (b1838)
Their Children:

- David Fellwood (1861 - 1881)
- Lily Fellwood (1862 – 1864)
- **ROBERT FELLWOOD** (b1863)
- Victoria Fellwood (b1863)
- Sarah Fellwood (b1870)
- Danny (b1880) (Adopted by Sabina Carter)

The Cutcliffe Family

John Cutcliffe
Married (1) Hannah Matthews (1846 - 1880)
Their Children:

- Daisy (b1873)
- Mary (b1874 - 1880)
- Rachael (b1876)
- Tommy (1879 - 1880)

Married (2) **Noeleen Gubb**
Her children:

- Clarice (b1867)
- Ruth (b1869)
- Susanna (b1872)

The Hammett Family

Isaac Hammett (1806 - 1880)
Married: **LIZA JONES** (b1810)

The Chugg Family

ALFRED CHUGG (b1815)
Married **JANE WATTS** (b1820)
12 children - one son still living at home: Jimmy Chugg (b1855)
Brother of Alfred Chugg: **CHARLIE CHUGG** (b1835)

The Rudd Family

Benjamin Rudd (1815 - 1881)
Married **Matilda Yeo** (b1820)
Their children:

- **Harry Rudd** (1851 - 1881) Married Annie Carter (b1864)
- Jacob Rudd (b1855)
- Francis Rudd (b1860)

The Webber Family

Peter Webber (b1815)
Married Mary Jane Watson (1818 – 1866)
Their son:
Arthur Webber (b1836)
Married Drucie Reynolds (1840 – 1866)
Their children:

- Christopher Webber (b1856)
- Dudley Webber (b1858)
- Elsie Webber (b1863)
- Maria Webber (b1866)

CHAPTER 1

Charles Fellwood glared up at his son from his wheelchair. The left side of his mouth drooped slightly, and his withered left arm lay uselessly across the thick blanket draped on his knees. His thin brown hair had receded from his highly domed forehead, and he looked older than his fifty-nine years. His eldest son, David, had died fighting in the Boer War, and that devastating news had brought on a severe stroke, leaving his left side paralysed and his speech impaired. Since that time three years ago, he had used a downstairs room as his bedroom, no longer sharing a bed with his wife, Eleanor.

The wealthy Fellwood family had owned Hartford Manor for generations. The estate covered over two thousand acres, divided into four farms. The home farm was the largest, with around eight hundred acres, and the other farms were smaller and rented out to tenant farmers. Many local men were employed as agricultural labourers or lime burners and lived rent-free in tied farm cottages. Since the death of David, his second son, Robert, had managed the estate, and it was this son who now stood angrily before his father.

His face ashen, Charles was almost incoherent with rage, and spittle flew from his lips. "You will not marry her! I forbid you. She's a common servant."

"I don't care what you think, Father. I shall marry Annie, and soon."

"I'll never give my permission, and I'll take the estate back off you."

"You forget the estate's already been signed over to me, and there's nothing you can do about it. Anyway, you will agree to our marriage when you hear what I have to tell you."

The young man went to the double doors that led into the garden and ushered in a young woman carrying a child. She was slightly built with pale white skin and freckles. Her vivid red hair hung in ringlets almost to her waist, and her eyes were a deep green. She seemed to be extremely nervous. The little girl in her arms was about two years old. Her hair was brown, with auburn highlights which shone in the sun, and she had her mother's green eyes. She buried her head shyly into her mother's neck.

"Father, this is Annie. I expect you remember her from when she worked here? And this is her daughter, Selina." Robert crossed the room to the washstand where a blue and white bowl and pitcher stood. He picked up a bar of white soap, put it to his nose, and inhaled deeply. He smiled at his father, but the smile did not reach his eyes. "Mmm, Sandalwood, I believe it's called; is that right? I know you buy it in London. Nice, isn't it? Annie, come here. Do you like the perfume of this soap?"

Charles Fellwood looked at his son as if he had taken leave of his senses. "What has my soap to do with anything?"

"Quite a lot as it happens."

Annie regarded the soap as if it were evil. She raised it cautiously to her nose and sniffed.

"Is it the same smell?"

She nodded, and Robert turned again to his father. "When Annie worked here, she was attacked and raped. She was grabbed in a dark corridor when she was clearing up after a New Year's Eve party. Someone put their hand over her mouth to keep her quiet and carried her to the West Wing and into the cellars. As you know, that part of the house is unused and the perfect place to be undisturbed."

More colour drained from his father's face. "So, what has it to do with me?"

"Annie didn't know who attacked her because she was also beaten. She was stunned, and it was dark. The only clue she had was the perfume the man wore, and now it seems it's the same as your soap."

"There would have been many guests present that night, and several must have used that same soap. It's not uncommon, and as you've said, we'd had a party. This doesn't prove I had anything to do with it."

"No, it doesn't, but it is significant, especially considering the other evidence. You see, Annie was left pregnant by the encounter and was then sacked by Miss Wetherby for her loose morals. This little girl is the result of what happened that night."

"So why are you telling me all this?"

"Annie, would you be so kind as to undress Selina and let my father see her shoulder, please?"

Annie nodded and started to undress the child. She slipped off her blue cardigan, dress, and bodice and stood the little girl before the old man. An ugly purple birthmark marred her shoulder. It was a strange shape, almost like a crescent moon. Charles Fellwood pursed his lips.

"Yes, that's right, father. It's the same birthmark that my sister, Victoria, has. I see you recognise it. Our old nanny used to say it runs in the family. Now, how could that have gotten onto Selina's shoulder? Let me see." Robert scratched his head theatrically. "Well, my brother, David, was fighting in the Boer War at the time, getting himself killed, and I was at boarding school in

Exeter, so you were the only Fellwood male in the house. Do you still deny this child is yours?"

Annie drew Selina to one side, stepped forward to address the old man and spoke sharply. "Look at me. Was it you? Was it you that raped me?"

"Well, what if it was?" Charles Fellwood suddenly glared at her defiantly. "You'd been flaunting yourself in front of me for weeks. This sort of thing happens all the time to servants, and it was only a bit of fun; you must know that. I had no idea you were with child or that you were dismissed, but what use is this to you now? I'll never let you marry my son."

"I've never flaunted myself at anybody, let alone an old man like you. I'll never forgive you as long as I live, and I hope you rot in hell!" Annie hissed at him furiously and then slapped him hard across the face.

Robert gently led her and the shocked child away from his father. "If you don't consent to our marriage, I'll tell Mama about this. I'll be twenty-one in May, and then I can marry whom I like, but it would look better to have your approval."

"Surely you wouldn't tell your mother, Robert? Think how much it would upset her."

"Oh, I'm afraid I would. You didn't worry how much you hurt Annie, did you? If this is not enough to convince you, I have another surprise for you today." Robert went to the doors again and called out.

"Willie, are you there? Can you bring Danny in, please?"

Annie's younger brother, Willie, appeared, leading a little boy by the hand. The child was about four years old and had dark curly hair and big brown eyes. He looked around in wonder at the grandeur of the room. His top lip was split up to his nose, and both feet turned inwards, one worse than the other, giving him a strange lopsided gait as he walked.

Charles Fellwood's eyes narrowed as he stared at Robert. "It's not …? It's not …?"

"Yes, it is, father. I've brought your youngest son to see you. This is Danny - the son you didn't want. Or, to be fair, the son that Mama didn't want because he wasn't perfect. As you can see, he's thriving, considering the difficulties he has to cope with. See how well Annie's mother looks after him; your money is well spent. Say hello to your son."

"Your mother; she might come in." Charles sounded breathless as he glanced anxiously at the door.

"No, it's all right, don't panic. She's visiting one of her friends this afternoon and won't return for a few hours yet. Now, I know this is blackmail, and I'm not proud of myself, but if you don't consent to our marriage, I'll ask Annie and Selina, Willie and Danny to stay here and meet Mama when she returns home. We might as well get this over with. I wonder what she'll say."

Charles Fellwood lowered his head briefly, then raised his eyes and looked coldly at his son. "I don't have much choice, do I? I've no idea how your mother will ever understand my apparent approval of your marriage. You do realise the gentry will shun you if you proceed with this relationship? And you, young lady, you may think that by marrying my son, you will never want again, but I can assure you it will not be like you think. You won't know how to behave or dress; you won't be accepted in society, and quite frankly, life will be difficult for you."

"That's our worry, Father, not yours. I don't care if the aristocracy ignores me; to be honest, that would almost be a bonus. I hate all the dressing up and the pretence that surrounds our life. As for Annie, well, I'm sure we can find someone to help her with the correct etiquette and dress sense, though as you've already pointed out, we're unlikely to be asked anywhere socially, anyway. If people want to come here, they must accept our marriage. As for Mama, you're right; I know she won't like it. That is a pity, but I love Annie, and she loves me, and I will not ruin our chance of happiness for the sake of appearances."

"Go, go now, before your mother comes home; please take these people away. She must not see them. Seeing these children and knowing what I've done would destroy our marriage. If only David were alive, none of this would be happening."

"No, it wouldn't, and I wish he were here too, but I would still want to marry Annie. We will go now. I would say I'm sorry to have upset you, but given what you did to Annie, I'm afraid I can't even pretend that I am. Just be aware, though, that I intend to announce our engagement at my and Victoria's twenty-first birthday party in a month. I'll need to tell Mama before that, so make sure you support me when I do. I can easily bring Selina and Danny back if I have to."

His father nodded and waved them away wearily.

As they left the Manor House, Annie and Robert walked ahead of Willie, who was leading Danny and Selina by the hand. Willie took his time, allowing his sister some privacy, for he knew she was upset. He had to walk slowly anyway, as Danny couldn't walk very fast. It was early April, and the boy helped the children gather primroses for his mother, Sabina. Willie was fifteen and a farm labourer on old Mr Houle's farm where he lived in, but today was his weekly half-day off, and he was pleased to help Annie and Robert.

Robert was delighted that the awkward meeting with his father was over and pleased they were one step closer to marriage. However, Annie was anxious. She still didn't believe she would ever be allowed to marry Robert, the son and heir of the Lord of Hartford Manor.

"Well, that's the hardest part over. Let's tell your mum and Liza now."

Before his death, Annie's father, Tom Carter, had been a labourer on the Hartford estate, living in a small cottage with his wife, Sabina, and their seven children. Tom suffered from consumption, and as his illness progressed, it became ever harder to hold down his job.

There were seven dwellings in the hamlet where they lived, all tied cottages with the inhabitants working on the estate in one way or another. Liza Hammett and her husband, Isaac, a childless couple in their seventies, lived a few doors from the Carters. Isaac just managed to earn a living as a rat catcher and handyman on the estate to enable him to keep a roof over their heads. However, one night, during a violent storm, a large oak tree was blown down in the wind, crushing their cottage roof and trapping Isaac in his bed as he lay sleeping. Somehow, the tree missed Liza, and she crawled to safety and summoned help. Annie's father, Tom, and other neighbours did all they could to save Isaac, but although they managed to free him from the wreckage, he died the next day. Unfortunately, exposure to the icy elements that night caused Tom Carter to become seriously ill with pneumonia, and with his body already weakened by consumption, he, too, had died within days, leaving his wife Sabina bereft.

In the days that followed, Sabina had been beside herself with worry. The cottage they lived in came with Tom's job, and she knew it would be needed for a new worker. Soon to be homeless and with no income, she feared they would all have to go into the workhouse. However, Liza Hammett suggested a solution that she thought might help them all. She offered to move in with Sabina and look after the children to allow their mother to continue working on the estate and keep a roof over their heads. The arrangement had worked well, though the work had been incredibly hard for Sabina, especially when she discovered she was pregnant with her ninth child.

Sabina and Liza were surprised to see Robert openly accompany Annie home, for they knew nothing of the recent encounter at the Manor House.

"Hello, Mum, Robert and I need to tell you something. Could you send the children out to play for a while? They shouldn't hear this yet."

"I've got a few spare coppers in my pocket. How about Willie takes you to Mrs Scott's shop in the village to buy some sweets?" Robert was rewarded with broad smiles, and Annie's siblings went off happily with their elder brother.

Liza reached for her shawl. "I'll go for a little walk as well and give you some time alone with your mother."

"No, don't go, Liza. We're happy for you to hear what we have to say. If it weren't for you, we'd all be in the workhouse." Annie bit her lip nervously. "Mum, we know who raped me and who Selina's father is."

"How have you found that out after all this time? She'll be three in a few months."

"Actually, we've known for some time, Mum. It was Robert's father, Charles Fellwood."

"What! No, surely not. You must be mistaken."

"No, there's no mistake, Sabina. The birthmark on Selina's shoulder runs in our family, and my father was the only male Fellwood at home at the time of the attack. We've just taken Selina to see him, and when we confronted him, he admitted it."

"We waited until now because I wanted to leave a respectful time after Harry's death. I didn't love him, but I was fond of him, and it was so kind of him to marry me, considering my condition. I'll always be grateful to him for that, and I'm so sorry he died in the way he did."

Sabina sat down unsteadily. "Your parents will never allow it, Robert; I've always said so."

"They've no choice, Sabina. The estate was formally signed over to me recently, and it's too late for my father to change that. That's also why we've had to wait until now. I've told him that if he doesn't give his blessing to our marriage, I'll show Selina's birthmark to Mama and tell her where Danny is living. Father is horrified, but there's nothing he can do about it. My twin sister, Victoria, and I are twenty-one next month, and after that, we can marry whomever we like anyway. I know my mother will be furious, but it will help if my marriage has my father's approval."

"I don't know what to say, Robert. I think the world of you and any mother would be proud to have you as a son-in-law, but how could this work? Where would you live?"

"Annie and I will live in the Manor House, of course. It may be a bit awkward, but that's a small price to pay for us to be together; we've waited so long. I'm glad you mentioned living arrangements, though, because you will no longer be able to live here." He turned to face Annie. "I'm sorry, I haven't even told you this yet."

"What do you mean? Surely you won't turn us out?"

"No, of course not, but I can hardly have my future mother-in-law working on my estate, milking the cows, and living in a farm worker's cottage, can I? I've given this a lot of thought, and I think the best thing is for you to move into the old Lodge House at the entrance to the Manor House driveway. Do you know the place, I mean? It was used as a gatehouse in years gone by. It's rather dilapidated because it's not been lived in for years, but we can get it repaired, and that would be quicker than building a new house. What do you think? Would it be suitable?"

Sabina's mouth had dropped open, but Annie had a wide smile. "That would be incredible. Mum, you'd love it there. Say something."

"I … I … don't know what to say. I'm just so shocked. I can't take it all in. The Lodge House is huge and so grand. We couldn't possibly live there. What would people say?"

"I think most people would be delighted for you, and the rest of them don't matter. I'll get the key from Jack Bater, and we'll look around to see if it's suitable. Keep all this to yourself for now, and get used to the idea. I'll also tell him he must find someone else to do your job."

Robert smiled at the three women. "It will all be fine, you'll see, though things will never be quite the same for any of you again, but that's no bad thing as far as I can see."

CHAPTER 2

A few days later, Robert met with his parents in the drawing room. His father was in his wheelchair, and his mother, Eleanor, was sitting on a sofa doing some embroidery. She was a handsome woman with dark brown curly hair and brown eyes. As tall as her husband, she was of statuesque build but still slim despite having borne six children, and she wore a light blue dress, elegant in its simplicity. His father looked ill with worry, but his mother smiled as her son entered the room.

"Ah, there you are, Robert. This is rather intriguing. What do you want to talk to us about? Is it about your birthday celebrations? I've been considering that, and we need to make plans."

"Yes, it is about my birthday, but I have some other news I need to tell you first. Mama and Papa, I intend to marry soon, and I want to announce my engagement at my and Victoria's birthday party in May."

"That truly is a surprise, Robert; I had no idea you were seeing any young ladies. Whom do you wish to marry?"

"I'm afraid this will be a big shock for you, Mama, but I've fallen in love with a girl in the village. In fact, before her first marriage, she was a servant in this house."

Eleanor gasped, and Charles looked uncomfortable; his pale face lost yet more colour and took on a ghastly sheen.

"I'm sorry, Mama. I know this is a surprise, but I hope you can give us your blessing."

"Don't be ridiculous, Robert. You're the heir to the Hartford estate, and there is no way you can marry a common village girl. Have you taken leave of your senses? Charles, say something, for goodness sake."

"It would be rather unconventional, Robert, and not something I would encourage. It is far better to marry someone of your own class. I'm sure there are plenty of young ladies who would be interested."

"Is that all you have to say? That it would be unconventional? The marriage is out of the question. Tell him you will not allow it."

"I'm sorry you feel that way, Mama, and I thought you might, but you see, once I'm twenty-one, I can marry whom I like. I don't need your permission, though I would like your blessing."

"You'll never get it. And as for the estate, well, if you persist with this foolishness, it will have to pass to Victoria instead of you."

"It's too late for that, Mama. The estate has already been signed over to me, and neither of you can change that. I'm sorry, I really am, because I don't want to upset you over this, but I love Annie. I'm sure you would like her if you would meet her."

"I am not receiving a village girl in this house. It's out of the question, particularly a former servant. If it's the girl I'm thinking of, didn't Miss Wetherby sack her for some reason? Charles, I can't believe you have nothing to say. Surely, you can't approve of this?"

"I'm afraid Robert is right, my dear. The estate is now legally his, and once he's twenty-one, he can marry whomever he likes. It's not what I would have wished for him, but there is nothing we can do. Perhaps we should meet the girl and make the best of it?"

Eleanor could not believe what she was hearing from her husband. He had always been so strong-minded, even since his stroke, and this was not like him. "I can't believe you're willing to accept this, Charles. Wait, did you already know of this? You don't seem surprised."

"I had mentioned it to him, Mama, and I know he's not happy with the situation, but he knows there is nothing he can do about it."

"We'll see about that. I shall visit Mr Billery at the bank to see if the estate can pass to Victoria instead of you."

"Do that if you must, but I've been managing the estate since Papa's stroke, and as I come of age in a few weeks, Mr Billery has already completed all the necessary paperwork, and it's been formally signed over to me. If you remember, you signed the forms yourself a few weeks ago. It was dealt with early, as there was no reason not to."

Eleanor was furious, not only with Robert but also with her husband. She could not believe he was accepting this. "I don't know where you intend to live with this girl, Robert, but it will not be in this house."

"I'm afraid it will be in this house, Mama, because it's mine now, and if you want to continue to live here, you must agree to receive her."

Charles quickly intervened. "Robert, please leave us now and let us discuss this. It's been a great shock for your mother. Give us some space before we all say things we might later regret."

"Very well, but I'll be bringing Annie to this house soon, and I will not have her upset. If you feel you can no longer live here after our marriage, then you must consider moving elsewhere, though I hope it will not come to that. I'm going to tell Sarah my news now, and I'll write to Victoria later. I might as well also tell you that I'm going to move Annie and her family into the Lodge House. It's stood empty for years, but it would be perfect for them. I'll get the key from Jack later and see what work needs to be done. I'm sure you can see that it's hardly appropriate for my future wife's family to live in a farm worker's cottage. I will also tell you that Annie was married before, and her late husband died in a fire. She has a small daughter called Selina, who is nearly three, and I hope she'll also be living here eventually." He held up his hands before either parent could speak. "All right, I'll leave you now because I know you're upset, but we will need to arrange a time for you to meet Annie soon."

As Robert left the room, Eleanor rounded on her husband.

"I can't believe you're just going to accept this, Charles. It's not like you."

"As I said, unfortunately, we can do nothing about it. Robert has chosen his timing carefully and knows he has the law on his side."

"If only David had not been so stupid as to run away and join the army, none of this would have happened. He would have inherited, and that would have been that."

"I'm sure David didn't plan to get killed in South Africa, my dear, but even if that had not happened, I think Robert would still have wanted to marry this girl. If you remember, we sent him back to school early because we could see he was infatuated with her when she worked here. He's been keen on her for a long time."

"He should know that a man in his position can't always have what he wants. There are standards to maintain, and people in our class seldom marry for love. Indeed, I hardly knew you when we married."

"Well, it's not worked out so bad, has it?"

"No, of course not, and that's just my point. He could easily marry a more suitable girl and come to love her."

"Talk to Tom Billery at the bank, by all means, but I think you'll find our hands are tied. I was always reluctant to let Robert run the estate because he has such a soft heart, and I thought he'd run us into debt, but I understand from Jack that he's making an excellent job of it, and we made an impressive profit last year."

Before his stroke, Charles had taken little interest in the estate, preferring to leave the day-to-day running of it to his manager, Jack Bater. David, too, had not wanted the responsibility of his inheritance, as he had always longed to join the army. However, Robert took after his late grandfather, Joshua, and knew and loved every inch of the countryside and house and took a keen interest in everything. Following David's untimely death, Robert took over the management of the estate despite the fact he was only eighteen. He enjoyed working with Jack, and together, they made many improvements. The tied farm cottages had been in a shocking state of repair. The roofs needed thatching, and the windows leaked. Charles Fellwood had refused to spend money on them for several years, but they were now fully refurbished. The farm workers had been given a slight wage increase, again something that had not happened for many years. Robert reaped the benefit of these actions, for the workers appreciated what he had done for them, and they worked hard in return. Their health improved once the cottages were no longer damp and draughty, and fewer deaths had occurred.

Leaving his parents, Robert searched for his youngest sister, Sarah, who was becoming quite the young lady at fourteen. She was taught at home by her governess, Jane Leworthy. Not having any school friends, Sarah had missed the company of her sister, Victoria, since her marriage, and she now spent a lot of time with her friend, Mabel, who lived nearby. Robert found Sarah in the stables, just dismounting from her pony, Jenny. She was a plain girl with long brown hair, which she wore in plaits.

"Hello, Robert, are you going for a ride? I've just been for miles over the moors, and it was wonderful. The gorse is in full bloom, and it looks amazing. You should get out there."

"Yes, I might later, and I'm glad you've had a pleasant ride. I hope you told someone where you were going; I don't like you going out alone."

"Oh, rubbish. I'm an experienced rider, but yes, I told Dodger where I was going, didn't I, Dodger?"

The stable boy took the horse from the young girl to rub it down. "Yes, she did tell me where she was going, sir, and she's an excellent rider."

"Well, make sure she always tells you, Dodger, good rider or not, accidents can happen."

"Aye, sir, I'll be sure to ask her." The young man led the horse away.

"I have some news to tell you, Sarah. I'm getting engaged on my birthday and plan to marry soon."

"Are you? I didn't know you were even seeing anyone. Who is it?"

"This has been a huge shock for Mama and Papa, but I'm going to marry Annie Carter. She used to work here. Do you remember her? She is a pretty girl with bright red curly hair and green eyes."

"My goodness, yes, I do remember her, but wasn't she sacked for getting pregnant?"

"Yes, she was, and she married Harry Rudd, but he was killed in a fire at the smithy a couple of years ago. She has a little girl called Selina."

"I can't see Mama and Papa ever agreeing to you marrying a servant, Robert. Are you sure about this?"

"Fortunately, they'll have no choice once I'm twenty-one, so I only have to wait until next month. The estate is already legally mine, so there's nothing they can do, but you're right, and they're furious. What do you think? Do I have your support? I love Annie, Sarah, so I hope you'll be nice to her?"

"Hey, if you love her, that's good enough for me, but I can see lots of problems ahead. Yes, of course, I'll be nice to her, and if there's anything I can do to help, just tell me, though I expect it will get me into trouble with Mama and Papa. Congratulations; I'm pleased for you. Now come here and give me a hug."

Robert embraced her warmly. "That means so much to me. You're the first person I've told who is pleased for me. If I tell you a secret, will you promise to keep it to yourself?"

"Of course; when have I ever let you down?"

"Do you remember that day, in the nursery, when we looked out of the upstairs window and saw a boy crawling along the path, dragging a sack of vegetables behind him? He thought by keeping low, no one could see him over the hedge."

"Yes, of course. It was raining, and he was covered in mud. We kept watch for days, but we never saw him again."

"Well, not long after that, you broke your ankle and were out of action, but I lay in wait for a couple of mornings to see if I could catch him, and I did."

"Oh, you meanie, you never said. I'd have liked to know that."

"I know, and I felt guilty not telling you, but the thing is, it wasn't a boy; it was a girl, and it was Annie."

"What! So not only do you want to marry a servant, but she's also a thief? This gets better and better."

"No, she's not a thief. Well, technically, I suppose she is, but she was only stealing vegetables because her family was starving. Her father had died of consumption, and her mother had seven children to feed and another on the way."

"Fair enough, though, I doubt Papa would see it that way."

"No, I know he wouldn't, and that's why you have to keep it a secret and tell no one. Anyway, I've been friendly with Annie and her family ever since. I would have liked to marry her before, but then she married Harry Rudd, and it was impossible. Sadly, for him, he died, but at least I can marry her now."

"Well, it's certainly going to be interesting around here. When can I meet her?"

"As soon as Mama and Papa can bring themselves to see her. I'm giving them some time to get used to the idea, but I'm going to write to Victoria now to tell her. I'll see you later." He kissed his little sister on the cheek and went to the library.

Robert's sister, Victoria, was his twin, though they were not alike. Whereas Robert had brown hair like his mother and younger sister, Victoria had raven black hair and was something of a beauty. She was not as tall as Robert and, since motherhood, had put on some weight, leaving her a little plump. Robert had been a skinny youth when he left school. However, the hard physical labour of working on the farm every day had honed his body, and strong muscles were now visible beneath his shirt.

Victoria had been married to Frank Eastleigh for a couple of years. He was a rich and handsome young man, and they lived in London. They had one daughter of eighteen months, called Caroline, and Victoria was now pregnant again with her second child. She was to return home to celebrate her joint birthday with Robert in May and planned to stay at Hartford Manor to await the birth in July. Robert and Frank had been friends since childhood, but on a visit to the Manor when Annie was working there, Frank made a pass at her, and he and Robert fought. There had been tension between them ever since, and, at first, Annie had suspected it was Frank who had raped her. However, Robert had confronted him about the attack, and Frank was so adamant it had nothing to do with him that Robert believed him. The relationship between the two men remained strained, though both had made an effort since his marriage to Victoria.

Robert sat in a chair by the window and selected some notepaper. He started to pen a letter to his sister and hoped she would react positively.

CHAPTER 3

After breaking the news of his forthcoming marriage, Robert kept out of his parents' way for the next week or so. It would not have surprised him if they had chosen to leave the house and turn their backs on him. He took his meals in the kitchen, where, in truth, he was more comfortable and enjoyed the easy company of Mrs Potts, the elderly cook, who had always spoilt him. The servants wondered what was going on but, of course, dared not ask.

Finally, he decided to find out whether his parents would meet Annie and presented himself for the evening meal. As he entered the dining room, he could immediately sense the hostile atmosphere, and it was clear his parents were barely speaking to each other. He sat down quietly, allowed the servants to serve the meal in silence, and then asked them to leave the room.

"Mama and Papa, I know you're both upset, but we need to discuss this. Have you come to terms with my news?"

"I'll never come to terms with your marriage plans, Robert, and I simply can't understand why your father does not have more to say on the subject. If it were practical for us to leave this house and live elsewhere, I would do that tomorrow, but unfortunately, it's not so easy. Your father is disabled and needs full-time nursing; arranging that elsewhere would be difficult. I've seen Tom Billery, and he has confirmed that the estate now formally belongs to you, and you will be free to marry whom you choose after your birthday. I'm extremely disappointed in your lack of compassion where we are concerned."

"You may not believe me, Mama, but I am genuinely sorry this is so difficult for you. However, I have been giving this some thought. This is a large house, and I think day to day, we would need to see little of each other. I, too, went to see Mr Billery the other day to go through the accounts, and he was pleased to tell me that the estate is showing a remarkable profit, so some of my ventures are working. I suggest we refurbish the West Wing, and Annie and I will live there. We would keep mostly to ourselves, and you and Papa would notice little change. What do you think?"

"That may be a compromise. What do you think, Eleanor? I know this is not what we would have chosen for Robert, but we must find a way to live under one roof. I was born here and don't want to leave the house; the Fellwood family has lived on this land since before the Domesday Book was written."

"I suppose it might be one way to make the best of a bad situation, though I suspect many of our friends will suddenly find they have other engagements and not want to come here once that girl's background is revealed."

Robert was encouraged that his mother was even willing to talk to him. "That's settled then. I'll survey the West Wing and see what needs doing, and then we can get the work started. I must ask, though, would you please both meet Annie? I'm sure you would like her if you would get to know her, but that's not the only reason. The servants will find this situation surprising, and one or two will be uncomfortable. Your housekeeper, Miss Wetherby, for one, because she unjustly sacked Annie for becoming pregnant when, in fact, she had been taken against her will by someone in this house."

"I didn't know that."

"I think there are probably quite a few things that go on in this house that you're unaware of, Mama." He glanced at his father, who was shuffling uncomfortably and staring intently at the ground. "What's important is that as far as the servants are concerned, everything is fine. We don't want them gossiping."

Charles grimaced. "I think that will be impossible to avoid, but I agree we must at least meet the girl. Eleanor, my dear, can you bring yourself to do that? It needn't be for long, and if we include Sarah, that might make it a bit easier."

His wife bit her lip and looked dismayed but nodded. "Make it as short a meeting as possible, Robert, and tell the girl to keep out of my way in the future."

"Thank you. I'm sure we can make this work if we all try, and who knows, in time, you might come to like Annie."

He left the Manor House in high spirits and went to tell Annie the excellent news. However, Annie was horrified. "Oh no, I can't. I can't meet your parents. They must hate me."

"Annie, if you want to be my wife, things must change, and you must do this. There will be things you won't want to do and will feel uncomfortable with, but if you want to spend your life with me, that's what you'll have to do. You don't need to worry, though, because I'll be there with you every step of the way, and Sarah is looking forward to your company. It will be all right. Now, do you have anything suitable to wear?"

"Goodness, no! The only decent dress I have is the one I wore to the Christmas party when I worked at the Manor, and that once belonged to your sister, Victoria, so I can't wear that one. All my others are far too shabby."

"It doesn't matter. I'll take you to Exeter to buy some. We could go on the train tomorrow if you like?"

Annie stared at him in amazement, for she had never been on a train nor ever expected to. She had also never had anyone want to buy not just one dress for her but several, and she suddenly realised how much her life would change.

"That does sound exciting, and I would like to do that one day, but for now, could we just buy some material and ask my Aunty Evie to make me a dress? She's an excellent dressmaker; I expect it would only take her a week or two. Would that be too long?"

"No, if that's what you want. Shall we buy some material from your Uncle George's shop?"

"It would certainly surprise him if I turned up there with you, but shouldn't we keep this quiet until after I've met your parents?"

"It's going to get out soon enough, but yes, I suppose so. Shall I give you some money, and you can go there with your Aunty Eveline?"

"Yes, that would be better, but I'll have to tell her. Is that all right?"

"Yes, of course. Here's some money, but let me know if it's not enough. Ask her to make you two dresses, and they will do until we can visit Exeter."

The Carter family had lived in Hartford for generations, many running The Red Lion Inn, where Annie's grandparents, Ned and Betsey, were now the innkeepers. They had been blessed with five children: one daughter called Eveline and four sons, George, Fred, Annie's father, Tom, and William. The eldest, Eveline, was now in her late forties and had never married.

George Carter ran the grocery and drapery store in the village. As the eldest son, he had been set up in the business by his father, Ned. At first, he had sold only groceries, but in recent years, he had expanded his range to include clothes and shoes. Until recently, Eveline had worked in the shop with him and had been a real asset, coming up with many ideas to improve the business. George was a hard worker, intent on making money. He was strictly religious and taught in the Sunday school at the Baptist Chapel. He was on the parish Board of Guardians and was heavily involved in managing the workhouse and distributing poor relief. He was teetotal and abhorred drunkenness, somewhat at odds with his father's profession of running the local inn.

George had three surviving children from his first marriage: Harriet, Francis, and Theresa. His first wife, Alice, had died of diphtheria, and though he missed her, it had not taken him long to turn his attention to his wife's younger sister, Mary Ann, who worked in the shop with him. After a respectable length of time had passed, they married. Their daughter, Nellie, was eighteen months old, and Mary Ann was due to give birth to her second child in August. In truth, George would have preferred not to start a second family at his age, but his attempts to avoid this had been unsuccessful, and Mary Ann was enjoying motherhood.

Eveline was amazed at the news of her niece's forthcoming engagement, though she knew Annie and Robert had been fond of each other for years, and she was more than willing to make the dresses.

"I hope it works out for you, Annie, but it won't be easy. The dresses might take me a while, though. You know how busy I am looking after Fred's and William's children."

"Yes, I know. I don't know how you manage with six of them."

"I can't pretend it's easy, but they're getting older now. I love them all to bits, so it's not a problem. Besides, Fred is as good as gold and helps out a lot, and what else could we do under the circumstances?"

"No, I know. With Fred's wife, Lucy, I suppose she couldn't help becoming mentally ill, though it was awful that she smothered two of her babies, but I think what William's wife, Sarah, did was even worse."

"Yes, I feel the same. Lucy couldn't help herself, and she died a terrible death in that asylum, poor girl, but as for Sarah, I'd still like to give her a good hiding for abandoning William's children in London. If that friend of William's hadn't happened to call at the inn to see Mum and Dad, we would never have known what had happened to them. Have you seen how she struts around the village now with William's baby?"

"Yes, I've seen her. Bentley's a lovely little boy, though, isn't he? I think he looks exactly like William."

"Yes, he does, though I tend to ignore her whenever I see her. Anyway, about these dresses, I only have Eddie at home with me now that all the others are at school, so it should be all right as long as we pick a fairly simple style. Shall we buy some material tomorrow? Your Uncle George will be surprised at us spending so much money."

Annie couldn't help smiling to herself about the prospect of buying so much material in her uncle's shop. As she left Eveline's house and walked up the path to the front gate, her Uncle George's second wife, Mary Ann, was passing by, pushing her daughter, Nellie, in the pram.

Annie smiled at Mary Ann because although she was not keen on her Uncle George, she had nothing against his wife. "Hello, Mary Ann, how are you keeping?"

"Very well, thanks, Annie, though I must admit pregnancy is more tiring the second time when you already have one child to run around after. This young lady keeps me busy."

"Yes, I can imagine. It's the same with Selina, though I only have her to worry about. Anyway, I'm glad to see you looking so well; bye for now."

CHAPTER 4

There was a dense early morning mist on the first day of May and a distinct chill in the air. However, the hot sun soon burned the fog away, and it promised to be a glorious day. Many villagers had been up since sunrise, for the custom was to gather flowers and branches to decorate their houses, in the belief that the greenery spirits would bring them good fortune. Young girls washed their faces in the morning dew, which was said to make them more beautiful the following year.

During the week, the children in the village had been following the tradition of garlanding. They made hoops out of thin, pliable branches at school and decorated them with flowers, greenery, and crepe paper. The garlands would be displayed at the May Day celebrations, and the vicar would pick the winner.

On the village green, Sam Symons and Richard Bedworth were using a horse to pull the maypole into a vertical position before dropping it into the hole, dug ready to receive it. They quickly filled the earth around the pole and stamped it down hard. The hole was deep enough for the pole to be secure. They walked away from it and stood at a distance to check that it was upright and admired their handiwork. The pole had been freshly painted with white paint, and long red, white, and blue streamers hung from the top and flapped gently in the breeze.

"I think that's it then, Sam. We'd better get the trestle tables from the cellar of The Red Lion next."

"The children will like dancing around that later. Yes, we'd better give Ned a hand; he'll never manage it all on his own."

Richard nodded towards one of the cottage gardens, where Clarice Gubb carefully collected dew from the rhubarb leaves. "I think it'll take more than a drop of dew to make her beautiful, don't you? Mother Nature needs all the help she can get there."

"Now, don't be unkind, Richard; she's a nice girl by all accounts, and they say beauty is only skin deep."

"Aye, that's true, and I hear they're pleased with her at the Manor House."

Clarice's mother, Noeleen Gubb, had married John Cutcliffe a year or so before, and she had two other teenage daughters, Ruth and Susanna, from her previous marriage. Of the three girls, Clarice, the eldest at seventeen, was the least good-looking or had been behind the door when the looks were handed out, as was the local saying. She had recently started work as a kitchen maid at the Manor House, and apart from her terrible acne, she was not a bad-looking girl. Noeleen was John's second wife. His first wife, Hannah, had died a few years earlier in the diphtheria outbreak that had decimated the village's population. He had also lost his young daughter, Mary, and toddler son, Tommy. His other two children, Daisy and Rachael, now aged nine and six, had survived but ended up in the workhouse with no one to look after them whilst John worked.

Hannah and John had been poor parents, and the diphtheria outbreak had started in their house with the death of Mary. Spending what little money they had on cider, their children were half-starved, filthy, and in poor health. Just before the epidemic, their neighbours Sabina and Annie Carter had tried to clean the family up, bathing the children, putting them in clean clothes, and scrubbing the house. Unfortunately, it had all been too little, too late, and John was left a broken man. To the villagers' amusement, John had turned over a new leaf. His second wife was a religious woman and a regular churchgoer and would not tolerate alcohol in the house. So far, John was abiding by the new rules, abstaining from drinking, and attending church every Sunday. Many wondered how long it would last.

John and Hannah had lived in a tied farm cottage on the Hartford Estate, where John worked. However, he had given up this cottage and moved in with Noeleen following their marriage, for her house was bigger and had become her own since her husband's death. Daisy and Rachael were brought home from the workhouse and overjoyed to return to their father. They had been reduced to little more than skin and bone, for the regime in the workhouse was harsh and food scarce. They soon noticed a difference, with Noeleen looking after them. She was a marvellous cook, scrupulously clean and tidy, and kept a tight rein on their father, so they had never had it so good. They began to put on weight, and the roses returned to their cheeks.

Clarice, Ruth, and Susanna carefully let the dew from the rhubarb leaves trickle into a small bowl until they thought they had enough.

"Do you think this will work, Clarice? It seems an awful lot of trouble to go to."

"That's what they say, Ruth. It can't do any harm, and it might get rid of these awful spots. It's worth a try anyway. I'm going to use this rag to put the dew on my face; here's one each for you two."

The girls carefully dabbed the water on their faces, and Susanna grinned at her two elder sisters.

"Who are you two trying to impress then? I know it's Christopher Webber for you, Clarice, but I'm not sure about you, Ruth?"

"I don't know what you mean."

"Yes, you do, Clarice; I've seen you making eyes at him in church. I expect you see him every day at the Manor now you work there. Does he like you?"

"Yes, I must admit I do like him, and he's asked me to go to the May Fair with him today. He's calling for me later. What about you, Ruth? Is there a boy you're keen on?"

"No, not really. Let me put more dew on your spots and see if we can get rid of them." She studied the ugly blemishes on her sister's face. "I hope I don't get any."

With the maypole safely erected, Sam and Richard strolled to The Red Lion Inn, where Ned Carter was sorting through the junk in his cellar. He picked out the long trestle tables that would be used for the villagers to sit around to consume food and drink. Though sprightly for his age, Ned was in his seventies and was glad to see the men.

"Morning, Ned. Can we give you a hand with those tables? They're pretty heavy."

"Yes, thanks, lads, that would be helpful, and with the amount of food Betsey's prepared, we'll need them. What a lovely day, though. We're so lucky after all the rain we've had."

May Day was an important event in the village of Hartford. The children had been practising their maypole dancing at the school for weeks. The result would be a neatly plaited pattern of ribbons around the pole or a tangled mess. Over the years, both results had occurred, so it was anyone's guess. Whilst they were getting the tables out of the cellar, Ned's daughter, Eveline, appeared.

"Good morning, Sam. Good morning, Richard. Thanks for helping Dad with the tables. Dad, don't you go doing too much now; let the younger men do the heavy lifting."

"Ah, don't fuss, lass, I'm all right. It's your mother you want to worry about; she's cooked that much food, and she's exhausted."

"I know; I've come to see how she's getting on. Today will be a good day for business, but I think she needs another servant to help; will you think about it?"

"Aye, I will, and I think you're right; it's time we took things a bit easier. Trouble is servants don't pay themselves, and you know what your mother's like; no one does the job half as well as she does it herself."

"No, I know. I'll see how she's doing, then visit Jane Chugg over at Hollyford Farm. I hear she's poorly. I'll be back later to help with the hog roast, though."

Eveline went through the bar and into the kitchen at the back, where Betsey was setting out pasties on large trays. They smelt delicious, and there were also dozens of sausage rolls. At one end of the long wooden table, a girl was cutting ham sandwiches; at the other, another was preparing cut rounds and cream with strawberry jam on top. "Hello, everyone, this looks wonderful; you have worked hard."

"I think we've almost finished now, thank goodness. Are you staying to help, Evie? And what have you done with the children?"

"No, I can't stay now, Mum. I've left the children with Fred this morning because I'm going to Hollyford Farm to see Jane Chugg; she's very poorly. Have you seen her lately?"

"Yes, a couple of days ago, and she'd taken to her bed, I'm afraid. I don't know what the trouble is, but she's lost weight and always liked her food. According to Alfred, the doctor thinks it might be a growth in her stomach, but he can't be sure. I shall try to get over and see her myself next week.

"All right, I'll tell her and see you later. Can I borrow Bess to ride over?"

Her mother nodded, and Evie went to the stables and saddled up the old horse. She could have walked the couple of miles to Hollyford, but she didn't get the opportunity to ride often these days, and certainly not on such a fine day. The sun was hot by this time, and Evie wished she had put on a hat. The countryside was stunning; the trees were clothed in fresh, vibrant green foliage, and the hedgerows teemed with primroses, violets, and red campion. In the distance, the sea was a startling blue, and she could see three fishing boats making their way out to deeper waters.

Alfred and Jane Chugg had lived at Hollyford Farm for many years and raised twelve children there. The farm was part of the Hartford Estate, and Alfred was a tenant farmer, just as his father and grandfather had been before him. The couple were in their early seventies, and only one son, Jimmy, remained at home. He was in his late thirties and still single. Times were hard in the countryside, with machines stealing much of the work previously done by farm labourers, and many young men had left for the towns in search of employment.

Recently, Alfred's youngest brother, Charlie, had returned home from a life at sea. He had travelled the world, and though he joked that he had a woman in every port, he had never married. He was a cheerful man in his late forties, and Alfred was delighted when he decided to settle down at the farm. They could certainly do with his help, and having been brought up there, Charlie knew what to do without being told. The two brothers were enjoying working together again.

Eveline tethered her horse to a rail outside the back door and knocked. Charlie opened the door and beamed at her. He was a tall, lean man with brown wavy hair and blue eyes, which twinkled when he smiled. His skin was deeply tanned from his travels.

"Hello, Eveline; it's good to see you again. Have you come to see Jane?"

"Hello, Charlie, yes, how is she?" As she gazed into those deep blue eyes, Eveline's stomach did a somersault, and she turned away for fear he would see her reaction.

"Not good, I'm afraid, but she'll be pleased to see you. She doesn't get that many visitors and likes to hear all the gossip."

"I hope you won't be offended, but I made some chicken soup yesterday and brought some for her. I know you aren't short of food here, but I thought she might like a drop."

"That's kind of you; I'm not sure if she'll eat it, but you can try. I'm afraid we're all missing her cooking since she took to her bed. We've taken on Maria Webber to help out, and she's a willing girl, but I'm afraid she isn't much of a cook."

"Oh dear, and you men need to eat plenty with all the work you do. Would you like me to show her how to make something for your dinner while I'm here?"

"If you have the time, it would be much appreciated. It was all right when Jane was up and about and telling her exactly what to do, but she doesn't seem to have much experience. I don't think it helps that her mother died when she was born."

"Right, I'll see Jane first and ask if she wants some soup, and then I can get that on to warm and tell Maria what to do."

Eveline could see that her friend was seriously ill, and even though it was only a week since she had last seen her, the change was remarkable. The weight had fallen from her bones, and her complexion was deathly pale. However, her face lit up with a smile when she saw Eveline. "Hello, Evie, thanks for coming."

"How are you, Jane? Charlie tells me you're not eating much, but I've brought you some chicken soup. Would you try some?"

"That's kind of you, Evie, but I'm afraid I can't eat anything. I don't feel hungry, and if I do eat, it just makes me sick. I can only just keep a sip of water down. I'd like Alfred to have it, though."

She winced as she tried to sit up, and Evie quickly plumped up the pillows behind her. "Are you in pain?"

"Yes, I have a terrible pain here under my ribs. It's been there a while, and I put it down to indigestion, but I can't ignore it anymore. Doctor Luckett's given me laudanum, which certainly helps with the pain, but it puts me straight to sleep. I'll have some when you go, but I wanted to stay awake to talk to you. I'm afraid I'm not long for this world, Evie."

"Oh, Jane, don't say that. You know what they say, where there's life, there's hope."

"Aye, I know, but I've seen too many others like it over the years. It doesn't matter, I've had a good life, and we all have to go sometime. I'll be sorry to leave Alfred and Jimmy on their own, though, and, of course, they won't talk about it."

Evie chatted with Jane for twenty minutes or so. She told her she would help Maria get the men's dinner, and Jane was pleased. She helped the old lady out of bed and onto the commode that Alfred had made and which housed the chamber pot. By the time Eveline got her back to bed, she was exhausted and gritting her teeth to cope with the pain. Eveline went quickly to the washstand and picked up a small brown bottle. She poured a teaspoon of the reddish-brown liquid, and Jane drank it quickly, pulling a face.

"My goodness, that's bitter. Could I have a sip of water, please?"

Eveline made her comfortable and went in search of Maria, whom she found scrubbing the kitchen floor.

The girl was not lazy, for everything was spotlessly clean. Together, they looked in the larder to see what could be cooked for dinner. There was a fresh chicken that Alfred had killed the day before. He had plucked and drawn it, so all it needed was cooking. They found a suitable dish for the bird, sprinkled it with salt and put some water and fresh herbs around it. Eveline instructed Maria to stoke up the old Bodley and cook the chicken for two hours. The cellar had plenty of potatoes, onions, swede, and carrots, so she helped Maria prepare the vegetables and told her how to cook them.

"Now, it should be ready by about one o'clock when the men arrive. Then, all you'll have to do is make the gravy and dish it all up. You can only learn carving by doing it, so don't worry about it; they won't mind if it's rough and ready as long as it's tasty, but you must make sure the chicken is cooked through. Stick a fork in it, and make sure no blood runs out. If it does, put it back in the oven for another quarter of an hour, and then try again. I spotted some apples in the cellar so you could make an apple crumble for a pudding. I can't stay and do it with you, but if I put you going, it should be all right. It's easy. Just peel and slice the apples, cook them gently with a little drop of water until they're soft, and then add sugar until they taste nice."

Evie put some flour and butter into a mixing bowl. "Just rub that in together with your fingers until it looks like breadcrumbs, and then put the cooked apple in a dish, put that on top, and cook it for about half an hour, or until it's brown. Put a dollop of cream on the top, and that should be delicious. All right?"

"Oh, yes, thanks, Evie. No one's ever shown me how to cook. Our Elsie has always done it at home, and I do the cleaning. She's never had the patience to teach me, and anyway, she's working at the Manor House now. Will you show me how to do a few more things the next time you come? I want to be able to look after Mr Chugg and Jimmy and Charlie properly because I know Mrs Chugg worries about it."

"Yes, I'll come again when I can, but I must go now because it's May Day, and my mother will exhaust herself trying to feed the entire village if I don't stop her."

Evie said goodbye to Alfred on her way out. "Jane's very poorly, Alfred."

"Aye, maid, I know what's happening. I'm not blind. I don't know what I'll do without her, though. We've been together over fifty years."

"I'm so sorry, Alfred. I think she needs to take that medicine regularly. She doesn't like to because it knocks her out, but she's in great pain. Why don't you leave the farm work to Charlie and Jimmy for a few days and sit with her a bit more? I think she'd like that."

"There's always such a lot to do, but happen you're right, and the work will still be here when she's gone."

"I'll come again as soon as I can, Alfred. In the meantime, I'm hoping Maria will have cooked you a tasty dinner."

CHAPTER 5

By the time Eveline returned from Hollyford Farm, the May Day festivities were underway. There was dancing on the village green, an archery contest, and some arm wrestling on one of Ned's trestle tables. A group of men surrounded the opponents, shouting encouragement to whichever one they had placed a bet on. Evie knew where her money would go if she were a betting woman: Francis Rudd. Although he was only a young man in his teens, Francis was as strong as an ox and well-suited to his job as a village blacksmith.

Following a terrible fire two years earlier, Francis had worked hard to rebuild the old smithy and was doing all he could to get the business thriving again. Sadly, his father, Ben, and brother, Harry, had perished. His mother, Matilda, had escaped unhurt, apart from the effects of smoke inhalation, but his brother, Jacob, had been badly burnt and was still not fully recovered. Jacob had always been slow-witted, and the trauma he had suffered had not helped matters, and he needed constant guidance for even the simplest of tasks. Ben Rudd had become forgetful in his later years, and it was thought he had accidentally caused the fire in the night. Matilda, previously a jolly woman who delivered most of the babies in the village and also laid out the dead, was a changed woman. She continued to wear black and had not recovered from the loss of both her husband and son. Following the fire, she sold some of her land to raise the money to rebuild the smithy and provide Francis and Jacob with a livelihood.

Eveline watched as Francis, red in the face, laughed, as with ease, he slowly pushed Christopher Webber's arm down onto the table for the second time. Christopher sighed deeply as he reluctantly handed over his money and walked off arm-in-arm with his girlfriend, Clarice. "I was sure I would beat him this year."

"Never mind, few people can beat Francis at that game, and I've not seen anyone do it yet today."

"Anyone else fancy a go?"

Eveline had seen Francis in action before and knew he could keep this up all day long. He would make a few shillings before the day was out. Most of his opponents were from neighbouring villages and were unaware of his reputation.

However, before another contest could begin, there was a shout for young men to carry the May Queen. This year, the Queen was Theresa Carter, a pretty girl of sixteen. Her long blond hair was adorned with flowers, and she wore a simple white dress. More flowers hung around her neck, and she sat on a chair lavishly decorated with greenery. Theresa was George Carter's youngest daughter, and Ned and Betsey were her grandparents.

The young men carried Theresa shoulder-high around the village. A small band preceded them, providing a reasonable rendition of local songs. Eventually, they reached the village green, where they placed the chair on a wooden cart so everyone could see it. Theresa cut a ceremonial red ribbon and declared the May Day celebrations officially open, although some had already started.

Eveline glanced around the crowds, looking for her brother, Fred, and the six children. She spotted him at last and waved to him. Eveline had moved in with Fred a couple of years earlier to help him bring up his three children, Llewellyn, Rosella, and Eddie, after their mother, Lucy, had committed suicide in a lunatic asylum. The other three children living with Fred and Eveline were the orphan children of their brother, William.

William had worked in China for many years. A widower, he had been granted a year off work to return to England and visit his family. He brought with him his three children: identical twins, Matthew and Joe, and his daughter, Amelia. Over the following months, he fell in love with Sarah Martin, a girl he had gone to school with, and the couple married and travelled to London en route to China.

Unfortunately, when they reached London to join a ship, William was taken seriously ill and died, leaving Sarah alone with the three children. Not a maternal woman, Sarah panicked and abandoned the children at the inn where she was staying. She returned to Hartford alone, pretending she had changed her mind, and William and the children had sailed to China without her.

Eventually, of course, the truth came out, and Fred and Eveline travelled to London, where they found their niece and nephews in a workhouse. They brought the children back to Devon and decided the best solution was to raise all six children together.

As soon as the story of Sarah abandoning William's children became known in the village, she was shunned by all who knew her. However, when he learnt she was pregnant with William's child, her father relented and reluctantly allowed her to return home to live. Her son, Bentley, was now two years old, but she was still ignored by all of William's family and most of the village.

"Hello, Fred. I was hoping to get here before the maypole dancing started."

"Yes, I think that will be any time now, Eveline. How was Jane Chugg today?

"I'm afraid she's seriously ill, and Alfred is worried about her. I'll need to see her again next week. Oh, there's Sabina with her children."

Eveline waved to her sister-in-law. "Let's walk to the maypole and get the children organised."

The twins, Matthew and Joe, and their sister, Amelia, stood alongside their cousins, Llewellyn and Rosella. Each took a coloured ribbon in readiness for the dance, but Eddie was a bit too young at four. Sabina joined them with her four youngest children, Edward, Stephen, Helen, and Danny.

"Hello, Fred, hello, Eveline; it's nice to see you both. Stephen, stand with Llewie and Rosie, ready for the dance."

Like Eddie, Helen and Danny were also four years old and too young to dance. Although at eight years old, their brother, Edward, should have been dancing, he had been deaf since birth, so teaching him to dance had proved difficult, and he stood with the younger children.

The band began to play, and the boys and girls, standing alternately around the base of the maypole, each took hold of the end of a long ribbon. They began to dance, the boys going one way and the girls the other as they weaved in and out and around each other. The teachers watched anxiously, willing the ceremony to reach a satisfactory conclusion. Fortunately, this year, it did, and the result was a neatly woven pattern of red, white, and blue ribbons running down the pole, and the crowd duly applauded the dancers.

Sabina grinned at her sister-in-law. "Well, that went better than I thought it might."

"Yes, it did, and I think most of the children were ours. I remember getting in a right old tangle when I did it as a child. Shall we get something to eat now?"

"Yes, I think we're all hungry. Are you coming, Fred?"

"No, not at the moment, Evie. You go with Sabina and the children and get them some dinner. I want to speak to Dad about a job he wants me to do for him."

"All right, Fred, you take your time. Come and join us when you're ready."

Eveline could see that her mother's food was selling like hotcakes, and many villagers were sitting at the long tables eating pasties, washed down with a pint of ale as they enjoyed the occasion.

"Come on, Sabina, I don't know about you, but I'm hungry, and these children always are. Oh, that's lucky. I think there are enough seats for all of us at this table. What about Annie? Is she coming with Selina?"

"Yes, she'll be here soon, I expect. I believe she's told you of her plans to marry Robert?"

"Yes, she told me in confidence because I've agreed to make some dresses for her. We're going to buy the material tomorrow. I find it hard to believe they'll be allowed to marry, though I know they were close before she married Harry."

"I know. They're adamant they'll wed, but I'll believe it when I see it. I don't want her to get hurt. Robert is even talking about all of us moving into the Lodge House. Can you believe it? It would be wonderful, but I think his mother would have a fit."

Eveline was about to reply when suddenly she fell silent and pursed her lips as she spotted her sister-in-law, Sarah Carter, approaching them.

Looking uncomfortable, Sarah sat close to Eveline and Sabina with her son, Bentley. Bentley had fair skin and curly red hair, common to many of the Carter family. He toddled over to Sabina and looked enviously at her pasty. Sarah quickly went to take his hand and lead him away, but Bentley did not want to go.

"Me want some."

Sabina hesitated, for she never could refuse a child, and this child was, of course, her nephew. Sarah scooped him up into her arms, where he kicked and screamed.

"It's all right, Sarah. Bentley, here's some for you."

Sabina broke a corner off her pasty, blew on it to cool it, and held it out to the little boy. He immediately rewarded her with a huge smile and said, "Ta."

Sabina's heart lurched as she looked into his blue eyes, which were so like his father's. Suddenly, she knew William would want her to be part of his son's life.

"Thank you, Sabina; I'm sorry he bothered you. There were no other seats, but we'll try to find somewhere else to sit."

"No, sit with us if you like, Sarah. Perhaps it's time Bentley got to know his cousins."

Eveline was surprised, but Sabina gave her a stern look, and she decided to go along with her sister-in-law.

"Thank you, Sabina, but I don't want to intrude because I know how you all feel about me. I've wished so many times I could turn the clock back and do things differently, but of course, I can't." She hung her head. "I'm so ashamed of myself, and I don't blame you all for hating me, but at the time, I panicked at the thought of caring for William's three children on my own."

"What's done is done, Sarah. I'd say it's what you do from now on that matters. Come on, join us. I think it's time to put the past behind us. What do you think, Eveline?"

Her sister-in-law was less sure, though she too had been struck by Bentley's likeness to her late brother.

"Yes, come and sit with us, Sarah, and let Bentley play with the others."

Sarah was delighted, and hesitantly at first, she joined in the conversation with the other two women. Since the truth had come out about William's death, she had led a lonely life, though she was grateful to her father for allowing her to move back home. She now dared to hope that if Sabina and Eveline would accept her, perhaps others in the village might follow their lead. When they had finished eating, the children all played with Bentley, who loved every minute.

Sabina stood up and brushed the crumbs from her dress. "Eveline, could you keep an eye on the children while I get us all another drink? Sarah, would you like one?"

Eveline nodded, and Sarah accepted gratefully. Sabina walked across the grass to the inn and through the bar on her way to the kitchen.

Arthur Webber was at the bar waiting to be served, and as everyone was busy, Sabina offered to get him his tankard of ale. Arthur was a tall, lean man of about fifty who worked as a labourer on the estate and lived with his family in Liza Hammett's former home. He was a widower, his wife, Drucie, having died in childbirth many years before. His sons, Christopher and Dudley, were also labourers on the estate, and it was Christopher who had recently been beaten at arm wrestling by Francis Rudd. Arthur's daughter, Elsie, was the second cook at the Manor House. She had always been a skilled cook and was now learning fast from Ethel Potts. Maria, his youngest daughter, had recently obtained a position at Hollyford Farm, and it was she that Eveline had helped to cook that morning. Arthur's father, Peter, a widower in his mid-seventies, lived with his son. Peter was disabled and had lost both his hands. A former miner, he had been seriously injured after an explosion and was lucky to escape with his life. He was an intelligent man who had struggled to come to terms with his disability and felt he was a burden on his family. With both Elsie and Maria now in service, life was difficult for the Webber menfolk, but they managed as best they could.

"There you are then, Arthur. You look ready for that."

"I certainly am, Sabina, thank you. The sun's hot today, and I rushed to finish my work this morning to come here for the afternoon. Luckily, I've got a half-day off."

"I thought I might have seen your father here today. How is he?"

"He's a bit under the weather. It's just a nasty cold, but he gets so depressed these days. I tried to persuade him to come because I thought it would do him good to get out, but he was having none of it. His accident hit him hard, and although it was a while ago, he's never come to terms with losing his hands. There's so little he can do now. As a younger man, he loved to paint pictures but never had the time or money to spend on them, and now, of course, he can't hold the brush. It's a pity because it would pass the time."

"That's a shame. Would he like me to call in and see him?"

"I don't know. He can be quite abrupt and plain rude these days, but if you're willing to risk it, it would do him good to see another face."

"That's settled then; I'll call and see him during the week. Now, I'm going to make my escape; otherwise, I'll be stuck behind this bar for hours."

By the time Sabina returned with the drinks, Annie had arrived with Selina, and as soon as she saw Sabina, the little girl ran to her granny, holding out her arms. Sabina picked her up and hugged her.

The Morris Men had just started dancing on the village green, and the children were fascinated. The eight men were arranged in two lines and wore white shirts with coloured belts or baldrics across their chests and small bells attached to their knees. They carried short sticks which they knocked against each other. Selina loved it and joined in, hopping from one foot to the other and clapping her hands.

The May Day celebrations continued until late into the night, but Sabina and Annie went home at tea time, for the little ones were tired. The women sat them around the table and fed them with some bread and dripping and hot milk before putting them to bed.

CHAPTER 6

The following day, Annie put Selina in the pram and went to call for her Aunty Eveline to buy the dress material. She was excited because she had never had any clothes that were brand new. They were usually hand-me-downs from other families or adult clothes cut and altered to fit. She decided to visit Matilda Rudd at the smithy on the way. Matilda was the nearest thing the village had to an experienced midwife, and with her practised eye, she had known that Annie was pregnant before the marriage to her son, Harry. She had gone along with the theory that the baby was early, and Selina had been a small baby, so it was plausible. However, she had always hoped that the child was Harry's, though the little girl was not like him in the slightest.

Matilda was on her knees washing the front steps as Annie approached, and she struggled to her feet with some difficulty and then shuffled over to speak to Selina. "Hello, my darling, come to see your old granny, have you?"

Selina beamed and held out her arms to be picked up. She was getting rather big for the pram, but it was too far for her to walk from Sabina's house to the smithy.

"Have you got time for a cup of tea, Annie?"

"Yes, please. I have something to tell you, Matilda, but you must keep it to yourself for now."

"That's intriguing. Let me make the tea and find Selina a biscuit, and then you can tell me your news."

Once they were comfortably seated, Annie plucked nervously at the tablecloth, trying to think how to start the conversation. Eventually, she looked up. "I wanted you to hear this from me and no one else, Matilda. I'm getting married again."

"Why, Annie, that's wonderful news. I'm so pleased for you, but whom are you going to marry? I didn't even know you were courting?"

"I'm going to marry Robert Fellwood."

"Never! Oh, Annie, I wish the best for you, of course I do, but that can never happen, surely you know that?"

"Normally, I would agree with you, but we have his parents' permission, and our engagement will be announced later this month."

"I can't believe they would allow it. I mean, why would they? You're a lovely girl, Annie, but you were a servant at the Manor House, and Robert will be Lord Fellwood one day. Oh, wait a minute." Matilda frowned and looked most uncomfortable. "Annie, I'm sorry to ask, but is Robert Selina's father? You see, I know you were with child before the wedding."

"No, Robert is not her father."

"Harry was her father, then?"

"No. You're right. I was already in the family way before we married, and Harry knew that when he proposed, but he insisted on marrying me, anyway, and we were happy, Matilda. I was attacked and raped at the Manor House one night after a late party. There were loads of guests, and I didn't even know who it was because it was so dark, and my attacker punched me, and I was stunned. Unfortunately for me, that once led to me being with child."

"Oh, Annie, I'm so sorry, but even so, I don't see why the Fellwoods would let you marry their son?"

"I can't say any more about it, Matilda. All I can tell you is that I now know who attacked me, and the Fellwood family would not want people to know who it was. They are agreeing to our marriage on the condition we keep it quiet. It wasn't Robert, though."

"Well, this is a strange do and no mistake. I always wondered if Selina was Harry's child."

"He treated her as if she was. He was a wonderful man, Matilda, and it was so kind of him to marry me and give me some respectability. I honestly do miss him."

"I shall always think of her as my first granddaughter. Is that all right? Can I still do that?"

"Yes, of course, and I'm so sorry if this is a shock, but I wanted you to know the truth. Could you keep my news to yourself until it's properly announced?"

"Yes, of course, my dear, and I wish you all the best, but I think you'll find your new life difficult."

"Thank you, and yes, I know it won't be easy. I'm on my way to buy some material from my Uncle George's shop because Aunty Eveline has agreed to make me two new dresses, one to wear when I meet Robert's parents, and the other for his birthday party when our engagement will be announced. The truth is, I'm dreading both occasions, though I am looking forward to seeing my Uncle George's face when I buy lots of new material."

Matilda laughed heartily, her blue eyes crinkling at the corners and dimples appearing in her old cheeks.

"Yes, he will be surprised."

"I hope Aunty Evie can make the dresses in time; I'll need them in a week or two."

"I'm handy with my needle, so if she needs some help, you tell her to come and see me. I'll gladly give her a hand, and we must have you looking your best."

"Oh, thanks, Matilda, that's kind of you, and yes, I'll tell Aunty Evie."

When Annie left, Matilda waved to Selina until they were out of sight. As the old lady went inside, she grinned at the thought of stuck-up George Carter serving Annie with his best material.

Eveline was waiting for Annie, and together, they walked to the shop, Eveline holding young Eddie by the hand. George's daughter, Harriet, had worked in the shop since Mary Ann married her father, and Eveline left to care for the children of her brothers, William and Fred. She was standing behind the counter serving people, and George was checking the stock.

"Good morning, Harriet, morning, Uncle George." Annie and Eveline smiled as they approached the counter.

"Hello, what can I get for you today?" Harriet was a little plump but a pretty girl with a sprinkling of freckles across her nose and light brown eyes. She wore her auburn hair tied up in a ponytail with a pink ribbon.

"I want to buy some material, please. Aunty Eveline is going to make me two new dresses."

Harriet was surprised, and George appeared from around the corner. "I'll see to this, Harriet. You carry on serving behind the counter." His daughter was annoyed, for she would have enjoyed showing the materials to her aunt and cousin.

"Our material might be a little expensive for you, I'm afraid, Annie, but we have a few ready-made cotton smocks that might be suitable?"

"No, I need enough material for two dresses, and it has to be of the best quality. Don't worry, I have the money. Can you show me what you have, please? I want two different colours."

"Of course, if you insist. The materials are over here on these shelves, but I warn you, they are not cheap."

Eveline and Annie chose two fabrics, one in mid-blue and the other in deep green. Eveline approved as she held each material up to Annie's face.

"These will be perfect, Annie. The green brings out the colour of your eyes, and both fabrics will hang nicely. Now, I've worked out how much we need. I can cut it if you like, George. I think I've done this more often than you or Harriet."

As Eveline measured and cut the cloth, George was curious. Not so long ago, Annie and her family were just one step away from the workhouse, and he had enraged Sabina by offering to arrange for her youngest children to go there. He couldn't imagine where Annie had got the money to pay for the material, and for a moment, he wondered if she had stolen it but then dismissed the thought, fairly sure his niece was no thief.

Eveline and Annie were smiling as they left the shop.

"Right then, Annie, I'll get cracking on these dresses. They shouldn't take me too long with my new sewing machine. Which one shall I make first?"

"Can you make the blue one first, because I thought I'd wear that to meet Robert's parents, and keep the green one for the party? Thanks so much for doing this, Aunty Eveline, and don't forget, Matilda will help you if you need her to."

"It's no problem. I shall enjoy it, but I'll ask Matilda if necessary. I'll let you know when I need you to try the dress on. Bye."

Annie hastened home with Selina. She had arranged to meet Robert after lunch and couldn't wait to tell him about her shopping trip. However, she was surprised to see him at her back door with his horse, Prince, and his sister, Sarah's pony, Jenny.

"Hello, Robert, you're early; I've not had my lunch yet. Is Sarah with you? That's her pony, isn't it?"

"No, she's not here, but she's let me borrow Jenny for the afternoon, and I thought I'd teach you how to ride. Have you ever been on a horse before?"

"Yes, I've ridden Grandad's horse several times, but he was always leading it. I've never ridden on my own."

"Well, now's your chance. I've brought some food, so if your mum will look after Selina, we could make an early start."

"Yes, of course, I'm sure she won't mind. I'm not sure I can ride on my own, though."

"I'll lead you for a while until you get used to it."

Having checked that her mother would mind Selina, Annie allowed Robert to help her onto the horse. She found it awkward to sit side-saddle and would have preferred to sit with one leg on either side of the pony. Robert led her through the woods, but she took the reins for herself once they reached the open countryside. She was nervous at first but soon gained confidence and began to enjoy herself. They trotted along together slowly until they came to the edge of the moors. Then they tethered their mounts to a tree and sat on the grass to eat the food Mrs Potts had packed.

From their vantage point, they had a marvellous view of the rolling countryside around them, with only one large house in sight. The gorse was in full bloom with its bright yellow flowers, and against the vivid blue of the sky, it was an amazing sight. Annie sighed as she munched on crusty bread, ham, and a boiled egg and drank the cold lemonade. She thought she couldn't be happier than at that moment, sitting there with Robert.

As they gazed down on the large house below them, they saw a woman arrive in a pony and trap. She was accompanied by a younger woman carrying a baby. They knocked on the door, and a tall woman answered and let them in.

"That place is called Buzzacott House, and a big family used to live there, but they left last year. I used to play with one of the daughters. Nobody seems to know much about the people who live there now; they seem to keep themselves to themselves. Do you know them, Robert?"

"No, I don't know them. Anyway, never mind them. I think it's high time you rewarded me with some attention, seeing as I've taken you riding and provided you with a tasty meal." He put his arm around Annie, pulled her to him, and kissed her gently. She lay back on the grass, and he leaned over her and kissed her more passionately. "Oh, Annie, I can't wait for us to be married; we've waited so long. When would you like to get married?"

Annie returned his kisses and murmured in his ear. "Mmm, how about tomorrow? Or could we make it later today?"

"If only we could. I was thinking more like August, around your birthday. You'll have to meet Mama and Papa in the next week or two." He was suddenly serious. "Annie, you realise that my sister, Victoria, and her husband, Frank, will be there too. I know you can't stand Frank, but at least we know now it wasn't him that attacked you."

"He wasn't the one that got me pregnant, but he did make a pass at me. It could have been a different matter if you hadn't saved me that day."

"I know, and I'll never forgive him, but he's my brother-in-law now, and I want to make my announcement whilst all the family are together."

"Just don't leave me alone with him."

"No, of course not. Our engagement will be announced next month, on my birthday. It will take a couple of months to refurbish the West Wing in the Manor House and plan the wedding, so I think we could hold the wedding in August. Can you wait that long?"

"Yes, that will be perfect."

CHAPTER 7

Eveline had made a superb job of Annie's new blue dress, which fit her perfectly. To her Uncle George's amazement, she bought some new black shoes and a ribbon for her hair. He badly wanted to know what was going on but didn't like to ask, and Annie and Eveline had no intention of telling him.

Annie was so nervous on the day of her visit to the Manor House that she was afraid she would be physically sick. Robert collected her in the pony and trap, for she couldn't walk to the house in all her finery. Robert took her hand as she alighted and led her up the steps to the imposing front door. He could feel her hand trembling beneath his, and he smiled encouragingly at her.

"Don't worry, it will be fine. You look beautiful."

Annie had never entered the house by the front door before, and when Sid Hobbs opened it, she almost laughed out loud, despite her nerves, for he was so surprised. The butler led them straight to the drawing room, where Charles sat in his wheelchair and Eleanor in an armchair.

Robert led Annie forward. "Mama, Papa, I'd like you to meet Anne Carter, my future wife."

Charles held out his right hand from his sitting position, for he was unable to stand. "Hello, Anne, I can't pretend we are pleased about this, but Robert is determined to marry you, and we cannot stop him, so I suppose we'll just have to make the best of it."

Annie made to curtsey, but Robert, fully expecting this, held on to her arm firmly and would not allow her to do so. Instead, she shook her future father-in-law's hand. She blushed to the roots of her hair but held Charles' gaze defiantly. "Yes, sir, I suppose we both will."

Eleanor glared at the girl, incensed at her impudence. "I would have you know you've come between mother and son, and I'll never forgive you for the situation you have placed us in."

Annie looked even more uncomfortable but held the woman's gaze. "At least we both know where we stand then. For what it's worth, I'd like you to know that I love your son and intend to do my best to make him happy." The two women did not shake hands.

Robert was so angry he could barely speak. "Right, now you've all had your say, may I suggest we sit down and ring for some tea? We must behave appropriately in front of the servants, and there are certain matters we need to discuss."

Robert rang the bell, and Maisie appeared at the door. Her jaw dropped when she saw Annie, and again, despite her nerves, Annie couldn't help but smile.

"Ah, Maisie, I see you have recognised Annie, and I know you two are friends. Would you bring us a tray of tea, please, and some of Mrs Potts' best cakes?"

"Yes, sir, of course." Maisie bobbed a curtsey and returned to the kitchen to pass on this hot gossip. In no time at all, she returned with a tray.

Only when Maisie had left the room did Robert speak as he poured the tea. He offered cake to all those present, but none could bring themselves to eat any.

"Right, now this is uncomfortable for all of us, so let's deal with the practicalities. I've already suggested that Anne and I will occupy the West Wing. It will need to be refurbished, so when we have finished here, I'll take Anne to see which rooms she'd like decorated first."

He paused, waiting for someone to comment, but as he was met with silence, he continued. "The next thing I have to get organised is the Lodge House for Anne's mother and family, and, of course, Anne herself, until we marry. I can't have my future mother-in-law milking the cows and living in a farm cottage, so this must be done as soon as possible. Annie, I'm sorry, I can't keep calling you, Anne. Annie, you and I will get the key from Jack Bater before we leave today. And, of course, the third matter is that of our engagement. Victoria and I will be celebrating our twenty-first birthday in a couple of weeks, and that's the ideal time to announce it. I believe Victoria, Frank, and Caroline are expected here in the next week or so, but I have already written to them with my news. Has no one got anything to say?"

Eleanor finally found her tongue. "Just who do you intend to invite to your party, Robert? How many of our friends do you think will come when they find out you're to marry a kitchen maid?"

"If you don't tell them, Mama, I don't think they'll even realise, but I don't intend to keep it a secret. Unless Victoria feels strongly, I think we should only invite immediate family and friends. I don't want a big party because it will all be strange to Annie, and she needs time to adjust to our way of life."

Charles snorted. "As if she ever will. I tell you, this will all end in tears."

"That remains to be seen, but can I take it you'll leave all the arrangements to me?" As he received no answer, Robert moved on. "Very well, now I hope we can all get along together as best we can. Come, Annie, I want to show you around the house." Once outside the room, Annie heaved a massive sigh of relief.

"Thank goodness that's over, but I can see they're furious, Robert."

"I know, but they'll just have to get over it. Come on, I'll show you the West Wing, though not the cellars; you don't need to see them again."

The West Wing had many rooms and more than enough space for the two of them. They selected a few rooms to be refurbished first, for the whole wing would take some time and a great deal of money. Annie vaguely knew the layout already, for it mirrored the other three wings of the house.

"Right, now that's settled, I'll take you to meet Sarah. Hopefully, you'll get a warmer welcome from her than you did from my parents."

They found Sarah in the music room playing the piano, the strains of Mozart giving away her presence. She didn't hear them enter the room, and they let her play on to the end of the piece, and then both applauded.

"That was excellent, Sarah. Can I introduce you to Annie? Annie, this is my little sister, Sarah."

"Hello, Sarah, I've heard a lot about you. I'm so pleased to meet you."

"Hello, Annie, welcome to the family. I don't suppose you've had much of a welcome from anyone else, but if you make Robert happy, that's all I will ever ask of you."

"Oh, thank you, Sarah. That means so much to me."

"Sarah, I want to ask you a favour. Would you help me to teach Annie how to behave at my birthday party? She needs to know which cutlery to use, what to drink, how to do her hair, how to dance, and all that. I think I need a woman's help."

"Yes, of course, and I'm sure Jane Leworthy, my governess, will help too. Why don't you come back tomorrow morning and join us in the schoolroom?. We can take care of it all there."

"Yes, come to the kitchen tomorrow, Annie, and I'll take you to the schoolroom." Robert hugged his sister. "Thanks, Sarah. I knew you wouldn't let me down."

As Robert led Annie away, she took his arm. "Could we go to the kitchen now, Robert? I'd love to see Mrs Potts, and Maisie, and all my other old friends."

"Of course, I was just going to suggest it."

When they entered the kitchen, there was a hushed silence until Annie broke it by exclaiming. "Well, is no one going to welcome me? Have you all lost your tongues?"

"Eh, lass, I don't know what to say. Young Maisie told us you were having tea with Lord and Lady Fellwood. What's going on?"

"You'll never believe it, but Robert and I are getting engaged to be married. What do you think of that?"

"Oh, Annie, I'm so pleased for you." Maisie's eyes shone with happiness for her friend, and she hugged her tightly.

Molly, the tweeny, and Mrs Potts also hugged Annie, and the elderly cook wiped a few tears from her eyes.

"I knew you had feelings for each other; that was always obvious, but I never thought this would happen. I can't imagine how you've brought this about, Master Robert, but I wish you both all the happiness in the world."

"Thank you, Mrs Potts. Now, have you got any of that cake left? I could manage a piece now with a cup of tea."

"Bless you, lad, sit down, and I'll get the kettle on." Mrs Potts sliced up a chocolate sponge and a ginger cake. "Annie, let me introduce you to some of our new servants, though you probably know most already. Caleb and Ethan are two of Jack Bater's sons. They're both footmen, and this is Elsie Webber; she's learning to be a cook like me, and her family live near your mum. Oh, and this is Clarice Gubb; her mum, Noeleen, is married to John Cutcliffe now."

"Yes, I know them all; hello, everyone."

Robert left Annie to gossip and went to get the Lodge House key from Jack Bater. Jack, of course, was curious as to why Robert wanted the key and was taken aback when Robert told him of his plans.

"My goodness, lad, that's a surprise; do your parents know?"

"Yes, they do, Jack; I've just told them. We're getting engaged on my birthday next month. I need the key now, though, because a lot of work will be needed to get the Lodge habitable."

"Of course, sir, I have it here. If you let me know what needs doing, I'll get some men onto it immediately. I wish you and Annie all the best, sir. You'll make a lovely couple."

"Thank you, Jack. The other thing is that Sabina can no longer do the milking and work on the estate. It's hardly a fitting role for my future mother-in-law. Can you find someone else to do the work?"

"Yes, of course, sir, that won't be a problem. There are always people wanting work."

"Fine, if you can arrange that as soon as possible, I'll tell Sabina. Carry on paying her wages, though, until we can sort out a more permanent arrangement."

"Yes, sir. I'm pleased for the Carter family; they deserve a bit of luck; they've had a hard time since poor Tom died."

CHAPTER 8

Robert had difficulty tearing Annie away from the kitchen, for she enjoyed talking to her old friends. Sid Hobbs said nothing but clearly disapproved. Fortunately, Miss Wetherby, the housekeeper who sacked Annie, was out for the afternoon. Annie was glad, for she had endured enough tension and unpleasantness for one day. She would tackle Miss Wetherby on another occasion.

Robert accompanied Annie home in the pony and trap. It stopped outside her front door, and as he held out his hand to help her alight, many neighbours came out of their cottages and cheered loudly. Since he had collected her earlier, Sabina had been besieged with questions and had told people the truth. They had been amazed at the news but delighted for Annie.

Sabina and Liza wanted to hear how they had gotten on. They were full of admiration for Annie, for they had not envied her, having to meet the Fellwoods, and were not sure they could have done so. Robert told Sabina that Jack would be passing her duties to another worker within days but that she would still be paid.

"Why, Robert, are you sure? It doesn't seem right to be paying me for no work."

"Just look at it as extra money for caring for Danny." He spoke quietly, for Danny was present and, of course, knew nothing of his parentage.

"I don't know what I shall do with myself all day if I don't work."

"You have four small children to care for, five, including Selina, so I don't suppose you'll be bored. Anyway, I have the key to the Lodge House, so we'll explore it in a couple of days; you should have finished work by then."

Annie went to see Robert off, and they longed to kiss and hold each other, but with so many neighbours watching their every move, they had to forego that pleasure. When Annie returned inside, Liza helped her out of her new dress, for Sabina had gone to visit Peter Webber.

Armed with a rabbit casserole, Sabina walked the short distance to the Webber's cottage, knocked on the door, and let herself in. Peter was sitting in a chair looking out of the window, and he smiled as she entered.

"Hello, Peter, how are you today?"

"Much the same as ever, lass, no use to man nor beast, I'm afraid."

"Don't say that."

"Well, 'tis true. There's not much a man can do with no hands." Peter lowered his head and would not meet her gaze, but she glimpsed tears shining in his eyes.

"It must be difficult, but you have a wise head on your shoulders, you know, and a lot of experience. I'm sure you could teach younger people. Anyway, are you hungry? I've just made a rabbit stew and brought some for us to share for our tea. There's enough for Arthur and the boys to have some when they get home."

"That's kind of you, Sabina. They will be grateful. With Elsie and Maria both in service, there are no women here to do things, and we miss them, but we need the money. If you leave the stew, I'll have some later because I can't feed myself, you see. I can't do anything for myself anymore. I don't usually have anything from breakfast to tea time because there's no one here to help me, but I'm used to it."

"That's no problem because I can help you. Now, where are the plates?"

Sabina delved into the cupboards and ladled two portions of the warm stew onto plates. She had also brought some freshly baked crusty bread. She sat beside Peter, spooned the stew into his mouth, and fed him with the bread, taking mouthfuls from her own plate in between. She told him all her news about Annie and the rest of the family.

"Oh, Sabina, this is delicious. I've not had such a tasty meal since Arthur's wife, Drucie, died many years ago. Thank you so much. I've enjoyed your company, too; you've brightened up my day."

"Good, because I've got a few ideas I want to talk to you about. I wanted to put you in a good mood first, and I thought a full belly might help. Now, I believe there's not much you don't know about farming and growing things and mining. Am I right?"

"Aye, I worked on the land for many years until I went into mining, but then I lost my hands in an accident, so all that's no use to me now."

"Maybe not, but it could be of use to other people. How would you feel about going into the school and telling the children how to do things concerned with farming?"

"I could, I suppose, but would the teachers want me interfering?"

"I could have a word with Mr Atkins and see what he thinks. He was from Exeter before he became headmaster, and I don't think he has any practical experience of working the land. Books are all very well, but they don't beat real experience. Shall I ask him?"

"Yes, all right. I think I might enjoy that."

"Excellent. Now Arthur mentioned that as a younger man, you enjoyed painting pictures, is that right?"

"Yes, I've always been able to draw, and at school, I was the best artist, but I've never had any paper or paints to use since. Why do you ask?"

"I was talking to the vicar one day, a long while back now, and he was telling me about this disabled lady he once knew, who, like you, had no hands. She was born without any arms at all. Anyway, she painted excellent pictures by holding the paintbrush between her teeth and sometimes even between her toes. It sounds incredibly difficult, but she mastered it well enough to sell the paintings, and I wondered if you'd be interested in trying. I could ask Fred to make you an easel, and we could probably beg a few paints and paper from Mr Atkins in return for your help in his lessons."

"You've certainly given all this some thought, Sabina. Goodness me, are you trying to reorganise my life?"

"I am that, Peter Webber, and you'd better know I'm not a woman to give up easily."

"I can see that. Yes, I'd be willing to give it a try. Anything to relieve this terrible boredom, and I've certainly got enough time on my hands if you'll pardon the pun."

Sabina was pleased he could joke about it. "Right now, I have just one other suggestion, and then I'll leave you in peace."

"Go on, then, what else?"

"Well, you've lost your arms, from the elbow down, on the left side, and from your mid-forearm on the right, but I wondered if anyone had ever tried strapping hooks to your arms? I know it would be nothing like hands, but it might be useful for some things. What do you think?"

"How would you attach the hooks to my arms?"

"If you're interested, I thought we could talk to Seth James, the saddler, to see if he could make some sort of harness to attach the hooks firmly to your arms. Do you think they might be helpful?"

"It might help with a few things, I suppose. I could carry a bucket of water by holding the handle and things like that. Yes, I'd like to give it a try; could you ask him?"

"Yes, and I'll also speak to Mr Atkins about the lessons and Fred about an easel. I'll have you busy again yet, Peter Webber; just you wait and see."

"I'm so glad you came today, Sabina. You have cheered me up. Thank you so much."

Sabina hugged the old man, made him comfortable, and then left him, promising to return when she had some news.

Sabina was keen to put her plans for Peter into action as soon as she could, for she feared he might change his mind if he had too much time to think about what she had suggested. The next day, she went to see Mr Atkins, and he listened to her carefully.

"Do you know, Sabina, I think that's a splendid idea. You're right; I don't have any first-hand knowledge of farming, and books are only so much help. Most of the youngsters I teach will end up working on the land in one way or another, so it would be helpful. Could you ask Peter to come along and see me, and we can discuss the best time for these lessons. I would have thought perhaps once or twice a week, depending on how much time he has to spare."

"Oh, he has lots of time to spare. Thank you so much, Mr Atkins; this will mean the world to him."

Encouraged that her plans were coming to fruition, she called at the smithy to ask Francis Rudd if he could make hooks to attach to Peter's forearms. Francis was sure it would be easy enough to do and thought it was an excellent idea. Whilst she was there, she called in to see Matilda, for the two women had been friends for a long time, and Matilda had delivered all of Sabina's babies.

"Sabina, Annie told me about her wedding plans."

"Oh, did she? We're supposed to be keeping it quiet until it's announced properly, but with Robert coming to pick her up today, I've had to tell people. I'm glad she told you herself, though, Matilda; it's only right you should know before the rest."

"That's not all she told me." Matilda looked keenly at her friend. "She told me that Harry was not Selina's father."

"I'm so sorry I couldn't tell you, Tilly. I wanted to, but Harry himself insisted no one should know. It was an awful business, and it was so kind of him to marry Annie under the circumstances, and they were happy, you know."

"Aye, I know, and I'm glad she told me because I've always wondered. I knew she was expecting before the wedding, and I hoped it was Harry's baby, but Selina is nothing like him. It's a sad tale, being attacked and not knowing your baby's father, but Selina will always be like a granddaughter to me, anyway, and Annie seems happy with that."

Sabina realised that Annie had not gone so far as to tell Matilda who Selina's father was, and she fervently hoped Matilda would never ask.

CHAPTER 9

Early one morning, Fred whistled a tune as he drove his horse and cart to a house on the outskirts of the village. The fine weather had continued, and he enjoyed the hot sun on his back. The house was over two hundred years old and in poor repair, and the elderly couple who occupied it had lived there for many years. The roof had been repaired many times but was now leaking badly, and Fred had been asked to supply an estimate for a new one. He would complete the timber work, and then Mark Watts, the local thatcher, would do his part. As the horse trundled along the lane, Fred spotted a young woman sitting on a bank. Her face was pale, and he noticed that she was heavily pregnant.

"Hello, lass, are you all right?"

"Yes, I'm fine, thanks; I'm just resting. I'm on my way to Warkley; do you know if it's much further?"

"Yes, it's a fair step. You need to make your way along here to the village and walk right to the other end, then carry on along that same road for about two miles."

"Oh, right. It's a bit further than I thought then, but at least I'm on the right road. Thanks, Mister."

"Mind how you go then. Goodbye."

Fred went on his way, thinking it was a long way for the girl to walk in her condition. She hadn't looked too well either. If he'd been going the same way, he'd have offered her a lift, but he had to see about this roofing business first because it would be a big job, and he didn't want to lose it. He reached the house and knocked on the solid front door for some time before an old man opened it slowly, the hinges creaking for want of a drop of oil.

"Hello, Mr Carter. I'm sorry to have kept you waiting, but my hearing's not what it was, and my arthritis doesn't let me move very quickly."

The man led Fred to a room at the back of the house where his wife was sitting on a settee with her feet up. Fred sat in the spare armchair and discussed the costs of a new roof with the couple. They haggled a bit, but Fred had expected that and purposely set his price slightly high. He came away with an agreement to carry out the work; he had achieved what he felt was a fair price, and the owners were pleased because they thought they had knocked his fee down a bit. Win, win. He always felt if everyone was happy, it was a good deal.

Not far from where he had first seen her, he saw the young girl sitting on the ground in a gateway; her face contorted in pain as she clutched tightly at her extended stomach. There was not much doubt as to the problem.

"Now then, lass, looks like you need a hand?"

"Yes, I think the baby's coming. I didn't feel well earlier, but this has come on suddenly. It's not due for another month."

"Can you stand? If I can get you onto the cart, I'll take you to the inn in the village. My parents own it, and they'll help you."

"I ain't got much money, mister. I can't pay for a room."

"Well, you can't have the child here at the side of the road, either. Come on, let's see if we can get you on the cart."

Between contractions, Fred helped the girl to her feet. To her embarrassment, fluid gushed down her legs as soon as she stood up. "Oh no, I'm so sorry. I can't stop it."

"It's all right; your waters have broken. That's nothing to worry about, but the baby is definitely on the way now, so we need to get you some help." He lifted the girl onto the cart and made her as comfortable as possible, propped up with a pile of hay he was carrying. "Right, hold on, and we'll soon be there."

He drove the horse along steadily, trying to avoid the worst ruts in the road, and when they came to the inn, he took the horse and cart to the back door and ran in to find his mother. Betsey didn't hesitate, telling him to bring the girl in and put her in one of the spare rooms. Fred carried the girl to the bedroom and laid her down gently.

"Off you go, Fred, and fetch Matilda. She's the expert in these matters. Don't worry, young lady, you're safe now, and there's nothing to worry about. Go on, Fred, make haste." Betsey waved her son off. "Now, lass, what's your name."

"It's Charlotte, missus, Charlotte Mackie. Thank you so much." The girl gasped as a strong contraction seized her, and Betsey held onto her hand.

"That's it, Charlotte, you hold my hand, and we'll get through this together. You'll be all right. How did you come to be in this state and all on your own?" The girl was downcast, and her face reddened. "Now, don't you worry, lass, whatever it is, I'll have heard it all before, and I'm not one to judge, but just tell me the truth. That's all I ask."

"My family lives in Exeter, and my father is a vicar, but I've been living with a friend for the last few months. Father threw me out because of the shame I've brought on the family. I'm not married, you see. My mother's been visiting me in secret and trying to help me. There, now I expect you'll want me to leave?"

"Nay, lass, of course, I don't want you to go. Not that you can, the state you're in. You're not the first, and you won't be the last, to find yourself in this predicament, but what of the father?"

"I'd been courting Martin, my young man, for over six months when I found out I was in the family way. Then he told me he was married with three young children and had no intention of leaving his wife. He gave me money to get rid of the child, but I couldn't do that." Charlotte paused to deal with another contraction and then continued. "I was on my way to see my aunt, who lives in Warkley. My mother has arranged for me to have the baby there and then get it adopted."

"Don't worry about any of that now. Let's get this baby born first."

It wasn't far from the inn to the smithy, and Fred was there in no time. "Matilda, Matilda, are you there? You're needed for a birth, Matilda."

"All right, Fred, don't knock my door down. Who's having a baby?"

"It's a young maid I found by the roadside. She was in a bad way, so I took her to the inn and Mum's looking after her, but she wants your help because the baby's about to come. I don't think there's a father in the picture. I didn't see a wedding ring, anyway."

"Poor girl, she was lucky you came along, Fred."

"Aye, I'm glad I did. I couldn't see her give birth in a gateway, now could I?"

"No, of course not. Now, just let me get my shawl. Can you take me back on the cart, Fred, or are you going somewhere else?"

"Yes, I can take you. It'll be quicker than you walking."

Matilda was still a little plump despite all the weight she had lost since the fire at the smithy, and Fred knew she could not walk very quickly. They were at the inn within a few minutes, and Fred helped Matilda down from the cart. Betsey met them at the back door and grasped her friend's hands.

"I'm so glad you're here, Matilda. I think the baby will be here soon. I'll see you later, Fred."

Leaving the girl in safe hands, Fred went on his way. He'd not gone far when he noticed Sabina walking along the road. He stopped to say hello and told her about the girl giving birth.

"Happens all too often, doesn't it? The woman is always left with the problem while the man escapes any responsibility. I'm glad I've seen you, though, Fred, because I have a favour to ask."

She quizzed him about making an easel for Peter Webber, and he smiled at his sister-in-law.

"You're so kind, Sabina. You're always helping someone, aren't you? I don't know how you do it with all your own family to look after, and what's this I hear about our Annie marrying Robert Fellwood?"

"My goodness, news travels fast. Aye, it's true enough, though I still can't believe it. Not only that, but Robert has made me give up my job. He's still paying me, and we're to move into the Lodge House when it's repaired. Can you believe that? The Carters in the Lodge House."

"I'm pleased for Annie and you, of course. No one deserves it more, and yes, of course, I can make Peter an easel. I'm not sure it will help him, though; you do know he has no hands?"

"Of course, but I've heard that people can paint by holding the brush between their teeth or even their toes, and he's willing to give it a try. He's so bored at the moment and feels useless. It'll give him something to do, even if the paintings aren't very good."

"I've plenty of bits of wood lying around, and it shouldn't take me long to make an easel, so I'll let you know when it's ready."

"Thanks, Fred, I'll see you soon, then."

Leaving Fred to go about his business, Sabina walked on to find Seth James, the saddler in the village.

"Sabina, of course, I'll help. I'm fortunate enough to have two sound hands. I'll need to give it some thought, though. I'll have a chat with Francis about a hook because what we make will have to fit together tightly if it's to be of any use. I should think some sort of harness to fit around his entire shoulder would be best. The hook will have to be secure. I'm not sure how comfortable it will be, though we can but try. I'll talk to Francis later, and then perhaps we can visit Peter together. He's a clever old man, so I think we need to talk to him before we start."

Sabina thanked Seth and went happily on her way, satisfied that her plan was coming together nicely.

CHAPTER 10

Eleanor Fellwood glanced anxiously out of her drawing room window and then at the ornate grandfather clock in the corner of the room. The carriage had been sent to the station to collect her daughter, Victoria, son-in-law, Frank, and granddaughter, Caroline, from the midday train, and she was impatient to see them. Since their marriage eighteen months earlier, Victoria and Frank had lived in London, and she had seen little of them, though she had visited them a couple of times. Victoria had become pregnant almost immediately after her marriage and had not wanted to undertake the long, arduous journey to the West Country too often.

However, although she was now heavily pregnant again, she had decided to come home to celebrate her twenty-first birthday with her twin brother. Eleanor was delighted, for she had missed her eldest daughter and was looking forward to seeing her again.

Frank was from a wealthy family of bankers living in Mayfair in London. He was a perfect match for Victoria, for although the Fellwoods were no paupers, they were not in nearly the same league as the Eastleigh family. The Fellwoods came from old blood, though, and were a highly respected family, and the fact that Victoria was a beauty was a bonus.

Charles Fellwood entered the room, pushed in his wheelchair by his valet. His shoulders drooped, and his complexion was pallid.

"Looking out of the window will not make them come any quicker, my dear."

"No, I know, but I'm longing to see Victoria and Caroline; we haven't seen the baby since she was a few months old. She won't know us."

They heard the sound of hooves on the cobbles, and the carriage swept up the drive. "Here they are now."

A few minutes later, Sid Hobbs ushered the visitors into the drawing room. Eleanor and Victoria embraced warmly, and the two men shook hands. Victoria held out her arms to her daughter and took her from her nanny.

"Come here, darling. Come and meet your grandma and grandpa."

The little girl was dressed all in white and had red ribbons in her brown hair. She was a plain child considering her attractive parents, but she smiled readily enough, and when she did so, it lit up her whole face. Victoria sat on a sofa and took her daughter on her knee. Eleanor sat next to her.

"My goodness, how she's grown. Is she walking yet?"

"Oh yes; the trouble is she gets at everything now. I'll show you."

Victoria put her daughter down, and she toddled around the room, pointing with her finger. She seemed quite at home until Eleanor attempted to pick her up, and then she cried loudly.

"Oh dear, I've rushed things. I forget she's not used to me. Victoria, do you want to calm her down?"

"No, she probably needs changing. Nanny, could you take her to the nursery and see to her, please?"

Elspeth, the nanny, immediately sprang forward, and Caroline thankfully buried herself in her arms.

"So, how are you, Victoria? Have you kept well with this pregnancy?"

"Not too bad. I had some morning sickness for a few weeks, but since then, I've been fine, and I'm certainly better than last time. I'll need Doctor Luckett to come and see me soon; we plan to stay until after the birth if that's all right?"

"Yes, of course, darling. We're pleased to have you here, aren't we, Charles?"

Her father nodded his head. "Do you have any plans whilst you're here, Frank?"

"Oh, I'm looking forward to a spot of hunting, hopefully. I don't suppose you can get out on horseback now?"

"No, sadly, that pleasure is no longer possible for me these days, though Robert goes occasionally when he has the time. Victoria always liked to join the hunt, but it's impossible in her present condition. Never mind, I'm sure we can organise something."

"How are Robert and Sarah? Will they be joining us?" Frank's eyes were full of mischief, a fact which did not go unnoticed by Eleanor.

"Sarah will be home soon; she had arranged to visit one of her friends for a couple of days before she knew you were coming today, but she'll be back for dinner. Grown into quite the young lady she has." Charles frowned. "I believe Robert has written to you about his intention to marry this girl from the village?" He raised his eyes questioningly and saw that the news was no surprise to them. "I'm sure you can appreciate how we feel about it, but he will not be dissuaded, and once he's twenty-one, we can't stop him. I've already signed the estate over to him because, since David's death and my stroke, there was no reason not to. Or so I thought." He grimaced. "Of course, I know differently now."

Victoria spoke before her husband could. "I was surprised, but I think he's been fond of this girl for a long time, even when she was a servant here. I agree it's not seemly, but if he loves her and will not be dissuaded, we must make the best of it."

Eleanor frowned. "As far as I'm concerned, she'll never be welcome in this house, and I am so disappointed in Robert, I can't begin to tell you. What our guests will make of it when he announces his engagement at the party, I do not know, and I'm dreading the occasion when I should be looking forward to it."

"I know, my dear. It's a difficult situation, but one I fear we cannot change."

After taking some tea, Victoria and Frank went to their rooms to rest and prepare for dinner. As they made their way along the landing, Frank took Victoria's arm.

"I hope you don't mind, my dear, but I've asked for a separate room whilst we are here. I know how tired you get this far on in pregnancy, and I thought you might prefer to be undisturbed?"

"How thoughtful of you, Frank; yes, whatever suits you. Please remember you're in my parent's house, though, so do not do anything to make me ashamed of you."

"I'm only thinking of you, my darling, and I believe my room is just along the corridor. I can share a room with you if you would prefer?"

"No, it suits me to have some peace and quiet at the moment. Will you escort me down to dinner? I need to rest now."

"Yes, I'll see you in a couple of hours."

He strolled along the corridor to his room. Although it was mild weather, a fire was burning merrily in the grate, for the bedrooms were always cold and draughty in such a big old house. Maisie knelt before the fire, adding some logs. She heard him open the door and immediately sprang to her feet.

"Why, Maisie, what a pleasant surprise. I haven't seen you in such a long time; how are you?"

"I'm fine, sir, thank you. I was seeing to your fire, but I've finished now."

Maisie turned to go, but Frank's hand gripped her arm.

"Now, what's the rush? Aren't you pleased to see me?"

"If you want the truth, sir, no, I'm not. Now, please let go of my arm."

"My, my, how you do bear a grudge. I'm only being friendly, and there's no need to rush off. Come on, give me a little kiss to welcome me back."

Maisie pulled her arm away from him determinedly and made hastily for the door.

"It's no good you trying it on with me, sir. I'm not interested."

"What a pity. We could have such fun together, you know, Maisie, my girl."

Maisie quickly let herself out of the door and hurried to the kitchen.

"Oh, Mrs Potts, that Mr Eastleigh! He's no different now he's married. In fact, he's worse, if anything."

"Is that a fact? We'll send one of the footmen to fetch and carry for him then; I'm not having any more trouble with you girls. Now come on, help me with the vegetables; we need to get a move on if dinner is to be on time tonight."

That evening, Robert went to dinner early, warmly greeted his two sisters, and shook Frank's hand. They had been firm friends as boys, but they had fought the last time they met. When Annie was a maid at Hartford Manor, Frank had lain in wait for her when she went to the garden to pick some parsley and pounced on her as she walked back through the barn. Had it not been for a stable lad fetching Robert, he would have forced himself on her. There had been a vicious fight between the two men, with each giving as good as the other, but it had allowed Annie to make her escape.

Frank looked at Robert with a mischievous smile on his lips. "Robert, old man, I've not seen you for a long time. How are you?"

"I'm fine, thanks, Frank, and yourself?"

"Yes, I'm well. I hear you're managing the estate now?"

They chatted for a few minutes until the gong sounded to summon them into dinner. A servant pushed Charles in his wheelchair alongside Eleanor, Frank took Victoria's arm, and Robert held his arm out to Sarah, who smiled and took it as they walked into the dining room.

Charles raised a toast to their guests and said how wonderful it was to have all his family around the table again.

"Father, before we start our meal, I would like to say something, please."

Charles Fellwood looked anxiously at Robert and narrowed his eyes.

"Could the servants leave us for a moment, please?" Robert paused to allow them time to leave the room.

"You all know by now that I plan to announce my engagement at our party on Saturday, when, of course, Annie will be present. I know most of you disapprove, but she is the kindest and most beautiful girl I have ever met, and I've loved her for a long time, so I hope you will all make her welcome."

There was a long silence that no one seemed prepared to break, though Frank looked highly amused.

"Robert, I have to say, old chap, that your parents are right for once. You simply can't proceed with this; it would be social suicide. I remember the girl, and she is a beauty, but not to marry. She used to work here as a kitchen maid, didn't she?"

"Yes, you know she did, Frank. Then she married Harry Rudd, and they had a child, but her husband was killed in a terrible fire at the smithy a couple of years ago. I've been friends with her and her family for several years since I started to take an interest in farming, but more recently, we've fallen in love. I know this has been a huge shock for you all, but I know what I'm doing and don't care what society makes of it."

"Robert, darling, please think again about what you're doing. I'm sure she is a lovely girl, and I've nothing against her personally, but you could have your pick of many young ladies. You are an eligible young man. Since poor David died, you have thrown yourself into running the estate and have done an excellent job, but I think perhaps you have forgotten how to have fun. We could organise hunting weekends, balls, parties, all sorts of things to allow you to meet someone more suitable for your social position. Once Victoria has had the baby, you could even return to London with her and Frank. I'm sure you would have the world at your feet. Please don't do this."

"I'm sorry, Mama, but I've made my decision. What do you think, Victoria?"

"Mama and Papa will not thank me for saying this, but I think you're right to follow your heart, Robert. If you love her, and she loves you, then how can it be wrong? I hope you'll both be happy."

"That means a lot to me; thank you so much." He turned to the rest of the family. "Despite what you may think, I'm not stupid, and I do appreciate how difficult this will be, but I'm sure we can all adjust if we try hard enough. I'll be moving Annie and her family into the Lodge House as soon as I can get it refurbished. I've also made arrangements for the West Wing to be modernised, and Annie and I will live there after we are married. Now, can we talk about other things because I'd like to hear all your news?"

Without waiting for a response, he rang the bell to ask the servants to bring the meal.

CHAPTER 11

It had been a few days since Charlotte Mackie gave birth to a daughter whom she named Doris. Betsey had taken to Charlotte, and they discovered that her granny, Gertie, had once lived in Hartford and played with Betsey as a child. What a small world. Gertie had married a soldier and moved to Exeter many years ago, but one of her children, Charlotte's Aunty Joan, lived in Warkley, and it was there that Charlotte was soon headed.

When Fred called at the inn to carry out an errand for his father, he stopped to admire the baby, and Charlotte thanked him again for caring for her.

"Ah, it was nothing. Anyone would have done the same. I could hardly leave you to give birth in a gateway, could I?"

"Well, I'm grateful, and I'm glad you called in so I could thank you properly because I'm just about to go to my aunt's house."

"I can give you a lift on the cart if you like because I'm going that way."

"That would be a big help, Fred. Thank you so much."

Betsey embraced the young girl and sent her on her way. She hoped the aunty might let Charlotte keep her baby, for she did not want to part with the child.

Fred helped Charlotte onto the cart and handed her the baby, then stopped to speak to Robert, Annie, and Sabina, who were passing on their way to the Lodge House. They were in high spirits, and the two women couldn't wait to see inside the house. However, they took the time to chat with Fred for a few minutes and admire Charlotte's new baby before continuing on their mission.

The Lodge House was at the entrance of the driveway to the Manor House, and in days gone by, old Tom Canning lived there as the lodgekeeper. He had been in charge of monitoring visitors, opening and closing the gates, and ensuring undesirables were refused entry. However, as he grew older, he did not carry out any of these duties for many years and was in his nineties when he died. After that, it was not felt necessary to replace him, and the house had stood empty for twenty years or more.

Robert put his finger through the hole in the back garden gate and tried to push the latch upwards, but it was rusted and wouldn't budge. He searched for a stick and, after a bit of manoeuvring, managed to prise it open. He had to put his shoulder to the gate to force it open, and once inside, it was clear why. The garden was not a bad size, but it had become a wilderness over the years. Large brambles had risen to head height, and the vicious prickles tore at their clothes and faces as they tried to push their way through. Sapling trees had taken root, and there was a lot of rubbish, undisturbed for many years. Here and there was the odd glimpse of a once-loved plant; honeysuckle and wisteria scrambled over the porch, both in full flower, and a pink rambling rose was just visible on the far wall. Stinging nettles were everywhere, and by the time they reached the back door, they were all rubbing themselves with dock leaves to relieve the irritation.

"It's funny how dock leaves always grow close to stinging nettles, isn't it? It must be Mother Nature's idea of a joke."

Annie grabbed another handful.

"It is, but at least they work, thank goodness." Sabina rubbed vigorously at some nasty weals on her arm.

Robert put the key into the keyhole and had to apply some pressure to get it to turn. He put his full weight behind the door to get it to open, which it eventually did, with a loud screech of protest. "Well, that's certainly going to need some oil and attention, or you'll never get in and out."

They found themselves in the dairy. The room was thick with dust, and giant cobwebs hung from the old wooden beams. The grimy windows let in little light, and as they gingerly picked their way across the room, there was a loud scuttling sound in the corner, and Annie glimpsed a large rat and shuddered. Abandoned equipment and utensils littered the floor, and Sabina noticed a cheese press and butter churns that could, no doubt, be cleaned up. The dairy led into a large kitchen with a long table running down the centre. Some benches, providing seating, were pushed under the table out of the way.

Sabina crossed the room to another door and found it was a pantry with a tiled floor and plastered walls. There were wooden shelves near the top, slate shelves further down, and a stone shelf at the bottom to keep the food cool. The small window had mesh across it to keep out the flies, and it faced north, on the cooler, shadier side of the house. The pantry still contained the remains of a large mouldy old cheese gnawed by rats and mice and some jars of pickle and preserves. There was a milk jug with a beaded cloth still hanging over the top and an old bread bin with the lid hanging off. In the ceiling were hooks for hanging game. Next to the pantry was another door, which Annie found gave access to a cupboard under the stairs. It was full of brushes, mops, buckets, and logs, as well as some candles and matches.

The kitchen had a sink under the large window and an enormous cooking range on the opposite side of the room. The floor was made of rough slabs, and the walls were lime-washed, but the rotten plaster was falling off in several places, exposing the stonework beneath. A large swill bucket by the range still contained old peelings and rotted food, probably collected for the pigs and poultry, but now completely dried out and like powder. Another small room leading off the kitchen housed an old copper for washing the clothes and a mangle for squeezing out the water. Sabina had always shared these facilities with several of her neighbours, and her eyes gleamed at the thought of having her own. There were two other large downstairs rooms, a parlour and a sitting room, and a hallway that led to the front door.

The sitting room had an ornate fireplace, but there did not appear to be one in the parlour, which seemed strange. Sabina commented on this, and Robert knocked on the wall to investigate.

"I suspect it's been bricked up, but I don't know why. I think if we knock this wall down, we'll find a fireplace behind it."

Sabina couldn't believe how much space there was. Her cottage had only two small rooms downstairs and two bedrooms upstairs. With such a large family, a few had always needed to sleep downstairs, leaving even less living accommodation.

They climbed the stairs, which turned a corner on the way up. The landing window faced the open countryside, and Sabina drew in her breath as she admired the view through the filthy glass. She couldn't believe she would soon live in such an incredible house. There were five large bedrooms, each with a double bed. One of the beds was still made up, and the bedding was rumpled and covered in thick dust. It looked as if it was just as old Tom had left it on the day he was carried out. All the windows had curtains, but they disintegrated into dust as soon as they were touched.

"What a state it's in," Robert exclaimed. "It's far worse than I expected; perhaps we had better think again?"

"What, no! You're joking." The words burst from Annie and Sabina at the same time.

"It's perfect; I can't believe we might live here."

"Oh, right. So, you like it, Sabina?"

"Yes, of course, I like it. It needs a huge spring clean and a bit of work, but other than that, it's amazing. Are you sure your parents will allow this?"

"It's no longer their decision. I'll get the farmhands to clear out all the rubbish and the maids to do the cleaning. Then we can get the walls re-plastered and that chimney sorted out. I wonder if the range still works."

"Robert, could Annie and I be here to sort everything out and help with the cleaning? That's if you want to, Annie."

"Of course, if that's what you want, Sabina. Annie, do you want to help; there's no need?"

"Oh, yes, I'd love to help Mum get this place looking nice. In fact, I can't wait. When can we start?"

"I think we need to get our engagement party over with first. I don't want you looking tired and jaded for that, and you'll need your wits about you."

Annie's face clouded as she was dreading the party. "Yes, I suppose so. How about next week, then?"

"Fine, who would you like to help you?"

"If we could have a couple of farmhands to shift the rubbish, then I'm sure Maisie, Mum, and myself could soon get this place shipshape."

Sabina left Annie and Robert at the Lodge House for some time together and walked home alone. Her mind was working furiously, and she could not hide the wide grin on her face.

"No need to ask what you thought of it then."

Liza smiled at her as she walked in. "It's a real treat to see you grinning like that. Not something we've seen a lot of lately."

"Well, I've definitely got something to grin about now, though I'm so afraid something will go wrong. Oh, Liza, it's such a comfortable house; I can't believe we'll live there. It needs a huge tidy-up, but I can't wait. Just wait until you see it."

"Sabina, I've been thinking about all this, and you won't need me now if you don't have to work; you'll be able to look after the children yourself. It's been a godsend living here with you since I lost Isaac, but I'll make a few enquiries about where I might be able to go. I'm so pleased for you, and I hope it works out for Annie and Robert, though I think it may be more difficult than they think."

"Yes, I think you're right about that, but Liza, there's no way you're going anywhere else to live. You'll be coming to the Lodge House with us. Why, we would have been in the workhouse long ago without you. Do you think I'd turn you away now? You'll end your days living with me, and that's final."

"Oh, Sabina, I'm so relieved to hear you say that; I've been worried to death, and that's the truth."

CHAPTER 12

Robert begged assistance from his sisters to transform Annie into a lady, and they readily agreed. A small spinet was taken to the West Wing. The room had been carefully chosen to be out of earshot of the main house, and with Victoria playing the music, Sarah and Robert endeavoured to teach Annie to dance. She soon mastered the waltz to a reasonable standard but struggled with the quadrille. She could not believe how tiring she found the lessons and amused the others by often exclaiming, this is far worse than a hard day's work!"

Victoria and Sarah had wondered how they would get on with the former servant, but before long, they were looking forward to their sessions together and truly enjoying them. Annie also needed to learn etiquette at the table, for she had no idea which knife, fork, or spoon to use. Robert smuggled the necessary cutlery from the kitchen, and they spread a cloth on the top of the closed spinet and taught Annie what she needed to know. However, the more they taught Annie, the more nervous she became, as she worried about how she would remember it all.

The night before the party, Annie couldn't sleep. Cross with herself, she got out of bed to get a drink. She tiptoed down the stairs as quietly as possible, for she didn't want to wake any of the family. In the past, her parents had slept downstairs on an old double bed, for there was not enough space in the two bedrooms. However, since her father, Tom, had died from consumption, and then John and Emma from diphtheria, there was more space, particularly since Willie and Mary had gone to live where they worked. Now, her mum and Liza shared the biggest bedroom with her brothers, Edward and Stephen, whilst Annie and Selina shared the other room with Helen and Danny. It was still cramped, and whilst the extra space downstairs was useful, they would have all preferred to have their loved ones back.

It was a moonlit night, and she could see quite well as she went into the kitchen and poured herself some water from a jug. Strolling around with the mug in her hand, she wandered into the sitting room where the dress her Aunty Eveline had made for the party hung from the curtain rail. It was a deep green and contrasted vividly with her fiery red hair and matched her remarkable eyes. She had purchased cream stockings, gloves, and black shoes to complete her outfit. She planned to decorate her hair with matching green ribbons and let it cascade over her pale shoulders in ringlets. Around her neck, she would wear the golden locket that Robert had given her so long ago but which, until now, she had kept hidden from sight. Sabina and Liza were speechless when she tried it all on, and tears glistened in their eyes.

She caressed the fine material between her finger and thumb. She loved the dress and longed to wear it but was worried about meeting her future in-laws and Frank Eastleigh. After a few minutes, she sighed and told herself it was time to go back to bed and that worrying would make no difference. Quietly, she climbed the creaky stairs and crept back into her bed, relieved that no one had heard her, but sleep was still elusive.

The following day, Robert arrived in the carriage to collect Annie. Many villagers living in the hamlet were outside to see Annie leave her house, and they gasped in disbelief, for they hardly recognised her in all her finery. Robert, too, was taken aback by how beautiful she looked and smiled as he noticed the gold locket around her neck. He helped her into the carriage and held her trembling hand.

"Don't look so worried. You'll be fine. You look amazing, and everyone is going to love you. I've instructed the servants that you are to be seated next to me and opposite Sarah, Victoria, and Frank. I know you don't care for Frank, but the girls will look after you, and I'll keep him in his place. There is one other thing, Annie. I haven't given you an engagement ring yet," he reached into his pocket and pulled out a small box, "I never knew my grandmother, but this was her ring. She owned a lot of jewellery, and Grandad left all the grandchildren something in his will when he died. I don't remember him either because I was only about five or six when he died. Anyway, I hope you like it, but if not, we can buy a different one."

He carefully removed the ring from the box and placed it on Annie's finger. It was made of gold and had a large cluster of sparkling diamonds.

"Oh, Robert, it's so beautiful, and it fits perfectly. Are you sure it's all right for me to have this? I shall be afraid to wear it in case I lose it."

"I'm glad you like it, and yes, of course, it's all right for you to have it. Now, give me a kiss while we have a moment to ourselves."

When the carriage stopped outside the sweeping steps to the house, Robert took her hand as she alighted and led her to the front door, which was opened by Sid Hobbs. The grumpy old man could not help but be impressed by her appearance, and to her astonishment, he smiled at her. Robert led her into the sitting room, where they were announced as they entered. Many people were already present, and all heads turned to look at Robert's future bride. Sarah immediately approached the couple and chatted with Annie, trying to put her at ease.

Robert led her around the room, introducing her to various aunts, uncles, cousins, and friends, and by the time the gong sounded for their evening meal, Annie longed to be anywhere else. Gratefully, she sat beside Robert, thankful she would only have to converse with those closest to her now. However, this relief was tempered by the worry of etiquette at the table. As Caleb and Ethan Bater served the food, they smiled encouragingly at Annie, and Caleb would have dearly liked to wink at her but knew it was more than his job was worth. The first course was watercress soup, and Annie smiled to herself, for she knew the recipe exactly from helping Mrs Potts in the past. She reached confidently for the soup spoon and tilted it away from her as she daintily took small mouthfuls from the bowl.

The second course was a lightly poached salmon, accompanied by hollandaise sauce, a small amount of grated carrot and beetroot, and a potato cake. Annie took her time and watched which knife and fork Robert and Sarah selected, then copied them, pleased to think it was the one she had suspected. Frank, seated between Sarah and Victoria on the other side of the table, was as fascinated by Annie as he always had been and found it difficult not to stare at her. Annie already felt she could not eat another mouthful as the main course arrived. The guests were served roast pork with sage and onion stuffing, apple sauce, and a medley of vegetables. The food was delicious, but she picked at it and allowed herself only the tiniest sips of the wines served with every course. Robert and Victoria had warned her not to drink much, for she was unused to alcohol, and they knew this could be disastrous.

There were several desserts to choose from: gooseberry fool, trifle, syllabub, and, of course, birthday cake. When everyone had finished eating, Robert rose to his feet and banged on the table with the back of a spoon.

"Ladies and gentlemen, may I have your attention for a few minutes, please? I want to say a few words and thank you all for coming here this evening. As you know, it's mine and Victoria's twenty-first birthday, so I'd like to wish her a happy birthday and thank you all for the wonderful gifts you have given us." He held up his hand to silence the loud cheers and clapping and continued. "You should also know that, although we are twins, she has never failed to boss me around and forever remind me that she is the eldest by some ten minutes." This comment made the guests laugh, and they clapped again. "Papa, I believe you wanted to say a few words too?"

Charles Fellwood remained seated because of his disability but forced a smile onto his face. "Yes, of course, thank you, Robert. Well, I don't have much to say, but may I wish our dear children, Robert and Victoria, a happy birthday and propose a toast to them." He raised his glass, and all the guests rose to their feet. "Robert and Victoria."

When the guests had settled down, Robert again took to his feet. "As some of you already know, I have another announcement to make. I want to introduce you to Anne Carter, this beautiful young lady at my side. She has made me the happiest man alive, for she has consented to become my wife, and tonight we are getting engaged."

Many of the guests knew nothing of Annie's background, and they raised their glasses, stamped their feet, and cheered loudly. Charles slowly toasted the couple and stared hard at his wife until she reluctantly did the same. With a broad grin on his face, Frank rose to his feet and raised his glass.

"To Robert and Annie." He grinned mischievously at Robert as he turned to Annie and said loudly, "Annie, are none of your own family here tonight? Could they not have some time off work? Robert, I think you should have invited Annie's mother to your party. Surely someone else could have milked the cows for one night."

Annie's eyes dropped to her lap as her face became bright red, and tears of embarrassment stung her eyes. Robert glared at the smirking man sitting opposite him.

"How could you be so cruel? There was no need for that."

Frank did not respond, for he was too weak with laughter. Victoria was furious, and Eleanor and Charles would have been happy if the ground had opened and swallowed them up.

Robert struggled to bring his temper under control as, taking to his feet, he faced his guests and forced himself to smile.

"Thanks to my brother-in-law and former friend, I must now make the situation clear, though I had hoped to leave this until a later date. I have known Annie for several years, and her family live in one of the tied cottages on our estate. Her father died of consumption a few years ago, and her mother has fought hard to support her children and stay out of the workhouse. Considering the hurdles this woman has had to overcome, she'd put most of us in this room to shame. For a time, Annie worked here as a kitchen maid before she left to get married. She has one child, a little girl called Selina, and her husband, Harry, died in a fire a couple of years ago. Since I have been managing the estate following David's death, I have gotten to know Annie better, and I am now in love with her. Her mother and family will soon move into the Lodge House on the estate."

Throughout this, Charles and Eleanor stared stonily at their son, and Annie kept her eyes in her lap. Robert calmly took a sip of his wine and then continued.

"Now, some of you may not approve of this relationship, but you should know that I will marry Annie, conventional or not, so please join me in a toast to my future bride."

He reached down and, taking Annie's hand, pulled her to her feet to stand beside him as he raised his glass and surveyed the shocked faces around the table. Victoria and then Sarah slowly rose to their feet, lifted their glasses, and spoke firmly. "Robert and Annie."

They looked around for support, and most of Robert's closest friends rose to their feet and joined in the toast. A few elderly relatives were tight-lipped as they pushed back their chairs and left the room silently, as did Charles and Eleanor.

"Right, folks, the excitement is over for the night. Perhaps I should thank you, Frank, for bringing all this out into the open; it's probably for the best. Come on, everyone, let's make our way to the hall, where the musicians will soon be playing, and we can relax, dance, and enjoy ourselves."

CHAPTER 13

Since Tom's death, Sabina had been helping with the milking on the estate. On six days a week, and often seven, she arose at four o'clock in the morning. On the day after Jack Bater found someone else to do her job, she woke early from habit, then realised she did not have to go to work. She found the option of staying in bed a rare treat, though, in truth, she was so excited about going to clean the Lodge House that she would have been content to get up at the usual time. As it was, she lay there until she heard the children stirring.

By eight o'clock, having got Edward and Stephen off to school and the little ones fed and organised for Liza to look after, Sabina and Annie set off for the Lodge House. Robert had left the gate slightly open and sent a workman to oil the lock of the back door so they could get in easily. By nine o'clock, having helped prepare breakfast at the Manor House, Maisie joined them, and she and Annie hugged each other.

"Oh, Annie, I can't believe you're going to marry Master Robert. Am I going to have to call you Miss Annie from now on?"

"No, silly; I shall always be Annie to you, when we're alone, anyway. I bet they were all surprised at the big house, weren't they?"

"It's been so funny. Miss Wetherby is disapproving, but everyone else is pleased for you, even Sid Hobbs, and Mrs Potts is delighted. How did it go at the engagement party?"

Annie pulled a face. "Badly, I think best describes it. She explained what had happened, and Maisie's eyes grew wide.

"Oh, how awful and how mean of Frank. Did many guests leave?"

"About a third of them, I suppose, but I quite enjoyed myself after that. At least we know now which people will accept our marriage and which won't. Anyway, I'm glad it's over. Now, where shall we start?"

"Sam Symons and John Cutcliffe will be here as soon as they've finished feeding the animals. Master Robert has told them to do as you say and remove all the rubbish. Fancy you having two men to boss around for the day."

They started in the sitting room, pulling down the ancient curtains, the dust making them cough as the material fell to pieces. With difficulty, they opened the sash windows wide and let in some much-needed fresh air. Clearing the sitting room and kitchen of rubbish took them most of the morning, and they could not believe where the time had gone, but suddenly they realised they were ravenous.

"We'll have to go back to the cottage to get something to eat." Sabina stood up and eased her aching back.

"No, it's all right. I've brought a food hamper from the Manor, and knowing Mrs Potts, there's probably enough in it to feed an army."

They went into the garden and found a stone bench to sit on, where they enjoyed hard-boiled eggs, ham and crusty, freshly baked bread. There was a large fruit cake as well, all washed down with ice-cold lemonade, that Maisie had stood in a bucket of cold water drawn from the well. With the hot sun beating down on them from a cloudless blue sky, Annie felt content.

After a short break, they continued working until the downstairs rooms were roughly swept. The two men had already removed one cartload of rubbish and were loading another. They were planning to have a bonfire in one of the fields.

Sabina flopped down onto a chair. "I'm afraid that's me done for today, girls. I'd love to carry on, but I'm exhausted; I don't know about you. Anyway, I need to get back and see how Liza's getting on; the children will be home from school by now, and I expect the little ones will have tired her out."

"I can stay another hour or so," said Maisie. "Miss Wetherby didn't say when I had to be back, but I know Mrs Potts would appreciate a hand with the evening meal. Goodness, I'm tired, too. It's hard work, but I've enjoyed it."

"Me, too. Robert would have got all this done for me, but I wouldn't have missed this for the world. It's been so enjoyable spending the whole day with you two. Shall we come again tomorrow?"

Over the next week, the three women worked hard in the Lodge House. When all the rubbish had been removed, the house looked more spacious than ever. Robert called in regularly, and Annie took him proudly around the house and showed him the work they would like carried out. Their priority was to investigate whether there was a fireplace in the parlour. Robert sent two workmen with pickaxes, and they hacked away at the plaster. It came off readily enough, and they soon exposed the bricked-up fireplace and set to work removing the bricks one by one. Across the mantel lay a huge oak beam, and they noticed some curious marks etched into it. Sabina shivered and was slightly uneasy when she saw them.

"Mum, what is it? Do you know what the marks are for?"

"Yes, I've seen them before. They're witches' marks. In the olden days, they were scratched onto places to ward off evil spirits. In this case, presumably to stop them coming down the chimney. They were often used in haunted houses; I hope that wasn't the case here."

"Is it going to worry you, Mum?"

"No, of course not. It will take more than a few scratches on a bit of wood to stop me from moving in here, and I've never heard of this house being haunted, have you?"

Annie shook her head. "No, but it's always been empty for as long as I can remember."

The men carried on removing the bricks one by one. It didn't take long for the ancient mortar was crumbling, and as the hole got bigger, debris began to fall down the chimney. Within minutes, the room was filled with an avalanche of billowing soot, dust, and ash, making it difficult to breathe, and they had no choice but to vacate the room. They ran coughing and sneezing into the garden, where they thankfully gulped in the clean, sweet air, and it was over an hour before the dust had settled enough to venture back in. There was a huge pile of debris by the fireplace, and Annie was glad they had not done too much cleaning before getting this job done. It would have been time wasted, for the soot and dust had gone everywhere, though, fortunately, they had closed the doors to the other rooms. As they started to shovel the dirt into sacks, they came across the skeletons of birds, the jawbone of a rat, a couple of bird's nests, and an old salt pot.

"What on earth was a salt pot doing in the chimney?"

"I expect it was put there on a ledge to keep the salt dry. You know, it always gets damp, and then it won't pour properly. Have you seen this?"

Sabina picked up a bunch of what had once been white feathers tied around the middle with a piece of string. She pursed her lips. "These were also put up chimneys to ward off evil spirits. I wonder how long ago the chimney was bricked up.

"A long time, I should think. We'll have to get this chimney swept before we do anything else."

The next day, all the chimneys were swept, and when that was done, the fires were lit to see if they drew correctly. Fortunately, they did, and the house was soon far too hot. Maisie spent two days cleaning the range, which occupied most of one wall in the kitchen. It was now black and sleek, with the fire on one side and the oven on the other. After all her hard work, Maisie was delighted that the range worked, and they decided to keep it lit. Above it, a long clothes airer called a 'Sheila's Maid' stretched from one wall to another, and Sabina knew it would be a godsend for drying clothes in the winter.

Soon, there was no more the women could do in the house, and they left the men to re-plaster the walls with lime mortar, replace the rotten windows and floorboards, and do all the other work needed before the house could be decorated and furnished.

Instead, they focused their attention on the garden and kept the two gardeners Robert had sent to help them very busy. Trees were felled, ground dug, and hedges trimmed. After a week of hard work, the garden was tidy and much larger than they had first thought. There was plenty of room for an extensive vegetable patch, and Sabina thought she might try keeping bees, for she loved honey. She told Annie she would like to continue keeping chickens, and before she knew it, Robert had sent workmen, who built not only a chicken run but a new chicken house as well. She sometimes had to pinch herself to ensure she was not dreaming..

CHAPTER 14

When all the work had been completed at the Lodge House, and it was ready to be furnished, Annie and Sabina invited Betsey, Liza, and Matilda to look around. It would still be a week or two until they could move in, as Robert had insisted on buying new furniture and household goods or sending spare ones from the Manor House. However, they could wait no longer to show off their new house.

The three older women were amazed at the space in the house as Annie and Sabina proudly showed them around. Until she married, Annie would have the largest bedroom to herself, as she now had delicate dresses to store, and soon, there would be wedding paraphernalia as well. Sabina and Liza would also have a room each, something neither of them could even imagine. With Willie and Mary no longer living at home, the boys and the girls would share the other two rooms, with Edward, Stephen, and Danny in the biggest one and Helen and Selina in the other.

Robert sent another hamper to the Lodge House, and when the women had finished their tour of the house, they sat at a new picnic table in the garden. The earlier rain had cleared up, but Sabina insisted they sit on some old blankets as the benches were still damp.

It was a jolly meal, and the women thoroughly enjoyed their afternoon. Betsey and Matilda were thrilled for Sabina, and Liza couldn't take in that she would soon be living in this magnificent dwelling. Eventually, Betsey said she must get back to the inn, or Ned would be wondering what had happened to her. As she stepped away from the picnic table, she slipped on the wet cobbles, and her leg twisted awkwardly below her as she fell heavily. At once, her companions were at her side, dismayed to see her leg lying at a ridiculous angle. Betsey was pale, and the sweat stood out on her brow as she tried not to cry out from the intense pain.

"Betsey, lie still, and Annie will get Doctor Luckett. It will be all right." Sabina tried to reassure her mother-in-law and nodded to Annie, who ran down the lane. She soon returned with the doctor, and his face was grim as he took in the situation at a glance.

"Now, Betsey, I can't pretend this isn't going to hurt because it is, but I'm going to have to pull your leg straight and put it in splints before I can take you to the hospital. If I don't do that, you could lose your leg." He looked at the others. "Can you get her something to bite on?"

The women watched in horror as he did what was necessary. Betsey bit down on a towel, and tears rolled down her old cheeks. Luckily, the procedure had taken place before Ned arrived, and he helped the doctor to get his wife onto the horse and cart and said he would accompany her to the hospital.

Ned returned many hours later, looking tired and upset, as he told his concerned customers at the inn what had happened. "She has to stay in the hospital overnight, and she should be home tomorrow. They've wrapped her leg in linen bandages, soaked in Plaster of Paris, and apparently, it will set hard into a cast to keep her leg still while it mends. They think it should heal all right, thanks to Doctor Luckett putting it into splints. It's marvellous what they can do these days."

The news of Betsey's accident soon spread around the village, and when Fred fetched her from the hospital the next day, there was quite a crowd outside the inn to welcome her home. She was pale and drawn and clearly in pain, but she smiled at everyone and thanked them for coming. Fred carried her inside and laid her on the bed, which they had already brought down from upstairs, and Eveline had made up with fresh sheets. Ned sat on the bed and held his wife's hand while Eveline made tea.

"Oh, Ned, I don't know how you'll cope with me laid up. You'll never be able to look after me and run the inn."

"It's certainly going to be difficult. I think we'll have to take on someone to help. If we could find a girl who could nurse you and help a bit with the chores, we'd probably be all right, but it's finding the right person quickly. Can you think of anyone?"

There was silence for a few moments until Fred spoke. "The only person I can think of is that girl, Charlotte, who had her baby here. When I gave her a lift to her aunt's house in Warkley, she mentioned that she used to work as a nurse at Exeter Hospital. I know she intended to have the baby adopted because she couldn't keep it and work. Perhaps she would come here for a while until you're better. You seemed to get on with each other."

"Oh, yes; she was such a pleasant girl, and I know her granny. Could you go to Warkley and ask her?"

"Yes, I'll go now because the horse and cart are already outside. Now, you take it easy, Mum, and I'll see you later."

It didn't take Fred long to travel to Warkley, and he hoped Charlotte hadn't already returned to Exeter. However, as he neared the cottage, he was relieved to see her hanging out some washing. She looked at him in surprise as he tethered the horse and entered the front gate.

"Hello, Fred, I didn't expect to see you again; what are you doing here?"

"Mother had a nasty fall yesterday and broke her leg. She's been to the hospital, and they've put it in plaster, but she'll be laid up for weeks. We need someone to nurse her and do a few chores, and you mentioned you're a nurse, so I wondered if you'd be interested. We'd pay you, of course."

"I see; how awful for poor Betsey. I'm so sorry. It's unfortunate to break a leg at her age, and it will probably take a while to mend."

"What about the baby? Is she still with you?"

At this, tears glistened in Charlotte's eyes and, to Fred's horror, began to trickle down her cheeks.

"No, she's not. She's gone, and I don't know where she is!"

"What do you mean? Has someone taken her?"

"Yes, my Aunty Joan. She sent me to the village yesterday to get some food and said she'd look after Doris, but when I got home, they were both gone. She's taken her somewhere to get her adopted. She says she didn't think I would do it. I think my father did know about the baby, and he's had a hand in this."

Fred put his arm around the girl to comfort her, for she was so upset. "I'm sorry you've had to give your baby up, Charlotte. Perhaps we could get her back?"

"Aunty Joan won't tell me where she took her, and in any case, I can't keep her and work. I knew I'd have to part with her, but I would have liked to keep her a little longer and at least say goodbye."

"Let me have a word with your Aunty and see if I can get the truth out of her. She should never have interfered."

"Thanks, Fred, but it's probably for the best. I kept putting it off. Anyway, I've no job to go to, and I would like to help Betsey and repay her kindness. I'd love to come and live at the inn for a few weeks. It will give me something else to think about. I could come with you now if you can wait until I pack my things. I can't wait to get away from here."

Charlotte would not let Fred go into the house with her because she knew he was longing to have words with her aunt. After a few minutes, she came out red-faced, clutching a bag with her few possessions, and slammed the door shut behind her. Fred said nothing but drove the horse and cart back to the inn and took Charlotte to his mother. Betsey was overjoyed to see the girl again, and relief was written all over Ned's face. Fred left them and returned to his work. He had finished the easel for Peter Webber and decided that he would deliver it to Sabina whilst he had the horse and cart out.

Sabina was busy packing up bits and pieces she wanted to take from the cottage to the Lodge House, and she was pleased to see Fred. "Hello, Fred, this is a surprise. How's Betsey? Is she home yet?"

"Yes, she's not too bad. I fetched her from the hospital earlier, and I've just persuaded Charlotte to come and nurse her for a few weeks because Dad would never have managed on his own. You know, the young girl who had the baby."

"Oh, I'm pleased to hear that; they will need help, and I know Betsey liked her. Does she still have the baby?"

"No, her aunt got her adopted, and Charlotte's upset, so this will help to distract her. Anyway, I'm here because I've finished making Peter's easel, so I thought I'd drop it in. I'll get it off the cart."

He returned with a fine wooden easel that could be adjusted to several heights.

"Oh, Fred, it's perfect; he'll be so pleased. What do I owe you?"

"Nothing, you know I'd do anything for you, Sabina, and the wood cost me next to nothing. I just hope he likes it."

"I'm sure he will, Fred, but here's a shilling, and thank you so much; I'll see you soon."

She pressed the money into his hand and refused to take it back, assuring him she could afford it.

Peter Webber had already started giving his talks at the school, and they had been well received. He was quite a character and could relate some amusing stories to the children, keeping their attention as they learned. Over his life, he had worked as a farm labourer, lime burner, and miner, so he had no shortage of tales to tell and knowledge to pass on. Mr Atkins soon realised he was an asset to the school. The children were fascinated by the loss of his hands and wanted to know all about the mining accident in which he had lost them.

For Peter, the twice-weekly sessions changed his life and gave him lots to think about as he planned what his next talks would be about. He didn't have the luxury of being able to make any notes, but he did try to think through the topics he would talk about, though, often on the day, he went off on a tangent.

Seth James and Francis Rudd visited Peter to discuss how best to help him.

"Would a hook be the best thing, Peter? Or would something of a different shape be best?"

"Since Sabina suggested this to me, I've thought about it a lot, and if you can make a harness to go around my shoulders, Seth, and strap onto my arms, then perhaps I could have a couple of different tools, one on each arm. My left arm finishes at my elbow, so perhaps a hook on the end would let me pull things toward me. My right arm's a bit better because I still have most of my forearm, which will give me better control. Do you think you could secure a fork to it? I could feed myself then, and that would be a godsend."

"Yes, that would be more useful than two hooks. Let's get you measured up then, and I'll see what I can do. I'll make a couple of hooks, and you can decide which is best, Peter. I think the difficult bit will be making them secure, but we can experiment and see what works best."

"I'm so grateful to you and Sabina for thinking of this. Anything you can do will be an improvement for me."

The men were about to leave when Sabina knocked gently on Peter's door and called out to him as she entered with the easel.

"Oh, hello, lads, I can guess what you're here for. Have you sorted something out?"

They told her what they had planned, and she looked thoughtful. "That's good, and look what I've brought for you, Peter; no excuse now, I shall expect a painting for Christmas."

Peter rose and inspected the easel. "Fred's made a wonderful job of it. How much do I owe him?"

"Nothing; he said it was only a few scraps of wood, and it didn't take him long. Now, let me adjust it to the right height for you. There, I think that's about right."

She stood back to survey it. "Now, have you got any paints and paper?"

"Yes, Mr Atkins has given me those over there look; quite a selection."

Sabina put a cloth, a cup of water, the paints, and the paintbrushes on the table near the easel and pegged a piece of paper to it. "There, you should be able to pick the brush you want from the jar with your teeth, rinse it in the water, and dry it slightly on the cloth. We might need to make some of the brushes a bit shorter for you to control them better. Mind you, I have another idea now." She turned to Seth and Francis. "I'm just wondering if a paintbrush could be fastened to Peter's arm instead of a fork when he wants to paint. It would be much easier to control than in his mouth."

"Yes, if we make something to hold a fork, I'm sure we could adapt a paintbrush to fit, and then he'd have a choice."

"It's incredible; thank you so much for everything you're doing for me. I enjoy going to the school, and I think the children like me coming."

"Aw, don't be daft. It was nothing, but I'm glad it's helped. Right, I'm going to leave you to it now, but I'll be back with a stew for you and Arthur and the boys later and to see how you're getting on. Now that I'm not working, I've got a lot more time to do things."

When she returned a few hours later, carrying a pot of stew with big fluffy dumplings, all the menfolk were at home and pleased to see her. They gathered around the easel, admiring Peter's efforts, which were not bad for a first attempt. He had outlined the scene from the kitchen window, capturing the row of cottages and the hills and trees in the background. Although far from perfect, Sabina thought it was probably better than she could do with two hands, and although there were a few drips and smudges here and there, from a distance, it was impressive.

As she went to leave, Arthur saw her out and took her hand in his. To her surprise, her heart fluttered in a way she had almost forgotten.

"Sabina, thank you so much. Dad was giving up on life, and what you've done has made such a difference to him. That stew smells delicious, and I insist on paying you for it. Here you are." He pressed a few coins into her hand and refused to take them back. "With Elsie and Maria in service, the meals you cook for us are much appreciated because none of us men are very good at it. We'll miss you when you move to the Lodge House, but I couldn't be more pleased for you. It couldn't happen to a nicer person."

Sabina was embarrassed at all the fuss but thanked him warmly and went home happily.

CHAPTER 15

Following the engagement party, Robert avoided his parents as much as possible and took his meals in his study. This arrangement suited him, for he was so involved in the running of the estate that whenever he was not outside working with Jack, he was to be found poring over the accounts. He found it difficult to fit everything into his busy schedule these days but loved every minute of it.

During the early spring, he delivered several lambs, believing it essential to have hands-on experience to understand farming fully and develop his knowledge. It was time to shear the sheep, and Robert watched for a while to see how it was done. It was essential to shear the sheep before the hot summer months to prevent blowflies from laying their eggs in the moist, warm wool. If this happened, the eggs would hatch, and the maggots would start to eat the sheep and cause infection. In some breeds, if the sheep were not shorn, their fleeces would become so heavy that if the animal rolled onto its back, it could not get up, and magpies had been known to peck out their eyes.

"Jack, it's time I had a go."

Robert had seen three sheep sheared efficiently by one of the most experienced farmworkers and decided that the task did not even look easy. He caught a sheep, held it between his knees, and started to cut away the wool. However, the animal was frightened, and sensing Robert's inexperience and nervousness, it struggled fiercely.

"Oh, for goodness sake, keep still." Robert became exasperated as the sheep writhed from side to side, making it impossible to cut the wool evenly.

"It's all right, just keep calm. You must hold the sheep more firmly. Let it know that you're in charge. You'll soon get the hang of it; we all had to learn."

Jack spoke calmly and glanced around at the other workmen, daring them to laugh. However, none of them did. They'd seen it all before and didn't want to put Robert off his task, for they had the greatest respect that he was even attempting to do the same work as them. "That's it. Now you're doing better. By the time you've shorn a hundred of them, you'll be pretty good." At this, the men did laugh.

"Yes, I'm getting there, but look at the state of that fleece. It's a disgrace compared to everyone else's, and it's taken me about five times as long."

"Never mind, as I say, you'll soon learn."

Jack was right, and by the end of the day, Robert could shear a sheep reasonably well. He was disappointed that he was still much slower than everyone else and unbelievably tired. His shoulders and back ached, and he had even greater respect for the men he employed who did this all day long without complaint.

Robert spent as much time as he could with Annie. They enjoyed riding over the moors, and Annie quickly became proficient in the saddle. She had been supervising the work in the Lodge House and was delighted with the result. Moving day arrived at last, and the children were excited, for they had not yet seen inside the house. Robert sent a horse and cart to their cottage to collect their personal belongings, and Sam Symons and John Cutcliffe spent the morning loading it up.

Sabina rounded up her family. "Right, come on, you lot. Say goodbye to our little house, and hop on the cart. I think there's just enough room for us to ride."

Sabina and Liza hadn't been to the house for a couple of weeks, and Annie couldn't wait to show them the newly painted rooms, now furnished with mostly new furniture.

Annie opened the front door, a broad smile on her face. "Welcome to your new home. I hope you'll like it here." She picked up Selina and carried her in, enjoying the gasps of amazement from her siblings. "Come on, Mum, I can't wait to show you and Liza the kitchen." She led the way, Sabina instructing all the children to stay with her and not wander off on their own.

"Oh, Annie, I can't believe we're going to live here."

Sabina and Liza were reduced to tears as they opened one cupboard after another and saw all the new pots and pans in the kitchen. The larder was bursting with food supplied by Mrs Potts. Enjoying herself immensely, Annie led them upstairs and showed them where they would sleep.

"Right, Mum, this bedroom is for you."

The room had lime-washed walls and blue curtains, her mother's favourite colour. The floorboards had been varnished and were adorned with blue rugs. The bed had a blue patchwork quilt and soft pillows, and on the sunny windowsill, Annie had placed a vase of late bluebells.

"Oh, Annie, I don't believe it. Honestly, I keep thinking I'll wake up in a minute." Sabina's eyes were round with wonder.

"Come on, we haven't finished yet. Next door is your bedroom, Liza. It's a bit smaller, but I think you'll like it." Again, the walls were lime-washed, and the floorboards varnished, but this time, the curtains, bedspread, and rugs were a pale green, and on the windowsill was a bottle-green vase of white roses.

"Annie, it looks amazing. Thank you so much. I never expected to sleep in a room as grand as this and in my own bed. I don't know what Isaac would have made of it all."

"You deserve it, Liza. Right now, I expect the rest of you would like to see where you'll be sleeping. Come on then, let's see what we can find."

None of the children had ever slept in a proper bed, having made do with a palliasse stuffed with feathers or straw on the floor. Annie led them along the landing and into another large bedroom where Edward, Stephen, and Danny would sleep. The room had three single beds, each with a red patterned bedspread. The curtains and rugs were also a dark red, contrasting nicely with the cream walls. In the corner was a large box of toys, and alongside it was the rocking horse, once so loved by Robert's sister, Sarah. The children gasped in amazement and ran to see what was in the box.

"Yes, I thought that box might interest you. Some of those toys were Robert's when he was a boy, and he has said you can have them. Now, you have to share the rocking horse with the girls, so don't forget that. There are some new books on that bookshelf, so now you need to learn to read properly. Come on, you can come back and play in a minute, but let's finish the tour of the house first."

Annie was thoroughly enjoying herself.

Across the corridor, a slightly smaller room held two single beds for Helen and Selina. The curtains and the bed covers were a deep pink, and the rugs were patterned with grey and maroon. Again, in one corner was a toy box, and on a shelf along the wall were six dolls. Next to the toy box were a doll's pram, a cot, and a doll's house. The two girls were wide-eyed as they made a beeline for the dolls. However, when they reached them, Helen turned nervously to Annie whilst Selina was braver and fingered the brocade on one of the doll's skirts.

"Can we touch them, Annie?" whispered Helen. She was four years old, a pretty little girl with blond hair and blue eyes. She had always been a placid, loving child, and she ran to Annie and put her arms around her waist as she gazed up at her.

"Yes, of course, you can, but you must look after them nicely and not be rough. That means you too, Selina." Annie took a doll from the shelf and handed it to her daughter. "You must be gentle, Selina. Nurse the dolly like this and cuddle her." Annie put the doll in the little girl's arms and showed her how to hold it and rock it to and fro. "There, now, when she is asleep, you can put her in the cot or take her for a walk around the room in the pram."

"This is nice, Mummy. I like this house. Can we stay here forever and ever?" Selina was much more mischievous than her Aunty Helen and had always been into everything, often running rings around poor Liza when she was looking after her. An intelligent child, at nearly three, she was beginning to settle down a bit.

"Yes, we can, but you must be careful not to break things and not come in with muddy feet. Can you do that?"

"Yes, Mummy, I promise." Annie smiled at her daughter's solemn face.

"Come on then, let's go downstairs again, and I'll finish showing you around down there."

Annie led the way and showed them the parlour and the sitting room, where they marvelled at the chairs and sofas they would have to sit on. The furniture had been brought from the big house and was not new, but the Carter family were impressed.

When they had seen their fill of the house, Annie led them outside, where John Cutcliffe was just releasing the hens into their new home. The garden had been forked over, and onions, potatoes, peas, and beans had been planted and were growing strongly. At the far end, where an enormous sweet chestnut tree stood, Annie had asked Fred to fix up a swing, a slide, and a see-saw. The children whooped with delight, and Selina struggled to be released from Annie's arms.

"Well, I don't think they'll be much trouble for a while. Shall we leave them to it and have a cup of tea? Oh, there's Robert. He said he'd come today."

Robert came in through the garden gate and surveyed the scene around him. "How's it going? Do you think you can all live here, all right?" He took Annie's hand and kissed it gently.

"Oh, Master Robert, we can never thank you enough. This house is incredible. I don't think I'll ever stop smiling." Sabina stood before her future son-in-law with tears in her eyes.

"I'm glad you like it, Sabina, but there is something you must do for me."

"Anything, anything at all. What is it you want me to do?"

"You must stop calling me Master Robert and just call me Robert, please; can you do that?"

"Yes, of course, if you're sure."

Robert nodded. "Now shall we look in the larder to see what we can have for our tea? I instructed Mrs Potts to make one of her big meat pies, and there should also be some potatoes and vegetables. She might even have made one of her famous trifles and a chocolate cake. I thought it would help to have an easy meal on moving day and one we can celebrate with."

When the Carter family sat down for their tea that night, they could not stop smiling, unable to believe their good fortune.

CHAPTER 16

Robert and Annie had set their wedding date for mid-August, and time was moving on. Now that the family had moved into their new home, Annie felt she could turn her attention to her wedding plans. With this in mind, she asked her Aunt Eveline if she would make her dress and the bridesmaids' dresses for Mary, Helen, and Selina. She would have liked Sarah to be a bridesmaid, too, but Eleanor and Charles were determined not to attend the wedding and planned to travel to London with Victoria and Frank after the baby was born.

Eveline was willing to make the dresses and went to George's shop with Annie again. The two women asked to see all the silks and satins suitable for a wedding dress, and George's daughter, Harriet, willingly laid out everything available. When George appeared, Annie could not resist provoking him.

"Hello, Uncle George. Aunty Eveline and I are looking for some material for my wedding dress."

"I heard you were getting married, Annie. Congratulations."

"Thank you. Yes, I'm very lucky, and my family is finding the Lodge House so much more comfortable than they would have been in the workhouse. Unfortunately, I'm not keen on any of these materials, so I think we'll have to look further afield. I wish you a good day."

Annie left the shop with her nose in the air and a smile on her face, and Eveline had to hurry to catch up with her. When she did so, she was laughing. "I should tell you off for what you just said to my brother, but it was so funny, I can't, and I have to say he did deserve it."

"Yes, it was a bit naughty of me, wasn't it, but I couldn't resist. He was so horrible to Mum after Dad died. The thing is, though, where can we get the material we need now?"

"Let's go to Exeter on the train and see if we can find what we want there. What do you think? We could take Sabina with us. We'd have to stay overnight because it's too far to travel there and back in one day and have time for shopping. Do you think Robert would take us to the station?"

"Yes, I'm sure he would, and if he'd let Maisie help Liza with the children, we could stay overnight. I'll ask him. We must get on with it, though, or you won't have time to make the dresses."

Annie went straight to the Manor House and, as usual, entered through the kitchen. She had been to see Sarah and Victoria a few times, for the three had become firm friends, much to Robert's delight. Mrs Potts was pleased to see her and made her a cup of tea whilst Maisie went to tell Robert that Annie was in the kitchen. Annie did not want to risk running into Miss Wetherby or Robert's parents if she could help it. Robert arrived, beaming, and suggested they walk around the grounds. As they strolled arm-in-arm to the lake, she told him what had happened earlier in George's shop, and he was amused.

"I think a trip to Exeter is an excellent idea, but I'll escort the three of you. I know I can't come shopping with you and see the new material, but that's no problem because I have some business I can attend to, and meet you all later for dinner. I don't want the three of you unprotected in Exeter, especially overnight. It's no problem about Maisie. She can spend a couple of days with Liza looking after the children; I'm sure she'll be delighted."

A few days later, Dodger took Robert and the three women to Eggleston Station to catch the first train and promised to collect them late the next day. Sabina and Annie were excited, for they had never been on a train, let alone visited the city. They were early, and as they waited on the platform for the train to arrive, Annie noticed a tall woman and thought she was familiar, but couldn't quite remember where she had seen her. She asked the others if they recognised her. Sabina and Eveline didn't, but Robert said he thought she was the woman they had seen answer the door at Buzzacott House.

"Yes, of course, that's it. She's so tall, she's quite distinctive."

When the train arrived, they boarded and found some seats, though it was not due to depart for another twenty minutes. While looking out the window, they noticed a young woman with a baby approaching the tall woman and speaking to her. The young mother kissed her baby tenderly and handed her over to the older woman, who cuddled the child affectionately. The mother seemed upset as she pressed something into the other woman's hand and then swiftly boarded the train. The older woman walked briskly out of the station with the baby in her arms.

The young woman moved along the train looking for a spare seat and found one close to Annie and her party. Tears were rolling down her cheeks as she sat down and searched for a handkerchief. Sabina couldn't bear to see someone so upset and went to the woman. "Is there anything I can do to help? I can see you're upset about something."

"No, there's nothing anyone can do but thank you; it's kind of you to ask. I've just had to part with my baby." The young woman sobbed as she told them she was called Jean.

"Oh dear, I'm so sorry. That's terrible. I would hate to part with any of my children. Is it a relative that has taken the child?"

"No, I've no one to help me, and I have to work, so I can't look after the baby. The father abandoned me as soon as he knew I was in the family way, and I don't know where he is now. I answered an advertisement in a newspaper. It said arrangements could be made for unwanted babies to be adopted or cared for until the mother could have them back. I'm hoping to find a job where I can keep the baby with me. I must admit I thought the woman I met would have been younger, but she seemed caring enough."

"Do you know where she lives?"

"Not exactly, but somewhere in Barnstaple, I believe, though she's moving house next week. We agreed to meet here at the station as it was about halfway for both of us. I had to pay her to take the child, of course, but she's promised to write to me every week, and when she's settled in her new home, she says I'll be able to see Rosie whenever I like, so at least I have that to look forward to."

Annie and Robert exchanged puzzled glances, for they were sure the woman lived at Buzzacott House, several miles from Barnstaple. However, they decided to say nothing as they didn't want to cause the woman more worry.

"Now, I'm sure your baby will be fine. As you say, the lady seemed pleased to take her, and no doubt, you'll hear from her in a week or two. It's not so bad if you can see the baby occasionally."

"Yes, I'm sure you're right; I'm just being silly, but thank you for your kindness."

Sabina resumed her seat beside Eveline and waited nervously for the train to depart. Annie, seated opposite them and beside Robert, was also impatient to find out what it was like to ride on a train. Robert and Eveline had allowed Sabina and Annie to sit by the window, and they enjoyed pointing out various landmarks as the train chuffed along the line to Exeter.

"I can't believe how fast we are travelling." Sabina was wide-eyed. "Are you sure it won't crash?"

"No, it's safe, and signals control the trains coming the other way, so they never end up on the same track. Relax, and enjoy the journey. Isn't the countryside beautiful?"

"Yes, and it's so interesting to see into all the farmyards and gardens as you pass. Look, some children are waving to us."

Three children sat on a garden wall, waved to the train as it passed, and laughing, the three women waved back.

All too soon, the train arrived in Exeter, and once outside the station, Robert waved down a carriage. "I know an inn near here where we can stay for the night, so if we go there first, we can leave our luggage, and then you can go shopping."

The carriage took them to the inn, where the innkeeper welcomed Robert and assured him he could find rooms for them all. Robert had a room to himself, whilst the three women shared a room with one double bed and a single. The carriage then took them into the centre of Exeter, where Robert went about his business and left Sabina and Annie in the expert hands of Eveline. They agreed to meet back at the inn for a meal later.

Eveline took them to a dressmaker's shop that she knew, and before long, all three were poring over luxurious fabrics.

"Oh, Annie, I like this one, but I shudder to think what it would cost." Sabina caressed the shiny white satin gently.

"It is lovely, but I have been married before. Do you think I should wear cream or another colour other than white?"

"I suppose that might be more fitting. How about this one?" Eveline held up a rich cream silk material.

"Oh, yes, that is lovely. Is it too expensive?"

"Of course not; Robert said you were to have what you liked. I think this would hang beautifully, and we could trim it with some of that lace." Eveline pointed to the top shelf. "Could we have a look at that lace, please?"

Mary Robbins, the shopkeeper, enjoyed their enthusiasm and was more than willing to show them any of her fabrics. She reached for the lace. "Here you are, and yes, I agree that cream fabric does hang nicely, and this lace will complement it perfectly. When is the wedding?"

"In just a few weeks, so there isn't much time. I hope you have enough fabric because we must buy some today."

"Now, don't you worry, I have everything here you'll need. We have sequins and pearls and ribbons and bows, so you'll be spoilt for choice."

Mary Robbins was right, and it took the three women more than two hours to choose everything they needed for Annie and the three bridesmaids. For Annie, they decided on the cream silk to be trimmed with delicate lace and tiny seed pearls. For the bridesmaids, Mary, Helen, and Selina, there was more deliberation, for there were so many gorgeous colours to choose from. They finally settled on a delicate lilac material, which they thought would suit all three children, and arranged to collect their purchases the following day. They enjoyed the rest of their afternoon, browsing in the shops, and then hailed a carriage to take them back to the inn.

CHAPTER 17

Eveline continued to visit Jane Chugg at Hollyford Farm regularly, and each time she went, she showed Maria Webber how to cook another meal. The girl was a keen learner and enjoyed their time together in the kitchen. One day, when Eveline visited, Doctor Luckett was just leaving the house as she arrived.

"Good morning, Doctor; how is Jane today?"

"I'm afraid she's seriously ill, Eveline, but she'll be pleased to see you."

"I didn't come last week as I had a cold, and I didn't want to risk passing it on to her, but I'm looking forward to seeing her today."

Eveline went into the kitchen and told Maria she would see Jane before they did any cooking. When she entered the bedroom, she was shocked at the change in Jane's appearance. The old lady was propped up on pillows, and her eyes were shut. Her face was ashen, and she had lost more weight. Eveline sat quietly beside her and waited. After a few moments, Jane's blue eyes opened, and when she saw her friend, she smiled weakly.

"Hello, Eveline, how nice to see you. Are you feeling better?"

"Yes, I'm fine, thanks, but I didn't want to pass my cold on to you. How are you feeling?"

"Not too good, as you can see. To be honest, I just want it to be over. I'm such a burden on everyone, and I know I won't get better. I wish the doctor would give me something to send me on my way."

"Now, you mustn't talk like that. You know what they say, where there's life, there's hope."

"Aye, I know, and you mean well, but we both know I won't be here much longer."

Eveline squeezed her friend's hand. "Is there anything I can get you?"

"No, I've had my medicine, and I'm not in pain. Just sit and tell me all that's going on. I like to hear the gossip."

Eveline told her all about Annie and Sabina moving into the Lodge House and how Annie was going to marry Master Robert.

"I'm making her wedding dress myself. Luckily, it's a simple design, and Matilda Rudd is helping me. She's a skilled seamstress, and having a sewing machine makes all the difference. We've already made the bridesmaids' dresses for Mary, Helen, and Selina, so I think we'll finish in good time, though I was a bit worried for a while. The banns were called for the first time last Sunday, so they'll be married in a couple of weeks."

"You tell Annie I'm pleased for her. She deserves to find happiness after what happened to Harry; it was such a tragedy."

They chatted for a while until Eveline could see Jane struggling to keep her eyes open. "I'm going to help Maria prepare the dinner now, Jane, so I'll see you later."

In the kitchen, Maria was chopping up steak and kidneys for a pie.

"Right then, Maria, let's see how you get on with the pastry. I showed you how to make it the other day, so hopefully, you can remember what to do. I'll dig some potatoes and pick a few peas to go with it."

Eveline was about to dig some early new potatoes when Charlie appeared.

"Hey, there's no need for you to do that. It's kind of you to teach Maria to cook, but I'm not having you digging potatoes."

"Nonsense, it's not a problem, and I'm sure you've other work to do."

"Nevertheless, I'll dig them, but you can pick the peas if you like. That's a fiddly job I don't care for."

Eveline's heart suddenly lurched as she looked into his vivid blue eyes. She blushed, and Charlie's eyes followed her thoughtfully. They continued their tasks in silence until Charlie straightened up and eased his back.

"There, I think that's enough teddies for today and tomorrow, and then I'll dig some more. They're better dug fresh; they scrape more easily. Have you finished picking the peas?"

"Yes, there are loads here, so it doesn't take long, but this is enough for a couple of meals. These are better gathered fresh, too."

"Come on, then, I'll carry these potatoes back to the kitchen for you."

"Thanks, Charlie, but I can manage if you're busy."

"No, it's no trouble. Anyway, I've been hoping for an opportunity to talk to you. I notice you always ride over to see Jane, and I wondered if you'd like to go riding with me one day. We could go out over Exmoor; the scenery's beautiful there. Could you leave the children for a few hours?"

"I love riding, though I have little time for it these days. I expect Sabina would mind the children for me. She never seems to mind how many children she has to look after."

"Is that a yes, then?" Charlie beamed at her, and once again, those bright blue eyes made her go weak at the knees.

Eveline blushed again. "Er, I don't know …"

Charlie put down the basket of potatoes and took her hand. "Eveline, I've become fond of you over the last few weeks, and I'd like to spend a day with you. Is there anything wrong with that?"

"Well, no, but ..."

"So, would you like to spend the day with me and go riding on Exmoor?"

"Yes, I would, but ..."

"What else is there to say, then? No buts. Can I take that as a yes?"

She suddenly smiled widely at him. "Yes, you can, Charlie Chugg. I'd like that. How about next Wednesday?"

"Grand, I'll look forward to it. Now I must go because Jack Bater has said Arthur Webber and I can go ferreting in the front meadow at the Manor Farm. It's teeming with rabbits, and they keep eating the crops. It'll be a bit of fun, and we can sell the rabbits in the village." As they reached the yard gate, Charlie put the basket down, swiftly took Eveline's hand, and kissed it gently, looking at her with laughter dancing in his eyes. "If I don't see you before, I'll see you here on Wednesday, about ten o'clock then. Bye."

Whistling happily, Charlie saddled his horse and rode to the farm cottages to meet Arthur Webber. He knocked loudly on the door and heard Arthur's father, Peter, shout to him to come in.

"Hello, Peter, how are you?"

"I'm fine, thank you, Charlie. Off ferreting, I hear?"

"Yes, that's right. Is Arthur around?"

"Aye, he's out the back choosing which ferrets to take. He's got plenty of them. Go through, lad."

"Thanks, Peter. This must be the easel I've been hearing all about then?"

"Yes, it gives me something to do, but it will take a lot of practice before I can produce anything worthwhile. Mind you, I've plenty of time."

Charlie surveyed the painting currently clipped to the easel. It was of a nearby cove surrounded by cliffs and seagulls wheeled in the foreground. "That looks like Raparree Beach if I'm not mistaken. Am I right?"

"Yes, I know it so well; I can picture it in my mind, though, of course, it would be better to go there and paint it. I'm pleased you recognised it, though."

"It's good, Peter, and far better than I could do with both hands, though that's not saying a great deal."

"You're very kind, but as I say, at least it gives me something to do. Go on now, out and find Arthur; he's expecting you."

Charlie found Arthur in his shed. He had ten cages, each housing a ferret, and one had newly born young.

"Hello, Arthur, you have a fine lot of ferrets. How many shall we take?"

"I think two will be plenty. These two here are both jills, and they're best for catching rabbits. They're not as aggressive as the males and less likely to kill the rabbits."

"Yes, I've heard that. I'm looking forward to this. It's not often a landowner gives his permission for ferreting."

"No, it isn't, but Jack said Master Robert doesn't mind, and we can keep all we catch and sell them in the village. It'll be a bit of extra money, won't it? I wish all the landowners were that sensible. The rabbit numbers need to be kept down, but most would have you sent to jail for daring to catch a few. Shall we get going?"

They put the ferrets into separate sacks and set off up the lane to the meadow. It was a large field with a slight incline and a stream running across the bottom. In one of the top corners was a large number of rabbit burrows.

"My goodness, there are a lot of burrows, Arthur. Have you brought enough nets?"

"Aye, I've plenty, and I mended several of them last night. Here, Charlie, you start pegging the nets around the burrows over that way, and I'll do the same over here."

Arthur handed Charlie a handful of nets, and half an hour or so later, the traps were pegged around each hole in the ground.

"Right, let's see how we get on." Arthur reached into the sack and retrieved the first ferret. "This here's Tinker, and she's my best ferret. She's getting on a bit now, but a grand rabbiter she is. Never lets me down." Arthur popped her down the first hole and then reached into another sack. "And this one here's Tinker's daughter, Titch. She's small for a ferret, and this is her first time, so I hope she'll do the business." He stroked the blond ferret and then carefully put her down a hole.

Both ferrets vanished immediately, and for a few minutes, nothing happened. Then two rabbits came bolting out of their burrows and straight into the nets, which immediately tightened around them. The men ran swiftly to the rabbits, peeling off the nets. Holding the rabbits' hind legs firmly in one hand and their necks in the other, they gave a sharp pull, and with a faint click, their necks were broken, and they lay lifeless. They quickly put the nets back over the burrows again. For the next hour or more, the two men were kept busy, as one after another, rabbits shot at speed out of the holes and into the nets. When Tinker reappeared, Arthur picked her up and stroked her fondly.

"Well, old girl, you've not lost your touch. You did a good job today. I wonder where that daughter of yours has got to. I hope she's not going to lead me a merry dance."

He put the older ferret back into a bag, and they removed the rest of the nets from around the holes. As Charlie gathered the last one, the younger ferret, Titch, poked her head out of the burrow and allowed him to pick her up. However, as he carried her across to Arthur, she gave him a sharp bite on his thumb, and he cried out in pain.

"Here, take the blasted animal. She's bitten my thumb, almost to the bone; vicious animal."

"Aye, they can give a nasty nip; their teeth are sharp. Make sure you wash that with salty water when we get back, Charlie. You don't want it going poisonous."

They counted the rabbits, now hung on a long stick that they carried between them. To their amazement, they had caught twenty-one rabbits.

"I think that's the most I've ever caught in one go; a nice little earner, wasn't it? A bit of fun, too. Shall we walk through the village and sell some?"

"Yes, might as well."

They walked through the village and found plenty of people wanting to buy a rabbit for their tea. They sold them for four pence each, which was a bargain, but after all, it had cost them nothing, and people were hungry. They debated whether to call at the Lodge House because Sabina had no need to buy rabbits these days.

"What do you think? Would Sabina think it a cheek if we called?"

"By the expression on your face, you'll be disappointed if we don't. Got a soft spot for her, have you? Well, I don't blame you; a lovely woman, she is."

"No, it's nothing like that, but she's been so kind to Dad, and I'd like to give her a few rabbits for free. I haven't got much else I can give her."

"Come on then, nothing ventured, nothing gained."

They raised the shiny brass knocker on the newly painted front door of the Lodge House, and Liza answered. "Hello, lads, looks like you've had a busy day. Selling them, are you?"

"Aye, Liza, we are, but is Sabina around? I wanted a word with her."

"Yes, come in, Arthur. She's in the kitchen making bread, but I know she'll be pleased to see you."

"Arthur, I'll go on now because I need to get back to the farm to do the milking. Alfred said he'd do it tonight, but I want to let him sit with Jane. I'll take these three rabbits, and you can sell the rest, all right?"

"Yes, if you're sure, Charlie. Thanks for your help. Shall we do it again sometime?"

"Yes, I'd like that; I enjoyed it. Bye for now."

Liza showed Arthur through to the kitchen, where Sabina was rosy-cheeked as she firmly kneaded a large lump of dough.

"Hello, Arthur, what brings you here? Is Peter all right?"

"What, of yes, he's fine, thanks. I've been rabbiting with Charlie Chugg, and would you believe we caught twenty-one of them? We've sold most of them in the village, but I wondered if you'd like a few."

"I would indeed. I love rabbit stew, even though we've eaten so much of it over the years. It's always a tasty meal. How much are they?"

"Oh no, I don't want anything for them. You've been so kind to us, Sabina. It would please me to give you something for a change."

"That's kind of you, Arthur, thank you. Leave a few rabbits with me, and I'll make a big pot of stew for us and you, too. I'll bring it over tomorrow if you like?"

"That would be grand, Sabina. There is one condition, though. Would you stay and eat with us? I only see you in passing, and it would be nice to sit and have a chat with you. Dad would enjoy it, too."

"Very well, thank you. I'll see you tomorrow at tea time."

CHAPTER 18

In the early hours of the fifteenth of July, Victoria went into labour and rang the bell to summon help.

"Maisie, the baby's coming; please wake my husband and arrange for someone to fetch Doctor Luckett."

The maid nodded and went swiftly along the corridor to Frank's room. It was two o'clock in the morning, but although she knocked loudly, she was unable to get an answer. However, the noise awoke Robert, who came to see what was happening.

"It's all right, Maisie, don't worry. I'll wake Frank. Ask Caleb to fetch Doctor Luckett."

Robert entered the room and pursed his lips when he saw that Frank's bed had not been slept in. He hurried downstairs to the drawing room to see if his brother-in-law had fallen asleep in a chair, but as he passed through the hallway, he heard Frank enter by the front door. It was immediately apparent he was drunk and smelt strongly of cheap perfume.

"God, how you disgust me. Your wife's in labour, and you roll home drunk, and goodness knows where you've been to smell the way you do." Robert glared at the man.

"Oh, come on, Robert, I'm only human. You must know that wives are not much fun when they're heavily pregnant. I suppose you don't know that yet, but you soon will, my friend."

"I'm no friend of yours, but for goodness sake, have a wash and sober up before you go to Victoria. She'll smell another woman on you."

"Oh, she's used to it. She doesn't seem that bothered. You have a most understanding sister, old man. Anyway, there's no point in me getting in the way until it's all over. With any luck, it should give me time to get my head down for a few hours."

Robert considered preventing the man from ascending the stairs but realised it was pointless and stood to one side, seething. Frank lurched past him, laughing loudly.

This being Victoria's second baby within a short time, her labour did not last long, and by six o'clock, she held her new son in her arms. Doctor Luckett stayed with her throughout and delivered the healthy baby. As the doctor descended the staircase, Robert approached him with questioning eyes.

"Hello, Robert, yes, good news. Your sister has a fine baby boy, and both mother and baby are doing well."

"Thank you, Doctor Luckett. May I see her?"

"Yes, of course, though I was expecting to see the father waiting?"

"Oh, he'll be here soon, I'm sure. Thanks for everything you've done."

Robert tore up the stairs and knocked on his sister's door. She was sitting up in bed, cradling her newborn son, and she smiled as Robert entered.

"Hello, Robert, what are you doing up this early?"

"I heard all the commotion in the night and waited up to see how things went. How are you?"

"I'm fine, thanks. This birth was so much easier than when I had Caroline. He's a bigger baby, too, but they say the first is the worst."

Robert pulled back the shawl and studied his new nephew. "He's lovely, Victoria. What are you going to call him?"

"If Frank agrees, I'd like to call him Joshua after our grandad."

"I like the name, and did you realise that today is Saint Swithin's Day? It looks like it will be fine, and I'm pleased about that because you know what they say: if it rains on Saint Swithin's Day, it will rain for forty days and forty nights."

"Oh, that's an old wives' tale."

"Maybe, but as we plan to cut the hay in the big field this morning, I'm pleased to see the sun shining."

"Is there any sign of Frank? I thought he might be waiting to see his new son."

"No, he was home quite late, and I've not seen him yet this morning. Do you want me to wake him?"

"No, don't bother. He won't come until he's ready. I'm afraid he's not exactly the doting or faithful husband I had hoped for, Robert, but at least he doesn't mistreat me. That's why I think you're right to marry for love. I realise now I didn't know Frank nearly well enough when I agreed to marry him. All I saw was a handsome face, and I fell for his charm."

"Well, the way he behaves is disgraceful, and I shall be telling him so when I see him."

"You'd be wasting your time, but thanks for coming to see me. Now, go and have your breakfast. I'm hoping to have a nap; I'm tired now."

"Yes, of course. I've got a busy day ahead because, as I say, we're cutting the hay this morning, and then I'm taking Annie and her family to the fair this afternoon. You know, it comes to the village every year, but I've never been. Have you?"

"No, of course not; we were never allowed as children, but have a good time."

"Thanks, I'm sure we will, and I'll see you this evening."

Robert spent the morning with Jack and the other farmhands, cutting the long grass with scythes. It was a big field, and the grass was thick, although it was the second cut of the year. The men were stripped to the waist, and the sun glistened on their sweat-drenched, rippling muscles as their blades cut through the long grass and laid it in swathes. It was essential to dry the hay quickly, for then it would be high in sugar content and more nourishing for the animals during the winter.

Jack straightened up to ease his aching back and mopped his brow, dripping with sweat. "It's a good year, Master Robert. The cows won't go hungry this winter."

"No, this grass should make excellent hay, especially if the weather stays dry for a few days."

"Yes, and I think it will. Why don't you get off now, sir? You said you were going to the fair this afternoon, and we've done more than three parts of the field now. The men and I will easily get it finished by supper."

Robert surveyed the field. "Yes, I think you're right, Jack. We've made excellent progress this morning. Why don't you call the men in now to have their lunch break, and then you could finish it this afternoon."

Jack nodded, and Robert went to wash and get something to eat before calling for Annie.

The Carter children were excited. They had been to the fair before but never with Robert, and they knew he would, no doubt, treat them to at least some sweets or perhaps a toffee apple. Annie answered the door herself and smiled at him happily.

"Hello, Robert, there are some rather impatient children here waiting for you. We're ready, so shall we go?"

They set off, Annie holding Robert's hand on one side and Selina's on the other. Danny held Robert's other hand, little knowing it was that of his big brother. They strolled at Danny's pace, and Edward, Stephen, and Helen skipped ahead happily. Sabina and Liza said they would come along a little later.

As they walked through the village, Noeleen Cutcliffe was leaving her house with her five daughters. From her first marriage, Clarice, Ruth, and Susanna were in their early teens and walked with their mother, but her stepdaughters, Daisy and Rachael, soon caught up to the Carter children and walked with them. On the way, they were joined by other villagers making their way to the fairground on the common, for it was to open at two o'clock.

A wooden archway had been erected at the entrance to the fair, and it was decorated with flowers and greenery. Across the top lay a white glove on a stick, symbolising the hand of friendship and a warm welcome to the fairground people. The mayor stood on a raised wooden platform, his gold chain gleaming brightly around his neck. A man beside him played a drum roll to silence the crowd. After a short speech, the mayor cut a red ribbon and declared the fair was open.

Annie suggested they walk around the fairground first and decide what they would like to spend their pennies on. They were spoilt for choice. Fairgrounds had been in decline just a couple of decades ago, but they were now popular once again. This year, there were three fairground rides to choose from. One, the Dobby Horses, they had seen before. The garishly painted horses were bolted to the wooden floor and went up and down as the carousel went round and round. The children were enthralled and would have happily spent all their money there and then to have a ride.

However, they walked on past many side stalls, some selling pasties and cakes, bacon and sausage sandwiches, and others with sweets called 'fairings' such as sugared almonds, gingerbread, and toffee apples. Sideshows costing tuppence a time included the Crazy Mirrors, showing distorted images, Gypsy Freda, the fortune teller, Robert Tipney, the Human Skeleton, and Charlie, the very tall man. The children were round-eyed as they listened to the fair hands trying to entice people inside and part with their money.

The two new fairground rides were even more exciting than the Dobby Horses, and they stood and watched in wonder. The Velocipede had bicycles, and the people riding them made the carousel turn by pedal power. With the combined effort of so many cyclists, it went surprisingly fast. The other ride was called the Sea on Land. Brightly coloured boats were bolted to the wooden floor of the carousel, but as well as revolving, the floor, which was painted blue and white, undulated as would the sea.

They continued past a boxing booth, where several young men were waiting to try their luck at beating an enormous giant of a man employed by the fair. Annie thought anyone taking him on must be mad. Next to that was a coconut shy, and the children were intrigued because they had never seen coconuts before. Towards the end of the fairground were pens containing all kinds of livestock, for many farmers bought and sold animals at the fair.

"Right then, which ride would you most like to go on?"

"Ooh, can we go on one, Robert?" Stephen was round-eyed as he had never for one moment expected to have a ride.

"Yes, I think we should all go on a ride together, and it looks to me as if the Dobby Horses would be best for all of us. Would you be happy with that?"

He could see from the smiling faces around him that his suggestion met with approval, so they strolled to the carousel and waited for it to stop. He lifted Edward, Stephen, and Helen onto three horses in a row and told them to hold on tight. Annie sat Selina in front of her on a white horse, and Robert settled Danny on a black horse next to Annie's and climbed up behind him. The carousel soon filled up with people, and Robert paid the man one shilling and tuppence.

Annie spotted Ruth Cutcliffe on a horse a few rows in front of her and wondered how she could afford a ride, for the Cutcliffes were not wealthy. Selina and Danny cried out excitedly as the horses started to go up and down, and the carousel began to turn, getting ever faster. Annie grinned at Robert, as she, too, had never been on a ride before.

The fairground attendant paid much attention to Ruth, and Annie watched in concern, for although he was good-looking, he was quite a bit older than Ruth. All too soon, the ride finished, and Annie and Robert helped the children to dismount from their horses. Annie saw that Ruth was staying on for another ride and that the man had his arm around her shoulders.

"I'm a bit concerned about Ruth. Look, she's flirting with that fair worker, and I don't like the look of him. Her mother will be cross if she sees her."

"There's nothing you can do about it, and she can't come to much harm here with all these people around. Now, what shall we do next? Would anyone like to see the Human Skeleton or perhaps the crazy mirrors?"

The children had seen enough starving people in their time, so they elected to see the crazy mirrors. They were soon laughing heartily at their reflections, as in some mirrors, they appeared very thin, and in others, short and fat. They wandered on, admiring the skill of the jugglers and marvelling at how a tightrope walker managed to keep his balance as he walked across a taut rope suspended between two wooden posts. Annie was pleased that none of the children asked for anything. Sabina had warned them they were not to ask, and they had behaved themselves.

When they reached the coconut shy, Robert stopped. "Who thinks I might be able to knock down a coconut?"

Stephen and Danny shouted, "I do, I do. Please see if you can."

Robert paid his money, but it was not as easy as he thought, and although he managed to hit a coconut, it didn't fall. Seeing the disappointed faces around him, he delved into his pocket once more, and this time, he was rewarded when a large coconut wobbled and slowly fell to the ground amid many cheers.

"We'll take this home and crack it open and see what's inside. I've never tried fresh coconut before, either, so it will be a new taste for all of us. I think it's time we went home now, but we'll get something to eat on the way. Start thinking about what you would like. Perhaps a pasty, or a toffee apple, or some sweets?"

As they made their way to the exit, Annie saw Ruth standing between two tents with the fairground man. They were kissing passionately, and Annie hesitated, concerned but reluctant to interfere. Ruth must have felt Annie's eyes on her, for she pulled away and looked at Annie angrily. "What are you looking at? Never seen two people kiss before?"

"I'm sorry, I didn't mean to stare, Ruth, but I wonder how well you know this man? Perhaps you'd like to walk home with us?"

"No, I'm fine, thank you, so please mind your own business. You're not the only one with a boyfriend, you know."

"No, of course not. I'm sorry." Annie moved on in embarrassment.

When they got back to Sabina's house, Robert drilled a hole in the coconut and drained the milk from inside. Then he smashed it open with a hammer, and they all tried a piece. They all liked it except Selina, who immediately spat it out and pulled a face that made them all laugh.

Annie escorted Robert outside and shut the back door behind her. They embraced and kissed, and he nuzzled her hair. "Not long now, Annie. The vicar will call the banns again on Sunday, and soon, you'll be my wife. What do you think about that?"

"I can't wait."

CHAPTER 19

A few days later, Sabina was awakened by a loud knocking on the door. She rose in haste, puzzled as to who it could be, for it was barely dawn. Pulling her shawl around her, she ran swiftly down the stairs and answered the door. She hoped the noise had not disturbed the children, for she treasured a few moments alone in the morning with a nice hot cup of tea. Outside, in the pouring rain, stood John Cutcliffe.

"Hello, John, what brings you here so early? Come in out of the rain."

"Thank you, Sabina; it's a nasty morning. I'm sorry to trouble you, but I wonder if you've seen anything of our Ruth? She didn't come home last night, and Noeleen's beside herself with worry."

"Sorry, no, I haven't seen her, John. I last saw her at the fair a few days ago."

"Aye, I think that could be the trouble. Kept going down there, she did, every day, you see. I don't know what the attraction was, but she certainly couldn't keep away, even though her mother forbade her to go there again. Then, last night, she didn't come home for her tea, which is not like her at all, and we're worried because she's only fifteen."

"Now, Annie did mention that she saw Ruth chatting to one of the fair workers, and she asked her if she'd like to walk home with her, but I'm afraid Ruth was a bit rude."

"Oh, I'm sorry. Youngsters, these days, I don't know. You try to bring 'em up properly, but they always think they know best. Would Annie be up yet, do you think?"

"She may be because Selina wakes early. Come into the kitchen, John, and I'll go and see."

Annie was awake and coming down the stairs with Selina sitting on her hip. "Morning, Mum. Are you looking for me?"

Sabina explained, and Annie agreed to have a chat with John.

"Hello, John, I'm sorry to hear Ruth's missing, but how can I help?"

"Sabina says you saw her at the fair with a man, is that right?"

"Yes, he was in charge of the Dobby Horses and was chatting Ruth up. Then, later, I saw them kissing, though I don't like to tell tales."

"The fair left last night, so it doesn't take a genius to know where she is then, does it? I don't know what her mother will make of this. What did the man look like?"

"I'd say he was about thirty, with long dark hair, and he wore a brown cap. Are you going to go after the fair?"

"I think it's the only thing I can do. The fair usually goes on to Barnstaple from here, but I can't go until after work, and it's a twelve-mile walk."

"John, I'll walk with you to the Manor and ask Robert if you can borrow a horse. Can you ride?"

"Aye, I can ride, but no, don't trouble yourself, Annie, I'll sort it out. It's not Master Robert's problem."

"He won't mind, John; I'm sure he won't. Come on, let's go and ask him."

Annie would not take no for an answer, and leaving Selina with Sabina, she pulled on her boots and shawl and trudged up the lane with John. The rain was easing, and it looked as if it might be a nice day after all.

"Annie, I'll have to find Jack Bater to ask for the time off to go after Ruth; I should start work in a few minutes."

"All right, John, tell him I'm asking Robert about borrowing a horse, and I'm sure he'll understand. You can make the time up, can't you?"

"Oh, yes, of course. I'll come and find you when I've spoken to Jack."

Annie entered the house through the kitchen door. Mrs Potts was surprised but pleased to see her.

"Hello, Annie, what a nice surprise. Come back to work, have you?"

"No, I'm afraid not, but it's nice to see you, Mrs Potts. Is Robert up yet?"

"No, my dear, it is rather early, you know, barely half-past five. Mind you, he usually comes down at about six o'clock. Would you like a cup of tea and some breakfast while you wait?"

Annie readily accepted the offer, for all food touched by Mrs Pott's was incredibly delicious, and she was soon tucking into a big bowl of creamy porridge. While eating, she explained what had brought her to see Robert so early. Mrs Potts was right, and before long, Robert appeared, yawning and surprised to see his future bride so early in the day.

"Hello, Annie. Is everything all right?"

Quickly she explained about the missing girl. "I wondered if we could ride after the fair with John and see if we can find Ruth. She may have gone of her own free will but might regret it now. Anyway, John wants to make sure she's all right. He's gone to ask Jack if he can have the morning off. Would you mind, Robert?"

"No, of course not. I'll have my breakfast, and then, if Mrs Potts could pack some lunch for us, we could make a day of it. John can borrow a horse, and we'll ride with him to Barnstaple to find Ruth. If that turns out all right, we can have a picnic on the way home. We were going riding today, anyway, weren't we?"

"Yes, thanks, Robert. While you eat, I'll find John and get Dodger to saddle up our horses. We can call and tell Mum on our way."

Before long, all three were on their way. Annie was surprised to find that John was an experienced rider, and he told her that as a boy, he had often ridden farm horses bareback. They urged their horses up the last hill, from where they could see the fair in the distance. The red and white helter-skelter and the garishly painted roofs of the other fairground rides were unmistakable.

"Well, at least it's here and not moved on somewhere else. Come on, I'm sure we'll soon find Ruth now."

Barnstaple was a sizeable and prosperous town that drew farmers from far and wide to the weekly market, where livestock was sold. The fair was traditionally held on the common ground at the edge of the town and close to a park with a lake. In the centre of the lake was an island known as Monkey Island, and during the summer, rowing boats could be hired for the trip across.

They trotted down the hill and into the fairground and tethered their horses to a fence. The campsite was a hive of activity as the fair people unloaded and rebuilt their stalls and rides, hurrying to prepare them for the afternoon opening. A man hammering tent pegs into the ground stood up as they approached.

"Is there something I can do for you, folk?" He was a man of about sixty and looked as if he might be in charge. He was unshaven, and though his hair was straggly, he was clean, and his manner was friendly.

"I hope you can. We've ridden from Hartford because my daughter didn't come home last night. We think she might have run away with a man from here, the chap in charge of the dobby horses. Have you seen her?"

"No, I can't say I have, but that tent is Luke's. There he is, look, just outside."

"Thanks, mate. We want a word with him."

As they approached the tent, Ruth appeared from inside. As soon as she saw her stepfather, her face reddened.

"Now then, Ruth, what are you playing at? Your mother is beside herself with worry."

The girl hung her head, and the young man left what he was doing and came striding over.

"What's going on? What do you want, Mister?"

"I want to know why my stepdaughter is in your tent. That's what I want to know. She's only fifteen, and her mother is worried to death."

"She came with me of her own free will. I never made her come, did I, Ruth?"

"No, I wanted to go with Luke, John. It's not his fault."

"With not a word to your mother or me, and what of your job at the bakery? It's not good enough, Ruth. Now, are you coming home with me?"

The young man intervened. "No, she isn't; she wants to come away with me, and she's old enough to make up her own mind. You needn't worry, though; I'll look after her."

"It's up to you, maid; we just wanted to know you're all right and hadn't been taken against your will. Are you sure you want to do this? The fair goes all over the country, and if you change your mind in a few weeks and find yourself miles from home, you'll be all on your own. You haven't had long to get to know this young man."

Ruth's lower lip trembled, and tears were bright in her eyes as she looked anxiously at Luke and then back to John. Annie put her arm around Ruth's shoulders.

"Ruth, you must think carefully. If you're sure this is what you want, then it sounds as if John will not stand in your way, but you'll be leaving all your family and friends, and it will be difficult for you to come back if you change your mind. It must be a hard life always on the road."

Ruth stared at her shoes for a moment, then raised her head, went to Luke, and put her arms around him. "Luke, could you leave the fair and stay in Hartford and get a job?"

"No, I'm sorry, Ruth; it's no use me pretending. I love the fair and travelling all over the country, and all my family are here."

"Just as mine are all in Hartford."

"Yes, I know, that's true. It's up to you. I'd like you to come away with me, but it's your choice. I'm afraid I can't live in one place; I'd hate it."

Slowly, she withdrew her arms and walked back to her stepfather. "I think I'd better come home, John."

John nodded and put his arm around her. "I know it's hard, but you're making the right decision, Ruth. Come on, get your bag, and then I'll give you a leg up on old Molly here, and you can ride home behind me."

Annie went into the tent with the girl and helped her pick up her few belongings. "Ruth, did anything happen between you and Luke last night? Is there any chance you could be in the family way?"

Ruth blushed. "No, we haven't done anything like that. I've got my monthly, you know?"

"Well, that's a relief. Come on, let's get going."

Ruth kissed her young man, and they promised to see each other again next year when the fair called again at Hartford.

CHAPTER 20

Robert and Annie rode most of the way back to Hartford with John and Ruth. Halfway back, Ruth changed horses and sat behind Robert to not tire John's horse too much. On the outskirts of the village, they dismounted before going their separate ways.

"I can't thank you enough for letting me have the morning off to find Ruth and for the use of the horse, sir." John shook Robert's hand firmly. "I'll make up the hours I owe in no time."

"Thank you, John. Just sort it out with Jack, will you? I'm glad we found Ruth safe and sound, but we'll leave you here because we're going the other way."

Ruth climbed up behind John again, and they galloped away. Robert and Annie also remounted their horses and rode through the woods to their favourite picnic spot overlooking Buzzacott House.

"Oh, what a wonderful view. It's the best one for miles around. Thank goodness that the early rain cleared up. Are you hungry?"

"Yes, I'm famished; let's have lunch straight away."

Robert took a rolled-up blanket from his saddle and spread it out on the ground, which was still damp. Annie removed a small wicker basket from her horse and set it on the blanket.

"Let's see what Mrs Potts has packed today. Oh, look, thick beef sandwiches and fruit cake. I love your cook, Robert, and I'll enjoy her cooking when we're married.

After eating their fill, they lay side by side on the blanket in the hot sun and kissed passionately until Robert suddenly pulled away from her.

"Come on; we've waited this long; we'd better get moving before we get too carried away. It will be difficult enough when we're married without you becoming pregnant before the ceremony."

"Mm, yes, I suppose so." Annie sat up reluctantly and glanced down the hill. "There's that woman again. I'm sure it was her we saw at the railway station. You know, the one Jean left her baby with. I wonder if she is moving house; I don't think she's been here long."

"Annie, you're so nosy!"

"I'm just curious. Come on then, where are you taking me?"

"Buzzacott woods are the start of my land, so if we ride through them and then on around the fields, I'll show you the work I've been doing since I took over the estate."

They mounted their horses and walked them slowly through the woods, for although there was a recognisable bridleway, it was uneven, with many exposed tree roots and low branches. The woods meandered gently downhill towards a humpback bridge across a stream. Near the stream was a small makeshift hut well-hidden between large boulders, trees, and bushes. They would probably have passed it by unseen had a man not peered out of the doorway as he heard voices.

"Hello, Sam, I haven't seen you for a long time. How are you?"

The old man smiled at Annie with blackened, broken teeth. His straggly grey hair was dirty and unkempt, and the wrinkles on his face were full of grime. He was thin, and his clothes hung from him and were full of holes. The only tidy part of his attire was his boots.

"Hello, my dear. It's nice to see you. That uncle of yours isn't around, is he?"

"No, you're all right, Sam. Are you living here?"

"Aye, for now, until someone moves me on, as they always do. I like it here in the woods, so I'd be obliged if you didn't mention my whereabouts to anyone." Sam eyed Robert anxiously. "Who's your friend, my dear?"

"This is Robert Fellwood, Sam. I'm going to marry him in a couple of weeks, so what do you think of that?" Leaving Sam to digest this information, she whispered to Robert. "Can Sam stay here, Robert? I'm sure he's doing no harm?"

"Hello, Sam. I own this land, and if you promise me you'll do no damage, I don't mind you staying here. Would you like that?"

"Oh, aye, sir, that would be marvellous. Can you tell the farm manager that 'tis all right? I'm always careful to make no mess, and I only catch the odd rabbit or two or perhaps a few fish."

"That's fine, but only you, mind. I don't want all your friends joining you."

"No, sir, I haven't got many friends, perhaps just young Annie, here. Always been kind to old Sam, she has. Mostly, I prefer my own company."

"Sam, do you know anything about that big house near here? Buzzacott House?"

Sam's face darkened. "No, not much, only that they sent me packing the other day when I tried to beg for some bread. I didn't hang about either because they've got a big dog. Luckily for me, it was chained up, but the woman threatened to set it loose on me if I didn't clear off. I think she would have, too; she was most unpleasant."

Robert pressed a few pennies into Sam's hand as they left and was rewarded with a beaming smile. He tried not to flinch at the old man's rank breath. As they rode off, Robert asked Annie how she knew the tramp.

"He used to beg in the village, and one day, he stole a pair of boots from my Uncle George's shop. I bumped into him in the woods when I was dragging home a sack of vegetables stolen from your garden. Poor old Sam was coughing and wheezing because Uncle George and Constable Folland were chasing him, and he would never have outrun them. I persuaded him to go through the gap in your hedge and hide in the Manor House gardens. I hid my sack down a badger hole and picked some flowers until the men appeared, and then I said he had gone the other way."

"You naughty girl fancy doing that to your uncle."

"Oh, I can't stand my Uncle George, and I was no better than Sam because I'd been stealing too. Thanks for letting him stay there, though; he's always getting moved on, poor old chap."

By this time, they had reached the edge of the woods, and Robert led the way down a grassy track and stopped at a gateway.

"This is one of our biggest fields, but the ground was so marshy and water-logged that we couldn't do much with it. Luckily, I bought a book about farming one day in Exeter, and it explained what to do. It's an interesting book by a chap called Henry Stephens, and I've found some useful information in it. Jack thinks I have these incredible ideas, but actually, they're from the book. If he could read, I'd let him borrow it. Anyway, last year, I got the men to dig deep ditches across the field, and we laid clay drainpipes to channel the water into the stream. It's worked a treat and just look at this crop of wheat we've grown. I think it's flourished because the ground here has never been planted before, though we used to let the cows graze here in the drier months."

Annie picked a sheaf of wheat and rubbed it in her hand. "Looks like it's ripe, too."

"Yes, we're going to harvest it tomorrow, and I want to be there to make sure it goes right. This is our first chance to try the new reaper I've bought."

"Oh, yes, of course, your new toy. I've heard the farmhands disapprove."

"Yes, they do. They think it will put them out of work, but it will be much quicker than cutting it all with a scythe. It's always a struggle to get it all in before it rains. I can't wait to see the reaper working. I've bought a new threshing machine, too, and the men aren't too pleased about that either."

"I won't see much of you tomorrow then, by the sound of it, but I hope it goes well."

"Another thing I learned in the book is how to rotate the crops. Until last year, we only planted two crops, wheat and barley, then left the field fallow for a year to rest. There's a new method now named after a chap from Norfolk. He's called Charles Townsend, but people call him 'Turnip Townsend'."

"Why does he have a head like a turnip?"

"No, of course not, but he suggests growing turnips and using a four-crop rotation. You see, in this field, we've grown wheat this year, then next year we'll grow clover or ryegrass, then oats or barley, and the fourth year, turnips or swedes. Growing the different crops puts the nutrients back into the soil, and you don't have to leave the ground fallow for a year. The best part of it is you can use the turnips and swedes to eat or feed the cattle during the winter. It's clever; I just hope it works. Am I boring you?"

"No, I like to hear all about it. What else have you done?"

"If we make our way back now, I'll show you the new animals I've bought."

They galloped back, laughing with exhilaration. Annie's red hair streamed out behind her, and Robert couldn't believe how skilfully she rode after such a short time. She showed no fear, and it was as if she had been born to the saddle. They took their horses to the stable and handed them over to Dodger's expert care.

"Come on; let's look at the pigsties first. Do you remember when I came to your house to see Henry, the old boar, killed? I was so shocked, but I've got used to it now. I remember you laughed at me because I was sick."

"Yes, you were a bit delicate then, weren't you?"

"I suppose so. Now, we have two sorts of pigs at the moment. These are Gloucester Old Spots; they're hardy animals and produce tasty meat. Do you know, people say the spots on them are bruises from falling apples because they're often kept in orchards? I think poor Henry was an Old Spot, wasn't he?"

"Yes, he was. He was a dear old pig. He used to like me scratching his back for him. It's always a shame when they're slaughtered, but people have to eat. As long as animals are looked after properly and killed quickly, I think that's what matters."

"Yes, I agree. This one is Peggy, and she's due to have her piglets in a day or two. Huge, isn't she?" Robert patted her back. "Mind you, her teats are bagging up with milk. I reckon they could be here by morning. Looks like she's nesting, too; see the straw and hay piled up in the corner? She's getting ready."

They moved to the next pigsty. "These are Tamworth pigs and a bit of an experiment. They're not popular these days, but I'm told they were bred from the Old English Forest pig. My book says they're exceptionally tasty, so I thought I'd rear a few. As you can see, Suzie had her litter last week."

Ten little piglets were suckling from their mother and squealing as they jostled for the best position. Suzie was a large pig with a long snout, and she was brown and hairy.

"We're too early to see the cows because it's not milking time yet, but I've built up a fine herd of over a hundred shorthorns. They are wonderful cows with a placid temperament and an impressive milk yield. That's why I've built more shippens and taken on extra men to do the milking. There are far too many cows now for the milkmaids to do the job in the meadows as they used to. Since the railway came to Devon, we can get the milk to London and all the other big cities on the train, and it makes an excellent profit. I'm pleased we can employ more men, too. At least it makes up for the Albion reaper taking their work away."

"I think you're very clever, and I know the men think the world of you. Now, I must go home and see my daughter, or she'll feel neglected, though she loves her Nanny and Liza."

"Yes, all right, just give me a kiss before you go."

They went into a corner of the big barn and embraced before she ran happily down the hill to the Lodge House.

CHAPTER 21

Since Charlie invited her to go riding with him, Eveline had wondered what possessed her to agree. In her early twenties, she had been engaged to a young man called Jimmy, but he had been killed by an explosion in the silver mine a few weeks before their wedding. She had known Jimmy all her life and had gone to school with him, and they had been inseparable. Following his death, she had withdrawn into herself, and despite several men taking an interest in her over the years, she had spurned all their advances, for none could ever measure up to her beloved Jimmy.

Since her brother, William, had died, leaving his three children, and her other brother, Fred, became widowed and left to cope alone with his three, she had moved in with Fred and cared for them all. This gave her a new lease on life and provided her with the family she had never had. Eveline was now in her forties and never expected romance to enter her life again, but somehow Charlie Chugg, with his bright blue eyes and wide smile, had melted her heart. She knew, if she was completely honest with herself, that her regular visits to Hollyford Farm were not only to see her sick friend but partly in the hope of seeing Charlie.

She had not dared to hope that her feelings would be reciprocated, and now that he had asked her out, she was suddenly so nervous she didn't know if she could go. She decided to have a chat with Sabina and see what she thought. If she did go, she would need to ask her to look after the children anyway, as they were all home from school for the summer holidays.

As soon as Sabina opened the door, Eveline could see she was unwell. Her eyes and nose were red and sore, and although she smiled at her friend when she spoke, it was in a hoarse whisper, which ended in a bout of frenzied coughing.

"Oh, Sabina, you look terrible, you poor thing."

"Thanks, I like you, too."

"Sorry, but you know what I mean. How long have you been poorly?"

"Since Saturday, but I feel much worse today. It's just a cold, but it has pulled me down. I'm just thankful I don't have to work anymore because I'd have had to go if we wanted to eat. We have a lot to thank Robert for. It's ridiculous that I worked in all weathers for years with barely a sniffle, and now, in a warm house, I'm like this. Do you want to come in? I don't want to pass it on to you."

"Oh, I'll risk it if you feel up to a chat?"

"Yes, I'd be glad of the company. Perhaps it will take my mind off it. Come on, I'll put the kettle on."

As they enjoyed a cup of tea, Eveline told Sabina about Charlie asking her to go riding.

"I don't know if I shall go. I mean, it would be stupid to start a relationship at my age, wouldn't it?"

"Of course, it wouldn't. You're not old, and anyway, why should your age matter? When are you going?"

"Tomorrow, and I must confess the reason I'm here, was to ask if you could look after the children, but I can see that's out of the question now with you looking so ill. I've left Fred to watch them for an hour, but I couldn't leave them with him all day; he'd never get any work done."

"Don't be silly. Of course, I'll have them, and they can play with my lot. Now they're all home from school, it's chaos here anyway, so a few more won't make much difference. I think it's wonderful, and I hope things progress; I'd love to see you married."

"Let's not get carried away; he's only asked me to go riding. Anyway, thanks for the offer, but you're too poorly. Luckily, I have one other option. I'll ask Mum if I can borrow Charlotte for the day, you know, the girl that had the baby. She misses that child something terrible, so I think she'd enjoy a day with mine. Between you and me, I think Fred's sweet on her, and I'd love him to find another woman, so it wouldn't hurt for them to see a bit more of each other."

"Can Betsey manage without her?"

"Yes, she's up and about on crutches, and her plaster will be taken off soon."

"If it's a problem, come back and tell me, and I'll have them. We can't have you missing a hot date!"

Eveline stayed half an hour drinking her tea with Sabina and then went to The Red Lion to see her mother. Betsey was in less pain now and could hobble around and do a few jobs. She was pleased to hear about Charlie and, like Sabina, was determined that Eveline would have no excuse not to go. She had long wanted to see her daughter happily married but had never thought it would happen.

Charlotte was willing to spend a day with the children, and the next morning, she arrived at Fred's house promptly at nine o'clock, having helped Betsey to wash and dress and have her breakfast.

"Good morning, Eveline. Good morning, Fred. It's a fine day again; we're having a lovely summer this year. Now, I've been thinking about what to do today. How about we pack up a picnic and go to the beach?" She was answered by squeals of delight and wide grins.

"Well, that seems to be a popular suggestion, but you can just take it easy here in the house if you want; they can play in the garden."

"No, I'd love to take them to the beach, and I'm looking forward to it. It will be a day off for me, too. Eveline, you be on your way and enjoy yourself. I can see to everything, so don't rush back. Take as long as you like; I can even put them to bed if necessary."

"Thank you so much; it's kind of you. Now, children, you behave yourselves for Charlotte, or there'll be trouble when I get home. Bye for now, and I'll see you later."

Fred closed the door behind Eveline. "Which beach are you going to, Charlotte?"

"I think it will have to be Rapparee because I won't be able to carry the picnic as far as Rockham, though it's a better beach. It will be fine; we can have fun in the rock pools and build sandcastles."

"Yes, I was just thinking Rockham would be the best one. I'll tell you what, you get the picnic packed, and I'll give you a lift there on the cart and pick you up again later."

"Oh, yes, Daddy, please take us to Rockham; it's much nicer there, and we haven't been for ages. Can you come too?" Rosella put her arms around her father's waist and looked at him pleadingly with her big brown eyes. She was eight years old and a pretty little girl with blond hair and a peaches and cream complexion who could twist her daddy around her little finger. "What do you think, Amelia?"

"Yes, I like Rockham Beach best. Please come with us, Uncle Fred." Amelia, also eight years old, gazed up at her uncle beseechingly.

"Well, I certainly can't stay with you all day; I have too much work to do, but I don't think I'm going to be able to get out of taking you there now, by the sounds of it. What do you think, Charlotte?"

"Oh, yes, I'd like to go to Rockham. I'll get a picnic ready and some towels and spare clothes because I expect they'll get wet. Now, children, see if you can find your sunhats if you have any because I don't want you getting sunstroke or sunburnt. Do you have any fishing nets or buckets and spades?"

Within half an hour, the cart was loaded with the children and all they required for a day at the beach. Charlotte sat beside Fred and chatted with him along the journey.

"How do you like working for my mother, then?"

"Oh, we get on well. Betsey's been so kind to me, and she's asked me to stay on permanently, even when her leg has healed."

"Are you going to stay?"

"Yes, I am. I don't think I've ever been happier than I am now living at the inn. I get along with my mother, but my father's so strict he's hard to live with. I want to stay around here in case I see my baby again."

"Yes, it must have been hard to give her up."

"It's the worst thing I've ever done, and I just can't forget her. Your mother says if I can get Doris back, I can keep her at the inn with me, but, of course, I don't know where she is."

"Are you going to ask your aunt where she took her?"

"Yes, I'm trying to pluck up the courage to do just that, but my aunt is not an easy person to get along with. I don't think she'll tell me. She said I'd disgraced the family by having a baby out of wedlock. She won't want me to have the baby back and risk humiliating the family."

"It's not up to her. Would you like me to go with you?"

"Oh, Fred, would you mind? I'd feel so much better with you by my side."

"Yes, of course. We'll sort something out soon. Right, here we are, then." Fred reined in the horse and jumped down to lift the smaller children off the cart. "I'll pick you up later. It's half past ten now, so if I come back about three o'clock, would that suit you?"

"Yes, that will be long enough. Thanks ever so much, Fred."

Charlotte led the way down the beach, carrying the heavy picnic basket, whilst the children followed with various buckets, spades, and fishing nets. She found a sheltered spot by some rocks and spread a rug on the ground.

"Right, you can all go off and play. Just make sure you can always see me, and then I'll be able to see you. I don't want to have to go home and tell your daddy I've lost one of you. Leave your shoes here with me, and go and find some crabs in the rock pools. Let's see who can find the biggest one. I'll sort things out here and then join you."

The children spent an hour looking for crabs and trying to catch the small fish that darted so quickly around the pools. They found several crabs, and Eddie was delighted to find the biggest. He was the youngest at four, so Charlotte was pleased for him. He was a friendly little boy with bright ginger hair and green eyes, familiar characteristics of the Carter family.

"Can we go in the water, Charlotte? It's so hot, and it would be nice to cool off." Llewellyn, or Llewie as he was known, gazed longingly at the gentle waves breaking onto the golden sand.

"Well, there's no one else here, so I think you could strip down to your underwear. I've brought spare clothes for all of you so you can change them afterwards. You mustn't go out too far, though, because I can't come in with you, and I can't swim. Can any of you swim?"

Llewie and the twins nodded. "Yes, we can, but I promise we won't go out too far."

"All right, put your clothes on the blanket, and I'll walk down to the water with you and have a paddle."

The children loved the water, splashing each other and swimming on the waves. It was a calm day, and the tide was coming in over the hot sand, making the water a pleasant temperature.

"Charlotte, what's this?"

"Now, are you Joe or Matthew?" I can't tell."

"I'm Matthew."

"Well, Matthew, I think it's a jellyfish."

Matthew shouted to the others. "Hey, come and see this jellyfish."

The children looked in awe at the large jellyfish. It was about the size of a dinner plate and brownish-purple in colour. They couldn't decide whether it was dead or alive but were certainly not going to touch it to find out.

"Just be careful if you see any more, and don't touch them. They have long tentacles hanging down, and they sting. Anyway, shall we have our picnic now?"

The children nodded their heads in agreement, for they were hungry. They sat in a circle with their towels draped around their shoulders. The sun was hot, and they soon dried out, the sand coating their legs like icing sugar. When they had finished their lunch of boiled egg sandwiches and bread pudding, Charlotte took them for a walk along the shoreline, and they collected seashells in their buckets.

At just after three o'clock, Fred arrived with the cart. The children groaned when they saw him coming down the road, for they didn't want to go home.

"Oh no, Dad's here already."

"Never mind, perhaps we can do it again one day."

As they travelled home on the cart, Fred thanked Charlotte for looking after the children.

"It was a pleasure, and we've had a wonderful day, so if you want me to do it again, please just ask."

"That's useful to know because I suspect there may be other days that Eveline will want to spend with Charlie. Anyway, I'm working at home for the rest of the day, so if you want to get back to the inn, you can. Of course, it would be nice if you'd like to stay for tea. Eveline made a beef casserole for us yesterday, so it only has to be warmed."

"I'd like that, Fred."

CHAPTER 22

Having left the children in safe hands, Eveline walked to the inn and saddled her horse. As she rode to Hollyford Farm, she became more nervous. When she arrived, Charlie was looking out of the kitchen window, and he waved and smiled widely.

"Hello, Eveline, it's great to see you. Fred didn't mind, did he?"

"No, of course not. Charlotte's looking after the children, and she's going to take them to the seaside. Is it all right to say hello to Jane before we go?"

"Yes, of course, but I'm afraid she's very poorly. Alfred's sitting with her."

Eveline had a quick word with Maria and then hurried up the stairs to see her friend. She knocked softly on the bedroom door, and Alfred called to her to come in. The room smelt stale and unpleasant, though it was scrupulously clean.

"Hello, Alfred. How are you?" Jane lay with her eyes closed. She looked even worse than she had the week before, and Eveline could see that she would not be with them much longer.

"I'm all right, lass, but as you can see, Jane's not good. She's taking a lot of medicine because she's in so much pain, and then it knocks her out. She's barely been conscious for days, but the doctor says it's best this way. I wish it were me instead of her."

"Oh, Alfred, I'm so sorry, poor Jane. It's so hard for you, too. Would you like me to stay with you today instead of riding with Charlie? We can do that anytime."

"No, you go off and enjoy yourself. Charlie's been looking forward to you coming for days."

Alfred smiled. "You do know he's quite besotted with you, don't you?" Eveline blushed. "I see the feeling's reciprocated then, and that's good because nothing would make Jane happier than you two getting together. I don't think Jane will wake for hours, and, anyway, I'm not leaving her side. Charlie and

Jimmy have done all the outside work that has to be done, and Maria will look after everything else."

Eveline squeezed his hand. "All right then, Alfred, if you're sure. I'll come and see Jane when we get back; perhaps she'll be awake then."

She rejoined Charlie in the kitchen. "Alfred insists we go out for the day although Jane's so poorly. I'll look in on her again when we get back. Maria, take care of Alfred, won't you? Make sure he eats something."

"Yes, of course, I will, don't worry. You two get off and enjoy your ride; I've packed you up some food."

Charlie picked up the picnic bag and led the way out of the kitchen. Once outside the door, he tentatively reached for Eveline's hand. "Where would you like to go?"

"What about Hangman's Hill? There's a fantastic view of the coast from the top. I've not been up there for such a long time, and I know a sheltered spot for a picnic. It's about five miles. What about you, though? Do you have anywhere in mind?"

"No, I hoped you would suggest somewhere, and that sounds perfect. I know the place you mean, but I haven't been there since I returned from the sea. Hangman's Hill it is, then."

Charlie secured the picnic bag to his saddle and helped Eveline onto her horse. She smiled at him. It was a long time since anyone had looked after her in such a way, and although she was perfectly capable of mounting her horse independently, she enjoyed the attention.

Leaving the farm track behind, they were soon trotting across the wild and rugged landscape of Exmoor, and when the opportunity arose, they let the horses have their heads and galloped down one hill and up the other side. Charlie reined in his horse, laughing.

"You're a skilled horsewoman, Eveline. I thought you said you hardly ever ride?"

"No, not these days, but as a youngster, I rode a lot, and you don't forget, do you? Come on, I'll race you to the top of the next hill; that's where I think we should have our picnic."

Before she had finished speaking, she kicked her horse and was off like the wind, laughing. Charlie was not far behind, but she had a head start on him, and try as he might, he couldn't catch her. She reined in her horse at the top of the hill and dismounted, still laughing. Her hair had escaped from its bun, and her face was flushed with exertion. Her eyes danced as, grinning widely, she tethered her horse to a tree. He thundered to a stop beside her.

"Hey, I hope you're not going to brag in The Red Lion that you outraced me; I'll never live it down."

"I might unless you can persuade me otherwise."

Needing no further encouragement, Charlie put his arms around her. "Hmm, I can but try then, I suppose." He kissed her gently on the lips, and as she melted into his embrace, he kissed her more passionately.

At length, she pulled away and smiled at him. "I think you've convinced me not to tell tales. Shall we find a nice spot and have something to eat? I'm starving."

They sat on a rug that Charlie removed from beneath his saddle and were soon munching on ham sandwiches.

"These sandwiches are delicious, aren't they? Maria's baking is improving. This bread is as good as any I could make."

"Yes, she's much better at everything since you started giving her lessons."

"She's keen to learn. It sounds like no one had taken the time to show her before. I was sorry to see how ill Jane is, though, and you have to feel for Alfred."

"Yes, I know; he hates seeing her suffering, and I think when the end does come, he'll naturally be sad but also relieved."

"I'm glad you've come home to live, Charlie. I know he has Jimmy to help, but I think he's glad to have you around. Don't you miss the sea, though? I know some sailors can't get used to life on land again."

"I do miss it, but I no longer want the long voyages. It's a hard life, and now I'm getting on a bit; I'd rather be on dry land with plenty of fresh food and water. I still go out in my fishing boat and sometimes sail across to France for a few days."

"Do you? What do you go there for?"

"Some things are best not talked about, but I expect you can guess?"

"Oh, I see. Do be careful then, won't you? If you got caught smuggling, you'd be sent to prison, you know, or may even be transported."

"Don't you worry; it's a little family tradition started by my great-grandfather, who farmed at Hollyford. My grandfather and father, too. Alfred never cared for the sea, so it was right he took on the farm, but I always loved going out in the boat with my father and grandfather. They taught me all I know, in every sense of the word. What I get up to is minor and hurts no one. It's just a bit of fun and helps make ends meet."

They had an enjoyable day, but as they slowly trotted up the farm lane, they saw Doctor Luckett's horse tethered in the yard.

"It looks like the doctor's here. I hope Jane's all right."

Maria met them at the door. "Jane's much worse. She hasn't woken up all day, not even to take her medicine, and Alfred and Jimmy are sitting with her."

Eveline frowned. "Oh dear, do you think I should go up or not?"

"I think Alfred would like you to. I'll wait down here with Maria, though. You don't want too many up there." Charlie squeezed her hand reassuringly.

Eveline knocked and entered the room just in time to see the doctor pulling the sheet over Jane's face.

"Oh no, oh, Alfred, Jimmy, I'm so sorry." She hugged the old man, and then his son, and they all sobbed, quite unable to speak. "At least she's at peace now, Alfred."

"Aye, she is that, maid, and she's not suffering now. I couldn't wish for her to carry on as she was. Eveline, it's a lot to ask, but could you help me to organise everything? Jane suggested I ask you."

"Yes, of course I will, Alfred, but we can talk about that later. For now, let's go downstairs and have a cup of tea. Come on." She took the old man by the arm and led him slowly from the room. The doctor gave her a thankful nod and said he would be on his way.

Eveline stayed and had a cup of tea, and she and Charlie told Alfred and Jimmy where they had been for their picnic, but inevitably, the conversation soon returned to Jane and the plans for her funeral.

"Well, naturally, she'll be buried in the churchyard in Hartford, but I'm not sure about the wake. I did think we could have it here, but it would be a lot for Maria to cope with because there'll be a lot of mourners. Jane reckoned having it at the inn would be best, especially as it's next to the church. It would save folk having to travel out here to the farm. "What do you think, Eveline?"

Alfred raised his watery blue eyes to hers.

"I think that's an excellent idea, Alfred. Mum thought the world of Jane, and I know she'd be more than pleased to put on a spread. I'll fetch Matilda now to do what's necessary for Jane. Hopefully, Fred will bring her on the cart, and then he can organise a coffin. Would you like me to see the vicar to arrange a time for the funeral? I could ride out again tomorrow to tell you the details."

"That would be grand. Thank you so much, Evie. It's one thing less for me to worry about."

"I'd better be going now, Charlie, or Fred and Charlotte will think I've run away. Don't worry about any of it, Alfred. I'll sort it all out and see you again sometime tomorrow."

Charlie went to the door with Eveline and kissed her briefly. "Thanks for coming today, Evie. I enjoyed our day out, though it's a pity it had such a sad ending. I'll look forward to seeing you tomorrow."

On her way home, Eveline called to tell Sabina about Jane, for the two women had been close. When Sabina opened the door, Eveline could see that her friend was still poorly.

"Hello, Sabina, are you any better?"

"My throat's a bit better, thanks, but this cough is driving me mad and keeping me up half the night, so I'm tired. Anyway, never mind that; how did you get on? I want all the details."

"There's time enough for that, though I can tell you I had a most enjoyable day with Charlie. I called in to tell you that Jane passed away earlier. She was asleep when I arrived this morning, and apparently, she never woke up again. You can imagine how upset Alfred is; they'd been married for over fifty years."

"Oh, poor Alfred, but I'm glad Jane's not suffering anymore. She's had an awful time of it for the last few months. Thanks for coming to tell me."

"I was passing the door anyway, and I knew you'd want to know. I'm organising the funeral for Alfred, and I've agreed to ask Mum if we can have the wake at the inn. Now, I must go because I've been out all day, and I don't want to take advantage of Charlotte's good nature, but I'll call in again soon for a chat."

As Sabina saw Eveline out of the house, two carriages from the Manor House passed by. The first contained Lord and Lady Fellwood and Sarah, and the second, Victoria, Frank, and their two young children.

"I wonder where they're all off to."

"From what Annie tells me, they're off to London. They're only going to avoid Annie and Robert's wedding. Pathetic, isn't it? You'd think they'd want to be at their only son's wedding, but they disapprove of Annie."

"Well, it will probably be all the more enjoyable for us if they don't go."

"Yes, that's true. Well, their loss is our gain."

CHAPTER 23

The next day, Eveline went to see the Reverend Rees to arrange Jane's funeral, and they agreed it should be held the following Monday. They both felt that the sooner it was dealt with, the better. The vicar had a busy week ahead as Annie and Robert's wedding was the following Saturday. Eveline then went to see her mother about the wake.

"Yes, of course, it must be held here. Mind you, I'll have to get some extra help because the Chuggs are a big family, and there will be a lot of mourners. I can't stand on this leg for long, and Charlotte can't do all the food alone. I must think whom I can ask." Betsey sat down, looking thoughtful.

"Why don't you ask Sabina and Annie if they would help on Sunday? I'm sure Liza can manage the children for a few hours, and I can come too because Fred will be at home all day. With Charlotte as well, we'll soon get it organised."

"Oh yes, of course, that would be fine."

"Good; I'll ride to the farm now to tell Alfred the arrangements."

Sabina and Annie agreed to help, and on Sunday morning, they met in the kitchen of the inn, where Betsey took charge.

"Right. Charlotte bought all the ingredients yesterday, so all we have to do is cook. We've got sausage meat for sausage rolls, beef skirt for pasties, and bacon and egg for pies. Then we could bake some cakes, scones, and a few puddings. What do you all prefer doing?"

"I'm best at the savoury stuff, so perhaps Eveline and I could do the sausage rolls, pasties, and pies. Annie and Charlotte, maybe you could make some cakes?"

The two girls glanced at each other, and Charlotte nodded. "Yes, I'm happy making cakes, especially if Annie can help me."

"That sounds like a plan, then. Perhaps we should finish all that and then make a few puddings between us. I can sit and peel the potatoes and onions and cut up the meat, so I'll do that." Betsey plonked herself down on a chair at the table, and Charlotte fetched the vegetables for her.

Charlotte was glad Sabina had suggested she work with Annie, for they were around the same age.

"What sort of cakes do you want to make, Annie?"

"I don't mind, but I'm probably better at rock buns than sponges. How about you?"

"I can make a couple of sponges. If there's time, we could make some scones and cut-rounds; they always go down a treat."

"We'd better get cracking then. How do you like working at the inn?"

"Oh, I love it here, and your granny's so kind. She's offered me a permanent job, even when her leg is better."

"Are you going to stay?"

"Yes, I am. I like it here, and I'm going to try to get my baby back. I hated giving her up, but my aunt left me no choice at the time. Betsey says I can keep her here if I can find her. Fred's going with me to my aunt's house soon to try to persuade her to tell us where she took Doris. She's such a fierce and scary lady; I'll be glad of his support."

"Oh, well, good luck. I can't even imagine what you went through, giving up your child. I would have hated to be parted from Selina. I'm glad Fred's going with you, too. He likes you, and he was pleased you gave the children such an enjoyable day at the seaside."

Charlotte blushed. "What do you mean? How do you know he likes me?"

"It's pretty obvious from the way he looks at you. Haven't you noticed?"

"No, not really."

"How about you? Do you like him?"

"Yes, of course, I like him. He's been so kind, and he rescued me when I was about to give birth to Doris in a gateway."

"What I mean is, do you really like him?" Charlotte blushed again and nodded.

"In that case, I'm going to suggest that he bring you to my wedding."

"Oh no, you can't do that."

"I can, and I will, and I think he'll be pleased. It will be nice for you, anyway. The reception will be at the Manor House, and I can tell you the food will be amazing because Mrs Potts is a wonderful cook. We were thinking of having the reception here, but there would be too many people, and anyway, now that Robert's family has gone to London, we can do what we like. Do say you'll come."

"See what Fred says, and if he wants to ask me, he can. Do you think Betsey will give me the time off?"

"Yes, I'm sure she will; she's my granny, after all."

By the end of the afternoon, Betsey's larder was full of pies, pasties, and sausage rolls, and the table was laden with cakes. They had also made two large trifles and dozens of scones and cut-rounds, which would be eaten with clotted cream and jam. When they finished washing up, the women sat around the table and enjoyed a well-earned cup of tea.

The funeral was arranged for ten o'clock, and unfortunately, it was raining heavily. Jane's six sons raised the coffin shoulder-high and carried it into the church. At the end, she weighed next to nothing, and there was no need for so many bearers, but they all wanted to do this one last thing for their mother. Eveline had somehow found time to decorate the church with wildflowers and other blooms from various people's gardens, and it looked and smelt beautiful. She knew Jane would have appreciated it, for she loved her flowers.

The church was packed, with many people standing, and some could not get inside at all. Alfred and Jane had lived in the village all their lives, and everyone knew them. Poor Alfred wept throughout the service, and he was not alone. On behalf of Alfred, the vicar invited the mourners to The Red Lion for the wake, and after the burial, they all trooped across the road to the inn. With her mother still not mobile, Eveline rushed around, refilling plates and offering cups of tea to those who did not want ale. As the crowds began to thin, Alfred called her over.

"Come here a minute, Evie; I want a word with you. Thank you so much for sorting everything out for me; I couldn't have faced it without you. You must tell me what I owe your mother; she's provided an amazing spread."

"I was fond of Jane, and I'm going to miss her, but I'll still come over and see you now and then, if that's all right, Alfred? I'll let you know what you owe Mum, too."

"Yes, of course, you must. Mind you, I think it might be our Charlie you want to see the most."

The old man smiled at her. "It would be wonderful if you two made a go of it. Jane would have been tickled pink, and it would be so good for Charlie. Anyway, I wanted to ask you something. I know we had twelve children, but our daughters are all married with families of their own now, and Jane always looked on you as another daughter. Is there any chance you would consider coming to live at the farm and become my housekeeper? Maria is a willing girl, but she's young and needs someone to tell her what to do. You've been so kind in teaching her to cook and helping while Jane was ill; it would be wonderful if you could always be there. What do you think?"

"Oh, Alfred, I would enjoy that, but I can't. You see, I live with Fred now and care for his three children and also William's three. He couldn't manage on his own and go out to work. Then, of course, I'm spending a bit of time with Charlie now, and it wouldn't be right for me to live under the same roof, now would it?"

"Oh, yes, of course, you do. I'd forgotten. Never mind, but if you ever want a job, you let me know."

"I'll continue teaching Maria to cook, but she's coming on, and I think she'll be fine. Now, if you'll excuse me, I want a quick word with Annie before she goes. It's her wedding on Saturday, and I want her to try her dress on again."

Loaded with leftover food, Sabina and Annie were about to leave when Eveline caught up with them.

"Annie, wait a minute; I need to speak to you. Hold on. Annie, I want you and the bridesmaids to try on the dresses once more before the wedding. Could you come tomorrow? That would give me time to do any last-minute alterations before Saturday."

"Yes, of course, no problem."

"My goodness, you're loaded down with food. Mum's given me lots to take home, too. We made far too much; still, it's better to have too much than too little. Fred's gone to get the cart, so why don't you have a lift back with us to save you carrying all this?"

"Oh, thanks, that would be a real help. Is that all right with you, Mum?"

"Yes, thanks, Eveline, that will save our arms. I'll get Fred to drop me off at the Webber's house, though, because I want to see how Peter is getting on. I've not seen him for a few days, and I thought I'd take him this apple pie."

Peter was delighted to see Sabina. "Aw, you never come empty-handed, do you, maid? You have a heart of gold, you do, but I expect you've been told that before. I'm glad you came, though, because I want to show you this."

A leather harness was attached to each of Peter's forearms. His left arm finished above the elbow, and on this arm, the harness had a hook embedded into it. On his right arm, which ended halfway down his forearm, there was also a harness and, inserted into this one, was a metal fork, which he was currently using to eat his sausages and potatoes.

"Oh, Peter, that's amazing! Look at you, feeding yourself. I'm so pleased for you."

Tears were running down the old man's wrinkled cheeks as he spiked a cold sausage, picked it up and bit a piece off. Despite the tears, he had a wide grin.

"Oh, my dear, you have no idea what this means to me. Just to be able to scratch my nose is amazing. I'll never be able to repay you for making all this possible. You have truly changed my life. The hook is permanently fixed to the harness, but I can slot in the fork, a knife or spoon, or even my paintbrush on my right hand. Just to be able to feed myself makes me feel so much better. I was so helpless before. Francis and Seth have done a wonderful job between them, and they wouldn't take a penny from me; I'm so grateful."

"How are you getting on with the harness, though? I was a bit worried it would be uncomfortable and chafe you."

"It is rubbing a bit, but I'm getting used to it, and it will wear in eventually. Arthur helps me to put it on before he goes to work, and he's padded it out with some soft rags where I'm a bit sore. I'm improving at changing the implements on the right arm with my teeth, though my language sometimes leaves a bit to be desired. I'll paint you a picture now that I have more control over the brush. You can hang it in your fancy new house then."

"I'd love to, and I can't wait to see it. Is Arthur not home yet?"

"No, he's been working overtime all week because he's asked for a few days off. He's off on a fishing trip tomorrow with Charlie Chugg."

"Oh, they'll enjoy that. Mind you, the weather isn't too promising. Is there anything I can do for you before I go?"

"No, I'm fine. Christopher will be home from work anytime, but thanks anyway. Please call again soon; Arthur will be sorry to have missed you."

The old man winked at her knowingly.

CHAPTER 24

The next day, the weather was atrocious, and it was hard to believe it was July and not February. High winds blew the torrential rain horizontally across the hills, and few folk ventured out. On the farms, the labourers brought in as many animals as they could and tried to find jobs to do undercover.

Annie wrapped cloaks around Mary, Helen, and Selina and, taking their hands, battled against the wind to walk to Fred's house to try on their dresses for the wedding. Eveline was looking out of the window and saw them coming.

"Oh, my goodness, what a day. Come in and dry yourselves by the fire. You can't put the dresses on until you're properly dry, or you'll ruin them. I hope it's not like this on Saturday."

Annie took off her cloak and shook it in the porch before helping the children to do the same.

"Goodness, no, it's so rough out there today. Still, it's nice and warm in here. You'd never think it was mid-summer. The waves on the sea are enormous."

A slight frown clouded Eveline's face.

"What's the matter, Aunty Evie? You look worried. You're not planning on going to the seaside, are you?"

"Just a minute, Annie, I can't hear myself think. Children, why don't you go upstairs and play in the bedrooms? Amelia and Rosella have some dolls and a dolls' house you girls could play with, or perhaps you could play cards?"

As the children tore off up the stairs, she turned to Annie.

"I shouldn't say anything, but I know I can trust you to keep this to yourself. Charlie Chugg and Arthur Webber are going on a fishing trip today and will be away for a few days. The thing is, it's not just a fishing trip because they're sailing to France, and you know what that means. I'm worried because the weather is so bad, and it's a long way. I'm hoping they've decided not to go."

"Well, Charlie was at sea for years, so I'm sure he won't take any unnecessary risks. As regards the other business, smuggling's been going on for donkey's years, and I've never heard of anyone around here getting caught. You like him, don't you?"

Eveline blushed. "Yes, I'm sure you're right, and he's an experienced sailor. I must confess I've become quite fond of Charlie. Do you think that's silly for a woman of my age?"

"No, of course not. Anyway, shall we have a cup of tea before we deal with the dresses? The children have settled down, so let's leave them while they're quiet."

Charlie and Arthur met at Charlie's boat at dawn, and they had to shout to each other, for the strong wind whipped their words away.

"I didn't expect the weather to be this stormy today, did you, Charlie? Do you think we should leave it for another day? The sea is extremely rough."

"It is pretty awful, but we can't cancel now because the men will be expecting to meet us on the French coast in a few days. They'll guess why if we don't turn up, but it's dangerous for them to hang on to the goods any longer than they need to. The excise men are taking far too much interest in these matters lately."

"You still intend to go, then?"

"Yes, if you're willing. It's a long trip from here to France, and I'll need your help, especially in this weather, so I can't go without you. In any case, you've asked for the time off work now. The wind's blowing in the right direction, though, so we should make good time. We'll sail along the north coast of Devon and Cornwall, then around Land's End and the Lizard, and across the channel to France. The trip will take us a few days, but I've put plenty of food onboard, and there are oilskins we can wrap ourselves up in. Hopefully, this storm will blow itself out in a few hours."

"All right, then, I know Ned's hoping we make the crossing because he's running out of brandy, and unless you get it for him, it's so expensive."

The first part of the journey was extremely rough, and even Charlie was surprised at the strength of the wind and the powerful waves, considering the time of year. However, he loved every minute and realised just how much he had missed the exhilaration of battling the elements. As time went by, they took turns to sail the boat, whilst the other got a few hours of rest. Eventually, the weather cleared up, and to their relief, the sun came out and warmed them. As they made their way across the channel, they could, at long last, make out the French coastline.

"The cove we want is just around the next headland. I know the landowner, and he's willing to look the other way for a bottle of brandy or two. It's sheltered once we get nearer to land, but we need to be mindful of the rocks; they're treacherous along this coast if you don't know what you're doing."

Skilfully, Charlie sailed the boat safely into a small cove and moored it to a nearby tree. Arthur was impressed at the way Charlie handled the boat.

"I'll tell the farmer we've arrived, and then he can pass the message on. Hopefully, the men will bring the goods later when it's dark. Can you stay here and keep an eye on the boat, Arthur?"

"Yes, of course. I'll get some food ready for when you get back."

It wasn't long before Charlie returned, smiling. "Everything is arranged, and the men will be here around midnight. We've time for a spot of fishing now, Arthur. If we get stopped on the way back, it looks better if we've got a sizable catch to show. Not only that, but we can sell the fish in the village."

The men spent an enjoyable few hours fishing and then settled down to sleep, for they knew there was a hard night ahead of them. When they awoke, it was dark, and they ate some bread and dripping and washed it down with a mug of ale. By the dim light of the moon, Charlie kept a close eye on the cliff path, and it wasn't long before he saw four men approaching, leading donkeys laden with boxes and kegs of brandy. He greeted the men warmly.

"Right, Arthur, if you can help unload the donkeys and get this lot on the boat, we'll be on our way in no time."

Arthur and three of the men swiftly moved all the contraband from the patiently waiting animals into the boat. Charlie and the fourth man stepped to one side, and Charlie handed him a packet.

"Here you are, Louis. Check it if you want, but it's all there as we agreed last time."

"Your word is good enough for me, Charlie; our families have been doing business long enough, non?"

"Indeed, they have, my friend, now thank you for all these goods. We'll be on our way soon and leave you in peace. I'll send word to you when I'm coming again. Probably in about three months, if that's all right?"

"Ah oui, mon ami, bon chance."

The two men shook hands and helped the others to finish loading the boat. Within minutes, Charlie deftly hoisted the sail, and the boat slowly made its way out of the cove to the open sea.

"They seem a friendly bunch for Frenchmen."

"Aye, they're trustworthy men, Arthur, and fortunately, they speak good English. I can get by in French, but it's so much easier if they speak English. Lazy of me, I suppose. Now, we'll get moving because the French get nervous and prefer us gone, and I'd like to get across the channel through the night. I'm always happier when I can see the English coastline. It looks like we'll be lucky with the wind, too. It's changed direction at just the right time for us to make good time going home."

In Hartford, Annie and Eveline put the new bridesmaids' dresses onto the three excited girls.

"Stand still, Selina. Let me do these buttons, and then we'll see what you look like."

The three little girls stood in a row, and Annie and Eveline surveyed them.

"What do you think, Annie? Are you pleased with them? Do you think they need any alterations?"

"Oh, Aunty Evie, they're amazing. Do you have a mirror?"

Yes, there's one in my bedroom. It's not full-length, but they'll be able to see most of themselves. Come on, girls, come upstairs, and you can see how you look. Pick up your dresses now, and walk nicely. I don't want you to fall over and rip them."

In the bedroom, the girls took turns surveying their reflections in the mirror. They couldn't believe they looked so elegant, just like young ladies. Annie swept Helen's blond hair up in her hands.

"What do you think? Should they have their hair tied up or hanging down?"

"They've all got fine hair. It might be less trouble to leave it hanging down. What if we made a garland of flowers to rest on their heads? A few white rosebuds with some lavender would look nice with their dresses."

"Oh, yes, perfect. If there are not enough flowers in the Lodge House garden, I'll get a few from the Manor House. At least I won't have to crawl through a hole in the hedge now and steal them."

"Annie, you didn't?"

"Ah, Aunty Eveline, you'd be surprised what I did to stop the family from starving after Dad died, but the less said, the better. Now, let's get you out of these fine clothes, girls, and then I'll put my dress on; fingers crossed it fits."

Annie was equally pleased with her dress. Made of cream silk, it was a simple dress that accentuated her slim figure perfectly. She circled in front of the mirror.

"What do you think? Will I do?" Her green eyes sparkled with happiness.

"You'll more than do; you look amazing. Now, girls, when Annie gets out of the carriage on her wedding day and walks into the church and up the aisle, you three must carry her train to save it from getting dirty. Can you pick it up and have a little practice?"

Obediently, Mary, Helen, and Sabina clutched a piece of the fine material in their hands, and Annie led the small procession around the room.

"Thank you so much, Aunty Evie; you've done a wonderful job."

"It wasn't just me, you know; Matilda did a lot of the sewing, too."

"Yes, of course, and I haven't forgotten. I'll call round soon and thank her. At least now, we know they all fit. Anyway, we had better get going. I want to call in the shop for a few things on the way home because it will save going out again later in this weather."

Annie hurried the girls along to the shop, and as she passed The Red Lion, she saw her grandfather, Ned, wheeling some empty barrels out of his shed and waved to him. She crossed the lane with the children, and they stood in the shed doorway to shelter from the rain.

"Hello, Grandad, are you all right?"

"Yes, I'm fine, thank you, Annie. What weather are we having, though? I hope this rain will clear up before your wedding this weekend. I'm looking forward to it. Who would ever have thought that old Ned Carter would be going to a wedding reception at the Manor House?"

"You'll be welcome, Grandad. Make sure you eat as much as you can."

"Oh, I will, maid, I've heard about Ethel Potts' cooking, but I never thought I'd sample it. I can't wait to see you happily married and settled; you deserve it."

Annie hugged him as he reached into his pocket and found a sweet for each of the girls.

"I suppose you want one too, maid? Never could resist one of your grandad's toffees, could you?"

"You know me too well, Grandad. See you on Saturday. Give my love to Granny."

"I will, Annie. We've just been to the hospital to get the plaster taken off her leg. She's so pleased they've removed it, though I think it was a bit too soon, myself. Her leg kept itching, and not being able to scratch it properly was driving her mad. Mind you, she did her best with her knitting needle, and I'm sure she shouldn't have. What they've done is marvellous, though. I don't mind telling you, when I saw how bad a break it was, I never thought she'd walk again, especially at her age. She must be careful for a few weeks until it strengthens."

"Oh, that's good; tell her I'll come and see her soon."

At the shop, Annie purchased some soap, tea, and flour. The bell on the shop door jingled as she was being served, and she turned to see who had come in. It was John Cutcliffe's wife, Noeleen, with her daughters, Ruth and Susanna.

"Oh, Annie, I'm glad I've seen you. I wanted to thank you for helping John get our Ruth back. Silly girl, going off like that with a practical stranger."

"Mum, he wasn't a stranger. I got to know him through the week the fair was here, and he's a nice young man."

"So, he might be, but a week's no time at all, Ruth. You should have known better than to just go off and leave me to worry about you. Mind you, he should have known better than to take you. Anyway, Annie, thank you so much, and I hope you'll be happy with Master Robert."

"It was no trouble at all, Noeleen, and I'm glad everything worked out all right. How is Clarice getting on at the Manor House?"

"Oh, fine, thank you, and now she lives in, there's one less mouth for me to feed. I think it's hard work, though, from what she tells me."

"I'm glad she's getting on all right. No doubt I'll see more of her when I'm married and living there. Right, come on, girls, let's get home in case the heavens open again, though I believe it will dry up. Goodbye, ladies."

After waving Annie and the girls off, Eveline carefully hung the dresses in her wardrobe, thinking that as soon as the weather improved, she'd get Fred to take them to the Lodge House ready for the wedding on Saturday. She would be relieved once the garments had gone and were no longer her responsibility. She heard the back door open and called out.

"Is that you, Fred? Have you come home for your dinner?"

"Aye, it's me, and yes, I'm hungry. What have we got?"

"I've made a chicken and leek pie with the leftovers from yesterday's roast dinner. It's in the oven, along with some roast potatoes, so we can have it now if you like?"

"Yes, please. I'm not working this afternoon because I'm taking Charlotte to Warkley to see her aunt. She wants to ask her where she took the baby. It was a dirty trick, sending the girl out on an errand like that and then getting rid of the child. It wasn't hers to part with."

"Perhaps she thought she was doing the right thing at the time. You know, wanted to spare Charlotte from having to hand over the child herself?"

"That could be it, I suppose, but from what I've heard, it doesn't sound as if she has a kind bone in her body. I'm not looking forward to meeting her, but she'd better not mess us about because I'm not leaving without an answer."

"I think you're sweet on Charlotte, Fred."

"I must confess I enjoy her company."

"It's time you found someone new to share your life with. What you went through with Lucy was awful, and you stayed faithful and devoted to her the whole time, and not many would."

"Yes, of course I did. I loved her, and she was so different before she became ill. She would never have harmed the children if she was in her right mind."

"No, I know, she wouldn't. It's difficult to understand, but it does happen. Anyway, let's eat."

Eveline called the six children to wash their hands and sit around the table. The cousins, Rosella and Amelia, both eight years old, sat with Eddie, the youngest, on one side of the table, and the three older boys, Llewie, Joe, and Matthew, sat on the other. Eddie wriggled in his seat and fidgeted.

"Eddie, I've told you before; sit still. You must behave at mealtimes, or you won't get any dinner."

"But, Daddy, Llewie keeps kicking me under the table."

"Do you want me to send you to your room, hungry, young man? Because I will. Why don't you behave like your cousins here? I never have to tell them off, do I?"

"No, Dad, I'm sorry."

Llewie looked anything but sorry and lowered his eyes to his plate. He sneaked a look at Matthew and Joe, but they were steadfastly ignoring him. Llewie found it tiresome that all three of his cousins were so well-behaved; it always made him look worse than ever when he was naughty. However, he had no notion of what Joe, Matthew, and Amelia had gone through, living in a workhouse in London before his father and Aunty Eveline had found them. They were so grateful to live with Fred and Eveline that they were careful not to put a foot wrong for fear of being sent back to London.

"Mm, Eveline, this is even better than the roast, I think, and that's saying something. You cook just like Mum does."

"Of course I do; she taught me everything I know."

CHAPTER 25

Fred harnessed Dolly, his old horse, and hitched her to the cart. It was over two miles to where Charlotte's Aunty Joan lived in Warkley, so it would be quicker than walking. He patted Dolly and gave her a carrot as she nuzzled his hand.

"Come on, then, old girl, no cartload of wood or a coffin for you to pull today. It should be a nice, easy afternoon for you. You deserve it; you're a good girl, aren't you?"

The horse munched happily on the carrot and stood quietly as Fred fastened the straps. As he approached The Red Lion, Fred pulled on the reins.

"Whoa then, Dolly, wait a minute while I fetch Charlotte; she should be ready, I hope." He entered the kitchen, where his parents and Charlotte had just finished their dinner. "Hello, Mum, how's your leg now, with the plaster off?"

"Fine, thanks, Fred. It's such a relief to be able to scratch my leg again. Why do things always itch when you can't get at them? It's still a bit bruised and swollen, but it's mended." She held out her foot for him to inspect.

"Oh, yes, it looks all right, doesn't it? Is it still painful?"

"It still aches, but nothing like it did. The doctor said I must be careful for a few weeks and not walk on it too much. Mind you, there's not much chance of me doing that, the way this pair fuss over me." The smile on her face took the sting out of her words.

"Make sure you listen to them, then, and make the most of it. Charlotte, are you ready to go? I've got Dolly and the cart outside."

"Yes, I'm ready; thanks for taking me, Fred. I feel nervous, which is silly because she's my aunt, but I feel better knowing you'll be with me. I think she might take more notice of you."

"Come on then, let's see if we can get some answers."

As they made their way along the country lanes to the next village, the hedgerows were full of summer flowers, and the foliage was lush and green. They saw smoke coming from the chimney of Joan Smith's cottage in the distance, and the knot in Charlotte's stomach tightened. Fred stopped Dolly at the front gate and tethered her to a post. Charlotte knocked on the front door, opened it, and called out.

"Hello, Aunty Joan, are you there? It's me, Charlotte. Hello."

"Hold on, I'm upstairs; I'll be there in a minute."

Fred had not seen Charlotte's aunty before, and he surveyed the elderly woman as she entered the room. She had brown hair sprinkled with grey streaks and swept up into a severe bun. Her clothes were plain and dark-coloured. When Charlotte introduced him, she shook his hand, but the tight smile on her lips did not reach her eyes.

"I thought you would have returned to Exeter by now, Charlotte. Is everything all right at home?"

"Oh, I didn't go back home, Aunty Joan. You know I left here to look after Fred's mother, Betsey, who had broken her leg? Well, it's mended now, but she's asked me to stay on to work at the inn, so that's what I'm going to do."

"I see. Well, I hope you told your parents you were not coming home. Were they happy about that? I thought your father wanted you to work in the church and the house?"

"I've written to mother but haven't heard back from her yet. Anyway, I would prefer to stay working here. Father and I never did get on, as you know."

"No, he isn't the easiest man to get along with; I'll grant you that, but at least with the baby adopted, you could go home. You have me to thank for that, and you're lucky your father is willing to have you back at all."

"I'm grateful for your help, but I wish you hadn't gotten rid of Doris. She was my baby, and it was up to me to decide what would happen to her. By giving her away behind my back, I didn't even get a chance to say goodbye."

"You kept putting it off, and with every day that passed, I could see you were growing fonder of the child. I just thought it was kinder to get the job done for you. Anyway, what's done is done. Now, would you like a cup of tea?"

"That's kind of you, but I'd better tell you the purpose of our visit and then see if the offer still stands. You see, Betsey is a kind soul, and she knows how upset I've been since I lost Doris. She has a large family herself and understands what it's like to lose a child. She says if I can get Doris back, I can keep her with me at the inn."

"I don't think that's a good idea at all. You've made the break now, and there's no point going back. No young man will ever look at you if you have a bastard to raise; surely you know that."

"I don't care about that; I just want my daughter back. I never expect to marry. I don't think I could ever trust a man again, anyway, so that doesn't matter. Now, where did you take her?"

"I'm not telling you. You're only thinking of yourself. People here know I'm your aunt, and I don't want the disgrace of a niece of mine bringing up a child born out of wedlock. Few people in Warkley know you had a child because we kept it quiet, and that's how it should stay."

All this time, Fred had remained silent, but now he stood up and confronted the old lady.

"Now, look, ma'am, you may feel this is none of my business, but Charlotte is a friend of mine, and she's been very kind to my mother. I'm determined to help her get the baby back, so please tell us where you took the child, and we'll be on our way and leave you in peace."

"You're right on one account, mister; it is none of your business. Now, I'll thank you both to leave my house."

"No, I'm sorry, but that's not going to happen. You haven't always lived hereabouts, but I have, and I know a great many people. If you don't tell us where you took the baby, then I'll make sure everyone knows what you did. You'll never be able to hold your head up in the village again, and if I put the word out, I doubt anyone locally will sell you anything you need. Now, you think about it: do you want to become an outcast? Because I swear to you, I can make it happen, and I will."

Her mouth a tight, thin line, and her face white with rage, the old woman scowled at him.

"I see how the land lies here, then. I'd heard you'd lost your wife; it's not difficult to see where your interests lie now, is it? You want to be careful, young lady or you'll find yourself in the family way for a second time, and I'll tell you now, I won't be helping you out again."

"You mind your foul tongue, woman! Now, will you tell us what we want to know or not? Because if you're not, we'll go to the inn for lunch and spread the word."

"Very well, if you must know, I took the child to Buzzacott House, not far from Hartford; do you know the place?"

"Yes, I do. Why did you take her there?"

"A mother and her daughter live there, and they advertise in the newspapers for unwanted babies to pass on to childless couples to adopt, though goodness knows why anyone would want to adopt a child. I would have thought being barren would be a godsend these days when most folks have so many children they don't know what to do with them. Anyway, I saw an advertisement in the North Devon Journal and saw the address was not far away. I think Lizzie Dymond, that's the woman's name, often meets mothers at the railway station if they don't live locally, but I just went and knocked on the door and explained the situation, and she was willing to take the child. It cost me five pounds, though, so I shall want that from you because she won't return it."

"Well, you took the ten pounds that Martin gave me to get rid of the baby, so it was my money, anyway."

"I deserved the rest for taking you in and feeding you. Money doesn't grow on trees, my girl, and you never went hungry here."

"I don't care about the money. Do you know if they had a couple in mind to take Doris?"

"I have no idea; I just wanted to get rid of her, and if you have any sense, you'll leave things as they are. Now, please leave me in peace; you've upset me enough for one day."

"Come on, Fred, we've got what we wanted. Let's go home."

Without another word, they left the house, Charlotte knowing it would be the last time she would ever set foot there. She would never forgive her aunt for giving Doris away. When they got outside, Fred took her arm.

"Are you all right, Charlotte? I know that was upsetting for you. What an unpleasant woman she is, but at least we know where she took the baby. It's not far either; we could go there on the way home if you like?"

"Oh, yes, please, if you don't mind, Fred, but I shouldn't take up any more of your time."

"Don't be daft. It would be stupid not to go when it's almost on the way home. Come on."

They stopped the horse and cart outside the front door of Buzzacott House and surveyed their surroundings. It was a large house, situated in extensive grounds, but sadly neglected, with nettles and brambles having taken over. The house needed repair, and the windows were covered in grime. Taking Charlotte's arm firmly, Fred walked her to the front door and knocked loudly. Charlotte looked as if her legs might give way at any moment, so Fred held on to her. A tall woman answered the door.

"Can I help you?"

"Yes, I hope so. This is my friend, Charlotte Mackie. She had a baby daughter recently, and without her permission, her aunt brought the baby here to be adopted. Charlotte's circumstances have changed, and she wants her baby back. Would that be possible?"

"No, I'm sorry, but as I would have told your aunt at the time, we don't keep the babies long. We arrange adoptions, and the babies are rehomed with childless couples. I can assure you we are always careful in selecting new parents, and your baby will be loved and cared for. How long ago was this, anyway?"

"My baby would have been two weeks old when she was brought here, about six weeks ago. My aunt is called Joan Smith. Could you ask for the baby back because I didn't give my permission?"

"No, of course not; it would be most unfair on the new parents. In most cases, they will have waited a long time trying to have a child, and it would be cruel to take the baby away."

"I can understand that, but could you tell us who took Charlotte's baby? Then, at least, she could see her and satisfy herself that she is all right?"

"No, I'm sorry, but it is made clear when we take the babies we cannot give out the names of the adoptive parents because they do not want to be contacted. Now, if you'll excuse me, I must get on. I'm busy."

The woman firmly shut the door, leaving them standing on the doorstep. As Fred led Charlotte away, the girl sobbed bitterly, and Fred hugged her.

"Come on, never mind. At least she'll be cared for. Any couple who adopts a baby must want the child, and I'll bet they had to pay dearly for it. You can bet your life; this woman didn't arrange everything for nothing. It seems to me she's onto a good thing. She charges the women who are giving up their babies and also the couples who adopt them. A nice little earner, I would say. I'm sorry we've come to a dead-end, but I'm sure you'll have more children one day."

"That may be so, but I'll never forget Doris and no other child could ever replace her."

"No, I understand that. Charlotte, I don't suppose you will have heard, but I, too, lost two babies. My wife, Lucy, had two children between Rosella and Eddie, and they died." He frowned. "But that's not quite the whole story; she killed Alfie and Grace when they were just a few weeks old, so I know what it's like to lose a child."

"Oh, Fred, that's terrible; I'm so sorry, but why did she kill her children?"

"I can't pretend to understand, but she had a mental illness. We found her trying to smother Eddie, and she admitted she had killed the other two and was committed to an asylum. Luckily, we saved Eddie, and the poor girl went through hell in that asylum. She took her own life in the end."

This time, Charlotte hugged Fred but could think of little to say to comfort him. He pulled away from her. "Come on, I'll take you back to the inn; I'm afraid we've done all we can here."

CHAPTER 26

Clarice Gubb was feeling pleased with herself. She had got all her jobs done and hoped to leave the Manor House on time for her half-day off. She knew from experience that Miss Wetherby would only let her go if all tasks were completed satisfactorily. The housekeeper seemed to take a real delight in finding fault and delaying the servants when it was their day off. With only one day's leave a month, this time was precious. Having said farewell to the kitchen staff, she let herself out the back door and took a shortcut through the barn to the lane behind. She wished her young man, Christopher Webber, could have the same time off as she did, but this never seemed to work out. Since working at the Manor House, she had seen Christopher every day, and they had struck up a friendship that had now become a romance. They found the same things funny, and he didn't seem to mind that she was plain-looking and suffering from acne. As she entered the barn, she heard her name called.

"Ah, there you are, Clarice. I was beginning to think I'd missed you; I came to get some tools, but Jack will be looking for me if I'm gone too long. I hoped you might be leaving around now."

"Hello, Chris. You made me jump, but it's lovely to see you alone for five minutes."

He put his arms around her and kissed her on the lips. She responded, and both were lost in their embrace and oblivious to their surroundings for a few moments.

"It's so annoying to sit with you at mealtimes and pretend we're not seeing each other. Miss Wetherby wouldn't approve if she knew, though, and neither of us can afford to lose our jobs. What are you doing on your afternoon off?"

"Mum will expect me to spend time with her and the family. I wish you and I could spend the afternoon together, but our leave never seems to coincide, does it?"

"No, and that's why I wanted to catch you now. I wondered if you'd like to meet me later for a walk up onto the cliffs. The only thing is, it would need to be quite late. What time do you have to be back?"

"It doesn't matter as long as I'm up at dawn tomorrow to do my jobs. Even if the back door is locked, I know where Jack keeps the spare key, so I can always let myself in and put the key back in the morning. Why do we have to walk so late?"

"Oh, well, keep this to yourself, but Dad and Charlie Chugg are coming home from France tonight with smuggled goods. I have to watch from the cliffs and signal with a lantern to tell them if it's safe to land. If the gaugers are lying in wait, Charlie will sail on to a different cove."

"Oh, Chris, I wish you hadn't said you'd do that; it's dangerous. You could go to prison if you're caught."

"It's unlikely the gaugers will be around. There aren't many of them, and they have the whole of the South West to keep an eye on. From what I've heard, they seem to concentrate more on the South Devon coastline. Nobody's ever been caught around here, but there's always a first time, and Charlie likes to take precautions. I looked for him last night, in case he was back early, but it was tonight he expected to arrive. It depends on the tides and the winds. I'll have to wait until it's dark before I can signal. Anyway, do you want to come?"

"I don't want to get into any trouble. What time do you want to meet?"

"Would around ten o'clock be too late?"

"No, that's all right. I'll meet you on the path to the cliffs when I leave home to go back to work."

"Excellent, I'll look forward to it and don't worry, I've done this a few times now and never seen anyone. Charlie's generous, too, so it gives me a bit more money to put by for a rainy day. I'll see you later."

He kissed her briefly and left the barn, clutching a bag of tools.

For the second time in as many minutes, Clarice's eyes drifted to the old clock on the mantelpiece. Having looked forward to her time off, she now found she wished the hours away until she could meet Christopher. Much to Ruth's discomfort, Clarice was told the story first-hand of how her sister had run off with the man from the fair. She tried to support her sister, saying that everyone makes mistakes, but her mother was having none of it.

"I keep telling her anything could have happened, and she's lucky to be here in one piece. Most men are only after one thing, and then they're off. Not you, John. I'm sure you were an honourable young man, but most aren't." Before her husband could answer, she continued. "If you girls have any sense, you'll stay away from men until you're older. Plenty of time to think of settling down and having a family when you're at least into your twenties."

Clarice shuffled uncomfortably, knowing her mother would not approve of her meeting with Christopher in a few hours. Her mother had cooked a satisfying meal of pigs' liver and onions with mashed potatoes and peas from the garden. To change the subject, Clarice complimented her on the meal. "That was delicious, Mum. Not even Ethel Potts could have bettered that."

John Cutcliffe pushed back his plate contentedly. "She's right, love; you can certainly cook. That was tasty, thank you. Did I see an apple pie in the oven?"

"You did, and I've scalded the milk to make some cream. Shall we have it now?"

Daisy and Rachael's eyes lit up at the mention of more food. There was never anything like this to eat in the workhouse. In their eyes, their stepmother could do no wrong. All the praying and attending church every Sunday was a nuisance, but nothing compared to near starvation.

Clarice helped Ruth and Susanna wash up whilst Noeleen read some of the Bible to Daisy and Rachael. At long last, it was time for Clarice to go.

"Bye, everyone; I'll see you all in a couple of weeks when I have another half-day off. I need to get back to the Manor House now."

"Yes, all right. Mind how you go, then, it's cloudy, making it dark early tonight."

Clarice waved goodbye to her mother and then, making sure she was not watching, took the footpath towards the cliffs instead of to the Manor House. She rounded a corner and jumped as Christopher stepped out from behind a bush.

"Oh, my goodness, you made me jump. Sorry I'm late, but the family kept me chatting."

"No, it's fine, and at least it's dark now. We have plenty of time, so shall we take the long path through the woods and then onto the headland? The boat won't be here for some time yet, and they won't land until I've signalled."

"How will they know it's safe to land?"

"If I flash the lantern quickly three times, and then wait for a few minutes, and do it again, they know it's safe, but if I flash it once, then count to sixty, and flash it again, and keep doing that, they'll know there's a problem, and they won't land."

"Very clever."

"It's simple enough, but it's worked so far."

They paused in the woods to kiss and cuddle until, eventually, Clarice thought Christopher was beginning to take rather too many liberties and pushed him away. "No, you don't, Chris Webber, you're not having your wicked way with me. Not that I wouldn't like you to."

"You know I'd never take advantage of you, Clarice; I love you."

That made the girl hesitate, and she looked at him thoughtfully. "Do you, Chris? Do you love me? I'm not pretty, and I've got all these beastly spots. You could probably have your pick of all the young ladies in the village. You do know that?"

"I doubt that, but it's you I want to be with, and I think you're beautiful. Anyway, everyone gets spots, and they'll go as you get older."

"In that case, I'll tell you something because I love you too. I love you very much."

They kissed again until, at last, he pulled away from her. "Come on, we'd better walk up to the headland now and get the lantern ready."

They puffed and panted as they climbed the cliff. At the top, stunted trees and gorse bushes grew at curious angles, showing clearly which way the strong winds blew. Christopher was sure-footed as he guided her along an indistinct path he was familiar with.

"This path's been used by generations of smugglers, but it's little known to most folk, and there's thick gorse on either side, so mind your step. You'll know all about it if you fall into a gorse bush."

They reached the top and gazed at the bay beneath them, taking the opportunity to catch their breath.

"This must be an amazing view in the daytime. Perhaps we could come here again sometime."

"Aye, maybe. Ah, there she is, *The Bountiful Lady*, Charlie's ship."

"Are you sure it's the right one?"

"Oh, yes, definitely, I'd know her anywhere, and anyway, Charlie always hangs a white vest from the topmast; can you see it? It's just about visible. Now, let's study the beach for a few minutes. The moon isn't bright tonight, which is both a good thing and a bad thing. It means the boat's not easily seen, but then, neither are the gaugers. I think it's all right. No, just a minute; can you see something glinting over there in the rocks?"

They strained their eyes, trying to see in the dim light.

"Yes, it's difficult to see, but the moonlight is shining on something."

Just then, the clouds cleared, revealing several men hiding behind the rocks on the beach. The moonlight glinted on their rifles.

"Oh no, the gaugers are out! I've never seen them before. They don't usually bother coming here because there isn't a lot of smuggling locally. Anyway, listen. We must flash the lantern as I told you, but then we must get away from here as quickly as possible because they'll have more men hidden here on the cliff, just looking for someone like me to signal. They know how it works. I think it's best if you go now and run straight back to the Manor House before I light the lantern; then you'll be in the clear."

"No, I'm not leaving you here on your own." She put her finger to his lips before he could object. "Listen, light the lantern and signal, then put it out and hide it. I'll put my cloak down, and if they find us, they'll think we're a courting couple. They'd never think I'd come here with you to signal to smugglers. You're much safer if I stay."

"Are you sure? They might not fall for it."

"They will, particularly if they know my mother. She's so upright and religious, they'll never think her daughter could be up to no good."

"But, Clarice, if any of them know you, they might tell your mother, and you'll be in trouble."

"I'll have to risk it, but it's better that I get a telling-off from my mother than you get jailed or transported to Australia. I think there's a hole here in the bank somewhere. I stepped in it just now; yes, there, look. It's probably a badger's hole. When you dowse the lantern, stick it in there, and we'll move away from it."

Chris carefully lit the lantern, hoisted it aloft and signalled once, then held it out of sight and counted to sixty. He repeated this five times whilst Clarice watched to see if any men came running.

"Chris, stop now; they must have seen it, surely? We must hide the lantern; otherwise, we'll be caught."

"Yes, Charlie is bound to have been watching. He'll sail the boat away now with any luck."

He dowsed the light and thrust the lantern into the badger's hole, pulling some bracken down over it. "Come on, let's get away from this spot and find somewhere to put your cloak down and sit it out. They retraced their footsteps and hurried back down the track until they came to a clearing that looked out to sea.

"Let's sit here. Oh, yes, look, Charlie's sailing away. Thank goodness."

They sat side by side on Clarice's cloak, looking out over the moonlit bay.

"This is romantic, isn't it? Shame to waste an opportunity." Clarice lay back and pulled him down to her.

"You're a naughty girl, Clarice Gubb, but you're not wrong, and we get so little time alone together."

He kissed her passionately, but within a few minutes, they were interrupted when men on horseback cantered into the clearing.

"Hey, you there. Get up and show yourself. What business do you have up here on the cliffs at this time of night?"

Christopher got up warily and held up his hands, for the man was pointing a rifle in his direction. "Nothing, mister, we ain't up to nothing. We were chatting and looking at the moonlight; nothing wrong with that, is there?"

"Who's that hiding behind you? Come out and show me your hands."

Clarice came out from behind Christopher with her hands held aloft. Christopher was shocked when he saw that her blouse was undone, partially revealing her breasts and that her hair had fallen around her shoulders. She looked embarrassed and hung her head. The man on the horse alighted and came towards them, swinging his lantern.

"Come here, let me see your faces. Who are you?"

Clarice's heart sank as she saw the man was a regular churchgoer and a close friend of her mother. She no longer had to pretend to be dismayed.

"Why, it's Clarice, isn't it? Clarice Gubb? I'm guessing your mother doesn't know what you're up to, young lady, but she soon will. Look at the disgraceful state of you. You should be ashamed of yourself. You wait until I tell her how I found you. And you, lad, what do you have to say for yourself? What's your name?"

"It's Christopher Webber, sir, and we were doing no harm. We've been seeing each other for a few months now, and we were only kissing. It would have gone no further, I promise you. I respect Clarice too much."

"Aye, I can see how much you were respecting her by her appearance. You can save your explanations for Noeleen, and I'll tell you now, rather you than me. Have you seen anyone else up here on the cliffs with a lantern?"

"No, sir, I swear we've seen no one else; why, what's the problem?"

"Smugglers are the problem, lad. There's too much of it going on, and it's our business to put a stop to it. There was a boat coming in tonight that we're sure was loaded with contraband. We've had reports of it being landed in this cove before, and tonight, we were ready for them, but someone signalled from this cliff to warn them. I saw it with my own eyes. Are you sure you've seen no one else? Clarice, don't you lie to me and make matters worse, or I surely will tell your mother what you've been up to."

"No, sir, I swear I haven't seen anyone else on the cliffs tonight. The only person I've seen is Christopher. I'd be so grateful if you didn't mention this to my mother. It would upset her so much, and there's no need; I wouldn't have let anything untoward happen, I promise you."

"Aye, well, I don't think it's your mother's feelings you're thinking of, but I was young myself once, and I may not tell her. I'll think about it for a day or two. Now, both of you step to one side. I want to make sure you have no lantern with you."

The couple dutifully stepped to one side, and Christopher tentatively took Clarice's shaking hand.

"All right, it looks as if your story's true, though you should know it's dangerous to come up here in the dark with no light to guide you back. I'll send one of my men back with you. I don't want to hear you've fallen off the cliff."

"That's kind of you, sir, but I know these cliffs, and now, in the moonlight, I promise you we'll be fine. The path is clear from here back to the village."

"Just as you like then; be on your way, and mind you, Clarice, I shall be keeping an eye on you from now on."

"Yes, sir, thank you. Come on, Christopher, I must get back to the Manor House now."

The young couple gratefully headed for the village, and as the men galloped off into the distance, Christopher pulled Clarice around to face him. "Clarice, what happened to your blouse? I didn't undo all those buttons and your hair; how did it get so messed up? I'll be surprised if he doesn't tell your mother."

"Oh, I undid the buttons and loosened my hair whilst I was standing behind you. I thought it would make our story more believable."

"It certainly did. I was horrified when I saw the state of you, but I think the sight of your open blouse certainly distracted them. That was clever. I just hope our friend keeps it to himself."

CHAPTER 27

It had been a long journey, and Charlie and Arthur were relieved to see the dim lights twinkling on the hillsides around Hartford. They were bone-tired and longed to be tucked up in their comfortable beds.

"Not long now, Arthur and our business will be done."

"Aye, and I shan't be sorry, though I have enjoyed it. I know Christopher will be up on the cliff, but how many men will meet us on the beach? We'll need some help to unload the goods and make them safe as quickly as possible."

"Yes, don't you worry. It's all organised, and it's lucky we got back tonight as expected. Alfred and Jimmy will be watching the cove, and as soon as they see we're going to land, they'll be there with four ponies to take the cargo away. We take the stuff to the farm and leave it there until we think it's safe to move it. We have a secret hiding place to store everything; it's been used for generations. I understand my great-grandfather built it."

"Right, come on, then, Chris, give us a signal. Oh, my God, there it is, but it's not the one we want. There must be gaugers lying in wait for us. That's never happened before. We can't land."

"What do we do now, then? It's only a matter of time before they'll come after us in another vessel."

"It's all right, Arthur, not to worry. We'll sail on to Lee Bay."

"Are you sure? The rocks there are treacherous."

"I know, but we don't have much choice. If we make a run for it now, they'll soon catch us because they have a bigger boat. They'll never think we'd try to take a boat this size into Lee Bay, and they sure as hell won't follow us. Don't worry; I've done it before because I knew this would happen one day."

"But what will we do with the goods, then?"

"Arthur, just trust me. This has been planned for, and we'll be all right, but I need to concentrate on getting the boat into the bay as soon as I can. When they see us making a run for it, they'll launch their vessel, and we must be out of sight before they see where we go."

Masterfully, Charlie sailed the boat out to sea. The men waiting on the beach saw what was happening, and the order was given to launch their vessel as quickly as possible. Fortunately for Charlie and Arthur, the wind was, yet again, in their favour, and they worked furiously to get the sails of *The Bountiful Lady* fully hoisted. Their boat was soon out of sight to the men on the beach, and Charlie immediately turned her sharply to sail into the next bay.

"Charlie, there are rocks everywhere; you'll never land it here and at this speed. We must get the sails down again."

Charlie shouted over the wind. "No, just wind in one sail and leave the others; it will be all right."

Skilfully, he manoeuvred the boat through the choppy water of an impossibly narrow channel, and suddenly the water was calm. He turned to Arthur with an enormous grin on his face. "See, I told you, I had done it before. I've practised this landing since I was a nipper and used to come out with Dad and Grandad. They wouldn't let me sail alone until I had mastered landing a boat in this bay, and I can tell you it's not easy. Now, if I sail in a bit closer, we'll be hidden from the eye out to sea. We'll start unloading, and then I'll tell you my other secret."

"That was amazing, Charlie. I honestly thought we would end up on the rocks."

"Oh, ye of little faith! It will come as no surprise to you that smuggling runs in my family, and I've been well-trained. This bay is inaccessible by land because high cliffs surround it, so we've nothing to fear there, although it's close to the village."

"Yes, I know, but how can we transport the goods anywhere; surely we're trapped here unless we sail out again?"

"We'll take everything to a cave just up the beach. From that cave, an ancient tunnel leads to the old silver mine, and the goods will be safe there for as long as we want. That part of the mine has not been worked for years because the silver petered out a long time ago, but the tunnels are still there. It's been a while, but I've been in the tunnel, and I know where it comes out the other end."

"Are you sure it's safe?"

"We don't have a lot of choices, do we? It was fine the last time I checked it, but I'm afraid there is some bad news."

"What?"

"Well, there are only the two of us now, and it will take us some time to unload everything and get it stashed in the tunnel. We'll have to get on with it, too, because I must sail out of here before the tide turns. Come on, let's get cracking."

For two hours, they worked non-stop. Charlie passed the goods off the boat to Arthur, and they trudged up to the cave countless times from the beach. Once inside the cave, Arthur held up the lantern to look for the tunnel.

"I bet you can't find it."

Arthur circled the cave unsuccessfully. "You're right. I can't see it; are you sure this is the cave?"

"Yes, here, look."

Along one side of the cave, fronds of seaweed hung from a ledge higher up. Charlie deftly swung himself up and pulled aside the curtain of seaweed. Behind it was a large hole into which he shone his lantern. Arthur could see that a passageway led uphill. Charlie hauled himself into the hole and pulled out a ladder.

"Here we are, the ladder's still sound. The water doesn't come up this far. If you pass the goods up to me, I'll stack them out of sight, and we can get off."

It took another hour before the men had accomplished their task, and they were both so tired they could barely stand.

"Come on, Arthur, I know you're tired, and so am I, but we must sail out of this cove before the tide turns, or we'll be stuck here for hours. Hopefully, the gaugers will have given up by now or have sailed off somewhere else. We'll have to risk it, anyway. Come on."

They sailed out of the cove without incident and were relieved to see no sign of the gaugers' boat. Charlie sailed away from the village and along the coast for a mile or two before heading out to the open sea and circling back to land at Hartford. As they reached the jetty, men came running at them from all directions.

"We are impounding this boat. Come off with your hands up."

"What for? Can a man not go fishing anymore? What is it you're looking for? We have an excellent catch, but as far as I know, that's not against the law."

They obligingly jumped off the boat, and one of the men pushed them to one side.

"Just sit down there on those rocks and wait. We have reason to believe you have smuggled goods on board from France, and we are going to search your boat. We know you've been sailing around, hoping we'd be gone."

"You search wherever you like, but I'll tell you now, all you'll find is fish, so you're wasting your time."

The men took no notice and, leaving one to watch Charlie and Arthur, the others boarded the boat and went through it with a fine-tooth comb. The man in charge came back to Charlie and Arthur.

"I expect you think you're clever, don't you, but I know you're a smuggler, Charlie Chugg, you and your father and grandfather, before you. We've been trying to catch your family for years, but your luck will run out one day, and then you'll go to jail for a long time."

"I don't know what you're talking about, and it seems you have no proof. If it's all the same to you, Arthur and I are tired, and we'd like to get to our beds; we have a lot of fish to sell tomorrow whilst it's fresh. Goodnight, gentlemen; I hope you catch your smugglers soon."

Watching discreetly from a safe distance, Christopher had been joined by Charlie's brother, Alfred, and his son, Jimmy. They watched with relief as they saw Charlie and Arthur make their way up the beach.

CHAPTER 28

The day before his wedding, Robert was busy harvesting corn in the fields. Jack had tried to persuade him to take a few days off to relax before the big day, but he would have none of it.

"Honestly, Jack, I'd much rather be out here working with you. The house is unbearable at the moment, with so many women fussing around. Mrs Potts and the maids are baking as if they have to feed the five thousand, and Annie, Sabina, and her Aunty Eveline are decorating everywhere with flowers. It's a kindness to let me spend the day with you in the sunshine."

"When you put it like that, sir, I can see why you'd rather be out here. This is the last field of corn to cut, and with your new reaper, it shouldn't take long."

They worked hard all morning until lunchtime when Dodger arrived on a small cart with Molly beside him. On the cart were two hampers of food that Robert had ordered for all the workers to celebrate the last harvest being gathered.

"Molly, come here a minute; stay and have a bite to eat with us because I've got a little job for you to do."

"Thank you, Master Robert, but I'd better not be too long, or Miss Wetherby will wonder where I am."

"If she asks, you can tell her I insisted you stay. Now, what I would like you to do is to make our corn dolly this year. Have you ever made one?"

"No, sir, but I'd like to try. What do I have to do?"

"That's a good question; does anyone here know how to make a corn dolly?"

Several of the men spoke up, including Dodger. Robert had always liked the stable lad, and he singled him out. "Right, come on, then Dodger, tell us how it's done."

"Folk all have their own way of doing it, but it doesn't matter as long as you end up with a doll at the end of it. You must wait for the straw to dry out, then take some straws from the last sheaf of corn to be cut and make a doll. You should try to leave a hollow space inside its tummy because that's where a spirit will live. Then, you must plough the dolly back into the first furrow ploughed for the new crop next year. The spirit can return to the soil then, and it will nurture the new crop."

"That sounds straightforward enough; do you think you could make some sort of dolly from the straw, Molly?"

"Yes, I'm sure I can, sir. I'll ask Maisie to help me. What happens to the dolly until the ploughing is done?"

"You just put it somewhere safe. Perhaps on the kitchen windowsill, or it could stay in the barn if Mrs Potts doesn't want it in the way."

Robert stayed for a couple of hours after lunch and saw the rest of the corn cut but then returned to the house to see how the preparations were coming along. The house had been decorated with many flowers, and their scent filled the air. Robert went to see how Mrs Potts was getting on in the kitchen and found her sitting in her favourite chair by the fireplace.

"Now then, what's all this? Are you slacking again, Mrs Potts?"

Mrs Potts immediately made to get up from her chair, but Robert put his hands firmly on her shoulders.

"Just teasing, Mrs Potts. I know you will have done the work of ten men today already. Do you want to show me what you've made for tomorrow?"

"Yes, sir. Well, of course, there's the wedding cake; it's over there look, and I hope it's to your liking?"

The wedding cake had three tiers, the bottom one being the largest, and each gradually getting smaller. Mrs Potts had decorated it with white icing and piped swirls and flowers on each layer.

"Mrs Potts, it's wonderful. Has Annie seen it yet?"

"Yes, sir, and she's pleased with it. Now, come and look in the pantry and the dairy at all the other food I've prepared for tomorrow; I hope there will be enough, but I think there will."

Mrs Potts had indeed surpassed herself, for every shelf was laden with cold joints of turkey, beef, ham, and pork, all waiting to be carved. There were pies of all shapes and sizes and two whole salmon. For dessert, she had made trifles and sponges, crumbles and possets.

"Mrs Potts, it's amazing. Thank you so much. There's enough food here to feed an army."

"I must admit I'm pleased with it all, sir, but it's not just my hard work; everyone here has pitched in."

"Yes, I'm sure they have, and I'll thank them all tomorrow. Right now, I'd better be on my way because I'm going to meet my cousin, Percy, at the railway station. He will be my best man tomorrow, which is kind of him because not many of my family will be coming. Do you remember, Percy? He came here quite often when we were growing up."

"I do, sir. Yes, he was a nice lad. I'd forgotten about him; have you seen much of him over the years?"

"No, not much because he lives in London now, but I visit him when possible."

Robert went in search of Dodger to take him to the station in the carriage. As they passed the Lodge House, Robert asked Dodger to stop for a moment, and he went in search of Annie. She came to the door and beamed when she saw it was him.

"Hello, Robert, come in." She kissed him briefly, shielded from Dodger's eyes by the porch.

"No, I can't stay because I'm off to the station to collect Percy. Anyway, I'm told I'm not supposed to see you until tomorrow, but I just wanted to make sure everything is all right."

"Yes, it's fine. I tried my dress on this morning, and it fitted perfectly. Aunty Eveline has done such an amazing job. Mary, Helen, and Selina tried their dresses on, too, and they looked beautiful. I can't wait for tomorrow; I'm so excited."

"That's all right, then. As long as you're not getting cold feet?"

"No, of course not, though I'm glad your family won't be there. I'd be far more nervous if they were, though I'm sorry for you that they won't come."

"Don't worry about it. It doesn't matter to me as long as you're there."

"Oh, I'll be there; there's no getting rid of me now. Have you seen all the food that Mrs Potts has cooked? And the cake is amazing. I don't know how she makes those flowers from icing. It's all so fiddly."

"The cake is a masterpiece, and, as usual, she's made enough food to feed the whole village, but that's all right because I want everyone to enjoy the day. Right then, I'll see you in church," he pulled her towards him and kissed her. "Until tomorrow."

Robert sat beside Dodger, for despite the difference in their stations in life, they were friends. They arrived just before the train was due, and leaving Dodger with the carriage, Robert went to find his cousin. He was one of the first passengers off the train, and Robert waved furiously.

"Percy, over here, old man. Percy, I'm here."

With a big grin, a young man hustled through the crowd. He was a good-looking lad, taller than Robert, and with mousey hair and brown eyes.

"Hello, Robert; it's so nice to see you." The two men shook hands.

"I can't thank you enough for being my best man, Percy. Not many of the family will be coming."

"That's their loss then, isn't it? Mind you, even I was surprised to hear you're marrying a former kitchen maid. I would have loved to be there when you told Aunt Eleanor. I bet her face was a picture."

"I think it's fair to say my mother wasn't pleased, and that's putting it mildly. I can't wait for you to meet Annie."

"I'm looking forward to it. Mind you, it will be difficult for you both; you are sure about this, aren't you?"

"I've never been more sure about anything; I've loved this girl for a long time. Now, let's get home because I want to hear all your news. I rather thought you might have brought a young lady with you?"

"Ah no, confirmed bachelor me; I'm not the marrying kind."

CHAPTER 29

The sound of birdsong awoke Annie on the day of her wedding, and she lay in bed and smiled to herself as she thought about the day ahead and how it would change her life forever. The birds always started to sing as soon as it became light, and she enjoyed listening to them, although it was so early. Her eyes adjusted to the gloomy light and moved from the window to her wedding dress, which hung on the wardrobe. It was a cream silk dress with a full skirt covered by a flimsy layer of lace, and it had a small train. The bodice had short sleeves and was also made of lace, and it fitted tightly, accentuating her tiny waist. She had chosen a long veil, which flowed down her back, and part of which could be pulled over her face for her walk to the altar.

The bridesmaids' dresses for Mary, Helen, and Selina hung alongside the wedding dress. They each had a full-length skirt and a simple sleeveless lacy top. They were a delicate lilac colour, and a slightly darker purple ribbon was tied at the back around the waistline.

Annie was to carry a bouquet of pale pink roses and lavender, picking up the colour of the bridesmaids' dresses. The bridesmaids would hold small posies of white rosebuds and lavender and would wear a few white roses in their hair. They all had long hair, and Sabina and Annie had practised various ways of plaiting and tying it until they found a style they were happy with and which would hold the flowers best. Annie would wear her long hair loose, allowing it to cascade around her shoulders in its natural ringlets.

She tossed back the covers, went to the window, and pulled back the curtains, praying it would be a dry day. However, the ground was wet, and it was drizzling slightly. She frowned and hoped it would dry up before the wedding at noon. Pulling a loose gown over her nightdress, she went to the kitchen for a cup of tea. She was pleased that no one else was up, for she liked a few minutes to herself in the morning. She pulled the kettle forward on the stove and was soon enjoying a strong cup of tea, which she drank sitting in the window seat.

The garden, which had been an overgrown wilderness only a few months before, was now planted with numerous vegetables and was her mother's pride and joy. Until she gave up work, there had never been enough hours in the day for gardening, but now, Sabina thoroughly enjoyed it and was learning all the time. There were two rows of runner beans, still producing scarlet flowers, and they picked masses of beans daily. Indeed, there were far too many for the family to eat, but Sabina was pleased to give the surplus to her neighbours. She had also tried her hand at growing potatoes, and they had flourished, supplying the family since early July, and the main crop would be harvested in October. It was so satisfying to wander into the garden and gather what they needed for a meal.

As she watched the raindrops race down the window pane, Annie was lost in thought. She didn't hear her mother approaching until she laid her hand on her shoulder.

"Oh, Mum, you made me jump; I didn't hear you coming."

"You were miles away; not changing your mind, are you?"

"No, of course not. Mind you, I'm half looking forward to the wedding and half dreading it. At least the Fellwoods won't be there; that would have been far worse."

"Yes, you have nothing to worry about. I'm sure it will all go without a hitch. Now, do you want your breakfast, or will you have a bath and wash your hair? It will take a while to dry, so you need to do it early."

"Yes, I'll bath first, then the bridesmaids and the boys could do with a scrub. What about you and Liza? Do you both want to have a bath? We might run out of hot water."

"No, Liza and I bathed yesterday, so we'll just wash, but there's plenty of hot water."

The Carters had a busy morning getting ready. Liza insisted they all had a hearty breakfast, starting with a bowl of creamy porridge, followed by bacon, eggs, and fresh crusty bread.

"Goodness, Liza, we won't get into our clothes at this rate."

"Never mind that you eat up. It will be a long day, and no doubt lunch will be late by the time the ceremony is over, and they've taken some photographs."

By half-past eleven, the family was dressed in their new finery. Robert had insisted no expense was spared, and George Carter had ordered several different outfits for them all to choose from. Sabina wore a long, sage-green dress that matched her eyes, and she wore a cream hat. Liza had chosen a pale blue dress and selected a navy hat. She couldn't stop stroking the soft fabric of the dress, for she had never worn anything so fine. The younger boys, Edward, Stephen, and Danny, wore navy velvet shorts with braces, over white silk shirts, and a bow tie, but Willie, at fifteen, wore long trousers. The boys fidgeted with the high collars, for they were unaccustomed to anything so tight around their necks.

Mary, Helen, and Selina longed to put on their new dresses, but Annie made them wait until the last minute in case they spilt anything. The family stood around waiting for Annie to make an appearance, and when, at last, she descended the stairs, they all looked at her in wonder.

"Well, do I look all right?"

"All right? You look beautiful, Annie; I'm so proud of you, and I wish your father could see you now."

"You all look incredibly smart, too. Who would have thought the Carter family would ever be dressed in such finery? I think the carriages have just pulled up outside. Most of you can go on in the first carriage, but I need to wait for Uncle Fred so he can give me away, and anyway, I must be a few minutes late. The bridesmaids will go with me."

Meanwhile, Robert had arrived at the church with Percy and was standing at the altar, waiting nervously for Annie to walk up the aisle. He kept turning around and looking anxiously over his shoulder, much to the amusement of the waiting congregation. They were enjoying the fact that the Squire's son was concerned about whether a village girl would turn up to marry him. The church was packed, mainly of Annie's family and the local people, though there were a few of Robert's relations and friends.

About ten minutes after noon, the organ started to play the Wedding March, and Robert was delighted to see his bride approaching on the arm of her Uncle Fred. He gasped at how lovely she looked, even with her veil over her face, and as she reached him, she pushed it back over her head and smiled widely at him. The ceremony went without a hitch, and after a few photographs had been taken outside the church, the carriages took the main guests to the Manor House, leaving the rest to make their own way.

Fortunately, it had stopped raining mid-morning, and the ground was mostly dry underfoot, though the day was still slightly overcast. Several servants, including Mrs Potts, Maisie, and Molly, had attended the wedding. It had taken some effort from Robert to persuade Mrs Potts to leave the kitchen long enough to attend the wedding, for she wanted the food to be perfect. She only agreed when he said she could travel back in a carriage to ensure she was there before the guests. Robert and Annie stood at the entrance to the hall and welcomed their guests.

"My dear, you look wonderful." An old lady shook Annie's hand warmly.

"Oh, Aunty Margery, I'm so pleased you accepted our invitation. Does Papa know?"

"Yes, Robert, he does, and he disapproves, but I don't care because I'm old enough to do as I like. I would have loved to be present when you told your mother you wanted to marry a servant. Now, this marriage isn't conventional, but then, neither am I and if you love each other, that's good enough for me. Mind you, young lady, woe betide you if you upset my favourite great-nephew."

"I've no intention of doing that, ma'am, and I'm so pleased you came; it's nice for Robert to have a few of his family here. There are more than enough of mine."

"There's no need to call me ma'am, my dear; Aunty Margery will do fine, but I'd better move along because I'm holding everyone up. Perhaps we could have a chat later? I want to get to know you better, and I don't live far away, so perhaps you could call on me?"

"Yes, I'd love to. Thank you so much."

"Aunty Margery, you'll be able to talk to Annie during the meal because you'll be sitting close to her. I hope that's all right?"

"Yes, of course, lad; it will be a pleasure."

The old lady hobbled off with her walking stick, and Robert winked at Annie. "There, you see, not all my family disapprove of you. If you can get on with Aunty Margery, she'll be a strong ally for you; she carries a lot of influence in the family."

Next in line was Annie's Uncle George and his wife, Mary Ann. Annie could see that the words of congratulation stuck in his throat, and it was all she could do not to laugh. Fortunately, Robert saved the situation by shaking George's hand and thanking him for his help obtaining clothes and shoes for so many people for the wedding.

"It was a pleasure, sir, and I hope I can continue to supply your household with many of its requirements."

"I'm sure we can put some business your way, George, now that you're part of the family."

Annie nearly choked with laughter, and as George walked away, she whispered to Robert. "He managed to swallow his pride long enough to try to get some extra business, didn't he?"

Welcoming all the guests took some time, and Annie was glad Liza had insisted she ate breakfast because she was getting hungry. It was nearly half past two before the guests were finally seated and could sample the spread Mrs Potts was so proud of. Robert had insisted Annie invite as many of the villagers as she wanted, and she fretted that they might have too much to drink and show themselves up. She shared this concern with Robert, and he told her not to worry.

"You'll find that not only poor people sometimes misbehave, so don't worry about it, and anyway, I don't think any of your friends or family will let you down."

Long tables had been set out in the hall, and extra servants were employed. Many of the guests could not read or write and couldn't understand the displayed table plans. Robert had anticipated this, and as the guests moved on from greeting the newly married couple, Ethan and Caleb Bater took their names and escorted them to their seats. Annie and Robert had spent a long time poring over the seating plan. Normally, the bride's family would be seated amidst the groom's family to allow the guests to get to know each other. However, that was a worrying prospect, given the different backgrounds of the people in this gathering. On the top table, the only guests from Robert's side of the family were Percy and Aunty Margery. Standing in for Annie's father, Tom, Fred sat next to Sabina and the three bridesmaids, Mary, Helen, and Sabina.

Annie had agonised over whether to invite Sarah Carter and her son Bentley. Since Sabina and Eveline had allowed Sarah to sit with them at the May Day celebrations, they had seen little of her, for she wisely kept herself to herself. Many in the village would never forgive her for abandoning William's children in London after his death and returning to Devon alone. Amongst these were Annie's grandparents, Ned and Betsey. Since the news had broken about what Sarah had done and William's children had been rescued from the workhouse in London, they had refused to have anything to do with their daughter-in-law. However, it was becoming increasingly difficult to ignore Sarah because of Bentley. He was the spitting image of William as a child, and whenever Betsey saw him in the village, she became upset. With this in mind, Annie visited her granny and asked if she felt it was time to forgive and forget.

"I'll never forgive or forget what she did, but I know William would want me to be part of his child's life. Mind you, whether I can persuade Ned to accept her is another matter. I'll think about it."

"My wedding might be the perfect opportunity to get you and all the family together with her. I don't like the thought of Bentley not knowing our family; he's such a sweet little boy, and I think Sarah is genuinely sorry for what she did. It sounds as if she panicked at the thought of bringing up William's children on her own after he died, and, of course, she had nowhere for them all to live."

"Aye, you can make excuses for her, but if she'd brought them back, we'd have worked something out. Anyway, I'll speak to your grandad and let you know."

So it was that at the wedding, Ned and Betsey sat with their grandchildren, Willie, Stephen, Edward, and Danny, and also Sarah and Bentley. Annie had also seated Liza at the same table to ensure her brothers behaved themselves. At Annie's insistence, Fred had invited Charlotte, and she would have dearly liked to seat them together, but as Fred had given her away, he had to sit on the top table. Therefore, Charlotte was seated with Eveline and the six children she cared for.

It was evident that romance was in the air, and Annie would have liked to do a bit more matchmaking, but it was difficult to achieve. She was aware that her Aunty Eveline was spending quite a bit of time at Hollyford Farm, and she was convinced this had a lot to do with Charlie Chugg. Also, though her mother would never admit it, she clearly thought the world of Arthur Webber and the visits to the Webber household were not all to do with cheering up his father, Peter. However, try as she might, she could not arrange for Charlie and Eveline, and her mother and Arthur, to sit together without raising curiosity. She just hoped they would get together after the meal.

Annie found she got on with Aunty Margery like a house on fire, just as Robert had hoped. Several different wines were served during the meal, but she carefully limited herself to one glass for fear she would show herself up. However, that one glass helped her relax, and she suddenly realised that she was enjoying herself despite all her fears. Once the meal and the speeches were out of the way, the tables were cleared, and the guests could spread out through several rooms. The band struck up a tune, and Robert and Annie took to the floor for the first dance, which was a waltz. To the amazement of her family, Annie danced it gracefully, and Robert wished Sarah and Victoria could have seen her, for it was largely thanks to their kindness and tuition that she could do so.

Annie was delighted to see Sabina dancing with Arthur Webber and Eveline dancing with Charlie Chugg. When the ladies went to powder their noses, Arthur leaned forward and whispered to Charlie.

"I didn't want to ask when the women were here, but when are we going to get the contraband from the silver mine; we don't want it discovered."

"Don't you worry about it, Arthur. Jimmy and I have already been there and fetched a couple of barrels of brandy to keep Ned going at the inn, but I think the rest of it's safer where it is for a few weeks. You don't quite know whom to trust these days. Don't worry, though; I'll pay you the rest of what I owe you as soon as I sell it. I'm grateful because I couldn't have done it without you. I'll see Christopher right, too; no need to worry."

"It's not that; I'd just sleep easier when all the evidence is gone. Does Eveline know what you do?"

"Aye, she does, and I can't say she particularly approves, but she knows it's gone on for years. We're becoming close, and I don't want to keep secrets from her. What about Sabina? Have you told her?"

"No, I'd like to, but I wouldn't want her to mention it to Annie and for her to tell Master Robert. I don't want us evicted from our cottage."

"I don't think you need to worry. Sabina would never betray you."

"No, I'm sure she wouldn't, but I don't want to put her in an awkward position. If we continue to see each other, I might have to give it a miss next time, Charlie."

"That's all right, Arthur, no problem. I can get someone else if needed, but I won't be going again for a while. This time, it was a close call, and the gaugers are getting better at their job. Anyway, here come the ladies."

It was likely that the party would continue into the early hours, but around ten o'clock, Robert banged on the table with a spoon and announced that he and his bride would be retiring for the night. This was met with loud cheers and raucous laughter as he swept Annie off her feet and carried her from the room.

"Robert, put me down; you don't have to carry me all the way. I'm no lightweight; now I eat so much."

"Rubbish, you're still as light as a feather, and anyway, I can't bear to put you down."

They reached their bedroom, which had been tastefully decorated with pale blue wallpaper and dark blue curtains, which the servants had already drawn. Robert gently placed Annie on the bed, lay beside her, and propped himself on one elbow.

"So, Lady Anne, here we are, alone at last. I've dreamt of this moment for nigh on four years now, and I can't believe we are finally here."

Annie giggled. "Am I really called Lady Anne?"

"No, not yet, but you will be one day. Now, I'm afraid you have promised to love, honour, and obey me, so you must do as you're told."

"I don't think that's going to be a problem." Annie pulled him towards her.

CHAPTER 30

Annie was not the only one keen to get Fred together with Charlotte. He, too, had the same thing in mind and thought the wedding would be a golden opportunity to get to know her better. However, with Arthur Webber and Charlie Chugg monopolising the time of Sabina and Eveline, he found that Charlotte was kept busy with the children.

Once he was able to move away from the top table, he went to sit with his mother and father to chat and immediately sensed an atmosphere. It was clear that Betsey and Ned were finding it difficult to spend time with their daughter-in-law. Sarah sat silently, watching her young son, Bentley, play with his cousins. Ned and Betsey sat in stony silence on the other side of the table.

Fred took his mother's hand. "Mum, Dad, you need to let this go for William's sake; please, for me?"

"It's not so easy, lad, and you'd feel the same way if this had happened to a son of yours. It's hard to forgive what happened. I wish we hadn't let Annie talk us into sitting at this table."

"Sarah, I know the family has ignored you since Bentley was born, but Annie arranged this to give you a chance to mend your bridges. Do you have nothing to say for yourself?"

"There's nothing I can say to make you all forgive me, Fred, but I would like you to know that now I have a son of my own; I understand how you feel, and I'm so ashamed of myself and so sorry. I don't know how I could have acted as I did, and if I could change things, I would, but I can't. I panicked and can't undo the past, so I don't blame you for how you feel. I'll leave now, and I promise to keep out of your way. If I had anywhere else I could go with Bentley, I would because hardly anyone in the village speaks to me, but unfortunately, there is nowhere. I'm lucky Dad lets us live with him because he was just as angry as you about what I did."

Betsey put her hand on Sarah's and squeezed it. "Well, maid, at least you've had the grace to apologise, and, for William's sake, I think I can accept your apology and move on, but it's up to Ned here because I won't go against him."

"Aye, I guess it's time to let bygones be bygones. We're too old to bear a grudge. I know it's what William would have wanted because he did love you, and his son looks so much like him it breaks my heart."

"In that case, I think it's high time you got to know him better. Bentley, come here and speak to your grandparents."

Pleased with his efforts, Fred felt he could now spend time with Charlotte. He found her in an anteroom with at least ten children around her.

"So here you are; I was beginning to think you were avoiding me."

"No, of course not, Fred, but the children were getting restless, so I brought them in here to play a few games and keep them amused. It looks like Sabina and Eveline are having a fine time with Arthur and Charlie, and I didn't want the children to cramp their style."

"It wouldn't surprise me if there are another couple of weddings before long, and I'd be pleased about that. I was hoping to dance with you before the evening's over; would you like that?"

"Yes, I would, Fred, thank you. Mind you, it's so long since I've danced, I've probably forgotten how."

"Well, I'm in the same boat, so we'll stumble around together." He looked at the children, three of them, his own. "Now, listen, I'm going to dance with Charlotte, so behave yourselves until I get back, or there'll be trouble; do you understand? Mary, you're old enough to keep an eye on them. Can I rely on you?"

"Yes, of course, Uncle Fred. You go and enjoy yourself; we'll be fine. I think we'll get some more to eat. The food here is delicious."

"Yes, it is, so make the most of it. Come on, then, Charlotte, let's see if we can get around the dance floor in one piece."

As Fred whirled Charlotte around the dancefloor, she had a wide grin.

"Oh, Fred, this is fun. I think it's the first time I've truly smiled since I lost Doris."

She faltered as tears welled up in her eyes.

"Now, come on, don't worry about that today. I've been thinking about that woman at Buzzacott House, and she seemed shifty, didn't she? I'm not sure I believed what she told us; she seemed nervous. I might see if I can find out more, and I'd like to speak to the daughter when her mother isn't around. Mind you, I've never seen the daughter, have you?"

"No, they never come to the village, so I don't know where they buy food. I'd be grateful if you could have another look, though I'm afraid Doris is gone for good."

"Don't worry about it now. Are you game for another dance? This one didn't go too badly, did it?"

"No, I enjoyed it, but Fred, if you keep dancing with me, tongues will wag; you know what the village is like for gossip."

"It's not going to worry me, and we're both single, so what's the problem?" Fred swept her into another waltz.

The day after the wedding, Annie awoke early, and for a few seconds, she wondered where she was. Then she saw that Robert was already awake and studying her intently.

"What are you looking at? Do I look terrible?"

"Don't be silly; you look beautiful. It's hard to believe you're by my side and in my bed. Did you sleep well?"

"I did, but I'm not sure about these curtains drawn around the bed; it's so hot. The bed's comfy, though. Who would have thought I'd ever sleep on a feather mattress in a four-poster bed? It's a bit different from my palliasse stuffed with straw."

"Is that what you slept on in the cottage?"

"Yes, of course, it's what we all slept on, though, since we moved to the Lodge House, we all have feather mattresses. Mum and Liza remark on it nearly every single day."

"Well, you won't ever be sleeping on straw again, Mrs Fellwood, or should I say, Lady Anne?"

Annie giggled. "I'll never get used to it, you know. I'll always be Annie to my family and friends, and that's how I want it to be."

"Yes, of course. Now, are you looking forward to our honeymoon?"

"I am. I can't wait to see London. I've heard Uncle Fred and Aunty Eveline talk about it, but I never thought I would go. They say there are so many people there, it's impossible to be alone. I'm not sure I'll like that, but I want to go. Can we see Buckingham Palace and the Houses of Parliament?"

"Yes, of course, and St Paul's Cathedral and the Tower of London. There's so much I want to show you; it's another world. I'm not sure a month will be long enough."

"Oh, it will have to be. I couldn't bear to be parted from Selina for longer than that. What time do we have to leave today? I'd like to see Mum and Selina before we go if that's all right?"

"Yes, there will be time if you go after breakfast, and then Dodger can take us to the station to catch the train. Anyway, it's still early, and I've given orders that we are not to be disturbed, so what do you think? How can we pass the time until breakfast?"

"Hmm, I'm sure we can think of something." Her words were cut short as he pressed his lips to hers.

CHAPTER 31

It was a sunny morning, and Sabina had promised herself a few hours in the garden. Life was so much easier for her now than at any time in her life. She wished her husband, Tom, was alive to enjoy everything with her. She missed him now, just as much as she ever had, and although family and friends had been telling her for some time that she should move on, it was easier said than done. However, devastating as it had been to lose her husband, she had known for some time it would happen. To some extent, she was glad he was no longer suffering from the terrible coughing spasms that racked his body and caused him to cough up blood. Consumption was a cruel killer.

This was not the case with her children, John and Emma. Considering their meagre diet, they had been in relatively good health until they caught diphtheria and died within hours of each other. Emma had seemed unaware of the serious implications of her illness, but John knew more, and Sabina would never forget the look in his eyes as he asked her, "Am I going to die, Mum? Please don't let me die." Even thinking of it now made the tears run down her cheeks as she remembered reassuring him she would do everything she could to make him better. Burying John, aged eight, and Emma, aged six, was the hardest thing she had ever had to do, and for a long time, she had thought that the crushing grief would kill her; indeed, some days, she wished it would.

Even now, when she knew she was falling in love with Arthur Webber, a part of her felt it was wrong and that she did not deserve to be happy again. Why should she be happy when her loved ones had not had the chance to live their lives? If she could have swapped places with any of them, she would have done so in a heartbeat. Liza knew how her mind worked and had given her more than one telling-off.

"That's not how it works, Sabina. We don't get to choose who lives and dies; only God can do that, and we must make the best of it. You might not like it, but you can do nothing about it. The worst thing you can do is waste your life worrying about it. Tom wouldn't want that; he'd want you to be happy."

Sabina knew that Liza was right. As he lay dying, Tom had urged her to marry again if she ever got the chance. Suddenly, she wanted to visit the churchyard and talk to Tom. She had told him before he died that she would go and talk to him, and he had said he would like that. Each time she was alone with Arthur these days, she was worried he might propose, and if he did, she had no idea what she would say. She loved him and thought they would be happy together, but it felt disrespectful to Tom to think of marrying another man. She walked around the garden and selected Sweet Williams, roses, and honeysuckle to put on the three graves.

"Liza, I'm going to take some flowers to the graves. Can you keep an eye on the children, please?"

"Aye, of course, I can. You take your time, maid."

It was still early as she wandered along the lane to the church, but the sun was already hot and the sky a perfect blue. The hedges were full of buttercups and celandines, and the bees and butterflies were busy collecting nectar. She pushed open the lych-gate to the church and was pleased to see the graveyard was deserted. She had come to talk to Tom regularly since he died, and she always worried someone would hear her and think she was going mad. Perhaps I am, she thought.

'Hello, Tom, it's me again. I don't suppose for a minute, you can hear what I'm telling you, but I told you I would come and talk to you, and so here I am. It gives me some small comfort. I've no great belief there is a God and that I'll see you again one day, but just in case, eh? Why would God take you and our two wonderful children, who never harmed anybody? It doesn't make any sense to me. Mind you, I'd better not let the vicar hear me talking like this. Anyway, Tom, our Annie, is married to Master Robert now, and one day, he'll be the Lord of the Manor, and she'll be Lady Fellwood. They've gone to London on their honeymoon. Goodness knows what you think about that. And guess what; we are all living in the Lodge House. I certainly didn't see that coming. Now I'm rambling on a bit, I know, because I don't know how to tell you this, Tom, but I'm courting again. I'm seeing a man called Arthur Webber. He lost his wife years ago and has four grown-up children. They moved into Liza and Isaac's old cottage after Isaac died. He's a kind man, Tom, and I think he will ask me to marry him, and if I'm honest, I want to say yes. Anyway, he may not ask me, but just in case he does, I wanted to tell you first. I hope you don't mind, and it doesn't mean I love you any less; it's just that you aren't here anymore, and I'm lonely. Right, that's enough self-pity for one day, I think. I'm going to get some water for your flowers now, and just so you know, I grew these myself.'

She bent over the grave and cleared the dead flowers. Then she picked up the old earthenware pot and took it to the stream to wash and refill it with clean water. She returned to the grave and seated on the wooden cross that marked her husband's grave was a robin. She watched it and listened as it sang to her. Tears flowed down her cheeks again. Tom had told her a saying he knew. 'When robins appear, a loved one is near.' She always laughed at him and told him it was a load of rubbish, but since his death, not many times had she visited his grave and not seen a robin.

As she approached to put the flowers on the grave, the bird flew a short distance away and sat on another cross. Sabina arranged the flowers to her liking, then told Tom once more how much she loved him and went to put flowers on John's and Emma's graves. As she moved away, she looked back, and the robin sat beside the flowers she had just arranged. She shook her head in wonder. 'Thank you, Tom; I know what to do now.'

The children spotted her coming as she approached the Lodge House and ran out to meet her. Selina was missing her mum and had been clinging to Sabina for the last few days. She ran to her granny, and Sabina swept her off her feet and cuddled her. Just as they were about to go through the garden gate, Sabina heard a carriage coming and told the four children to stand still at the side of the lane. They obediently did as they were told. She knew Edward and Stephen would stand still, but she put her hand out in front of Helen and Danny, just in case they took it in their heads to wander out. Although there was only a month or two between them, to look at them, it could easily have been a year. Helen was the eldest but was several inches shorter than Danny. She was petite with blond hair and blue eyes, a delicate child. Danny could not have been more different. He was a stocky, thick-set child with dark brown, almost black, curly hair and brown eyes. His harelip, which had made it difficult for him to feed as a baby, did not hold him back now, and he loved his food. Sabina was pleased with his progress. When she had taken him in at Robert's request, she had not expected him to survive, and the doctor had said with his club feet, he would never walk. However, as a baby, she had put his twisted legs into splints, and whether this had made a difference, she would never know, but walk he did, albeit with a pronounced limp. He had no idea that Sabina was not his mother and, at nearly four, was not yet old enough to question the fact. Sabina knew that one day he would, and then he would be told how Annie had found him abandoned in the woods.

The carriage slowed to a walking pace to squeeze past the Carter family because the lane was narrow. As it passed, Charles Fellwood saw the family lined up, and his heart was in his mouth because he immediately recognised his son. He tried to distract his wife's attention by talking to her and even taking her hand, but Danny stood out amongst all the fair and red-headed Carter family, and she could not take her eyes off him. She banged on the roof with her stick.

"Driver, stop. Stop the carriage."

"Why are we stopping, Mama?" Sarah was surprised, for her mother never acknowledged any of the villagers. Her mother didn't answer.

Dodger reined in the horses in surprise, wondering if he had done something wrong. He descended and went to the door.

"Yes, ma'am. Is there something I can help you with?"

Eleanor waved Dodger aside and stared, first at Danny and then at Sabina. "Are these your children?"

"Yes, ma'am."

"All of them?"

"Yes, ma'am. I'm Annie's mother. I'm pleased to meet you." Sabina dipped a curtsey.

"I've not stopped because I want to meet you. I've stopped because this child," she pointed at Danny, "looks different from the others, and I'm curious."

"Yes, he does, ma'am, we've always said so, but there it is." Sabina held her ground and risked a glance at Charles Fellwood, who was shaking his head at her. Sarah saw this and was even more puzzled.

"What's wrong with his mouth?"

"He was born like that, ma'am. There's nothing to be done, but he gets by."

"Is there anything else wrong with him?"

"I'm not sure what you mean, ma'am?"

"Is he an imbecile? Is he slow-witted?"

"Oh no, he's as bright as a button and quick to learn. The only problem he has is that he limps because of his twisted feet."

Danny disliked the intense scrutiny and began to fidget. "Mum, can I go inside now, please? I don't like this lady." He stared at Eleanor with his wide brown eyes, and she knew he was her son.

"Don't be rude, Danny. Now, say sorry to the lady, and then you can all go inside."

Danny mumbled an apology, and Sabina pushed the children through the gate.

"Will that be all, ma'am?"

She looked Eleanor straight in the eye, and both women knew the truth.

CHAPTER 32

A few days after Annie and Robert's wedding, Arthur went to see Fred in his workshop.

"Hello, Fred, I'm just on my way home from work, but I've been meaning to call in and thank you again for making Dad that easel. He loves it. I'm not saying he'll ever be an artist, but he's getting better at it, especially now he can hold the brush in his makeshift hand. At least it gives him something to do."

"Oh, I'm pleased to hear it. It must be awful for him to be handicapped like that. We never know what's around the corner for us, do we? It just shows you must live for today and let tomorrow take care of itself. I'm glad you called because I've wanted a word with you since the wedding."

"It's not about me dancing with Sabina, is it?"

"What? Oh no, of course not. I was delighted to see you both enjoying yourself, and anyway, it's none of my business; she's a wonderful woman, though, Arthur, so don't mess her around."

"You don't have to tell me, and no, of course, I won't. Always thinking of someone else she is, and it's thanks to her that Dad finally thinks life's worth living again. What can I do for you?"

"I want to ask a favour. I expect you've noticed that I'm friendly with Charlotte. You know, the girl that had the baby a few weeks ago? She works at the inn for Mum now."

"Yes, I know."

"I only got to know her because I found her having the baby in a gateway, and I took her to the inn. Eventually, she went with the baby to her aunt's house in Warkley. I thought that would be the last I saw of her, but then Mum broke her leg, and I asked Charlotte if she'd come back to the inn to look after her. She'd worked as a nurse before she had the baby, you see. When I went to fetch her from Warkley, she was upset because her aunt had sent her to the village on an errand, and whilst she was gone, she had taken the baby somewhere for adoption."

"That's awful, but how can I help?"

"It turns out my mum knew Charlotte's granny, and not only that, but Mum gets on well with the girl, and she's offered her a permanent job. Mum's told her she can keep the baby at the inn if she can get her back; my mum's a real soft touch sometimes. Sorry, Arthur, I'm rambling; I'll get to the point. I took Charlotte to see her aunt again recently, and we persuaded her to tell us where she took the child. It wasn't easy because she didn't want Charlotte to have the child back. She says it will bring more shame on the family, and it's best to leave things as they are. Eventually, though, she told us she took the baby to Buzzacott House. Do you know where I mean? It's that big house on the edge of Exmoor."

"Aye, I know it. I don't know the people that live there, though."

"No, neither do I, but I took Charlotte there, and we asked about the baby. The woman told us that she takes the babies for a fee and then arranges for childless couples to adopt them, no doubt for another fee. She said the baby had gone, and she couldn't get her back."

"So, what do you want me to do about it?"

"I'm just suspicious, I suppose, Arthur. The house was neglected, and it looked filthy from the outside. You'd think with people coming to swap babies, they'd keep it clean and tidy. The woman wasn't at all friendly and seemed shifty to me. It's a long shot, but Charlotte's desperate to get her daughter back, so I wondered if you'd go with me to snoop around; I'd feel better if I had company. I can't explain it, but I feel something's not right. I thought if we go when they're out, we could have a snoop around, and they'd be none the wiser."

"It sounds harmless enough, but we need to know when they will likely be out. We can't just go wandering around their property and then find they're in. They'd have the police after us and probably think we were planning to rob them."

"Yes, I know. Annie says the old tramp who used to hang around the village lives nearby in some ramshackle hut. Sam, I think he's called. Apparently, Master Robert said he didn't mind him living there. According to Annie, poor old Sam has already fallen foul of the woman living there. I thought if I rode out and asked him about their comings and goings, he might be able to tell us a regular time when they're likely to be out. What do you think? Are you game?"

"I wouldn't mind going with you, but it's difficult. I'm not self-employed like you, so I can't come and go as I please, and I've recently had a few days off to sail to France with Charlie Chugg. I can't ask for time off again so soon, and Sunday is the only day I don't work, so unless they're churchgoers, I might not be much help. I'm seeing Charlie tonight, though, and he can come and go as he likes on his brother's farm. I'm sure he'd go with you. Take it from me; he likes an adventure, does Charlie."

"I've heard he does. Yes, ask him, please. Tell him there'll be a pint or two in it for him. I'll ride out and see Sam tomorrow and find out if he knows the best time to go. You won't say anything to anyone, will you, Arthur?"

"You need to ask?"

"No, sorry, of course, I don't."

Despite some heavy drizzle the next day, Fred saddled up his horse and rode towards Exmoor. It was a shame it was so misty because he knew that all around him, the scenery was beautiful, and he didn't get many opportunities to enjoy it. By trade, he was a carpenter, and the mainstay of his business was making coffins, for all too many people died young of this or that ailment. He could turn his hand to most jobs, but when he had the time, he liked to make furniture and keep it in stock to sell. Ideally, he would have loved a shop to display it all. Fortunately, much business came his way by word of mouth, for he was well-known for his craftsmanship. He couldn't complain. He made a decent living to support himself, his sister, Eveline, his three children, and those of his brother, William. They didn't go hungry, and the children were fairly well clothed, though keeping them in shoes was a challenge. He was grateful to Eveline, for he could never have managed without her.

When his wife, Lucy, had been alive, she had been unable to cope with the children, and it had been so difficult to keep an eye on things in the house and work enough hours to support them all. His sister, Eveline, was much more efficient. Since she had moved in, the arrangement had worked perfectly for everyone, but he wondered how long it would last. He knew Charlie and Eveline were becoming an item, however much she might deny it, for only a blind man could have failed to see they were a couple in love when they danced at Annie's wedding. Ah, well, he thought to himself, she deserves to be happy, and I wouldn't deny her. At least the children were not babies anymore.

Despite the wet weather, he enjoyed his ride, for he seldom took to the saddle. Usually, he was taking wood or tools to or from a job, so he needed his horse and cart. When he came to the woods on the edge of the Manor House land, he looked around for Sam. The undergrowth was dense, and he meandered along the track, keeping an eye out on either side. He didn't want to call out as he thought Sam probably valued his privacy and might hide. In the end, he found him by following the delicious smell of cooking. He followed his nose through the trees to where he found the old man sitting by a campfire. A large pot was suspended above the fire, and the smell of whatever he was cooking was surprisingly tempting. He climbed down and led his horse forward.

"Hello, Sam, I'm Annie's Uncle Fred. Could I speak to you for a few minutes?"

"I ain't doing no harm, and Annie's young man said I could stay here as long as I like; I ain't doing no harm, mister."

"No, I can see that, Sam, and I'm not here to make trouble for you. I just want to talk to you about something."

"Well, there's usually trouble when people want to speak to me, but I've just been here minding me own business for weeks now. I ain't stole nothin'."

"No, really, there's no trouble. I'm just hoping you can help me with something. Sam, what are you cooking? It smells wonderful."

"Aye, it does, doesn't it? 'Tis some trout I caught earlier, and I've sprinkled a few wild herbs on them. Me mother taught me to cook when I was a nipper. Sam, she said, if you can cook, you'll never starve. And she was right, and I can make a tasty meal out of next to nothing. Knew what she was talking about, did my old mum."

"It just so happens I have some fresh bread and cheese in my saddlebag. Would you like to share your fish and my lunch, and we could eat together? Your cooking has made me hungry."

"That sounds like a good idea, young man, and if you're a friend of Annie's, then you can't be all bad. Mind you, her other uncle, he must be your brother; I've no time for him. A nasty piece of work he is for all his religion."

"That's got to be our George you're talking about, and I don't disagree with you; he's not the easiest man to get along with, nor the kindest."

"You can say that again."

Fred went to get his lunch, and the old man vanished into his hut and came out with two plates. He poked about in the coals of the fire with a stick and pushed out a tin with a lid on it. Deftly, he removed the top, and inside were some small potatoes. He raised his eyes to Fred. "Don't ask where I got 'em, but I don't eat much."

Sam slid some potatoes and one fish onto each plate. Fred broke off a piece of bread and a lump of cheese each, and the two men settled down to their meal.

"Here you are. I've only got one fork, but you can have it. I learned to eat with my fingers long before I learned to use a fork." Fred took the implement gratefully, and they munched away in silence for a few minutes.

"Do you know, Sam, this is one of the most delicious meals I've ever eaten. I don't know what herbs you've put on the fish, but it's so tasty."

The old man grinned, showing all his decayed teeth and much of his last mouthful of food.

"Aye, I told you my mother knew how to cook. This cheese is delicious, too. Now, what do you want to know?"

"Annie mentioned that you'd fallen foul of the people living in Buzzacott House, and I wanted to know if you see much of them. It seems they take in babies from people who don't want them or can't keep them and then pass them on to people who do. All for a price, of course. The baby of a friend of mine was taken there a few weeks ago, and now she wants her daughter back. We asked the woman who lives there, but she said the baby was adopted. I think she was hiding something, and I'd like another look around, preferably when the house is empty. Do you know if they go out on a regular day each week?"

"A horrible woman, she is. I went there once to beg for a crust of bread on a day when the fish weren't biting, and she threatened to set her dog on me. A great brute, he is. I think she would have, too, so I haven't been there since. She goes out together with her daughter about once a week."

"Do you know what day of the week it is?"

"No, but they take the horse and cart, and I think they go into the next town for their shopping, so I expect it's on market day; that's what most folks do. Anyway, they go off with the cart empty and come back with shopping on it and food for the horse. They don't go in the direction of Hartford, so they must go to Eggleston. Is that any help to you, Fred?"

"Yes, Sam, I think it is. Do they go in the morning or the afternoon?"

"About mid-morning usually, and they don't return until a couple of hours after dinner."

"Sam, I'm grateful to you, and when I next pass this way, I'll bring you a loaf of bread and some more cheese. Would you like that? I've got an old tarpaulin at home that I don't use anymore. Would you like it to cover the roof of your hut? It might make it a bit more waterproof. I can give you a hand to get it up there."

Fred was treated to another glimpse of Sam's rotten teeth as the old man grinned at him in thanks.

CHAPTER 33

Not a word was spoken in the carriage as it made its way along the tree-lined avenue that led to Hartford Manor. The enormous oak trees had been planted many years before by a long-dead ancestor who could never have lived long enough to see them in all their glory. They cast dappled shade across the lane and, as intended, successfully hid the old house from sight until the last bend had been negotiated, and then it was revealed in all its splendour. Hartford Manor had been virtually rebuilt in the late eighteenth century after a fire, though old manuscripts found in the library proved that a house had stood on the site for hundreds of years.

Sarah wasn't sure what the problem was, but from the icy atmosphere which had pervaded the carriage, she knew something quite serious had upset her mother. She debated whether to ask or even introduce an innocent topic of conversation, but one look at her parents' faces persuaded her it was better not to interfere. It was with some relief that she alighted from the carriage when it arrived outside the Manor House, and the footman opened the door for her. Now, she did risk turning back to her parents.

"Mama and Papa, may I go for a ride, please? It's not the same in London riding around the park, and I'd love to take Jenny out for a gallop over the moors. I'm so pleased to be home, and it's a sunny day."

Her parents glanced at her distractedly as if they had forgotten she was there. Her father smiled weakly at her. "Yes, of course, darling, but tell the stable boy where you're going, please, and be back in time for our evening meal."

"Yes, Papa, thank you." She raced to her room to change her clothes, delighted to be out of the carriage and free to do as she pleased.

Eleanor stepped down from the carriage and headed straight for the house; tight-lipped and grim-faced, she ignored the servants who stood in a line waiting to welcome their employers back home. Two footmen lifted Charles out of the carriage and placed him gently in the waiting wheelchair. He bade them push him over to Sid Hobbs, where he spoke a few words to him, permitting the servants to resume their duties. As the servants ambled back into the house, one or two whispered to each other.

"Blimey, did you see the face on her Ladyship? I wonder what's upset her." Sid Hobbs silenced them with a stern look.

The footmen took Charles to his downstairs room, and his valet arrived to make him comfortable. He was tired, for it had been a long journey home, and his body ached. He closed his eyes and hoped to get some rest before answering the questions from his wife that he knew were inevitable.

However, this hope was not fulfilled when, twenty minutes later, Eleanor came into the room. Charles opened his eyes tiredly.

"The journey has exhausted me, my dear, and I feel quite unwell. Would you mind if we spoke later when I've rested?"

"I'm sorry, Charles; I know you're tired, and so am I, but this cannot wait. I need to know, though I think I already do, is that child our son?"

"It's no use me telling you otherwise, is it when you already know the answer? Yes, that was our son. I'm sorry, Eleanor. I hoped you would never see him again, but I could not foresee the future. I had no idea the Carter family would move into the Lodge House; how could I?"

"When the child was born, I asked you to send it far away to be looked after so that I would never have to see it again. It was so deformed, and you knew it reminded me of my younger brother. I begged you to do that. Why did you not do as I asked?"

"It was more difficult than you think. I didn't know anyone who lived far away who would take a deformed child. More than that, it needed to be someone who could wet nurse it. The doctor didn't think the baby would survive on cow's milk, so it had to be a woman feeding her own baby. What did you expect me to do with the child? Throw it down a mine shaft or into the local pond? I've heard it happens, but I didn't think you meant for me to do that when you insisted I get rid of it."

"No, of course, I didn't, but I thought Doctor Luckett would help you to arrange something. I thought he would have colleagues all over the country who could help. I've always thought the child was miles away from here being cared for by someone, and now I find he's been living in the village all along. Everyone must know, and we must be the laughing stock for miles around. How could you disgrace us like this?"

"No, that's where you're wrong. When Robert came into your bedroom and saw his deformed brother, he was upset, and it was too late then to tell him the story that the child had been stillborn, as we intended. He was keen on this servant girl even then and had befriended the whole Carter family. He told me that Sabina, the mother, had recently given birth and would be able to feed our baby, and he offered to ask her if she would take the child. She had recently lost her husband to consumption and had eight children of her own. The family were near starvation, and he thought if I paid her, she would look after our baby, and that's what she agreed to do. Doctor Luckett told me the family was poor but clean and tidy and that she was a good mother. He thought the child would be cared for there, as well as anywhere, and so that's what we did. Robert took the baby and handed it over to the servant girl, and she pretended she'd found it in the woods. It's not uncommon for these things to happen when girls get in the family way, and the story was accepted by local folk. Few people know the truth, and they know better than to tell anyone, or I'd make their life very uncomfortable."

"Is this why you agreed to Robert marrying that girl?"

"Yes, he threatened to tell you about the boy, and I didn't want that to happen. However, in truth, I would have had no say in the matter because he is of age, and we had already signed the estate over to him. You may want to blame me, but I couldn't have stopped him, anyway."

"You must have known I would eventually see the boy if they lived in the Lodge House; we pass it every time we go out."

"Well, again, I didn't know they would move there, and there was nothing I could do to stop it."

"So, is that all your secrets, or do you have any more? Is there anything else I should know about?"

Charles grimaced inwardly but kept his face composed. "Of course not; what else could there be?"

"I don't know, Charles. We've never been madly in love, but I did think we were always honest with each other. Now, I'm not so sure."

He reached out, and she allowed him to take her hand. "I'm sorry, my dear; I know this has been a terrible shock for you, but nothing needs to change. From what I hear and from the way the boy looked, he's well cared for and is thriving. He may never know it, but at least he has his brother in his life, and you can rest assured Robert will see that he never wants for anything. What did you think of him? Besides his deformed lip and limping, I thought he looked quite normal. He looked intelligent, and the woman said he was."

Eleanor drew her hand away. "That's all very well, but as a mother, how do you think I'm going to feel when I drive by in the carriage and see a son of mine playing in the road with all the local riff-raff?"

"I'm sorry to say this, Eleanor, but perhaps you should have thought a bit longer before rejecting him so quickly and so finally. I wanted to keep him to see how he progressed, and now, I think he would have been fine."

"That's easy to say now, but at the time, the doctor thought that in addition to his physical disabilities, he would also be an imbecile. I saw enough of what that entails with my brother, Sydney. It was heartbreaking to see, and I didn't want to watch a child of mine suffer like that."

"No, I know, and I do understand, but I don't think this child is an imbecile; when I looked into his eyes, I thought he looked normal. Anyway, it's too late now; what's done is done, and we must make the best of it."

"Well, the family will have to move. I'm not having them living there right under our noses. That woman was looking down her nose at me. How dare she? A commoner like her! As soon as Robert returns from his honeymoon, he must make other arrangements."

"I don't think he will, my dear, and we can't make him. Perhaps we could have another driveway made in the other direction. Then, you would not need to go that way. Now, I'm sorry, but I must rest." The old man laid his head back and closed his eyes. He was relieved when he heard his bedroom door close.

Difficult questions were also being asked in the Lodge House. Edward had only been four, and Stephen two, when Annie appeared with the newborn baby and the tale she had found him in the woods. They had never considered that Danny was not their brother. Sabina was glad that her two eldest children, Willie, fifteen, and Mary, thirteen, now lived with their employers. They knew the truth and may have given something away to Lady Fellwood, though they, too, knew the subject was not for discussion.

Stephen, now aged six, was curious. He pulled at Sabina's skirt. "Mum, what did the lady want? Why did she look at Danny?" The other children pricked up their ears, also keen to hear the answer.

"I think she was just taking an interest now that Annie has married Master Robert. Danny stands out because he has dark hair, and all of you have red and fair hair." She ruffled Danny's dark curls. "And, of course, he is so handsome. Anyway, Liza, I believe you made some scones this morning, didn't you? Shall we have some with jam and cream for our tea?"

Liza came swiftly to the rescue. "I did, so you children sit at the table, and I'll put the kettle on." Sabina smiled at her gratefully over the children's heads and heaved a sigh of relief.

CHAPTER 34

Charlie agreed to go to Buzzacott House with Fred, and they knew that Friday was market day in Eggleston. Charlie helped Jimmy and Alfred with the milking and then rode over to call for Fred at nine o'clock. They knew it was pointless arriving too early at the house before the two women had left for their day's shopping. Eveline was delighted to see Charlie and cooked both men a hearty breakfast of sausages, bacon, and eggs with large doorsteps of fresh bread and field mushrooms.

"My goodness, that went down well. You're a marvellous cook, Eveline." Charlie contentedly pushed back his empty plate. "You're a lucky man getting meals like that cooked for you every day, Fred. Maria is getting better at her cooking all the time, mind, but she's got a way to go to match you, Eveline. I don't think we'll need any dinner."

"I must remember to take a loaf of bread and a chunk of cheese for Sam because I promised him, and that old tarpaulin too. If you could give me a hand, Charlie, we can get going then. By the time we've put the tarpaulin on Sam's roof, I should think the women will have gone."

Eveline started to clear the table. "Just be careful what you're doing, you two. You don't want the police after you for trespassing. I don't see what good this will do, Fred, and I'd rather you let it be."

"Don't you worry; no one will even know we've been there. Now, we'll see you later. Bye"

The men galloped off toward Exmoor. It was a dry day, so this time, Fred was able to enjoy the views of the countryside all around him. It didn't take long to reach Sam's hut, though, once again, they smelt the smoke from his campfire before they saw him. They dismounted and tied their horses to a tree, and Fred began to unload the tarpaulin as Sam appeared, trudging up the hill from the stream below.

"Hello, Sam, how are you?"

"I'm all right, Fred, thank you. Who's this?" Sam eyed Charlie warily.

"Oh, this is Charlie; he's a friend of mine. You don't need to worry about Charlie. He's come to help me put this tarpaulin on your roof, and we've brought some nails to keep it in place. Would you like us to do that for you?"

"Aye, I'd be grateful. It leaks when there's a heavy downpour, and then I get so cold. I've got a makeshift ladder I made here; that might help."

The tarpaulin was heavy, and the two men struggled to lift it onto the roof, then took turns climbing the rickety ladder and nailing it down.

"There, that will be better, Sam, and now it's nailed down, it shouldn't blow off in the wind. Oh, I've just remembered; I've got some bread and cheese in my saddle bag for you. In return for that delicious fish you cooked for me the last time I saw you."

"I'll cook some more for you if you like. I caught some trout earlier this morning, so it's all fresh. It's a pleasure for me to have a bit of company. I don't see many folk, and that suits me fine because they often bring trouble, but you're different, Fred. I like you."

"That is tempting, but my sister cooked us a plateful of bacon and eggs before we came out, so we'll give it a miss today. Thanks for the offer, though. Now, Sam, have you seen the women from the house pass this morning on their way to market?"

"Aye, they went by not ten minutes before you showed up."

"Did they speak to you?"

"Nay, they wouldn't speak to me. And come to that, I don't want to speak to them, so that's all right."

"What time do you think they'll be back, Sam?"

"I don't know what time it will be, but it's usually late afternoon, so not for a while. Are you going to the house?"

"Yes, we want to have a bit of a nose around, but we don't want them to know."

"Well, if they pass before you come back, I'll warn you so you can scarper."

"How will you do that?"

"I'll show you."

Sam vanished into the hut and came out carrying a hunting trumpet. He put it to his lips and blew hard, managing a long but not very tuneful note.

"That's perfect, thanks, Sam. I'm not even going to ask how you came by a hunting trumpet, but that would be helpful. We'll see you later. It shouldn't take us long, anyway."

They left their horses tied up near Sam's hut and returned to the road. They didn't see a soul, for it was an isolated spot. They did not have to walk far before they came to a pair of large wrought iron gates, which were wide open. In better days, the gates must have been a grand entrance to a house of some note, but the years had not been kind. One gate was leaning on its side, and both were rusty and had not been painted for years. The driveway was full of weeds, and there was a desolate atmosphere as they made their way to the house.

"Creepy, isn't it, Fred? I don't think I'd like to live here, though, with some attention, it could be a lovely place again. It must be years since this undergrowth was cut back, and it makes it so dark and gloomy. I can see why you wanted some company. I wouldn't be comfortable coming here on my own."

They went to the front door and tried the handle and found it was locked. The large windows on either side of the door were covered in grime, and it was difficult to see in. Fred was careful not to make too many obvious marks but went to the side window and rubbed off some dirt to peer in. Both of the rooms that they could see into were sparsely furnished, with no sign that any babies were being cared for. Charlie went around the side of the house, where he came to a wooden door set into a high fence. He tried the handle but found that, too, was locked.

"We're not going to be able to see much, Fred, unless we can get over this fence, and it's pretty high. I don't know why they need a fence like this out here in the middle of nowhere. It doesn't look that old, either. What do you think, shall we climb over?"

"Yes, I'm game if you are. The front garden's fairly small for a house of this size, so I think most of the land must be out the back. Is there something we can stand on?"

They searched around and found an empty barrel and rolled it over to the fence. "We must remember to put it back when we go."

Charlie took a rope from his waist, tied it around the barrel, and threw the other end over the fence.

"You may think I've done this before. I always like to make sure I've got a way out if I'm going into a tricky situation."

"You think of everything, Charlie. You're a handy chap to have around. Here goes then."

Fred hauled himself up and over the fence, followed swiftly by Charlie. The back garden was huge and overgrown. The neglected feel of the property continued, and they went to a window that looked into a kitchen. Here, there were more signs of someone living there, but the room was dirty, with unwashed dishes stacked high near the sink and a pile of laundry. They tried the handle to the back door, but again, it was locked. They found this surprising, for few folk bothered to lock their doors locally, and for a house this remote, it seemed unnecessary. They didn't get the chance to explore further, for suddenly, a large dog appeared, baring its teeth and growling at them.

"Don't run, Fred! If you run, it will chase you, and I think it means business. I've got a stick, so you just back away slowly and get over the fence. I'll keep it busy until you're over, and then I'll run for it. Gingerly, Fred retreated whilst Charlie brandished the stick at the dog. However, as soon as it saw Fred start to climb the fence, it ran towards him, barking. Charlie lunged and whacked it across the rear haunches. The dog yelped sharply and turned his attention to Charlie, leaving Fred time to get to the top of the fence.

"Come on, Charlie. Run for it, and I'll help you up."

The dog held on to the stick with its large yellow fangs, and Charlie slowly edged backwards towards the fence. Battling with the stick in one hand, he grabbed the rope in the other but had to turn his attention to getting over the fence. Immediately, the animal saw its chance and sunk its teeth deeply into Charlie's leg. He screamed in pain and kicked viciously at the brute's head. The dog held on, but a second kick sent it spinning away, yelping, and with Fred's help, he managed to get onto the fence. The two men virtually fell down the other side, and Charlie bent to survey the damage to his leg. He had a nasty bite, which was bleeding heavily.

"Bloody animal!

Talk about vicious. Now, why would they need a nasty dog like that out here?"

"Come on, Charlie, I'll put this barrel back where we found it, and then we'd better make ourselves scarce. There's nothing else we can do, anyway."

Leaning on Fred, Charlie limped back to Sam, who was waiting for them.

"How did you get on? Oh, what's wrong with your leg? Did the dog get you? I thought I heard barking."

"Yes, damn the brute, he's had a right go at my leg." Charlie rolled up his trouser leg to reveal a deep bite. The blood was running freely down his ankle and over his boots.

"You'd better let me see to that, or you could lose your leg. Sit down, and take off your boot and sock so I can see what I'm doing. I know a thing or two about medicine. Living the life I do, I've had to take care of myself, and my mother didn't just teach me to cook. Fred, can you fetch a bucket of clean water from the stream, please?"

The two men were amazed at the efficiency of the old man as he made Charlie plunge his whole leg into the icy cold water. He went to his hut and came out with a package of white powder, which he added to the bucket.

"Don't worry, it's only salt so it won't hurt you, but it will clean the wound, so give it a soak. I've seen that dog, and trust me, you don't want your leg to become infected. I've seen what can happen many times over the years."

Eventually, when he let Charlie take his leg out of the cold water, they could see that the wound was clean, and the bleeding had almost stopped. Sam vanished into his hut again and came out with an old tin and some rags. He passed the container to Fred. "Here, Fred, see if you can get the lid off that, will you?"

Fred prized off the lid to reveal some greyish-green ointment inside.

"I haven't had cause to use this for a long time, fortunately, but it's made of all sorts of herbs, and it helps wounds to heal. We'll put some of that on, and I'll bind your leg tightly with these rags."

The old man worked swiftly, and before long, Charlie's leg was bound, and Sam allowed him to replace his clothing and boots.

"There, now, if I were you, I'd ride home and rest that for a few days. It should be all right now, but keep an eye on it, and if it starts to go red around the wound, you'd better see a doctor or come back and see me. I think I know nearly as much as any doctor, or I wouldn't have lived as long as I have. What did you find at the house, anyway?"

"Not much, but it's run down and neglected. I would have thought if you want folk to come and buy babies, you'd need to make it a bit more welcoming. And why would you need a high fence and a vicious dog like that? It doesn't make sense. I don't feel inclined to go back, though. I think we need to ask Constable Folland to make a few enquiries and see what he can find out. He can visit the house officially to ask a few questions. Anyway, Sam, thank you so much for your help. No doubt, we'll see you again soon."

The two men mounted their horses and galloped back to the village.

CHAPTER 35

Annie was having the time of her life in London, though she missed her daughter and the rest of the family. Until she met Robert, she had never been further than the neighbouring villages and had been amazed at the number of people and shops in Exeter when she visited on the train. However, that experience had done little to prepare her for the sights of London. Every street was teeming with people, all apparently on important business, for they hurried past with no time to stop and chat. Everywhere she looked, people were trying to sell something to make a few pence. Flower girls, matchstick girls, and shoeshine boys, carters selling fish, meat, and vegetables, and even people acting, singing and dancing with their caps out in front of them, hoping for a few coppers.

Annie was spellbound but saddened by the number of homeless people wandering around aimlessly, trying to find something, anything, to eat. What upset her the most were the ragamuffin children, all as thin as rakes but as ready as the next man to pick your pocket and rob you. In Hartford, although many lived at a subsistence level, there was usually a small amount of help available from the Overseers of the Poor. Even neighbours would often help if one fell on tough times. Here, no one seemed to care for the plight of orphans and poor people. It was all Robert could do to stop Annie from handing all her money to the children who constantly begged.

"Annie, you mustn't show your money in public, or you may be attacked. It doesn't matter how much you hand out; there will always be a crowd wanting more. I know it upsets you, and it is awful, but we can't save them all."

"No, I know, but it's so sad, and don't forget I know what it's like to be hungry. It's not right; we have so much, and they have so little."

He took her hand and led her firmly to the waiting carriage.

"What would you like to do now? Shall we go back to the house and have some lunch, and then go somewhere else this afternoon? You haven't been to

St Paul's Cathedral yet, and that's worth seeing. Or we could take a boat trip down the Thames? What do you think?"

The honeymoon couple were staying at Percy's house in Grosvenor Square, a wealthy district in the Mayfair area of London. Fortunately, Percy was broadminded and cared, not in the slightest, that Robert had married a servant girl. He was much of the mind to live and let live. His late father, Algernon, was Robert's maternal uncle and by far the wealthiest member of the family. Percy had lost his mother several years earlier, and Algernon had died five years ago. Until his father's death, Percy had dated young women and made a pretence of his intention to marry one. He hated leading the girls on but knew his father would never understand his sexual preference for young men and didn't want to risk being disinherited. However, now that his fortune was safe, as long as he was discreet, he could do as he liked.

Grosvenor Square, or Little America, as it was sometimes known, was a desirable area of London. Percy's house had a basement, four floors, and large attics and was lavishly furnished. Outside, an extensive park with tall trees provided a safe and pleasant area for the residents to enjoy walking or riding in.

"Why is it called Little America?"

"John Adams, the second president of the United States, lived at number nine at one time. He was an ambassador here."

"I see." Annie had no idea what an ambassador was but decided to leave it there. "There is one thing I'd like to do while we are in London."

"What's that, then? Shopping for presents for all the family? That's fine if you'd like to."

"I would like to do that, but not today. You once told me about your friend, Stephen Turner, who was at Westford School with you. Do you remember?"

"Yes, of course. He's a good friend. I hoped he'd come to the wedding so you could meet him, but he's working in Europe, and couldn't get back. So, what about Stephen?"

"Well, you told me that his father is a famous Harley Street surgeon, and I wondered if he could do anything for Danny. You know, about his lip or his twisted feet. Of course, it would probably cost a fortune, so if it's impossible, you must say so."

"That's an excellent idea. I always intended to do that and never got around to it. I know Stephen's parents, so I think they will see us. It might be best to visit his father's surgery because I can't quite remember where they live in London, though I know they have a house in Devon. We'll get some lunch and then go to Harley Street. If he can't see us today, we can make an appointment."

Later that afternoon, the carriage stopped outside the Harley Street premises in Marylebone, and Annie and Robert made their way up the steps.

They stepped into a waiting room where an elderly woman was sitting behind a desk.

"May I help you?"

"Yes, I hope so. I'm a friend of Doctor Turner's son, Stephen, and I wondered if the doctor could spare me a few minutes of his time?"

"It's unlikely if you don't have an appointment; the doctor is busy."

"Is it possible you could at least ask for us, please?"

"If you'd like to take a seat, I'll mention your presence to Doctor Turner when he is next free. May I ask your names, please?"

"Yes, of course. Tell him it's Lord and Lady Fellwood, thank you." The receptionist looked suitably impressed whilst Annie stifled a giggle.

"Oh, Robert, that sounds so grand. It doesn't sound like us at all.

"Well, it's close to the truth. The titles will be ours one day. We might as well make use of them."

They waited for nearly half an hour before an elderly man limped out of the door in front of them and went to the receptionist to make another appointment. That done, the woman then knocked on her employer's door and went in. After a few minutes, she held the door open and said the doctor could spare them a few minutes.

Robert entered first and was greeted by an elderly, distinguished-looking gentleman with white hair and a beard. He shook Robert's hand warmly. "Robert, my boy, I'm pleased to see you. I can't think how many years it has been since I last saw you. It must be four or five, at least, since you came to stay for a week or two in Devon. How are you? Is this your lovely wife?"

"Hello, sir; it's good to see you too, and yes, it is a few years. Please may I introduce my wife, Anne? We're on our honeymoon in London."

The doctor took Annie's hand, leaned over and touched it with his lips. "My dear, I'm pleased to meet you; I'll have you know you've married a fine young man."

"Thank you, sir, yes, I already know that."

"I'm sure you do. Now, I expect you know that Stephen is still working in Italy."

"Yes, sir, how is he?"

"Oh, fine, fine, as far as I know. He came home last Christmas, but we haven't seen him since, though he writes occasionally. We're planning to see him this Christmas. Now, is this just a social call, or is there something I can help you with?"

"It's a bit of both, sir. I wanted to look in and say hello whilst we're in the city, but I would also like your advice. Anne has a younger brother who was born with a hare lip and club feet, and I wondered if there is any treatment you could suggest that would be helpful. I know that if nothing can be done, you'll be honest and tell me so, whereas some doctors would be after our money. I wouldn't want the child to suffer any unnecessary treatment."

"That is a sad statement, but probably true. How old is the child?"

"He's four, sir. He struggled to thrive as a baby because feeding him was difficult, but he manages to eat most things now. He walks, but with a limp."

"Do you know what caused the deformities? I mean, does it run in the family?"

"No, sir, not as far as we know."

"Is he mentally impaired?"

"No, sir, he's intelligent and able to speak, though not clearly."

"I see. It's difficult to say without seeing the child for myself because every case is different. I do treat patients with deformities with increasing success. Possibly, we could break and reset his ankles so that his limp would be improved. With his hare lip, I would need to examine the inside of his mouth because it depends on how extensive the deformity is. Is the child here with you in London?"

"No, sir, he's in North Devon. I was seeking your opinion as to whether it's worth me making further enquiries."

"Yes, I would say it is. As you know, I have a property in North Devon where my wife, Clara, prefers to live. She doesn't like the city, and the countryside is better for her health. Stephen lived there in the holidays when he attended Westford School. I go there as often as possible, and Clara occasionally joins me here in London. I shall retire there, eventually. Now, young lady, would you like me to take a look at your little brother?"

"Yes, sir, I'd be grateful, but how can we arrange that? Would we have to bring Danny to London?"

"That would be one way of doing things, but I'm going to Devon for a few days next month, and I could examine him whilst I'm there."

"That's extremely kind of you, sir. If you think something can be done, we would also need to have some idea of the cost, if possible."

"One step at a time, Robert. I can't promise he can be helped until I see him, but I'm willing to take a look. Now, I must see my next patient, but would you like to come to dinner this evening? Then we can discuss it further and hear each other's news. I didn't know you'd taken over the Hartford Estate from your father. Is he in good health?"

"Yes, sir, he's quite well, but since he had a stroke, he's found it all too much to manage. Anyway, we would love to come to dinner this evening. Where do you live?"

"Here, of course. My surgery is only on the lower floor. Would you like to come back at seven o'clock this evening, and we can eat together?"

"Yes, thank you. We'll see you later."

As Annie and Robert walked away from Harley Street, Robert took her hand.

"That went well, didn't it? Are you happy to dine with him tonight? It was difficult to refuse."

"Yes, of course, and it was kind of him to say he'll see Danny."

"What would you like to do now? Shall we get a carriage back to Percy's house and relax before we need to leave for dinner, or is there anywhere else you'd like to go?"

"There is one more place I'd like to visit if it's all right with you."

"Of course, where do you have in mind?"

"Highgate Cemetery. It's where my Uncle William is buried, and I know Gran would be pleased if I visited. I was fond of him too, so I'd like to go, anyway. The only trouble is I don't know where the grave is, and I think it's a big cemetery."

"We can have a look. Is there a headstone?"

"Yes, there should be. My Uncle Fred paid to have one put there, but no one has visited since. The landlady William and Sarah stayed with showed Uncle Fred where the grave was because she went to the funeral. I never thought to ask him or Aunty Eveline where the grave was before we left home."

"We might be able to find the vicar or someone to ask. I'm not exactly sure where Highgate is, but we'd better get a carriage because I don't think it's within walking distance."

It was fortunate they hailed a carriage because the cemetery was over four miles from where they were and too far to walk in the time they had available. They entered the imposing gates to the cemetery and started walking down the first path, keeping an eye open for William's grave. It was a hauntingly beautiful place, with old trees covered in ancient ivy and many ornate tombs, some with sculptured angels adorning them. It was very peaceful. The cemetery had been opened some forty-odd years before when the graveyards in central London were becoming full and considered a health risk. There had been a lot of burials since then, and they looked around to find someone to help them find the grave they sought. The only man they found, besides visitors like themselves, was a labourer digging a grave. He asked how long ago the burial took place and was able to direct them to the more recent excavations. They thanked him and continued going methodically up and down the rows of tombstones.

After half an hour or so, Annie gave a yell. "Robert, here it is! I've found it."

He hurried over to join her, and together, they surveyed the granite tombstone and read the inscription.

"In Loving Memory of William Edward Carter,
who died on 14 June 1881, aged 36 years.
A native of North Devon and the
Imperial Maritime Customs, China.
Rest in Peace."

Annie had tears in her eyes. "I'm so glad we found it. I'm sure he'd be pleased that one of his family took the trouble to visit."

"Yes, I expect he would. What did he do in China? It sounds impressive."

"I'm not sure, but I know he was regarded as extremely clever, and he had a well-paid job. They kept it open for him for a year to allow him to come home and see his family. I'm glad Uncle Fred put that he was from North Devon because he's a long way from home. At least, I can tell the family he has a nice gravestone."

"Yes, now, if you've seen enough, we'd better get a carriage back to Percy's house and get ready for dinner with Doctor Turner."

They retraced their steps down the path and waved their thanks to the gravedigger as they passed.

CHAPTER 36

Charlie's leg throbbed as he galloped back from Sam's hut with Fred. They rode to Fred's house as it was nearer than Hollyford Farm, and Charlie was more than glad of an excuse to see Eveline again. She was busy making pastry and had flour all over the table, and her forearms were covered in it. Her face was flushed with the heat of the kitchen, and wisps of her slightly greying hair had escaped from her bun. Charlie thought she looked beautiful. Hearing them come in, she glanced up from her task.

"Hello, I'm glad you're back. How did you get on?"

"Yes, all right; we didn't get caught, anyway, but there was a huge dog there, and he's taken a chunk out of Charlie's leg."

"Oh no, Fred, I told you not to go. Charlie, I'd better bathe your leg."

"No, it's all right; you finish making your pastry. Old Sam bathed and bandaged it for me so the wound's clean. He put some ointment on it, which he says will stop it festering, so I think it's best left alone for now."

"I hope he knows what he's doing. Dog bites can be serious if they get infected. You must keep an eye on it."

"Sam certainly seemed to know what he was doing, and he's had to look after himself for years, so I trust him. He's a nice man when you get to know him. I don't know how he came to be living like he is, but I think he prefers it."

"How about you, Fred? Did the dog bite you?"

"No, luckily for me, Charlie took the brunt of it. It's a nasty bite, too."

"I'm making this pastry for a pie for tea, but I have some crusty bread, cheese, and pickled onions if you're hungry. Charlie, if you'd like some too, it would give you a chance to rest your leg before you ride home."

"That's kind of you, but you've already cooked me breakfast, and I'm not hungry. I wouldn't say no to a cup of tea, though."

"Fine, sit yourself down then because I want to hear what happened. You don't mind if Charlie stays, do you, Fred?"

"No, of course not. I was grateful for your company this morning, Charlie, and I don't like to think what would have happened if I'd faced that dog on my own. He was vicious. Please stay for a cup of tea by all means. If you don't, Eveline will only be cross with me."

Eveline blushed furiously and slapped her brother on the arm. "Behave yourself, Fred Carter, or you'll get no dinner later."

As they drank their tea, they told Eveline all that had happened that morning.

"It does seem strange, as you say, but I don't see what you can do about it. I mean, they aren't breaking any laws, are they? If they want to neglect their house and have a wild dog roaming in their garden, then it's their business."

"Yes, I know it is, but if they're taking in babies and selling them on, then surely they'd want the place to be a bit more welcoming? And why live in the middle of nowhere with a dog like that? It must be difficult for people to find, particularly mothers with no easy way of getting there. I think it's suspicious, and after lunch, I'm going to visit Constable Folland to see what he thinks. There's nothing to lose, anyway."

"I don't think many mothers go to the house. When I went on the train to Exeter to buy Annie's wedding dress material, there was a woman at the station who took a child off her mother. Annie and Robert were sure it was the same woman they had seen at Buzzacott House; she's quite distinctive because she's unusually tall. Anyway, the mother of the child then got on the train. She was distressed about parting with her child, and Sabina went to comfort her. You know what a soft heart Sabina has, and she couldn't bear to see the young girl so upset. Jean, she was called. She told us that she'd seen an advertisement in a newspaper. It said babies could be found adoptive parents or looked after until the mother could have them back. The tall lady had arranged to collect the child at the station as it was a convenient meeting place for them both. Jean said the woman was moving house and that when she had, she would write to Jean to let her know the new address so she could visit the child. She didn't want her baby fully adopted; she wanted to pay to have it looked after until she could find a way to have it back."

"That's interesting; if she collects the babies from the railway station, it wouldn't matter what state the house was in. Mind you, if they look after babies there, surely we would have seen nappies on the line or some sign of children? Would they leave the babies alone while they go into Eggleston on market day? It just doesn't make sense."

Having finished his tea, Charlie pushed back his chair and winced as he put his weight on his leg, which had stiffened up.

"Right, I must get going, or Jimmy and Alfred will be complaining that I've left all the work to them today. Now, Eveline, since you have fed me today, I must insist on repaying the favour. Would you like to come to the farm one day soon and have some lunch? Maybe we could go riding again?"

"I'd like that, Charlie, and now all the children are back at school, I can get away for a few hours. Would you mind if I did that, Fred?"

"No, of course not; why should I mind? You take care of all of us, Evie, but you have your own life to lead. I'm glad you're friendly with Charlie. You visit the farm whenever you like, and even if the children are not at school, I've plenty of work to keep me in the yard for a day. In any case, now they're bigger, they can more or less look after themselves as long as I'm around to keep an eye on them."

"How about tomorrow then, Eveline?"

"Would you mind if we made it the day after? I can make some food ready for everyone's tea, then. It will save me from doing it when I get home. I'm not organised enough to do that for tomorrow. I think your leg might be painful tomorrow, too. If it is sore, we needn't go riding; I'll just come for lunch."

"I'll look forward to it. Bye then, Fred, I hope you get on all right with the constable, but whatever you do, don't go to that house on your own, will you?"

"No, I won't. If I can repay the favour and help you with anything, Charlie, you only have to ask; you know that, don't you?"

"Ah, now, there's a thing; I thought you'd never ask."

"Go on, then. How can I help you?"

"Let's just say I have some items that need moving from the old silver mine. I've got Arthur Webber and my nephew, Jimmy, lined up to help, but you know what they say: many hands make light work. Could you spare me a couple of hours on Saturday?"

"Yes, of course. Where do you want it taken to?"

"Some to Eveline's dad at the inn, and the rest to the farm. Alfred has a secure storage place. Not a word to Constable Folland, mind."

"No, I understand, and my lips are sealed. All right then, where shall I meet you?"

"Is ten o'clock, just inside the entrance to the silver mine, on Saturday all right?"

"Fine, I'll walk out with you because I'm going to find Folland now. See you later, Eveline."

Constable Folland lived in a small cottage at the far end of the village. His wife, Ada, was in the garden picking peas. "Hello, Fred, how are you?"

"I'm fine, thanks, Ada. Is Wilfred around?"

"Yes, he's in the kitchen and not long finished his lunch. Let yourself in, will you? I want to finish picking these peas for tea."

Fred strolled along the path to the back door and knocked before opening the door and calling out. "Hello, Wilfred, are you there? It's Fred Carter. Can I have a word, please?"

Wilfred was still sitting at the table with a cup of tea in front of him.

"Oh, hello, Fred, yes, come on in. I've not seen you for a long time. Is anything wrong?"

"I'm not sure, Wilfred, but I want to talk to you about something."

"Sit down then, lad. I'm a good listener. I have to be in my profession."

Fred told him about Charlotte's baby and the woman at Eggleston station and then about his and Charlie's activities that morning.

"You do know I should arrest you for trespass, Fred Carter? It's a bit of a risk you telling me all this, you know. By rights, I should arrest you and Charlie and make sure you're up in front of the magistrates. It's lucky I know you both, isn't it?"

"I know it puts you in an awkward position, Wilfred, but that's a chance I had to take. What do you think? Does it sound suspicious to you?"

"It certainly seems odd, but I'm not sure what you want me to do. I mean, from what you've told me, you've no proof the woman has broken any laws."

"Could you just talk to her and see what she has to say? I mean, what's happening to these babies? I've no proof, Wilfred, but I think something's not right at that house. It can't do any harm, can it?"

"No, I suppose not. All right, I haven't got much on tomorrow, so I'll ride out and have a chat. What's the woman called; do you know?"

"No, I don't know anything about her, but I think she has a daughter living there with her. Thanks, Wilfred; please let me know how you get on."

CHAPTER 37

The next day, true to his word and on what should have been his day off, Wilfred saddled up his horse and rode towards Buzzacott House. He stopped on the way, hoping for a chat with Sam to find out what he made of the situation, but as soon as Sam saw the constable coming, he was off as fast as his legs would carry him.

"Sam, stop. There's nothing to worry about; I just want to talk to you." He hurried after the old man and soon gained on him, for Sam was not that nimble.

"Sam, you can't escape from me, so please stop."

The tramp eyed the man suspiciously. "I ain't done nothing wrong, and Annie's young man said I could stop here as long as I like."

"That's fine, Sam. You're not bothering anyone here. Can I talk to you for a few minutes?"

"Aye, well, I don't suppose I've much choice. What do you want to know?"

"Fred Carter has asked me to look around Buzzacott House, and I wondered if you know the people there?"

"Not really. There's a woman and her daughter, but I ain't seen no man about the place. They've made it clear I'm not welcome, so I keep away."

"Do you ever see people calling at the house?"

"Sometimes. A few young women with babies. They seem to bring them and then leave without them, but I don't know what happens to them. The woman goes out quite a bit with the pony and trap, mostly into Eggleston, but I've only seen the daughter go out with her once a week to the market. Perhaps she stays at home and looks after the babies. They've got a vicious dog out the back; he bit Charlie's Chugg's leg almost to the bone. That's all I know, mister."

Leaving Sam in peace, Wilfred knocked on the door of the big house. The sound from the tarnished brass knocker echoed for some time before a woman eventually answered.

"Can I help you?"

"Good morning, ma'am. My name is Constable Folland, and I'm from Hartford. I want to come in and ask you a few questions, if I may?"

"Surely we can talk here? I don't like people coming into my house."

"No, I'd rather come in, if you don't mind. I've had reports of babies being brought to this house, and I need to ask you what's going on?"

"Very well, you'd better come in." The woman led the way and escorted Wilfred into the front drawing room. The heavy curtains made the room dull, as did the grime on the windows. The room was furnished with dark, heavy furniture and had not been dusted for some time. "Please sit down."

"First of all, what's your name?"

"It's Lizzie Dymond."

"Can you tell me why women bring babies here?"

"I've fostered a few babies for various friends, just temporarily, you understand. As I'm sure you're aware, many young girls find themselves in the family way these days with no means of supporting a child. Unfortunately, when a man finds out a baby is on the way, he often vanishes without a trace. I used to be a nurse, and sometimes my ex-colleagues contact me to ask if I can care for a baby for a short time until the mother can make better arrangements and take the child back. Usually, I only take a baby for a few weeks, then it returns to its mother."

"Do you have any babies here at the moment?"

"No, it doesn't happen often."

"Do you charge for looking after them?"

"Yes, of course, I can't do this for nothing."

"Do you also arrange full adoptions?"

"Yes, I have once or twice, and in those circumstances, the child is always better off living with a couple who want it and can provide for its needs. Why do you ask?"

"Do you remember an elderly woman from Warkley who brought a baby girl to you several weeks ago?"

"Yes, it was the daughter of her niece, I believe. The girl had no means of supporting the child, and the aunt felt she was doing her a favour in getting it adopted."

"Is the child still here?"

"No, a couple in Exeter had been waiting for just such an opportunity, and I delivered the child to them within days of receiving it. An excellent outcome for all concerned. They were overjoyed."

"Can you give me the details of the adoptive parents, please?"

"No, I'm sorry. I'm not trying to be difficult, but as I explained to the child's mother when she called here the other day, I don't pass on any details of adoptive parents. My discretion is part of the deal, and I keep no records for precisely that reason. They pay me in cash for my trouble, and that's the end of the matter."

"You must remember where you took the child?"

"No, I met them at the railway station. I never want to know where a child is going, and then I can't divulge any information even if I wanted to. It's better this way and gives the adoptive parents peace of mind."

"Do you live here alone?"

"No, my daughter, Thurza, lives here with me."

"Do you have a husband?"

"No, he died some years ago."

"May I see your daughter, please?"

"I don't see how that's relevant, but yes, I suppose so. I must tell you she is slightly slow-witted."

The woman rose and went to the door. "Thurza, can you come here a moment, please? A gentleman wants to speak to you."

A dark-haired girl in her thirties appeared. She was nervous and unwilling to look Wilfred in the eye.

"Hello, Thurza. Can I ask you a few questions, please?"

The girl looked anxiously at her mother and then down at her feet and said nothing.

"I'm sorry, as I said, she's not quite right; never has been. Strangers make her even worse. I'm surprised she even came into the room. Come here, darling. There's nothing to worry about."

The woman crossed the room and put her arm around her daughter. "Is this necessary, constable? We've done nothing wrong besides looking after a few babies for close friends, and your visit will unsettle my daughter. She'll probably keep me awake all night after this. I'd like you to leave now."

"Yes, ma'am. I can see she's uncomfortable. I'm sorry to have troubled you, but you understand we have to be seen to follow up on such matters."

"Yes, of course. I hope I've put your mind at rest. We are just living here quietly and minding our own business. The remoteness of this spot would not suit everyone, but it's perfect for my daughter as she is so nervous around people."

Giving Wilfred no opportunity to see anything of the rest of the house, she firmly showed him to the door.

Wilfred galloped back to the village and called in to see Fred, who was putting the finishing touches to a fine table he had been working on for weeks.

"My, that's a handsome piece of furniture, Fred; it should fetch a pretty penny. Is it for anyone in particular?"

"It would make me a handsome profit, it's true, but I didn't give my niece, Annie, and her husband, Robert, a wedding present, and I thought this might be acceptable. It isn't easy to know what to buy when your niece marries into the gentry, and I don't have a lot to spare. I've been rushing to get it finished because they'll be back from their honeymoon soon. They're going to live in the West Wing of the Manor House, and I thought they might like this. I hope so, anyway."

"You've made a fine job of it; I should think they'll be delighted."

"Fingers crossed, but if they don't want it, I can easily sell it. I'd like to make more furniture, but most of my time is spent making coffins and doing other woodwork for folk. I mustn't grumble, though. I've always got plenty of work, and that's a godsend."

"Have you ever thought about taking on an apprentice? Then you could put more time into your furniture making."

"Yes, I have been thinking about that for a while, but my eldest son, Llewie, is ten, so I've been waiting for him to be big enough to learn the trade. He helps a bit already, but I'd like him to stay at school as long as possible. Not something I was able to do, but we all like to make a better life for our children, don't we? Anyway, how did you get on at Buzzacott?"

"I had a word with the old tramp, and he said he'd seen some women leaving babies there. I had to smile because back along, some boots were stolen from your brother George's shop, and we were sure Sam stole them. We chased after him, and I don't know how he got away, but we never caught him. Anyway, today, his clothes are all rags and tatters, but he has on a sound pair of boots. I'm pretty sure I know where they came from, but I can't prove it now."

"Well, I know it's not right, but I expect Sam needed them, and to be honest, George could afford to give him a pair of boots. Not that he ever would, of course. He counts every penny; he always has. So, what about the woman at the big house?"

"Yes, I went there, and she didn't want to let me in, though she did, eventually. I only went into one room, though, and it was pretty dirty, but that's not a crime. She admitted she takes in babies, either for a short time until they can return to their mothers or for full adoption. She said she was a nurse and that previous work colleagues sometimes contacted her to see if she could help. It sounded all right. I asked about your friend Charlotte's baby, but she said a couple in Exeter adopted the child, and she wouldn't tell me who they were."

"No, she wouldn't tell us either."

"She said she doesn't keep records so that the adoptive parents can't be traced. She even hands the children over at a railway station, so she doesn't know their home addresses. She says that's the deal she offers, and it provides the adoptive parents with peace of mind. I suppose I can understand that because if you've taken in a child and got attached to it, you wouldn't want it taken away again. Not so good for the natural mother if she changes her mind, of course, but I don't think circumstances would allow that to happen often."

"Does she have babies there now?"

"She said not, and I certainly didn't see any evidence of any or hear any crying. Her husband died years ago, and she has a daughter living with her, who doesn't seem quite right. I asked to see the girl, and she came into the room, but she was uncomfortable and wouldn't speak to me. Her mother said it suits them living in the middle of nowhere because the girl is nervous of strangers, and that did seem to be the case."

"We're no further forward, then?"

"I don't think what she's doing is illegal, and unless we find evidence that she's mistreating these babies, there's nothing more to be done. I'm sorry, Fred, but I think Charlotte will have to accept that her baby is gone for good, though by the sound of it, to a family who will love her and bring her up as their own. That must be some comfort, surely?"

"Yes, I suppose so. Thanks for making enquiries, Wilfred. I'm much obliged."

CHAPTER 38

Annie fidgeted in her seat and couldn't wait for the train to pull into Eggleston station. She leaned against the window, trying to see how far away they were.

"We won't get there any quicker, you know. You might as well relax and enjoy the rest of the journey. It won't be long now before we're home. Dodger should be waiting with the carriage, hopefully."

"I know, but I can't wait to see Selina, Mum, and everyone. I've never been parted from Selina before, and I feel so guilty leaving her."

"She'll have been fine with her granny, and anyway, she'll love the presents you've bought her. I think all your family will be pleased with what you've bought them."

"Yes, they will. It was such a treat to be able to buy them presents. Thank you, Robert. We spent so much money; I can't believe it. Probably more than Dad would have earned in a lifetime."

"Well, you're a lady now, Anne Fellwood, so you can spend money now and then. Not all the time, though; we must make sure the estate pays its way, so we'll need to be a bit careful now. I'm planning on making more changes to the way the estate is run. We must move with the times, and I'm looking forward to it."

"I'm not looking forward to seeing your parents again."

"No, I know, but you won't have to see much of them. The West Wing refurbishment should be finished by now. There's even a separate entrance we can use, so we don't have to see my parents at all."

"I don't want to stop you from seeing them; they're your family, after all, but I think they would rather not see me, and the feeling is mutual."

"If they can't, or won't, accept you, then I don't plan on seeing much of them. I despise my father every time I see him for what he did to you, and I'll never forgive him for that. They have their own servants, so they're well cared for, and they've still got Victoria and Sarah and their grandchildren, so they're all right."

As the train slowed and the countryside became more familiar, Annie's excitement grew. "Oh, there's Dodger with the carriage. It won't be long until we're home now. Do you mind if we call at the Lodge House before the Manor House?"

"No, of course not. I thought we would probably stay and have a meal with your family before going to the Manor. Dodger can go ahead with the carriage, and the servants can unload our luggage and sort it out, and we'll walk there when we're ready. Annie, have you thought about Selina? I mean, do you want her to come and live at the Manor House?"

"Yes, of course. She's my daughter. That's not a problem, is it?"

"No, not to me, but have you talked to her about it?"

"No, not yet. I thought it could wait until we got back from our honeymoon. Why?"

"I just want you to be prepared if she doesn't want to come. She's always lived with your mother and all the other children, and she may not be comfortable leaving them. It may be best to take it slowly and just let her come for a few hours at a time."

"Oh, yes, I suppose so, though I hope she'll want to be with me."

"She probably will, but she's not seen you for over a month. Anyway, here we are, home at last."

They alighted from the train and walked to the waiting carriage whilst a porter dealt with their luggage.

"Hello, Dodger, it's great to see you."

"Yes, Annie, sorry, I mean, ma'am, it's nice to see you, too. Did you enjoy yourselves in London?"

"We did, thank you. Is everyone in good health at home?"

"As far as I know, ma'am. Shall we get going now, sir?

"Yes, please, Dodger; can you drop us at the Lodge House and take the luggage to the Manor House, please? We'll take these bags in with us."

As soon as the carriage pulled up outside the Lodge House, the entire Carter family and Liza came spilling out the door to greet the newly married couple. To Annie's disappointment, Selina held on to Sabina's skirt and looked shyly at her mother.

"Hello, darling, do you have a hug for me?" Annie held out her arms.

The child hesitated, but after encouragement from Sabina, she moved towards Annie and was soon gathered into her arms. "Have you been a good girl for your granny? I missed you so much. Did you miss me?"

Selina nodded and clung to her mother.

"She's been as good as gold, but she has missed you, especially the first week or so. Anyway, did you enjoy yourself?" Sabina hugged her daughter.

Edward, Stephen, Helen, and Danny gathered around Annie, trying to hug her. "We had a great time, but let's go inside, and I'll tell you all about it. I might have some presents for you all, too."

Once inside the house, Annie delved into her bag and found gifts for them all: thick shawls for Sabina and Liza and warm winter coats for the children.

"There, hopefully, you'll all be warm this winter. I think the coats will be too big, but I thought it was better that way than too small, and you'll soon grow into them. Do you want to try them on?"

The children did just that, and although a little on the large side, the garments were perfect.

"Now, it just so happens I also found a few toys, so let's see what we have here. They're wrapped up, so just let me find them, and then you can sit in a circle and take turns opening your presents. It had better be the youngest first, so that's you, Selina. Here, what do you think this is?"

The five children sat cross-legged on the floor in a circle, and Annie handed each of them a gift wrapped in pretty tissue paper.

"It's a dolly; look, Granny, I've got a dolly. Thank you, Mummy."

The children unwrapped their presents in turn. Helen also received a doll, Danny, some alphabet-building bricks, Stephen, a spinning top, and Edward, a toy train. The children were overjoyed, for presents seldom came their way.

"Right, now the excitement is over, how about some tea? I've got a chicken in the oven, roasting with some parsley stuffing and potatoes, and it should be ready. Who's hungry?"

"Oh, Liza, I've missed your cooking, and I'm starving, so yes, please, let's eat."

Annie hugged the old lady.

Over a simple but enjoyable meal, Annie and Robert told them all about London and also their visit to Stephen Turner's father.

"Do you think he can make things better for Danny?"

"We don't know yet, but at least he'll take a look. Is that all right with you, Danny? Will you let a doctor look at your feet and mouth to see if he can fix them?"

"Yes, it would be nice if I didn't limp so much. Some of the boys at school tease me because I can't run."

"We'll see if we can make that a bit better then, but we can't promise, so don't be too disappointed if it can't be done."

Soon, it was time for Annie and Robert to go to the Manor House. She hugged her mother. "I'm not looking forward to this."

"You knew when you married Robert what it would entail, so hold your head up high and take no nonsense from anyone. You'll be fine, and from what Robert's been saying, you needn't see his parents often at all. What about Selina?"

"Is it all right if I get settled in first and then take her for a visit and see if she's happy to come and live with us? I want her to, but I don't want to upset her." Annie picked up her little daughter and hugged her. "Selina, I have to go now, but I'll be back again in the morning; is that all right?"

"Don't go away again, Mummy."

"No, I promise I'll be back tomorrow to see you. Why don't you take your new dolly to bed to cuddle tonight?"

"All right, then."

CHAPTER 39

It was almost dusk as Robert and Annie walked the half-mile or so to the Manor House. It was a pleasant walk along the tree-lined avenue, and they meandered through the gardens on their way to the West Wing. Although the summer was nearly over, the roses were still in full bloom, and in the early evening, their scent could be smelt in the air. Hand in hand, they strolled through the walled vegetable garden, smiling as they traversed the path where, a few years before, Annie had crawled in torrential rain, dragging a sack of stolen vegetables behind her.

Moving on, they passed through orchards of apples, pears, and mazzards. The mazzards were long gone, picked by the gardeners and made into pies or bottled for the winter by Mrs Potts, but the apple and pear trees were heavily laden with ripe fruit. They walked on, enjoying the last rays of the sun until they reached the lake and sat on a seat, watching the trout jump to catch flies. It was an idyllic spot and so quiet and peaceful after all the hustle and bustle of London. Robert put his arm around Annie, and she laid her head on his shoulder.

"Oh, Robert, it's wonderful to be home, isn't it?"

"Yes, it is. I enjoyed London, but I wouldn't want to live there. I'm looking forward to going around the estate with Jack tomorrow to see how things are doing." She lifted her head, and he kissed her gently on the lips. "Come on, shall we explore our new home?"

She nodded, and they made their way to the new entrance in the West Wing. At Robert's request, no new servants had been employed. He wanted Annie to choose her own household staff, so they let themselves in by the front door and explored their new home alone.

The painters and decorators had done an excellent job, and everything was bright and new. In the hallway, the tiled floor had been scrubbed and was covered here and there with thick rugs. The oak panelwork had been varnished, and the few brass ornaments dotted around gleamed in the last rays of sun that shone through the sparkling windows.

"Oh, Robert," breathed Annie, "doesn't it look wonderful?"

"Yes, it does. Who would have thought the dilapidated old West Wing could look so amazing? Let's look at the other rooms. See, the drawing room is next."

Slowly, they made their way from room to room, taking in all the sumptuous furnishings. Comfortable chairs, vibrant tapestries, and new curtains adorned each room. Having explored the drawing room, study, parlour, and dining room, they made their way up the magnificent staircase. On the first floor were six bedrooms, all decorated according to Annie's wishes. In the master bedroom, the lower half of the walls were panelled with ancient oak, now highly polished. Above that, the walls had been replastered and painted a pale green. The carpet was a darker green, as were the curtains, including the ones that adorned the large four-poster bed in the centre of the room. Everywhere they looked, there were vases of flowers from the garden and hothouses, and the scent was intoxicating.

"I can't believe we'll be living here, Robert. This must have cost a small fortune."

"It cost a lot of money, but they've done a fantastic job, haven't they? The poor old West Wing was in a terrible state, so it was necessary. Anyway, the estate has made excellent profits since I took over. The bank manager, Mr Billery, approved all the expenditure, and he likes my plans for the future. Nothing will need doing for a long time now, but we need to get busy in the next few days employing some servants. I thought you would like to choose who works here, yourself."

"Really? Can I choose the servants?"

"Yes, of course."

"Could I take some of the old servants I used to work with?"

"That may not go down too well, but if they want to come here to work, I don't see why not. Whom do you have in mind?"

"Definitely, Mrs Potts, Maisie, and Molly. They were all so kind to me when I worked here, especially when I was attacked. Miss Wetherby will have a fit if I take them from her, though."

"Good; it will serve her right. Now, I'd better let my parents know we're back. I'll tell them you would like those three servants to work here, and I don't suppose they'll mind. They might not want to lose Mrs Potts, but I'll see what I can do. We might have to share them until replacements can be found, but that's all right, isn't it?"

"Yes, of course. I don't want to cause any trouble, but it would be so lovely to have my friends working here."

"That's fine, but you must remember you're the lady of the house now and not a kitchen maid. Are you sure it wouldn't be difficult for you?"

"No, it would be a real comfort to me to know I have people close to me whom I can trust and care for me."

"Very well, then, will you be all right if I leave you for a while?"

"Of course, I'll go to the old kitchen and see my friends. I won't say anything about them changing jobs, though, until we know if it's possible."

The door from the West Wing to the main house had, at Robert's request, been bricked up, and the only access connecting the two dwellings was on the lower floor where the kitchens were situated. He knew this would make it easier for some staff to service both households. He went down the old staircase, through the new kitchen, which was to serve the West Wing, and down a passageway to the kitchen of the main house.

"Why, hello, Master Robert, how nice to see you, sir. I forgot you could come in that way now. Are you pleased with your new accommodation?"

"Yes, it's all looking lovely, thanks, Mrs Potts. How are you?"

"I'm fine, sir, and how is Annie? Oh, dear, I must stop calling her that. I'm sorry, sir."

"Don't worry about it, Mrs Potts; I don't think Annie will mind what you call her; you know she thinks the world of you. She's fine, thank you, and we had a wonderful time in London, but I'll leave her to tell you all about it."

He heard footsteps on the stairs. "Oh, hello, Hobbs. Could you let my parents know I'm here, please?"

"Of course, sir. They are in the dining room. Would you like to come with me?"

The butler advised the Fellwoods that their son was waiting to see them, and Robert entered the room. He noticed that his father was looking frail. He had lost weight, and his face had an unhealthy pallor. His mother was not particularly pleased to see him. "Hello, Mama and Papa; how are you both?"

"Your father is not in the best health, but I'm fine, thank you. Where is Anne?"

"She's looking around the West Wing. The workmen have made a wonderful job of it, and you wouldn't know it was the same place. She feels awkward and didn't think you would want to see her. She intends to keep out of your way as much as possible. With the new entrance to our quarters, you'll barely see her at all, so hopefully, we can all dwell peacefully and get on with our lives."

His father shifted uncomfortably in his chair. "That sounds like the best plan, but there is something we must talk to you about."

Eleanor took over the conversation. "When we returned from London, we came past the Lodge House, where you have installed that family and the children were playing outside. It was quite obvious that one child was the odd one out. The whole family had bright ginger or fair hair, and there was one child with dark locks. As we passed, I noticed that he limped, and I could see his mouth was deformed. If there was any doubt in my mind that he was my son, it was dispelled as soon as I looked into his eyes. It was like looking into the eyes of David. Do you deny he is my son?"

"No, I can't lie to you, Mama. He is your child. At the time, you wanted nothing to do with him, and we had to find someone who could breastfeed him and who we knew would take care of him. Sabina, Annie's mother, had recently given birth and was feeding her daughter, Helen. Whatever you may think, Sabina is a fine woman, and she dotes on her children. I knew that no one would care for him better. The only problem was that you wanted him taken far away, where you would never see him, but that was difficult to arrange. Of course, at the time, I had no way of knowing that Harry Rudd would be killed in a fire or that Annie and I could ever be together. When that happened, it made sense for the Carter family to move into the Lodge House. I'm sorry if seeing him was a shock to you; I am."

"It disgusts me that you used this information to blackmail your father into letting you marry the kitchen maid. I'd rather he had told me the truth and put a stop to this ridiculous marriage."

Robert glanced again at his father, who gave an almost imperceptible shake of his head. "That's not quite true, Mama, though Papa didn't want you to find out about Danny. Neither of you could prevent me from marrying whom I like. We've already discussed this. The estate is in my name, and I'm over twenty-one, so I had no need to blackmail anyone, though I did keep quiet about Danny rather than upset you."

"Well, they'll have to move. They cannot continue to live on my doorstep, where I shall probably see the child every time I go out in the carriage. How do you think it will make me feel seeing him every time I pass?"

"I don't know, Mama. I really don't. I never understood how you could part with him as you did, especially knowing how much care he would need. I'll tell you now: it's thanks to Sabina's patience and care that he survived at all. He had great difficulty feeding, and he didn't thrive for a long time. At the same time, she had to care for all her other children and work on the farm to earn money; to be honest, I don't know how she coped with it all. If anyone deserves to live in the Lodge House and enjoy a better standard of living, it's Sabina Carter, and she will not be moving."

"Robert, I can see your mother's point of view, and I can also see yours. This woman, Sabina, has done her best for the child. The only solution I can see is to build another driveway in the other direction, and we could use that one. What do you think?"

"I think it would cost a great deal of money, Papa, and is unnecessary. I'll give it some thought, but I don't think it's practical. A new driveway would have to be of considerable length to join up to the other lane that goes into Hartford. I'll discuss it with Jack Bater and see what he thinks. There is one more thing I need to tell you about Danny, seeing as you now know he's your son. When we were in London, I went to see Stephen Turner's father. You may remember I was at school with Stephen, and we stayed at each other's houses in the holidays sometimes. His father is a highly-respected surgeon and physician with premises in Harley Street. Stephen is working in Europe, but Annie and I spent a pleasant evening with Doctor Turner, and he has agreed to examine Danny to see if he can improve his mouth and feet. He has a house near Cullompton, where his wife lives most of the time because she dislikes London; he intends to retire there when the time comes."

"That is of no interest to us, Robert; we do not intend to become involved with the child, but if his quality of life can be improved, then, of course, that would be a good thing. I would like to know, though, is the child intelligent or lacking, mentally?"

"Oh, I can tell you he doesn't miss a thing; he's a clever and altogether lovely little boy. I'm fond of him and glad I'm in his life, though, of course, he has no idea I'm his brother. Now, there is one other matter that I need to speak to you about. I have purposely waited until Annie and I returned from London before engaging any servants for the West Wing. We must get on with this now, so we'll seek new servants within the next few days. Would you have any objection if some of the current staff came to work for us, and the new people worked in the main house? Annie is friendly with Mrs Potts and two kitchen maids, Maisie and Molly, and she'd like them to work in the West Wing. We wouldn't take them until suitable replacements had been found, of course."

Charles Fellwood spoke quickly before his wife could voice her views. "I can't see a problem with that, can you, my dear?"

"I don't mind about the kitchen maids, but Ethel Potts is an excellent and reliable cook who's been with us for many years, and I'd be sorry to part with her. It's whether we can find someone of an equal standard."

"I suspect Elsie Webber, the girl that Ethel has been training, would probably be able to step up, but it depends on what Mrs Potts thinks; she'll know best. Are you happy for me to have a word with her and also Miss Wetherby, of course?"

"What about Miss Wetherby? Do you want her to manage both households?"

"No, I haven't spoken to Annie about a housekeeper yet, but I suspect she'll either want to manage things herself or employ someone new. Miss Wetherby was rather unkind to Annie when she worked here." Robert could not believe he had nearly divulged the real reason his father had not objected to his marriage.

"Very well, you may ask the servants involved. Of course, they may not want to change."

"Thank you. I'll do my best to sort it out satisfactorily for everyone. Now, I'll bid you goodnight; I'm tired after the journey back from London."

CHAPTER 40

Since dancing together at Annie and Robert's wedding, Fred and Charlotte's feelings for each other had intensified. Fred visited the inn more often, usually with the excuse of making sure his parents were all right, but Betsey was not fooled for a moment.

"We're seeing quite a bit of you, Fred; not that I'm complaining, mind."

"Well, what with you breaking your leg and Dad getting on a bit, I like to make sure you're both all right. I don't suppose George does much for you?"

"You tell yourself that if you want, Fred. I don't see much of George, it's true, but I think we both know the reason you're here so often and at the moment, she's hanging out the washing. Why don't you go out to see her? In fact, when will you make an honest woman of her? You're both single, and your feelings are easy to read."

"Am I that obvious? It's true, I think the world of Charlotte, and I hope she feels the same way."

"What are you waiting for then?"

"She's not got over losing her baby yet, and for me, it feels like I'm betraying Lucy to think of marrying another woman. I've only known Charlotte a few months, anyway."

"That's rubbish, Fred Carter; listen to yourself. The best thing for Charlotte would be for her to have another child, and as for Lucy, she's been dead and gone for over three years now. She would not have wanted you to be miserable and lonely for the rest of your life. If I've learned one thing in my time, it's that you have to grab happiness when you get the chance. Life's too short to waste time. You deserve to be happy, Fred, and so does Charlotte."

"Maybe, but it's not so easy, is it? There's Eveline to consider. I don't think it would work with both women trying to run the house. Evie's been so good to me, I couldn't ask her to leave, and then, of course, if we married, Charlotte would have to leave the inn, and you need her here to help you."

"Eveline would be the first to tell you to follow your heart. She'll want you to be happy, Fred. She could always come back here to live. As long as she was here to look after them, she could move back with William's three children. As for Charlotte, yes, of course, I'd miss her, but there are always people looking for work, and I'd soon get someone else, and if Eveline were here, she'd lend a hand like she used to. Anyway, I wouldn't be losing Charlotte because she'd be my daughter-in-law. It's up to you, of course, Fred, and only you know your true feelings, but I would like to see you settled again."

"Aye, well, I'll think about it. Is it all right with you if I ask her out for a walk later?"

"Yes, of course, and don't hurry back."

Fred went up the steep steps to the back garden, where Charlotte had nearly finished hanging out a basket of washing.

"Hello, Fred. I didn't know you were coming here today."

"I just called in to see if Mum and Dad are all right, but I wondered if you'd like to come for a walk later? Mum says you can take the afternoon off, and it would be nice to have some time to ourselves."

"I'd like that, Fred. What time do you want to go out?"

"I'll call for you about two o'clock if that's all right with you?"

"Yes, fine, I can help Ned at lunchtime first. It's busy, then. See you later."

Fred duly called for Charlotte, and as they left the village behind, he took her hand, and they headed towards the open moorland. The sun was shining, and the heather was still in full bloom, creating a purple haze as far as the eye could see.

"This is such a pretty walk, Fred, my favourite, I think. Oh, look, there's a squirrel. Did you see it? It just vanished up that tree."

"Yes, I just caught a glimpse. They move so fast, don't they? I like them, but Dad says they're dirty rats with fluffy tails."

"Have you heard any more about that woman at Buzzacott House?"

"No, I've not been back there since Charlie got bitten. His leg's healing well, thank goodness. Old Sam's ointment certainly did the trick. Despite what Wilf Folland said, I still think they're up to mischief. I might visit Sam again and ask if he's noticed any more comings and goings."

"You might as well let it drop, Fred. I think Doris is gone for good. I know I must put it behind me, but 'tis hard."

Seeing tears in her eyes, Fred stopped and pulled her to him, leaning his back against a tree.

"Don't cry, Charlotte. I can't bear to see you so upset. At least from what we heard, Doris is loved and cared for, and that's something, surely?"

"Yes, of course, it is, but I'll never stop wanting her back."

Fred wiped her tears away with his thumbs and then kissed her eyes, nose, and finally her mouth. "There's something I want to ask you, Charlotte. I don't know if it's too soon, but I know I love you, and I hope you have feelings for me. Charlotte, will you marry me?"

"Do you mean it, Fred? Do you really want to marry me?"

"Yes, of course, I wouldn't have asked otherwise, would I? Do you want to think about it?"

"I don't need to think about it, Fred; I love you, too."

"Oh, Charlotte, you've made me such a happy man, and I didn't think that would ever be the case again. Thank goodness, I came across you in that gateway all those months ago."

"Fred, how would we manage, though? I mean, your mother needs me, and then there's Eveline to consider. Her home is with you, and I'm fond of her, but I'm not sure it would work with both of us living there."

"Actually, my mother came up with a solution."

"You've discussed this with Betsey?"

"Not intentionally, but she told me it was time to make an honest woman of you, and the more I thought about it, the more I thought she was right."

"What are you, a man or a mouse, Fred Carter? Did it take your mother to make you propose to me?"

"Yes, I suppose it did, if I'm honest. I've been thinking about it for some time, but I didn't want to rush you because I know you're still sad about Doris. Mum said that if we did marry, Eveline could live at the inn like she used to and maybe take Joe, Matthew, and Amelia with her. I wouldn't mind if the children stayed with us, and I don't suppose you would, but it would be cruel to take them all away from her; she's loved looking after them."

"That sounds like an excellent plan. Come on, let's climb to the top of that tor, and then we can go back and tell Betsey and Ned our news and talk to Eveline and see what she thinks. The last thing I want to do is upset her."

Betsey was amused to hear that Fred had proposed so quickly. "My goodness, lad, you soon acted on that advice; even I didn't see that coming. Still, I'm pleased, and I hope you'll be happy together."

Charlotte's eyes were shining with excitement. "Thank you, Betsey. If it weren't for you, I wouldn't even be here, so you made this possible. It sounds as if it's thanks to you that Fred proposed at all, and I couldn't wish for a nicer mother-in-law." She hugged the old woman.

When Ned heard the news, he shook his son by the hand and kissed Charlotte on the cheek. "I'm glad for both of you; you already have somewhere to live, and with Fred's three children to look after, that should help to take your mind off your baby."

"Mum and Dad, just one thing. Please keep this to yourself for now because we are going to tell Eveline, and I want her to be the first to know. I just hope she won't mind."

"I think you may find she's half expecting it."

Eveline was delighted for them and said she had started to feel in the way, so it was something of a relief.

"Are you sure you don't mind? I'd feel terrible if you felt I had pushed you out."

"No, it's fine, Charlotte; I know you'll make Fred happy, and that's all I want. I've loved looking after all the children, but it's a busy job, I can tell you. If Mum's willing for me to live at the inn with William's three, then I think that's a good solution. If I do that, I can help and keep an eye on Mum and Dad, too, because they're not getting any younger. The children may miss each other, but they'll see each other at school, and we all live near each other, anyway. Shall we leave things as they are until after the wedding, and then I'll move to the inn with the children?"

"Yes, that sounds like a good plan. We haven't had time to even think about when the wedding will be, and we'll have to talk to the vicar, but I don't see any point in waiting, do you, Charlotte?"

"No, the sooner, the better for me. I still can't believe it; this has happened so fast."

CHAPTER 41

Eveline had become a regular visitor at Hollyford Farm. She went on the pretext of visiting Alfred, but after each visit, she counted the hours and days until she could go again. As she neared the farm, she steadied the horse to a trot. Charlie appeared from the barn, carrying a bundle of hay high on a pitchfork over his shoulder. He grinned widely, and her stomach did its usual somersault as she looked into his blue eyes and mentally reprimanded herself for behaving like a lovesick schoolgirl.

"Hello, Evie, I was hoping you'd come today. Let me just put this hay in the shippen for the cows, and then I can speak to you."

She dismounted and tethered her horse, smiling at him as he reappeared. He took her hand and drew her into a corner of the barn. He pulled her into his arms and kissed her passionately. "I've missed you, Evie."

She returned his kisses until they heard Alfred enter by the back door of the barn, and they hastily pulled apart.

The old man chuckled when he saw them. "No need for you two to worry on my account. I'm glad to see you're getting on so well." He went on his way, still grinning to himself.

"Oh, Charlie, what must he think of me? Allowing you to kiss me in a dark corner of the barn! What a way to behave."

"Don't be daft. Alfred doesn't care. We've made his day, and he'll be teasing me about this for days."

"Let's go to the kitchen so I can check your leg because I'm not sure you're looking after that bite."

"It's fine, there's no need."

"Nevertheless, I'd like to make sure. Dog bites can be serious."

"Oh, come on, then."

They found the sitting room deserted, but they could hear Maria moving around upstairs. Charlie sat in a comfy chair, and Eveline perched on a stool before him. She took his foot in her lap and peeled away the layers of cloth.

"Right, let's have a look. The dressings will need replacing, anyway. These are the same bandages I put on the other day, aren't they? You've not even looked at it."

"No, I haven't, but it isn't bothering me, and it would if it was infected."

"Oh, my goodness, it's still nasty. You're right, though; it's not inflamed, and it's healing nicely. You have a lot to thank Sam for; I'd like to know what he puts in his ointment."

"I'll ask him next time I see him, but I don't know if he'll tell me."

"I've got some news to tell you; you'll never guess what. Fred has proposed to Charlotte, and she's accepted. It's all a bit sudden, but anyone can see they think the world of each other, and I'm pleased for them. Mind you, it will mean big changes for me."

"That's great news; I'm glad for them. They've got on since day one, haven't they? It must have been love at first sight. What do you mean about the big changes for you?"

"Well, I can hardly carry on living in Fred's house when they're married, can I? I'm sure we'd get on all right, but Charlotte will want to run her own house without me watching her every move. To be honest, I've been feeling a bit in the way lately. It's been obvious they want to be alone."

"What will you do, then?"

"It's all sorted. As soon as they're married, or probably just before, I'll move back to the inn with William's three children. That will leave Charlotte with Fred's three, and I'll still have Joe, Matthew, and Amelia. I'd miss them if I had to give them all up now. It will be helpful for Mum and Dad to have me around again, too, because Charlotte will no longer work at the inn."

"I see; you seem to have it all worked out, which is a shame because it doesn't quite fit in with my plans at all."

"What do you mean? It won't affect you at all."

"Ah, well, you don't know what my plans are, do you?"

Eveline was puzzled as Charlie sank to one knee and then cried out in pain as he remembered his dog bite. He grimaced and quickly swapped legs.

"Ouch, ah, that's better. Sorry, I forgot about my sore leg." He took her hand, "Eveline Carter, will you marry me?"

"Are you joking, Charlie? Or are you just saying this because I have to move out of Fred's house? Because I'll be fine at the inn."

"Of course, I'm not joking; now, will you answer me, or do you want to think about it and cause me days of anguish?"

"Oh, Charlie, do you mean it?"

"Yes, of course, I mean it; I love you, Eveline. I've wanted to ask you for a long time, but I couldn't see a solution to your domestic arrangements. I couldn't ask you to let Fred down, but it sounds as if that problem has resolved itself now. What do you say?"

She put her arms around him and gazed into his vivid blue eyes. "Oh, Charlie, I love you too, and yes, I'd love to marry you."

Laughing, he pulled her to him and kissed her happily. "That's amazing. I'm such a lucky man. Let's get married tomorrow."

"Whoa, steady on; you've swept me off my feet, but there are still William's children to consider. Mum and Dad can't look after them on their own, and it wouldn't be fair to expect Charlotte to take on all six, though I suspect she would. I can't abandon them; I love them like my own, and I'd never let William down. It's unlikely Sarah would take them because there's no room in her dad's house."

"They can come here with you, of course. I'd never ask you to give them up. There's loads of room here on the farm. Alfred and Jane had twelve children, and I'm one of ten, so it's nothing new here to have a houseful. More than half the bedrooms are empty. Do you think they'd be happy to come here?"

"Oh, yes, they'd love it. After spending months in that workhouse in London, they're grateful for anything. I don't think they've gotten over that ordeal yet. Perhaps they never will; Sarah has a lot to answer for. Do you think Alfred and Jimmy would mind if they came here, though? I mean, they aren't related to the children, and it will be three extra mouths to feed."

"I'm sure they won't mind, but if they do, I'll get a job somewhere else with a tied cottage. It's not a problem. People around here know I'm a reliable worker, and I can turn my hand to most things. Shall we tell Alfred and Jimmy now? I can't wait to tell somebody."

In the kitchen, Maria was laying the table for dinner when Charlie and Eveline walked in hand-in-hand, grinning widely. Alfred and Jimmy had come in from the fields and were scrubbing their hands at the sink. Maria glanced up.

"Hello, Eveline, would you like to eat with us? It's roast pork, and there's plenty of it. I'd love you to have some and see if you think my cooking has improved."

"Yes, please, and if the smell is anything to go by, it will be delicious."

Charlie waited until they were all seated. Maria, too, for she was treated as one of the family. "We've got some news to tell you."

Jimmy and Alfred glanced at each other. "I think we can guess, can't we, Dad? Go on, then, tell us."

"I've just asked Eveline to marry me, and she's agreed. What do you think of that?"

Alfred had tears in his eyes as he took Eveline's hand. "This would have made Jane so happy. I wish she were here. She thought the world of you, Eveline, and she hoped this would happen; she told me so. I couldn't be more pleased. What about all those children you look after, though? I asked you to come here as a housekeeper longer ago, and you said you couldn't leave them."

"No, but things are changing at quite a pace at the moment, Alfred. Our Fred is marrying Charlotte Mackie. I don't suppose you know her, but she's a young girl who's been working at the inn. She'll move in with Fred after they're married and will look after his three children, and we need to sort out what will happen to my other two nephews and niece. They were my brother William's children."

"Aye, I remember William and the news they were abandoned in London; it was a terrible business. You're not sending them to live with his widow, are you? Not after what she did?"

"No, though, she is sorry about it all now." Eveline glanced at Charlie, her eyes pleading for him to help her.

"Alfred, if it's all right with you and Jimmy, I'd like the children to live here with us after we're married. Would you mind?"

"Mind, no, of course not. It would be wonderful to have children in the house again. This table needs a few more seated around it. What do you think, Jimmy?"

"Yes, that's fine with me. I was more worried you might say you were going to leave the farm, and Dad and I wouldn't want that. We need your help."

"This girl, Charlotte, is she the one whose aunt gave up her baby for adoption a few months ago?"

"Yes, that's right, Jimmy. I went to Buzzacott House with Fred to see if we could find out anything about where the child had been taken. That's where I got bitten by that brute of a dog. Charlotte still frets over her daughter, and Fred would love to get the baby back for her. We still think there's something fishy going on there, and I don't think Fred will rest until he gets to the bottom of it. If you two can manage this afternoon, I thought I'd ride back with Eveline because, by rights, I should ask Ned if I can have her hand in marriage, even though she's already said yes. I'd better do things right. I want to visit Sam today because I'd like to thank him for looking after my leg. Is that all right with you, Eveline?"

"Yes, that's fine with me. Maria, this pork is perfectly cooked. If there's enough left, perhaps we could take Sam a pork sandwich?"

After they had eaten their fill, Eveline made a pork sandwich for Sam, cutting thick slices of fresh bread and spreading it generously with butter. "There, I think he'll enjoy that."

They galloped towards Buzzacott Woods, where they knew they would find Sam.

"That's strange. Sam usually has a fire going, but I don't see any smoke, and I don't think he ever lets it out if he can help it. I wonder if he's decided to move on. I thought he'd stay here for the winter because his hut is waterproof now. Anyway, let's go and see."

Charlie led the way through the thick wood to a clearing, where Sam's hut was all but invisible if you didn't know it was there. There was no sign of the old man, and the hut door was shut, whereas it had always been open when Charlie had visited before. He carefully climbed down from his horse, putting his sound leg down first to take his weight.

"Hello, Sam; are you there?" Charlie pushed the door open. As his eyes grew accustomed to the dimness, he could see a body huddled on the pallet Sam slept on. His fears grew as his friend showed no sign of movement, and he felt for a pulse on the old man's neck. To his relief, Sam stirred and then panicked as he realised someone was bent over him.

"It's all right, Sam, it's all right, it's me, Charlie. Are you poorly or just having a nap?"

Sam opened his eyes and gazed at Charlie. He didn't recognise him for a few moments, but as realisation dawned, he gave a weak smile. "Oh, hello, Charlie. I was fast asleep. Just a minute, and I'll get up."

With some difficulty, Sam swung his legs to the floor and pushed himself into a sitting position, groaning loudly. He sat there for a few minutes as if summoning the strength to stand.

"Sam, what's wrong? Are you hurt?" Charlie could see the tramp was thinner and even more unkempt than usual.

"Aye, I'm not too good. That's why I was resting. Hold on, and I'll come outside. There's not much room in here."

Charlie led the way from the hut and signalled to Eveline to dismount from her horse. He glanced back to talk to Sam and gasped in shock. Sam's hair was crusted with blood, and there were dark purple bruises and weals all down one side of his grimy face. He swayed as he stumbled towards where the fire should be burning merrily.

"Oh, Sam, what's happened? Has someone beaten you?"

"No, I'm all right; I fell over the other day and bumped my head, but I'm on the mend. Oh, now, my fire's gone out." The sight of the cold, grey ashes seemed more than the injured man could take, and suddenly, tears coursed down his wrinkled cheeks.

Charlie quickly pulled forward the tree stump, which seemed to be Sam's favourite seat. "Here, sit down, Sam and tell us what happened."

"Nothing happened. Like I told you, I fell over."

Charlie persisted gently. "I don't think you did, Sam. Your injuries don't look like the result of a fall. I think someone beat you with a stick. Tell me who did it, and I'll give them a hiding they'll never forget."

Sam shook his head. "No, I don't want you getting into trouble. How's that dog bite?"

"Still sore, but thanks to you, it's healing nicely. That's why I'm here; I wanted to thank you. I might have lost my leg if it wasn't for you. That ointment was amazing stuff, Sam. This is my friend, Eveline. She's Annie's aunt, and she'd like to know your secret ingredients."

"Aye, I'll be bet she would; well, if you come when I'm better, my dear, I'll show you how to make it. I've always kept it a secret and told no one else, but maybe it's time I did. I may not be around a great while longer."

"Hello, Sam, I'm pleased to meet you again. I've seen you before when you came to the inn."

Sam squinted at her out of his left eye, which wasn't swollen shut. "Oh, yes, I remember you. You gave me food more than once, if I remember rightly."

"Yes, I did, Sam. I've brought some food for you today, too. Have you eaten?"

"No, I haven't eaten for days. I've been too sore and too poorly to move from my bed."

"In that case, see if you can manage a few mouthfuls of this pork sandwich; it's nice and tender. Here you are." He took half of the sandwich from her gratefully and slowly nibbled at it gingerly, trying to avoid his split lip.

"Charlie, could you get the fire going for Sam, please? I can heat some water then and bathe his injuries when he's finished eating. Perhaps we could make a hot drink for him too. Do you have any tea, Sam?"

"No, I don't have any tea, but there's some dried mint in that tin. I could have a cup of that. You too, if you like."

Whilst he ate his sandwich, Eveline went into the hut to find some rags and then sat beside him. Charlie got the fire going and went to gather more firewood.

"Sam, tell me, who did this? I won't let Charlie go after them, but tell me. How many men were there? Did they steal much?"

At that, the old man did smile. "Nay, 'twasn't men. To my shame, 'twas a woman. Fancy me getting beaten up like this by a woman. 'Tis a sad state of affairs."

"So, who was it, and why did they beat you like this? Oh, wait a minute, was it the woman at Buzzacott House?"

"Aye, you're a smart maid. I was doing no harm. Mind you, I was spying on her, so I suppose she had some cause. I saw another woman bring a baby to the house, and I knew Fred and Charlie wanted to know all about that, so I followed her and hid in the bushes. The girl handed over her baby to the tall woman and then made off back the way she came. Unfortunately, I sneezed a couple of times, and the woman heard me. She passed the baby to her daughter and came running over to find out who was there. As soon as she saw me, she set about me something vicious with a big stick she was carrying. Beat me black and blue, she did. I'm bruised all over. She said if she ever saw me near the house again, I'd be sorry, and she'd set the dog on me. I don't want Charlie going there and saying anything to her because it's me who will suffer for it when he's gone. If I could move on, I would, but my hut's here, and I'm not fit to travel. I might roam again when I'm better, but my hut's cosy, and young Fellwood did say I could stay, and that doesn't happen often."

"Oh, Sam, I'm so sorry. What an awful thing for her to do."

"Aye, she showed no mercy, even though I was screaming. She's a big woman too, almost as strong as a man, and there's not much to me these days. Just a bag of old skin and bones."

"Sam, will you let me bathe your wounds and put some of your ointment on them?"

He nodded. "Yes, all right. I haven't felt well enough to attend to them or get food or firewood. I feel better for that pork sandwich, though. I think you and Charlie might just have saved my life between you."

By this time, Charlie had the fire burning, and the water was soon hot. He made Sam some mint tea, and Eveline bathed his wounds and daubed ointment on them, but he refused to undress and let her see his other injuries. Charlie fetched a supply of firewood and stacked it near the fire.

"Sam, we'll come again tomorrow to see how you are. There's enough firewood there to last you until then, and we'll bring more food and clothes. The ones you have on are covered in blood. Will you be all right on your own until then?"

"I will now, and thank you so much for your kindness. To tell you the truth, I'd given up and was just waiting for the end to come, but perhaps it's not my time yet after all."

"Of course, it's not. We'll see you tomorrow, Sam."

Charlie and Eveline galloped back to the inn, where Ned was delighted to accept Charlie's request for his daughter's hand in marriage. Betsey was overjoyed at the thought of both her daughter and her son getting married.

CHAPTER 42

Robert and Jack Bater strolled around the farm, discussing the work that needed doing. Jack was delighted Robert took such an interest in the work on the farm. A lesser manager might have disliked the interference from his employer, but Robert had studied farming in detail and could tell Jack newer and better ways of doing things despite Jack's considerable experience. Together, they made a great team, and the profits were better than they had been for many a year.

"I thought we could plant this field with winter wheat, Jack. I've read that Squarehead Master gives a reliable crop. Have you grown it before?"

"No, not that variety. We usually sow Yeoman or New Harvester, but it's good to try new things. I've heard Squarehead is excellent for thatching, too."

"That's what I thought. We'll have the grain and the extra income from selling it for thatching. Perhaps we could start the ploughing towards the end of next month?"

"Yes, we've got all the hay in now, so we can do that. It'll take a week or two to get the ground ready because I like to leave it to settle for a few days after ploughing before we drag it to break it down."

"Then is it ready to sow the seed?"

"Yes, I usually sow winter wheat around the middle of November. It gives it a better chance to germinate before the ground turns too cold, and with your new seed drill, it will be much easier than it used to be with the seed fiddle. My goodness, I've walked miles in my time, walking up and down, up and down a field, scattering seed. It makes your arms ache, too."

"It's an amazing invention, and I'm glad it will save you some leg work. We have a lot to thank Jethro Tull for."

"Who's Jethro Tull?"

"He invented the seed drill sometime back in the 1700s. I don't know why my grandfather or father never bought one. They were probably more expensive back then, and my father certainly didn't like to spend money, but it's so much more efficient than using a seed fiddle. Once the seed's sown and we've put the roller over it, we'll lose far less seed to the birds."

They walked on to the next field, where a crop of mangelwurzels was looking healthy.

"These are a good size this year, aren't they? Are they ready for harvesting yet, Jack?"

"Yes, but there's plenty of time; I plan to get the men on to that in the next day or two. We might get them in then before the next rain."

"I can help; what do we have to do?"

"Oh, you just pull them up by the leaves with your left hand, like this, and chop off the leaves with a knife." Jack demonstrated. "Then we come along with a horse and cart and pick them up and store them in the barn. Hopefully, they'll feed the cows and pigs for most of the winter."

"What happens to the leaves?"

"We just plough them back in, which puts a bit of goodness back into the soil. Shall we walk on to the orchards now? I want to look at the apples."

They entered the orchard and surveyed the many rows of fruit trees. Some of the fruit had fallen to the ground in the recent winds.

"What sort is this one, Jack? I know little about apples."

"That's a Russet. A lovely apple; it can be kept for eating until April if you store it carefully, and some people think it makes the best cider of all. We have four rows of them. The next lot is Coxes Orange Pippins. Again, a useful apple, with the orange and red skin." He picked one off the nearest tree. "Nice yellow flesh and juicy, delicious to eat, but also ideal for cider. Then we come to the largest and oldest trees, and these are Bramleys. Not an eating apple, but excellent for apple pies, and having sampled many of Mrs Potts' pies, I'm sure you know that."

"Yes, her pies are wonderful. What do we do with all these apples?"

"We sell some in the Pannier Market in Barnstaple each week, store some for use in the house during the winter, and make the rest into cider. Cider has become popular in recent years, and I think we should make more of it this year. We used to only sell it locally, but now we can send produce to London on the train; I think we should make a lot more. We use it to pay people too, especially the casual labourers that we need from time to time. Mind you, I never give them any until they've finished the work."

"That sounds like a splendid idea. Do we mix the apples to make the cider?"

"I thought this year we might make a separate batch from each variety and then one combining all three and see which sells the best. What do you think?"

"Yes, another good idea, Jack. Now, you can probably put my mind to rest over something that old Arthur Potts told me the other day. I think he was teasing me because I know nothing about it, but he was enjoying a drink from a stone flagon of cider, and he said it was good because of the rat he put in it. Surely not?"

"I'm afraid it's true, sir. We usually put in a dead rat or two."

"Oh no, I can't believe it. Why would you do that?"

"It can be any meat. I once heard of a farmer whose best pig went missing, and they never found the animal. That year, the cider was outstanding, and when it was all gone, there were the bones of the pig in the bottom of the vat. The poor old sow must have toppled in while drinking the fermenting juice and drowned. The farmer swore it was the meat of the pig that made the cider so good. Mind you, it wasn't an exercise he wanted to repeat because pigs cost too much. That's why most farmers chuck in a dead rat or two."

"But how does it make it taste better; it's disgusting."

"Cider is corrosive because of its high acidity, and it dissolves the meat off the bones. It's the protein in the meat, you see; it feeds the yeast and speeds up fermentation. In any case, it's all gone before you drink it. All adds to the taste, as they say."

Robert grimaced as they walked across the fields to continue their tour.

Annie didn't think she had ever been so happy. To finally be able to express her feelings for Robert openly filled her with joy. She had lived at the Manor House for a couple of weeks and had seen nothing of her in-laws, for which she was grateful, but she was finding it difficult to settle in. Sarah had come to see her a few times and had admired the new furnishings, hardly believing the West Wing was the same dilapidated place she had explored as a child.

Annie had taken Selina to her new home several times, but the child was not content there. A bedroom had been prepared for her, with all sorts of toys, but she was not to be swayed. The little girl was willing to visit and spend time with her mother but always wanted to go home to her granny. Annie was upset by this but could understand it because she, too, felt out of place. She was no longer one of the servants, yet did not fit the life of a lady. She was unused to having time to herself and found it difficult to fill the hours when Robert was out with Jack, where he loved to be.

So far, the servants from the main house had also catered for the needs of Annie and Robert in the West Wing, but this was causing problems, and it was clear the matter must be addressed. Having put the issue off until now, Annie determinedly rang the bell and, when Molly appeared, asked her to bring tea and cakes for two. When Molly duly reappeared with a loaded tray some twenty minutes later, Annie told her to ask Mrs Potts to come and see her. Annie welcomed the old lady into the room and invited her to sit.

"This is a change of circumstances, Mrs Potts, isn't it? I'm used to you telling me what to do, and now we have to get used to me doing the opposite. I need your help with something."

"Of course, my dear. I've always had a soft spot for you and Master Robert, too, so if there's anything I can help with, you have only to ask."

"I know it's put extra pressure on the servants, looking after the main house and us here in the West Wing. Having done the chores myself at one time, I appreciate how difficult it must be to carry all our meals here from the main kitchen, let alone cope with the rest of the work, so I need to make changes. I need to employ our own servants, and Robert has decided to leave this to me. He's spoken to his parents, and they're willing for me to choose some of the existing servants, and they will employ new ones. I wondered if you would like to come to the West Wing and work for me. What do you think?"

"Yes, of course, I'd be delighted to cook for you and Master Robert. Would any of the maids be coming with me? It would be hard work to train new ones from scratch, particularly at my time of life."

"If you want to be employed as the cook here, that's fine because I love your cooking, but I have another idea. How about if you became the housekeeper, in charge of all the servants in the West Wing, like Miss Wetherby is in the main house? You know everything there is to know about running a kitchen, ordering the food, and keeping accounts. Would you like to do that? It would be a bit more money for you, and I thought it may be a little easier than being on your feet all day cooking."

"I appreciate the offer, thank you, but who would be the cook?"

"Well, you'll know better than me, but Maisie has worked for you for several years, so would she be ready to step up as cook? You'd be on hand if she weren't sure of anything, and you've always got on together, haven't you? It would be more money for her, too."

"The girl does deserve it; she's always been a hard worker. Yes, I think that would work. What about the main house, though? Who would be the cook?"

"It would be up to Miss Wetherby, but I thought maybe Elsie Webber could take that on?"

"Yes, I'm sure she could. I've been training her for over a year now, and she was experienced before she came here. Will you ask any other servants to come and work for you?"

Yes, I'd like Molly as a kitchen maid to assist Maisie and possibly Ethan or Caleb Bater to become a butler. Which one do you think would be the most suitable?

"They're both fine young men, but Ethan is the eldest, so by rights, it should probably be him."

"I'll take your advice; thank you, Mrs Potts. I will talk to Miss Wetherby and advise her she'll need to seek new servants, and then I'll speak to Maisie, Molly, and Ethan. We'll have to do this gradually because we can't leave the main house short of servants, but hopefully, within a week or two, we should be able to get it all in place. We may need to employ one or two new servants here, but we'll see how this works out first. Now, let's enjoy our tea and cakes, shall we?"

CHAPTER 43

Robert was pleased to hear that Annie had taken steps to sort out the staffing.

"Well done. It can't have been easy, especially the meeting with Miss Wetherby."

"No, it wasn't, but I was determined to establish my authority where she was concerned, and I have to say she took it well. I was surprised."

"She knew it was useless to argue. Now you're married to me; she daren't."

"I quite enjoyed it. Anyway, Mrs Potts and the others are pleased with their new positions, and Miss Wetherby already knew of people waiting for an opportunity to work here, so the new servants will start next week."

"That's excellent because we'll have our first little dinner party the week after. I had a letter from Doctor Turner this morning saying he's staying in Devon for a couple of weeks, and he offered to come here and see Danny. I thought we could invite him for dinner and ask him to stay overnight with his wife and then take him to see Danny the next day. I think Danny would be more comfortable seeing him at the Lodge House than here, don't you?"

"Yes, without a doubt. Goodness, I'm not sure I'm ready to host a dinner party, though. Will it be just the Turners?"

"It can be, but I'm tempted to ask Sarah and Aunty Margery; would you like that?"

"Yes, I think it would help if Sarah were here, and Aunty Margery seemed to be on our side at the wedding, didn't she? She asked me to visit, but I haven't done so yet. Is it far to where she lives?"

"No, not far; perhaps ten miles or so. Why don't you visit and invite her to dinner?"

"I can't just arrive unannounced, can I?"

"There isn't time to write first, but I'm sure she won't mind, and if she's out or can't see you, well, so be it. You can leave the invitation. Would you like me to go with you?"

"No, I think I'll go alone. I must get used to all this, Robert, and I think Aunty Margery will be a good ally. Can you write the invitation to dinner, though? Your writing is far better than mine."

The next day, Dodger drove Annie to Enderby House, where Robert's Aunty Margery lived alone. She had lost her husband several years before, and they had no children. Annie would have liked to ride up front with Dodger and chat along the way, but she knew this was unacceptable, so she sat inside the carriage. She enjoyed the journey, looking out across the fields and into peoples' gardens as they drove by, but couldn't help thinking that Dodger had a better view than she did.

The stable boy drove the carriage carefully up the impressive drive to the large house. He helped Annie from the carriage, and as she walked slowly up the steps, the door opened, and the butler came out to greet her.

"Can I help you, ma'am? I saw the carriage arrive from the window."

"Yes, thank you. I would like to see Lady Margery if she can spare the time. Please ask her to accept my apologies for arriving unannounced."

"Of course, ma'am. I'll see if she is willing to receive you. May I take your name, please?"

"Yes, please tell her Anne Fellwood would appreciate a few moments of her time. Thank you."

The butler showed Annie into the drawing room, and she seated herself near the window. She did not have to wait long before the old lady swept into the room.

"Annie, my dear, what a pleasant surprise. I'm so glad you came; I wondered if you would."

"Thank you so much for seeing me unannounced. Robert didn't think you would mind, and there wasn't time to write. I'm sorry, but should I call you Aunty Margery?"

"You're welcome here any time, my dear, and yes, of course, you should call me Aunty Margery; I've already told you that. So why the hurry to come and see me?"

Annie explained about Doctor Turner and his wife and the reason for their visit. "We wondered if you would like to come to dinner and stay the night. We would love to show you all the improvements we've made to the West Wing. I suppose you must remember it from your childhood when you lived there?"

"It wasn't used even then, though it was in better repair than in recent years. I'm glad it's had a new lease of life, and yes, I'd love to come to dinner. I know Clara Turner, so it will be good to catch up with her. It's strange your little brother should have a hare lip, as my brother, George, also had one, and he died young. Joshua, Charles' father, was the eldest, so of course, he inherited the estate. I had a few other brothers and sisters, but they have all passed on now, and I'm the only one left. I take it Charles and Eleanor are not invited to your dinner party?"

"No, they wouldn't come anyway, but we will ask Sarah. She's been so kind to me."

Annie was keen to keep the conversation moving forward, for she did not want Aunty Margery to read too much into the fact that the hare lip seemed to run in the Fellwood family. She was a sharp old lady, and Annie didn't want her putting two and two together.

"Oh, that's good; I always enjoy her company. How are you getting on living at the Manor House?"

"Well, I've engaged my own servants. I worked with some of them at the Manor House when I was a kitchen maid; they're my friends, and I need them around me. They understand that my station has changed, and they're respectful, but I know I can rely on them, and that's important to me just now. This dinner will be something of a test for them as well as me because they're only starting next week, and the dinner is soon after."

"Can I give you a bit of advice?"

"Yes, of course, I'd be grateful."

"On the day they start, go into the kitchen and welcome them and tell them you're relying on them. Seek Mrs Potts' advice about the menu for your dinner party, and keep it simple. She has years of experience, and she'll know what to serve. I'm sure it will be a splendid evening, and I'm looking forward to it already. You'll be amongst friends, and you mustn't worry about any of it. Now, I hope you have time for lunch before you depart?"

"Yes, I'll do that, and I'd love to stay for lunch. Thank you."

A week later, Annie and Robert waited on the doorstep of the West Wing to welcome the doctor and his wife. Aunty Margery had arrived earlier in the day and had gone to her room for a rest. Robert squeezed Annie's hand reassuringly and whispered. "It will be fine. They're good people, and you look beautiful."

The couple alighted from their carriage and mounted the steps, and Doctor Turner did the introductions.

"My dear, this is Robert and Anne, though I believe she is known as Annie to her friends, so I suggest that is what we call her if she doesn't mind?"

"Oh, yes, Doctor Turner, of course, that's fine." Annie smiled at the elderly couple and, responding to firm pressure on her arm from Robert, resisted the urge to curtsey.

"Good, now we have established we are friends; you can't continue to call me Doctor Turner. I am Geoffrey, and this is my wife, Clara. She's been longing to meet you, Annie."

The grey-haired lady on his arm smiled at Annie. "It's a pleasure to meet you, my dear. Thank you so much for inviting us. I haven't been too well lately, and we haven't socialised much, so this is a real change."

"Oh, I'm sorry to hear that. Are you better now?"

"Yes, I'm fine now, thank you. Geoffrey tells me you have invited Lady Margery. I'm so pleased because we've known each other for years and will have much to catch up on."

"Oh, yes, my aunt told Annie she knew you. Now, we'll get you settled into your rooms, and then, by all means, join us in the drawing room if you like, or you could have a rest if you prefer. Dinner will be served at seven o'clock." Robert led the way down the hall, where Molly was waiting to show the couple to their room.

Despite her nerves, Annie thoroughly enjoyed the evening, for the other three women present were determined to make her feel comfortable. Mrs Potts had chosen to serve a starter of leek and potato soup, with fresh crusty rolls, followed by roast beef and all the trimmings. "You'll find you can't go far wrong with that." Mrs Potts had told her. The new housekeeper was right, and the meal was delicious. For pudding, there was a choice of apple pie, lemon posset, or bread and butter pudding, and Robert entertained his guests with his new knowledge about his apple orchards.

When the party ended, the guests went to their rooms, and Sarah took a shortcut to the main house through the kitchens. "You did well, Annie. No one would have known you weren't born a lady." Sarah hugged her. "See you soon."

The next day, after breakfast, Robert and Annie took the doctor to the Lodge House to see Danny, leaving Clara and Marjorie to enjoy the morning together, strolling around the gardens. Annie told Robert about Aunty Margery's comment about hare lips, and they were both glad she was not going to see Danny because, for sure, she would have picked up a family resemblance. It was a dry morning, and the three of them decided to walk the short distance to the Lodge House. Sabina and Liza waited anxiously with Danny, having sent the rest of the children outside to play in the garden.

The doctor did his best to put Sabina and Liza at ease and then focused on Danny.

"Now, young man, I've come to examine your mouth and your feet. Is that all right with you?" Danny nodded nervously. "I'm not going to hurt you, so there's nothing to worry about, and I might find you a special treat when I'm finished. How does that sound?"

Danny grinned, making the split in his upper lip even more prominent.

The doctor laid him on the table and peered into his mouth. "Thank you, Danny. Now, can I have a look at your feet? Let's take off these boots so I can have a proper look. That's it."

The doctor moved Danny's ankles this way and that and then asked him to stand up and walk slowly around the room. "That's fine, Danny. Thank you. Now, I promised you a treat, and so I've brought you a small present. Do you like sweets?" Danny nodded. "Yes, I rather thought you might. Here you are, then. There's a special lollipop for you, and here are some toffees you might like to share with your brothers and sisters. Would you like to join them in the garden?"

The little boy limped off happily. He was delighted that only he had a red lollipop and pleased to be able to share the toffees with the other children. Liza brought in a pot of tea and some cakes, and the doctor waited until they were all settled before he spoke.

"Right, now I'm pleased to say I can help Danny with all his deformities, though it's a pity I didn't get my hands on him when he was a baby. It's always better to treat these things as soon as possible. How old is he now?

"He's four, sir."

"I thought he must be about that. You've done an excellent job of looking after him, Mrs Carter. I expect he was difficult to feed when he was born, wasn't he?"

"Yes, it took a long time to feed him because he couldn't suck well. He struggled for the first six months of his life, and of course, I was also feeding my daughter, Helen, at the time, so I didn't have much milk to spare."

"I see; I didn't realise he had a twin."

"Oh, no, sir, he's not my child; he's a foundling. Annie found him abandoned in the woods, and because I had milk, I agreed to take him in. I couldn't see him starve."

"That's even more commendable. Tell me, has someone already treated his feet?"

"Just me, sir. I saw how they turned in, one worse than the other, and I bound them tightly with splints for several months. He didn't seem to mind, and I thought it might encourage them to grow straight. At the time, I didn't think he would ever walk, but he manages as best he can, though, of course, he limps."

"You did an excellent job, Mrs Carter. That is precisely the treatment any physician would have suggested. Now, I can help Danny with his mouth and feet, and I suggest we tackle the problems one at a time because the procedures will cause him some discomfort. However, with modern treatments, this is considerably minimised compared to how it used to be. That is thanks to two men who, between them, have revolutionised surgery. Thanks to a man called James Simpson, we now use a gas called chloroform to anaesthetise patients. It puts them to sleep while we operate. This saves a lot of pain, though Danny will be uncomfortable when he wakes up. We also have to thank another man, Joseph Lister, for initiating the use of carbolic acid. We sterilise our equipment in it and also use it on wounds. In both cases, it reduces the chance of infection. Now, I'm not sure if you needed the history lesson, but I'm trying to reassure you that I can correct Danny's deformities without causing him too much pain or risk to his life."

"It would be wonderful for Danny to eat properly and not limp. Children can be so cruel, and he gets teased at school. Where would the operation be done?"

"It would be best done in London. My surgery there is well-equipped, and I could keep an eye on him for a few weeks after the operation. Maybe you could come to London with him and stay with us?"

"There is just one thing, Geoffrey. I must ask how much the operations will cost. I'm willing to pay, but I need to know how much is involved?"

"There will be no cost, Robert; it will be my pleasure to help such a deserving little boy. I'm not short of money, and I always carry out a few operations for free every year. I prefer to charge the affluent patients who see me in Harley Street. All too frequently, there is little wrong with them that more exercise and a little less port would not cure. Maybe you could organise the transport for Danny and his mother? Now, the operation on his mouth will be the more complicated procedure because it involves his palate, though it's not the worst case I've dealt with. I suggest we do that one first, perhaps after Christmas, if that suits you. I'm quite busy for the next couple of months."

"Oh, that is generous of you, Geoffrey. Are you sure? I'm willing to pay."

"No, really, it will be a pleasure. Now, shall we get the young man back in and see what he has to say about it?" Danny and his siblings returned to the room, where the doctor explained to Danny what he was going to do. "You'll be asleep, Danny, whilst I repair your mouth, but it will be sore for a few days. I'll be able to give you some medicine to ease it, though. Would you like me to fix it?"

"Yes, please. Can you do my feet, too?"

"Yes, I can, but we'll do your mouth first and let that get better, and then we'll think about your feet. Is that all right with you?"

"Yes, please."

"Fine, I'll say goodbye for now then, and when I see you in London after Christmas, we'll get it all sorted out. Robert, I'll leave you to make the arrangements if that's all right?"

"Yes, of course. Thank you so much, Geoffrey. I've always wanted to get this done for Danny. Thank you for making it possible. Come on; we'll return to the Manor House and get lunch. Goodbye, Sabina."

CHAPTER 44

Since Sam's beating, Charlie and Fred had made a point of keeping an eye on the old man. This was partly due to Eveline insisting they do so but also because they were still suspicious of Lizzie Dymond at Buzzacott House. They could see no reason for her to beat the poor man if she had nothing to hide. Sam was still recovering from his injuries, and the bruises on his grimy face were purple and yellow. His eye was now open, although it was still bloodshot. He was glad to see Charlie and Fred, for he enjoyed their company, and since Eveline had been involved, she had sent him food regularly, and he looked the better for it. She had even sent him a parcel of old clothes, and he had not been as tidy or as warm for many a year.

A couple of weeks after Sam's beating, Charlie was helping Fred with a difficult roofing job not far from Sam's hut, and they decided to call in and see him. As they trotted side by side, they discussed their wedding plans.

"Not long now, Charlie, before we both get hitched. Have you been married before?"

"No, I've always travelled too much to get tied down, which always suited me. I'm ready now, though, and I'm looking forward to marrying Eveline. I'll take care of her, Fred; you don't need to worry."

"I'm not worried. Eveline's a strong woman, and she can look after herself. Mind you, I've heard about you sailors with a girl in every port; she won't stand for that, you know."

"No, there'll be none of that, I can assure you; I'll be faithful. It's generous of your Annie to offer to have the reception at the big house, isn't it? It'll cost a pretty penny, and I'm willing to pay my share. It will be good to have the extra space, seeing as we're having a double wedding."

"Yes, I know. I've offered to pay, too, but I doubt Robert will take anything. He's enjoying being part of a real family; I don't think he's ever known much affection from his own. I'm glad we're having a joint wedding. It makes sense, seeing as it would be pretty much all the same guests at both ceremonies. Are you going on a honeymoon?"

"No, not straight away. Eveline wants to get the children settled in at the farm before we consider going anywhere. Maybe one day, we'll manage a day or two away, but not for a while, not until they would be comfortable staying with Alfred, Jimmy, and Maria. How about you and Charlotte?"

"No, the same thing. I can't afford to take time off work at the moment because I'm busy, and anyway, it's the same with my three children. They know Charlotte, of course, and they get on well with her, but they're bound to miss Eveline looking after them every day, so we want to take it slowly. William's children and mine have been through enough upheaval in their short lives already."

"I can't believe how perfectly it's all worked out. Anyway, here we are; there's the smoke from Sam's fire. When I see that from a distance, I think he must be all right."

"He should be, what with Eveline feeding and clothing him and us getting firewood for him; he's never had it so good."

Sam heard the horses' hooves and came out of his shed, beaming his familiar toothy smile. "Hello, lads, it's nice to see you again. Sit yourselves down. I'm just cooking some fresh fish, and I know you're partial to that, so would you like some?"

"It smells delicious, so it's hard to say no, but we don't want to take your food away, Sam."

"Nay lad, there's plenty more trout in that stream, and I've nothing better to do than catch them. I've nothing to go with the fish, though."

"I can help you out there, Sam, because Eveline has sent you two loaves of bread and some cheese. I'll get it from my saddlebag."

As the three men ate their food, the conversation inevitably turned to Buzzacott House and the woman who lived there. "She's not bothered you since, has she, Sam?"

"No, I've kept away, though it was a close shave yesterday. I went near the house picking herbs because that's where the ones I wanted grow, and she came out carrying a bundle. I dropped to the ground and lay still on my belly because the last thing I wanted was for her to see me and beat me again. I'm only just getting over the last lot. I had to lie there for quite a while, and I was worried I'd get the cramp."

"Why was she there so long; what was she doing?"

"She had a spade with her, and she dug a hole and put the bundle into it, so I suppose it was some rubbish or perhaps a dead cat or something. Anyway, the ground was hard and full of thick roots, so it wasn't an easy job, but she kept at it. I waited until she had gone back into the house before I dared to move, and then, of course, it took me a while to get my stiff old joints moving before I could get up. At least she didn't see me, though, thank goodness."

"Today's Friday, so it's market day in Eggleston. Did you see her go out with the pony and trap?"

"Aye, she passed by early this morning. No sign of the daughter, though, so she must be in the house."

"I'm not worried about her. Shall we take a look at what she buried, Charlie?"

"Yes, we can if you want, but it's probably a smelly old cat or her kittens. What else would she be burying? I hope it was that beastly dog."

"Nay, lad, it wasn't the dog. The bundle wasn't big enough; she'd struggle to carry that great brute. No, I reckon it will be a cat."

Sam took them to a glade just outside the garden wall, and they could see where the earth had been disturbed. Sam wouldn't stay with them but returned to his hut. "I'll leave you to it. I don't want to risk her coming back and seeing me. She might beat me again, and I'm not sure I'd survive another hiding. You should be all right, though; she isn't usually back until later. I'll keep watch and blow my horn if I see her coming along the road."

Using Sam's spade, Fred gently dug away the soil. He got down about six inches and could see some blue material showing. "Whatever it is, she didn't dig down far. Mind you, these tree roots make it hard going. There, I can pull the bundle out now, I think."

Fred pulled at the material, and it came free of the hole. "Right, let's have a look. Oh, my God, no!"

Both men gasped in horror as a child's tiny foot fell free of the material.

"Oh, Charlie, it's a baby. Oh, please, God, don't let it be Doris."

Fred's face was as white as a sheet as he peeled back the patterned curtain material and exposed the naked body of a tiny baby. It was so emaciated it was impossible to tell how old the child was, but one thing was clear: it was the body of a male child. There were no apparent signs of injury.

"What do you think happened to it? There are no injuries. Do you think it just died, and she wanted to get rid of it? What a terrible thing to do. The poor child deserved a decent burial."

Charlie pulled anxiously at Fred's sleeve. "Fred, I've got a horrible feeling there might be more; the ground is disturbed in other places." Both men felt physically sick. "Let's not look for anymore; let's get Wilf Folland. He needs to sort this out, not us. He can't ignore this. Wrap the child up again, and we'll take it back to Sam's." They scraped the soil back into the hole, and Fred carried the tiny body.

"I knew they were up to something, but even I didn't suspect this. I hope we don't find Charlotte's baby here too. It would truly break her heart."

They left the child's corpse near Sam's hut, and he promised to keep an eye on it. Even the tramp had tears when he heard what they had found.

Charlie and Fred galloped back to the village and told Wilfred what they had found. He was flabbergasted. "I can't believe it. Do you think they murdered the child? I mean, why would they, if they could get it adopted and make money? It doesn't make sense."

"Wilfred, what do you want to do? Shall we go back and explore the house and see if there are more babies?"

"Yes, I think we'd better, but what about the dog? Perhaps we'd better wait until the woman is in?"

"I think it would be best to look around while she's out of the way. The daughter's there, so she can let us in the front door."

"I'm not sure she will. She didn't seem quite right to me when I saw her."

"I know what we'll do."

"What?"

"We've still got some laudanum that the doctor gave Jane when she was so ill and in a lot of pain. It used to put her to sleep quickly. We could soak some meat in it and feed it to the dog. It won't take long to ride to the farm first; I know where the medicine is. I kept it in case I ever have a toothache again."

The constable took charge. "Yes, I think that's justified in this case. If the girl will answer the door, so be it, but if not, we'll dope the dog and go in through the back. If I get questioned about it, I'll say we did it in case there were any other babies in danger. I can't see anyone arguing with that."

With several pieces of pork soaked in laudanum, the three men rode as fast as they could back to Sam, where they showed Wilfred the body of the child. Although he had been warned of what to expect, he was shocked when he saw the sad little corpse. "Even if this child died from natural causes, deaths have to be registered. You can't just bury bodies in the woods. This woman has a lot to answer for. Come on."

Wilfred knocked loudly on the front door, but there was no response. "Are you sure there's someone in there?"

"Yes, Sam said she wasn't on the pony and trap with her mother, and I think I just saw a curtain twitch in that window. The front door is too sturdy to break in; shall we see if we can get in through the back?"

Fred led the way to the back of the property and wheeled over the old barrel they had used before to get up and peer the fence. Immediately, they could hear deep-throated growls as the dog spotted Fred.

"It's here, and it's not happy. Charlie, pass me that meat."

Fred threw a piece of meat over the fence, and the dog immediately gulped it down hungrily. Fred kept throwing the meat until it was all gone.

"He doesn't seem to mind the taste, mind you; he looks half-starved. No wonder he fancied a piece of your leg, Charlie. There's no sign of him going to sleep yet. Oh, wait a minute, he looks a bit unsteady."

Within a few minutes, the dog keeled over and was fast asleep. The three men climbed over the fence, with Fred and Charlie hauling Wilfred over between them, for he was an older man and carried more weight.

"Well, I won't be coming back this way, and that's for sure." Wilfred was red in the face and gasping for breath with the exertion.

They tried the back door and, luckily, this time found it was unlocked. They called out as they walked through a scullery and into a large, untidy kitchen, but no one answered. Dishes were piled high in the sink, and there were mounds of dirty washing. They wandered through another room and into the front room, where the girl was sitting near the window, tightly cradling a sleeping child.

"It's all right, lass; we won't hurt you. We just want to talk to you."

"My mother's not here."

"No, we know, but that's all right. We want to talk to you about the baby."

"It's mine. This one is mine. I'm keeping this one. Mum said I could."

Slowly, Wilfred sat down on a chair near her. Did you have the baby yourself, Thurza? That is your name, isn't it?"

"Yes, that's my name, but Mum says I mustn't talk to strangers."

"You met me the other day, Thurza, so it's all right to talk to me. May I see your baby? Is it a boy or a girl?"

Gently, he pulled the shawl away from the baby's face and was relieved to see the child was breathing, though it didn't stir. It was malnourished, and it was impossible to tell how old it was.

"What a lovely baby. What is it called?"

"It's called Thurza, like me."

"So, it's a little girl then, is it?"

"Yes, of course, it is. She's tired now. She needs to sleep. She needs lots of sleep. Mum says so."

"Are there any other babies here, Thurza?"

"I'm not allowed to talk about the babies. Please go away, or Mum will be cross. Please go. Mum might give me the stick if she finds you here. Please, go now, before she comes home."

"I'll make sure your mum doesn't hurt you, Thurza, I promise, but you do need to tell us about the other babies. Where are they?"

The girl sat in stubborn silence, rocking to and fro, once more in a world of her own. Wilf put his hand on her arm, and she flinched as if she had forgotten he was there. "Leave me alone; I'll tell Mum, and she'll beat you."

"No, she can't do that, Thurza. Now, you must take me to the other babies, or I'll have to take you off to jail. Where are they?"

The girl got to her feet and, still hugging the child, silently led the way from the room and into the hallway. She walked to a door under the stairs, opened it, and led them down some dimly lit stairs. In the basement, a little light came through two grimy windows. As their eyes adjusted to the gloom, the men looked around the filthy, sparsely furnished space.

"There are no babies here, Thurza. Why have you brought us here?" Where are the babies?"

"They're over there on the bed." She led the way to an old double bed in the far corner and pulled back a shawl covering three small bodies. "There they are, look. They'll soon be angels, but I'm keeping Thurza. Mum said I could."

The men gazed at the babies in disbelief. "Are they alive?" Fred was the first to move and picked up the nearest child. It was warm but floppy and unresponsive. "This one is, but there's something wrong with it. Here, take this one, Charlie."

Fred picked up the second and then the third child to find they, too, were alive but in the same condition.

"I don't know what's wrong with them, but they are alive."

Wilfred inspected the three children. "I think they're drugged. I've heard about this; people drug them to keep them quiet. It saves feeding and looking after them. They use stuff called Godfrey's Cordial; it's got morphine in it. Thurza, why aren't you looking after these babies, too?

"Mum won't let me. Mum's an angel-maker. She sends most of them to heaven to be with Jesus because he wants them more than their mothers did. They don't suffer, and they don't cry. They just fall asleep."

They heard a key in the lock of the front door and a voice shouting, "Thurza, where are you?"

CHAPTER 45

On hearing her mother's voice, Thurza panicked. "Oh no, it's my mother. She'll kill me for bringing you down here. We must hide." She ran to the corner of the room and crouched behind the bed, a terrified expression on her face and tears running down her cheeks.

Charlie pushed past her and ran straight up the stairs. Lizzie Dymond was standing at the open door to the basement, and as soon as she saw Charlie, she slammed the door shut, and he could hear her fumbling with a key.

"No, you don't." He twisted the handle and pushed it hard. The door moved an inch or so, but she was putting all her weight behind it on the other side. She was a strong woman but no match for Charlie, and he soon had the door open. As soon as she realised she could not lock him in the basement, she ran swiftly for the front door, but Charlie was too quick for her and grabbed her from behind. She kicked and fought like a wildcat, scratching at his face and trying to bite him.

"Stop it, stop it now, or I'll make you! You're not going to win, so stand still."

She ignored him and continued to fight with all her might. Charlie did his best to hold her, but when she bit him on the hand and finally pulled free, he slapped her hard across the face, and she fell to the ground, stunned. By this time, Wilfred and Fred had joined in, and together, the three men pulled her to her feet, sat her on a chair, and tied her to it.

"Lizzie Dymond, you are under arrest for the neglect and murder of, I don't know how many babies. I'll be making arrangements to take you to Barnstaple jail. Do you have anything to say for yourself?"

"Where's Thurza? Did she let you in? I told her not to answer the door."

"No, she didn't, so don't blame her. We came in through the back door. Now, what's wrong with those babies downstairs? Have you doped them?"

"I'm telling you nothing."

"Fred, can you ride to the village and come back with a couple of carts, please? Charlie and I will stay here and wait for you. We'll need some women to care for the babies on the way home. If they've got any spare nappies and clothes, that would be useful because those babies are soaking wet."

"Yes, Wilfred, of course. Charlie, is that bite all right? She's drawn blood."

"Aye, I'm all right, but I've had just about enough of getting bitten in this house. First the dog, and now a madwoman. I hope neither of them has rabies!"

Fred galloped back to the village. He could scarcely believe what they had found. He wondered if any of the surviving babies could be Doris. "No use worrying about that now, Fred Carter." He said to himself. "Pull yourself together, man, and do what you must."

He hitched the cart to his horse and went to find his sister. Eveline was in the garden, gathering the dry washing.

"Hello, Fred, you're back early. Tea won't be ready for a while."

"No, I'm not here for tea. I've come to ask for your help." He told her what they had found at Buzzacott House.

"Oh no, Fred, that's awful. Is Doris there?"

"I don't know. She might be, but the babies are in such a state it's difficult to know, and of course, I only saw her once. Anyway, we need to get back there as soon as possible and get those babies attended to. I thought we could take our children to the Lodge House and ask Liza to keep an eye on them all. It's asking a lot of a woman of her age, but I want to take Sabina with us. I did consider fetching Charlotte from the inn, but I can't take her to that house. We'll need Doctor Luckett to examine the babies and see if they can be saved. I have my doubts, and I don't want Charlotte to see them until we know if they will live."

Eveline rounded up the six children and put them on the cart. "We're going to the Lodge House, where you can play with your cousins for the afternoon, and you must behave yourselves for Liza because she is an old lady. If you're naughty, I'll hear about it, and there will be trouble. Do I make myself clear?" Six heads nodded. Eveline could be strict when she wanted to be.

At the Lodge House, Sabina and Liza were astonished to see Fred and Eveline arrive with all the children but more than willing to help when they heard what had happened.

"Liza, are you sure you'll be all right with all these children? You can go with Eveline if you like, and I'll stay here."

"No, I'll be all right, Sabina. It's a dry afternoon, and they can play in the garden. There's plenty here for them to do. I'm too old and stiff to be jolted about on a cart all the way to Buzzacott, and you'll cope better with the babies than me. I don't want to see them, poor little mites."

Leaving Liza with the eleven children, they went to the smithy to find Francis Rudd. They could hear the blacksmith hard at work long before they saw him. Francis hammering on his anvil was a familiar sound in the village.

Sure enough, there he was, sweat dripping from his brow as he took mighty swipes at a lump of metal and hammered it into shape. When Fred pulled up in the cart, he went out to meet him, mopping his brow.

"Hello, Fred, ladies, is everything all right? You look a bit flustered."

Quickly, Fred told him what had happened and asked if he could help. "We need two carts, you see, Francis. Wilf Folland wants to take the two women straight to Barnstaple jail because there's no jail here in Hartford, and they certainly need locking up. In fact, I hope they throw away the key. If you could do that with Wilfred, we can bring the babies back here. Can you leave the forge for a few hours?"

"Aye, I'll make the fire safe and then tell Mum, or she'll wonder where I am. You go on with the women, and I'll follow when I'm ready. I know where it is. I'll be there as soon as I can."

Wilfred heard the horse and cart coming along the track and went to meet it.

"Ah, there you are, Fred. Hello, Sabina, hello, Eveline. Thanks so much for coming. The girl is still in the cellar with the baby she was holding. She won't come upstairs; she's that frightened of her mother, but she'll have to now, and we need to take the baby away from her, too. Would you ladies like to see if you can persuade her to part with it?"

They went into the house where Lizzie was still tied to the chair. Sabina went over to her. "You evil bitch; I hope you hang." She slapped her hard across the face. "That's for all the mothers whose hearts you've broken, especially our Charlotte's."

"Come on, Sabina. Leave her alone; I'll make sure justice is done. Oh, there's Francis outside with his cart. He didn't hang about, did he? Charlie, can you stay here and keep an eye on her."

Fred led the way down the stairs to the cellar, with Wilfred, Eveline, and Sabina following. "You're not going to like what you see, I'm afraid."

Thurza was still crouched behind the bed, peering out to see who was coming. The child in her arms was whimpering, and Sabina went to her. "Hello, Thurza, my name's Sabina. Can I see your baby? I like babies. I have lots of my own." The girl held the baby tightly and ignored Sabina. "Your baby's crying; does it need feeding? Shall we get it some milk?"

"There's none left unless Mother got some. Go away, and leave me alone."

"Thurza, your baby's poorly, and we need to take it to a doctor to make it better. Will you let me do that for you?"

"Babies don't get better. They turn into angels and go to heaven. Mother told me, but I like this one, so Mother said I can keep her for a while."

"Thurza, the doctor can make this baby better. Will you let me take her to the doctor? You don't want this one to become an angel, do you?"

"No, I like this one. She's pretty."

"Come on then, let me have a look at her. I can see you've looked after her. You're a good girl, Thurza." Sabina smiled at her reassuringly.

"All right, then." Reluctantly, the girl handed the baby over to Sabina.

"Thank you. Now, we'll take her upstairs together."

"Is my mother up there?"

"Yes, but she won't hurt you, Thurza. We've told her you didn't let us in. Come on, I'll go first."

Sabina took the child from the girl and looked at it sadly. It was thin and weighed next to nothing. She led the way up the stairs, and Wilfred followed. As soon as Thurza saw her mother tied to a chair, she tried to bolt back down the stairs.

Wilfred stepped forward quickly to block her path. "Now, it's all right, Thurza. We had to keep your mother quiet because she was fighting us, but we didn't hurt her. We're going to take you both for a ride on a cart, so you come outside with me, and you can get on it first. Charlie, I'll get Thurza settled, and then I'll come back to help you with this one."

Leaving Thurza with Francis, who had stayed on the cart, Wilfred returned to the room and looked down at the woman. "Now, are you going to behave yourself? You'd better because you're going nowhere with us three men to deal with you. It will be easier for you if you come quietly because it wouldn't upset us too much to give you a good hiding."

The constable untied the ropes that were holding her to the chair but left her hands tied behind her back and pushed her out of the door. Once she was loaded onto the cart, he tethered his and Charlie's horses to the back of the cart and beckoned to Sabina, who was at the door holding the baby.

"Sabina, Charlie and I will ride back on the cart with Francis to keep an eye on these women. We'll call on Sam and collect the body of the dead child. That will have to be taken to Barnstaple. You, Fred, and Eveline do what you can to make the babies comfortable and bring them back to the village. Would you mind taking them to your house for the time being? I want to get these two locked up in Barnstaple, and then I'll come and see what's to be done about the babies. I'll fetch Doctor Luckett and bring him to examine them."

"Yes, that's fine, Wilfred. We'll see you later."

"Just a minute, Wilfred. What about the dog? We can't leave it here to starve, and it's too dangerous to let it go."

"Would you mind putting it down, Fred? It's a shame, but it's so vicious I don't see any alternative. See if you can find a gun in the house. If not, we must come back to see to it."

Fred and Eveline brought the other three babies upstairs, and together with Sabina, they set about changing all four into dry clothes, for they were saturated in urine. As they peeled off their wet clothes, which no doubt some heartbroken mother had lovingly dressed them in, they were saddened to see how emaciated they were. The three little girls and one boy were heavily drugged, for apart from the odd whimper, they lay limp and lifeless, barely breathing. The little girl Thurza had been so fond of had fared slightly better. She wasn't as thin as the others, and she had been changed more regularly.

"Oh, look at their poor little bottoms. They're so sore; it's a wonder they aren't screaming."

"I don't think they can at the moment, but I don't know what they'll be like when the drugs wear off. We need to get them to Doctor Luckett as soon as possible and see if he can do anything for them."

"How old do you think they are?"

"It's impossible to tell, isn't it; they're so starved. Fred, how old would Charlotte's baby be now?"

"I think she was born in early May, so I suppose she'd be about six months old by now. Do you think any of these babies could be Doris? They don't seem big enough."

"Doctor Luckett might be able to tell us, but the first thing is to try to save them, then worry about whom they belong to. No doubt the police will search the house for any records, and, of course, the woman will know if she can be persuaded to talk."

"Right, that's all four changed. Fred, do you want to deal with the dog while we get the babies onto the cart? That's if you can find a gun. Mind the beast doesn't bite you."

Fred searched for a gun and finally found a rifle on top of a cupboard in the kitchen, and luckily, it was fully loaded. Cautiously, he opened the back door and peered out to see if the dog had regained consciousness. It was just stirring and getting shakily to its feet. Swiftly, he shot it in the head. "There, you'll never bite anyone else, but at least you didn't suffer." He wondered whether he should bury it but decided it was more important to get the babies back to the village. No doubt the police would be coming to investigate so they could deal with it. He'd seen enough unpleasantness for one day.

CHAPTER 46

Liza saw Sabina and Eveline step down carefully from the cart with the babies in their arms and opened the door for them. "Oh, the poor little dears. Do you think they'll live?"

"I don't know, Liza, but could you warm some milk? We'll see if they'll feed. I think there are some bottles and teats in that cupboard near the sink." Sabina put the two babies she was carrying in one of the armchairs. "Eveline, put the other two in that chair if you like."

"I've already found the bottles and washed them, and the milk is ready to go on the stove. We only have two bottles, though, and one teat. I would have gone to the shop to get some more, but I couldn't leave all the children."

"Have they behaved themselves? You look exhausted, Liza, but thank you so much for looking after them."

"Oh, yes, they've been good, Eveline, but I'm afraid at my age, it doesn't take much to tire me out."

"Fred, there are some bottles in our kitchen, but I'm not sure about teats. Would you mind going to fetch them and buy some teats from the shop?

"Yes, of course, I will, but then I must tell Charlotte what we've found. It will upset her, but she'll never forgive me if I don't, and she has to know sooner or later."

Fred returned with the bottles and teats, and Sabina and Eveline coaxed the babies to feed. The little girl that Thurza had favoured soon sucked hungrily at the teat, and Sabina heaved a sigh of relief. "I think this one will live. She wants to anyway, and that's half the battle."

"That's good. This one is sucking a little bit, but still sleepy. How about yours, Liza?"

"No, this one seems too sleepy. I think I'll leave her a bit longer and try the boy. Mind you, he looks in a worse state than the girls." She picked up the tiny child and put the bottle to his lips. He stirred slightly and opened his mouth. "Oh, yes, I think he might take a little drop."

They heard a knocking at the door, and Sabina told Stephen to open it. "It's Charlie, the doctor, and the constable, Mum. Shall I let them in?"

"Yes, of course."

The three men trooped in, and the doctor went straight to the babies. "Goodness me, how could anyone let babies get into this state? Don't give them too much milk. That could do more harm than good because they aren't used to it. Just give them a little drop and often. I think we'll probably need to mix some morphine with it and wean them off it gradually. We won't give them any yet and see how they react, but they'll undoubtedly miss it if we stop it completely."

"Have you come across this problem before then, doctor?"

"Sadly, yes. The mixture most commonly used is called Godfrey's Cordial or Mother's Friend, and lots of families use it to make the children sleep so they can work. The parents have to get some sleep to work the long hours they do, and this keeps the children quiet. It's mostly just morphine mixed with treacle. Unfortunately, children quickly become addicted to it. It's not a problem here in Hartford because we only have one shop, and thankfully, George refuses to sell it. I used to work in a big town, and the shops there sold it by the jugful. Over time, the treacle separates from the morphine, so the further down the barrel you get, the stronger the dose becomes. I've known one dose to kill a child; it's pretty lethal. Apart from being malnourished, is there anything else wrong with them that you know of?"

"They've been asleep all the time, even when we changed them because they were soaking wet. There are no wounds on them, but their bottoms are sore from lying in soiled nappies."

"I can give you some ointment for that. If you can leave them in a warm room with their nappies off and let the air get to their skin, that will help. What's going to happen to these babies? It will be hard work looking after them once the drugs wear off. Are they going to the workhouse because I can't see them getting the right care there?"

"That was my next question. I'm grateful to you, ladies, for what you have done, but this isn't your problem. I'm afraid I'll have to take them to the workhouse because there's nowhere else. Unless the hospital would take them, doctor?"

"Yes, Wilfred, it would, but the hospital is struggling to cope with several cases of measles, and if any of these babies caught that, they would likely perish. Probably the workhouse is the better option, though a poor option, it may be."

Before they could further discuss the babies' future, there was another knock on the door, and Stephen ran to answer it. It was Fred and Charlotte, and she didn't wait to be invited in. Pushing past Stephen, she ran into the room and put her hand to her mouth. "Oh my God! Is one of them, Doris?"

"We don't know, Charlotte. Wilf, is it all right if Charlotte has a look to see if she thinks any of them is her daughter?"

"Yes, of course, Fred. Take your time, my dear."

"None of them seem big enough to be six months old."

"No, but they've been starved, so naturally, they're small. Think carefully: did Doris have any distinguishing marks on her body, like a mole or a birthmark?"

"No, doctor, there was nothing like that." Charlotte took each baby in turn and looked closely. She kept returning to the one Thurza had favoured. "I think this one is Doris. Her features are familiar, and her hair is blond like mine. I think the other two will be dark-haired. I'm pretty sure she's Doris; may I keep her?"

"Well, she needs looking after at the moment, and if you're willing to do that, then I'm grateful. However, I have to make more enquiries about all this and search the house to see if there is any evidence of who these babies belong to. If we find this baby girl belongs to someone else, we would have to give her back if they wanted her, and I don't want to upset you further, ma'am. Maybe you shouldn't become attached to her until we know."

"Wilf's right, Charlotte. It would be best to leave this to someone else until we know for sure. I couldn't bear for you to give her up a second time."

"I understand what you're saying, Fred, but I'm convinced this is Doris. Anyway, if there is evidence to the contrary, I will hand her back, I promise, but I want to care for this child. If she goes to the workhouse, she may not live long enough to go anywhere. I'd rather look after her, even if I do have to give her back."

"Very well, as long as you understand the situation. So that leaves the other three. If you ladies can wrap them up, I'll take them to the workhouse when I leave."

Eveline and Fred exchanged glances, and he gave an almost imperceptible nod. Eveline then looked at Sabina for confirmation of what she was thinking.

"It's all right, Wilf; we'll look after them, at least until you find out whom they belong to. Eveline, if you can take one, I'll look after the other two because I have Liza to help me, and no doubt when Annie hears about all this, she'll help too."

"That's kind of you, ladies, and I'm sure these babies will stand a much better chance of survival in your tender care. Now, I was just going to tell you what will happen next. The two women are locked up in the Barnstaple jail, where I suspect they will be in for a hard time when the other women find out what they're in for. Few women like to hear of babies being mistreated."

"What about Thurza? Is she locked up with her mother? She's frightened of her, and I don't think Thurza understood what was going on; she's simple-minded."

"I'm afraid she's in with her mother at the moment, Sabina, because there's nowhere else for her to go, and they'll need to stick together in there. Tomorrow, I'll take two officers with me, and we'll search the house for any information about the babies, and we'll also dig in the woods to see if there are any further bodies. What about the dog, Fred? Did you shoot it?"

"Yes, luckily, it was still too groggy from the laudanum to attack me, and I shot it before it knew what was happening, so it didn't suffer."

"We'll bury it when we go there tomorrow, then. Thanks for doing that; not a pleasant task. Now, I'll leave you good people, and I'll be in touch soon. Are you coming, doctor?"

"Yes, there's no more I can do here, and the babies are in safe hands. Here's a small bottle of morphine for each of you ladies. If the babies are fretful when they wake up, just put a couple of drops in their bottle, and that should help. It's difficult to know what dose to give them because we don't know what they've been having, and we mustn't overdose them. I'll visit each of you in the morning to see how things are. I bid you all goodnight."

CHAPTER 47

A few days later, Charlie went to see Sam. When they found the babies at the house, there was no time to tell him all that had happened, and Charlie thought he deserved to know. Sam had been involved in the investigations concerning the babies, and no doubt, he would be delighted to hear that the woman and her daughter were safely locked up and could do him no further harm. However, Sam was better informed than Charlie, for he had been speaking to the police.

"They called here and asked me a few questions, and I showed them where that baby was buried. A nasty business, all of it. They told me the pair of them were locked up in jail. I should think they'll hang. I hope so, anyway."

"I'm not sure the daughter deserves that, Sam; she was scared to death of her mother."

"I'm not surprised; I was too. She was a great bully and built more like a man than a woman. Did you know they found two more bodies?"

"No, I didn't. Oh, that's awful, but I'm not surprised. It looked like there had been more digging. When they've finished investigating, Wilfred will tell us what's happening."

"How are the babies that you found? Will they live?"

"We think so, though it's touch and go with one little girl. The one Charlotte is looking after, the one she thinks is Doris, is thriving. She was better looked after than the others because Thurza had taken a liking to her, and I think she got most of whatever milk was available. Eveline is looking after another little girl, and Sabina, Annie's mother, is looking after two of them, a boy and a girl. It's that baby girl who's struggling, but if anyone can nurse her back to health, it will be Sabina. Mind you, those women have their work cut out. Now the drugs are wearing off, those babies are crying night and day. Doctor Luckett keeps raising the dose of morphine, but he has to be careful in case he overdoses them. I think it will take a long time for them to recover completely if they ever do. Anyway, I'm not just here about that; Fred and I wondered if you'd like to come to our weddings? You know, Fred and Charlotte, and me and Eveline are all getting married? It's on Saturday, and we'd like you to come. The reception is at the Manor House, thanks to Annie and Master Robert."

"Eh, lad, I wouldn't know how to behave at a do like that, and what would I wear? They won't want a smelly old tramp like me going to the Manor House. Whatever next. I'm tickled to have been asked, though, and no mistake."

"If you'd like to come, you can have a bath at my house, and we can find you some tidy clothes. You'd be all right, Sam. I can make sure I get you a seat near someone you can talk to. You deserve a treat for helping us to rescue those babies."

"You're so kind, Charlie, but surely you don't want me there?"

"Yes, I do, Sam, and so do Eveline and Fred. If you want to come, you can ride home with me in the cart now. What do you say?"

"How many days is it until Saturday?"

"Today is Thursday, so it's the day after tomorrow. If you come back with me today, you can have a good scrub tomorrow, and I'll sort you out some clothes to wear. Alfred has some he can't get into anymore, and he won't throw them away, but I think they'd fit you."

"But where would I stay until Saturday? I can't walk back here to my hut; it's too far for me these days."

"I've been thinking about that. There's a loft above the old stables we don't use nowadays. In the past, one of the grooms used to live there, and it's quite pleasant. It's cosy and warm all year round above the animals, too. You can stay there if you like. In fact, if you want to do a few odd jobs around the farm, you can stay there as long as you like. We couldn't pay you, but we could feed you. Would you like to live there, or would you prefer to be on the road? I know some people do."

"I've been on the road all my life, so I don't know anything else, but it's becoming more of a struggle the older I get. Are you sure, Charlie? I don't want to be a nuisance, and I can't remember the last time someone wanted me anywhere. Usually, they can't drive me away fast enough."

"I've talked to Alfred, Jimmy, and Eveline, and they're all happy for you to live there. As I say, we can't run to another wage, but we could find you enough food, or you can still catch fish and rabbits."

Well, 'tis kind of you. Yes, all right then, I'd like to give it a try. I can always come back here if I don't like it, can't I? What about all my stuff that's here, though?"

"We can take most of it on the cart today; that's why I brought it. If you bring what you need the most, we can always come back another time if you decide to stay. It's pretty deserted here, so I doubt anything will get stolen."

Sam hadn't much in the way of possessions, and it didn't take Charlie long to load what he needed onto the cart. As they travelled back to the village, Sam occasionally burst out laughing.

"What are you laughing at, Sam?"

"I'm that tickled to think I'm going to the Manor House. I wish my old mum were still here; she'd surely pee her pants laughing."

When they reached the farm, Charlie took Sam up into the loft. "What do you think, Sam? Could you be comfortable here?"

"My goodness, yes. Look, there's a bed and even a table and chair. What more could I want?"

"I'll fetch your bits and pieces, and then I'll get you something for your supper, and tomorrow you can have a bath."

The next day, Charlie put the old tin bath in front of the kitchen stove and helped Maria fill it with hot water. He told her she could have a few hours off to go into Hartford.

"I don't suppose he's got anything I haven't seen before, Charlie. I've had to clean up Grandad times enough since he lost his hands."

"Yes, I suppose you have, Maria, but Sam may not see it like that. I think putting his body in water is going to be quite a shock, let alone having a young girl like you watching. You make the most of it and enjoy a few hours off." She went off laughing as he went to fetch the old man.

"Come on, Sam, take your clothes off and get in. I've put some old clothes there you can wear for today, and then some better ones for the wedding tomorrow. There's no one around. I've sent Maria to the village, and Alfred and Jimmy are out in the fields. Do you want me to leave you to it?"

"It doesn't matter to me, lad. I've nothing to hide."

He stripped off his clothes and gingerly lowered his thin, grimy body into the hot, soapy water, some bruises from his beating still showing. "My goodness, that feels amazing. I can't remember when I last had a bath. In fact, I'm not sure I've ever had one since I was a nipper. I used to swim in Shebworthy Pond now and then in the summer months when I was younger."

"Here you are; use this cloth with the soap and give yourself a good scrub. If I wash your hair, would you like me to cut it for you and shave you?"

"You can if you like. Do you know what you're doing, or will it be a basin on my head? That's what my mum used to do."

"I should be able to make a fairly good job of it. When I was at sea for months on end, we often used to cut each other's hair when it got too long, and the weather was hot."

Charlie snipped away at the thick grey hair and then at the long and matted beard before he fetched a cut-throat razor to finish the job. "Now, keep still, Sam; I don't want to nick you."

When they were both satisfied that he was clean, he stepped out of the bathtub carefully and dried himself on the rough towel Maria had left for him.

"You get dressed in those clothes, Sam, and I'll get rid of this bathwater. Good heavens, the water's filthy. I'll have to clean the bath afterwards, or Maria will grumble. Leave your dirty clothes there, and I'll get Maria to wash them."

"I'm sorry about the dirt, Charlie, but you did insist on bringing me here. Do you have any scissors that I could use to cut my toenails? They've been troubling me for a long time, and now they're soft, they should cut easily."

"Yes, here you are."

Charlie busied himself emptying and cleaning the bath, then took it out to the washhouse and hung it on a nail on the wall. He entered the kitchen just as Sam was tucking his clean shirt into his trousers and pulling on a coat.

"Good Lord, Sam, no one will know you. Come with me. There's a mirror in Alfred's bedroom."

The two men climbed the stairs, and Sam surveyed himself in the mirror. "Will you look at that? I've never seen myself in a full-length mirror; I look quite respectable, don't I?"

"You certainly do, Sam. Now, don't get dirty until after the wedding. There are a few other people who will want to bathe before then, including me."

CHAPTER 48

Fred and Charlie fidgeted as they waited nervously at the altar in Hartford Church. Fred's brother, George, was his best man, and Jimmy was Charlie's.

"I hope they're coming; they're late."

"Of course, they're coming, Charlie; brides are always late. It's what they do."

"I didn't think Eveline would put me through this, I ..."

Before he could finish his sentence, the organ started to play the wedding march, and both men rose to their feet and looked down the aisle. With broad smiles on their faces, Charlotte and Eveline stood one on each side of Ned, who proudly escorted them up the aisle to give them away.

Eveline wore a full-length white dress with a long train and embroidered bodice. An intricate lace veil, one of Charlie's many spoils from France, hung over her face, and she carried some late pink roses from the Manor House greenhouses. Charlotte's dress was cream, again full-length, but much plainer, though it suited her slight figure. She, too, had a veil over her face and carried a bouquet identical to Eveline's. There were no bridesmaids. They had decided there were so many girls in the family it was easier to have none. That being the case, they handed their bouquets to Betsey as they reached their future husbands. Both brides lifted the veils from their faces, and the Reverend Rees began the service.

Everything went without a hitch, and before long, the happy couples were seated in a carriage to take them to the Manor House. As was traditional, they waited in the hallway of the West Wing to welcome each guest.

First in the queue were Annie and Robert with William's children, Joe, Matthew, and Amelia; Fred's children, Llewellyn, Rosella, and Eddie; and Selina. Sabina and Liza followed with the Carter children, Willie, Mary, Edward, Stephen, Helen, and Danny. Robert whispered to Annie. "Goodness, Annie, you have a lot of children in your family."

"There's more yet. Here comes Uncle George and his lot."

Annie's Uncle George shook Fred's hand, then Charlie's, and lightly kissed the hands of his sister, Eveline, and Charlotte. As he bent over Eveline's hand, she whispered to him. "George, be nice to everyone today." She looked into his eyes. "Please, no preaching."

"Don't worry, I'm on my best behaviour. I won't show you up. You look amazing, Evie; I'm so pleased for you."

Charlotte had not invited any of her family, for they had not supported her in her hour of need. She would have liked her mother there, but that would have meant asking her father, and she felt she was better off without him and his opinions. However, there were plenty of relatives on Charlie's side, for he was one of ten children. Having been at sea for years, even Charlie had not met some of his nieces and nephews, and he had to rely on Alfred to make the introductions.

Strictly speaking, the wedding had nothing to do with Robert's family. However, he had asked Sarah and Aunty Margery, now firm friends of Annie. He had decided against asking his sister, Victoria, as it would have meant her travelling from London with two young babies, and Annie preferred not to see her husband, Frank, if it could be avoided.

Most of the furniture had been removed from the dining room to make way for several long tables to accommodate all the guests. The great hall in the main house would have been far more suitable for so many people, but Robert knew his mother would be horrified at the thought of people from the village being entertained in her house, so they had decided to make do with what they had. It just wasn't worth the upset.

Together, Annie and Eveline had worked out a seating plan, for they knew it was important for people to sit where they felt comfortable. Families sat together, of course, but they weren't sure where to seat Aunty Margery and Sarah, or for that matter, Sam.

They giggled together as they considered the options. "It's difficult, isn't it? I mean, how many weddings have a titled lady and a tramp to accommodate."

"It would be funny to sit Sam on George's table, don't you think? He's convinced Sam stole those boots from his shop, and he'll never forgive him."

"No, I don't think we'd better do that. Anyway, George is the best man for Fred, so he'll be sitting at the top table. So will Jimmy, Ned, Betsey, and your mother. What about if we sit Sam with Liza and the children? Liza won't mind, and she'll keep an eye on him."

When it was Sam's turn to shake hands with the newly married couples, Fred looked at him in amazement. "My goodness, Sam, I didn't recognise you. What has Charlie done to you?"

In truth, Fred had not been sure who the guest was until he smiled his toothy grin, which gave the game away. There was not much Charlie could do about that.

"I know, I've not been so clean for many a year or had such fine clothes. What kind people you all are. I can't believe I'm here at the Manor House for my dinner; I never thought this would happen. I keep thinking I must be dreaming. Thank you so much."

"It's you we have to thank, Sam. You helped a lot in saving those babies."

Charlotte shook his hand warmly. "Yes, thank you so much, Sam. I'm pleased to meet you at last; I've heard a lot about you." She winked at him and whispered in his ear. "I know what it's like to be hungry and have nowhere to go, so enjoy yourself and eat as much as you can; you deserve it."

Eventually, all the guests were welcomed and shown to their designated seats. Annie and Eveline had decided against displaying the seating plan, for many present could not read and write. Instead, the footmen escorted people to their seats, just as they had for Annie's wedding. Aunty Margery and Sarah sat with Annie and Robert, a fair distance from Sam, although he now looked respectable. Selina, William's children, and Fred's children also sat with Annie, and she just hoped they would behave.

Maisie had been nervous about catering for such a large party, and this was her first big test since being promoted to cook. However, she still had Ethel Potts in the background to advise her, and all went well. The meal started with chicken soup or salmon, followed by roast pork and all the trimmings. A whole pig had been turning on a spit in the kitchen for hours and was incredibly tasty and tender. There were several desserts to choose from, followed by cheese and biscuits.

During the meal, Annie told Aunty Margery and Sarah about the babies they had found in Buzzacott House, and they were horrified.

Aunty Margery nodded her head. "I've heard about this before. When I was younger, I lived in London and was involved in charity work, though my husband disapproved. These women take in children, either to foster in the short term until the mother can have them back or, in some cases, to arrange a full adoption. Mind you, most do their best for the children, and doctors are often involved. Unfortunately, you always get a few who are only in it for the money, and they don't care what happens to the children. It's so sad. Where are the babies today?"

"A lady in the village, Matilda Rudd, is looking after them so that all the family can come to the wedding. Matilda is an old lady now, but she still delivers many of the babies in the village. We know they will be safe with her."

"How are they doing? Are they all expected to live?"

"Yes, it was touch and go, especially with one little girl, but it's been a couple of weeks now, so Doctor Luckett is hopeful they will all pull through. They're taking a little milk and often, but the most difficult thing is weaning them off the morphine. Without it, they cry all the time. We're reducing it gradually, but it will take a long time, and it's hard work looking after them."

"What will happen to them?"

"We're not sure yet; we're waiting for the police to tell us if they've traced any of the parents. My mother is looking after a boy and a girl, and my Aunty Eveline, another little girl. If they have to give them back, it won't be too bad, but we're hoping and praying that the baby Charlotte is looking after is her daughter, Doris. If she has to give that child back, it will break her heart. It would be like losing her all over again."

Once the meal was over, the guests left the dining room to allow the servants to remove the tables and make room for dancing later. The guests circulated, and Sabina was able to sit with Arthur Webber and his father, Peter. She was glad Peter had agreed to come but had been concerned about how he would manage to eat the meal. She wondered if he was confident enough to eat in public with the newly made attachments to his arms. However, she needn't have worried because he coped admirably, having opted for salmon instead of soup, which would have been more difficult.

Under the table, Arthur took her hand and squeezed it. "There's no denying both brides look beautiful today, but not as beautiful as you."

"Ssh Arthur, someone will hear you."

"It doesn't matter if they do. We're both unmarried, so why shouldn't we be courting?"

"Is that what we're doing then, courting?"

"I would have thought that was obvious by now."

"I can't stay too long today. Matilda's looking after all four babies, and they're hard work. It's kind of her to do it, and I don't want to leave her alone for too long."

"She'll be all right for a while, and I know she'd want you to stay and have a few dances with me. You will, won't you?"

"Yes, just a few."

Looking up, Sabina was surprised to see Robert's Aunty Margery at her side.

"Hello, I don't think we've met, but I'm Robert's Aunty Margery, and I believe you are Annie's mother, Sabina, aren't you?"

"Yes, ma'am, I am; it's a pleasure to meet you."

Sabina got up to curtsey, but the old lady pushed her back down. "No need for any of that. I don't stand on ceremony. I've always been the black sheep of the family, but now I am old, and I can do what I like. I wanted to congratulate you on your lovely daughter. I know Charles and Eleanor disapprove of her, but I can see she makes Robert happy. Now, these must be Annie's brothers and sisters; will you introduce me, please? I'll know whom she is talking about then. We've become firm friends, and it's always good to put a face to a name."

Sabina introduced all of her children, staring intently at each one as if trying to communicate by telepathy, the necessity to be polite. She needn't have worried, for the children had seen that look before, and anyway, they wouldn't upset Robert for anything.

"Sabina, could you tell me who that gentleman is? The one who is sitting with the older lady. Is he her husband?"

"Oh no, ma'am, that's Liza. She's a widow, and she lives with me and the family at the Lodge House. The man she is with is Sam. He's an old tramp who's lived rough in the village for as long as I can remember. The reason he's here is that he was camping near Buzzacott House, and he helped Fred and Charlie when they were curious about what was going on there. Charlie's letting him live at Hollyford Farm now, in a loft above the stables. I'm pleased for him because he's getting on a bit now. I don't know his story, but he always seems like a nice man. I've never seen him so clean, though. Why do you ask?"

"Oh, no reason, but he looks familiar. I guess I must have seen him in the village over the years. And who do we have here, then? More relatives?"

"No, this is my friend, Arthur Webber; he works here on the estate, and this is his father, Peter."

"I'm pleased to meet you, Arthur. What do you do on the estate?"

"I'm a farm labourer, ma'am."

"A very worthwhile job; do you enjoy it?"

"Yes, I can't grumble, thank you."

Lady Margery turned her attention to Peter Webber. "Now, I've heard everything about you from Annie, Mr Webber, and I'm impressed at how well you manage your disability. Some men would have given up; you should be proud of yourself."

"Why, thank you, ma'am. It's all thanks to Sabina. She got people to make me this harness, and now I can use all sorts of implements. I've got a knife, fork, and spoon that I can use, and even a paintbrush. Sabina's brother, Fred, made me an easel, and I pass the time painting. I'm not very good, but I'm improving."

"That is interesting, Peter. May I call you Peter?" He nodded. "Well, Peter, I like painting too, so perhaps I could see your paintings sometime."

"Why yes, ma'am, of course; it would be a pleasure. There is one hanging in the hallway here. Annie insisted on buying it, though I don't think it was worth anything like what she paid me. She was being kind, I think."

"In that case, would you take me to see it, Peter?"

"Yes, of course, ma'am. If you follow me, I'll take you to it."

As Peter and Margery walked out to the hallway, Arthur and Sabina looked at each other in surprise. "I didn't see that coming. What a dear old lady; not a bit snobbish, is she? Do you think she fancies my dad?"

"Behave yourself, Arthur Webber. Now, the band is starting up, so will you give me that dance you promised?"

CHAPTER 49

The time following the wedding was a busy one for Annie. The newlyweds could not afford a honeymoon, but to let them have some time to themselves, she had offered to have William and Fred's children stay at the Manor House for a week. She was delighted when Selina agreed to come too, and the little girl seemed happier in the house with the company of the other children. Finally, she slept in the bedroom Annie had lovingly prepared for her, albeit shared with Amelia and Rosella. The twins, Joe and Matthew, and Llewie and Eddie, all shared another room. Annie had arranged for the children to have lessons with Sarah's governess, Jane Leworthy, instead of attending the local school. The children found this a novelty, and Jane was delighted to have her classroom full of children for a change. Sarah moved from pupil to deputy teacher for the week and enjoyed her new role.

Annie was also looking after Charlotte's baby, Doris, and the little girl that Eveline had been caring for. Eveline had named her Martha, though she was trying not to become too attached to her in case she had to hand her back. Annie enlisted Molly's help for the week, particularly with the babies, who took up far more of her time than anticipated.

She was surprised one morning when Ethan came to ask if she would receive Aunty Margery. "This is a surprise, Aunty Margery; how nice you have come to see us. I'll call for some tea."

"That would be most welcome, my dear. I hope you don't mind me turning up unannounced?"

"No, of course not; you're welcome here any time. Mind you, I am busy this week because I'm looking after Selina and all of Uncle Fred and Uncle William's children, as well as two of the rescued babies. The children are no trouble at all. They're content playing in the gardens and with all the toys in the nursery. What with that, and enjoying Mrs Potts' cooking, they have no reason to be naughty. It's the babies that are taking up Molly's and my time, and she still has to help in the kitchen quite a lot of the time."

"That's why I'm here. Robert mentioned that you were looking after all these children, and I wondered if I could help. I'm only sitting at home with nothing to do, and I've always loved children, though I was never blessed with any of my own. Would you like me to stay and help for a few days? You'd be doing me a favour because I get bored at home with too much time to myself."

"Yes, of course; you're more than welcome to stay. You don't have to help with the babies, though."

"I'd like to. There is one other thing I want to do while I'm here, though. I want to see Peter Webber, that man who paints. He showed me the painting in your hallway, and I like it. It's a seascape, and he's caught the light amazingly well. I like to paint too, but I've never produced anything as fine as that, and I'd like his advice. I want to ask him to paint me a picture. It's remarkable how he can paint as well as he does when he has no hands. He's an inspiration to us all, and I'd like to help him sell more of his paintings. I suspect your mother, Sabina, is rather fond of his son, Arthur."

"She's not admitting it, but yes, I think you're right. I'd like to see her settle down with Arthur. It's several years since she lost my dad, and she's still a young woman. I'll ask Molly to keep an eye on the children this afternoon, and we could take the babies for a walk to the Webber's house. Would that be too far for you to walk? It's only in the village near the church. The fresh air might make the babies sleep better tonight, too."

"Fine, I'll get my servant to bring my luggage in then. I brought a few changes of clothes, just in case you were happy for me to stay. Where is Robert this morning?"

"Oh, he's out and about with Jack Bater, our farm manager. Robert loves looking after the estate; he was born to do it, and he's made lots of improvements. He's thinking of introducing shooting parties here next year. He says they bring in a lot of money, so he and Jack are discussing breeding pheasants."

"On my estate, we have shooting parties, and I understand they're lucrative, though I leave it all to my manager, I'm afraid. You need to ensure the money is coming in these days because estates like this seem to get ever more expensive to run."

Margery stayed the whole week, and Annie enjoyed her company and help. However, she had to admit that she would not be sorry to hand the children and the babies back to Eveline and Charlotte. Charlotte had moved to Fred's house and Eveline to Hollyford Farm, and both women appreciated the time to make a few changes to their new homes. Annie asked Selina if she would like to stay at the Manor House, but she wanted to go home with the other children. "I like it here with you, Mummy, but I don't have anybody to play with. Can you come and live with Granny again? That would be best."

Annie explained that would not be possible now that she was married to Robert, but Selina did agree to come and stay for a couple of nights again soon, so Annie felt that at least she was making progress.

A few days after all the families had returned to their respective households, Wilfred Folland visited Sabina.

"Now that our investigations at Buzzacott House are complete, I have some news, and it would be easier to tell everyone all together."

She agreed to invite everyone involved to the Lodge House, and so Annie, Fred, Charlotte, Charlie and Eveline all waited in Sabina's parlour for the constable to arrive. Charlotte was anxious, for she feared losing the baby for the second time. Fred held her hand and tried to comfort her, though he, too, was nervous. Eventually, they heard a knock on the door, and Annie answered it and showed Wilfred in.

"Hello, everyone. Thanks for organising this, Sabina; it's so much easier to see you all together. I have a lot to tell you. Following the discovery of the babies at Buzzacott House, I went there with my colleagues, and sadly, we recovered another two bodies of young infants buried close to where you found the first child. I suspect they were not buried in the garden because the dog would have dug them up. Incidentally, we buried the dog in the same hole, so thanks for dealing with that, Fred. We searched the house from top to bottom for any records that might help us to identify the babies, both dead and alive, but we found nothing. However, we sent a photograph of Lizzie and Thurza Dymond to police stations throughout the country, and they were recognised in several areas. It seems they've been doing this for years and kept moving on to avoid getting caught. We also put their photographs in the newspapers to see if any mothers recognised them, and two have come forward."

Charlotte gasped, and Fred held her hand tighter and put his other arm around her. Wilfred picked up on her anxiety.

"You'll be pleased to know, Mrs Carter, that the little girl you're looking after is indeed your daughter, and so you can keep her."

"Oh, thank God!" Charlotte burst into tears of relief, and Fred held her tight.

"The two mothers who have come forward gave up a boy and a girl to be looked after but wanted them back at a later date. They didn't want them fully adopted. Lizzie Dymond met both of them at the railway station and assured them she would write as soon as she had moved to her new address. Of course, she never intended to do so, and they never heard anymore. This seems to be how she got her money. The mothers paid her to take their babies, and she just let them die rather than spend time and money looking after them."

"Do you know which ones are their babies?"

"It's going to be difficult to know. We'll have to bring the mothers here to see the babies and establish whether they can identify them. The two bodies we found were both of little girls, so it's likely the boy does belong to the mother who has come forward. They both want them back."

"What about Lizzie? Has she told you anything?"

"Yes, she's been cooperating because she wants to avoid the death penalty, though I don't think she will. She admitted that the baby Thurza had taken a liking to is yours, Mrs Carter, but she didn't want to upset her daughter by making her part with it. She said when she first started this business, she cared for the babies properly and found new parents for those destined for full adoption. However, as she became older, it got too much trouble, and she realised there was an easier way to make money. She admitted she's been drugging the babies to keep them quiet and need little care. It seems she couldn't quite bring herself to kill the infants, but she had no problem in letting them slowly starve to death."

"Where is she now? Is she still in Barnstaple jail, and what about Thurza?"

"Lizzie has been sent to Exeter jail and will stand trial for murder after Christmas. I think it is more than likely she'll hang, and rightly so. There was another famous case back in 1870; you may remember it. It was in all the papers. A woman called Margaret Walters was hanged. She was known as the Brixton Baby Farmer. That's what they call these women: baby farmers. As for Thurza, I'm not sure if it might not be better for her if she hanged too, but she's been sent to an asylum because it's clear she has mental problems."

"She'd be better off hanged, I can assure you."

"It's not for us to say, Fred. Now, can I arrange for the mothers to come and see the babies, please? It seems more than likely that the baby boy does belong to the mother who has come forward, and the other mother says her daughter had a crooked little finger. She says she was born like it. Do either of the female babies you're looking after have a deformed finger?"

"Yes, the little girl I'm looking after has a crooked finger, and I'm also looking after the boy, so you'd better tell the mothers to come here."

"I'm so sorry, Sabina. Did you want to keep them?"

"No, it's all right, Eveline. I've become fond of them, but I've had nine of my own and watched three die. Mabel was a newborn baby, and then John and Emma were young children. I can do without further heartbreak and worry because although they're beginning to thrive, I don't think these babies are out of the woods yet. These two have been hard work, or maybe it's because I'm getting older. Do you want to keep Martha?"

"Oh, yes, I've never had any children of my own, and I'm too old now. I love William's three, but none were babies when I started looking after them. Is it all right if I keep the baby, Wilfred? It's what Charlie and I have been hoping for."

"Yes, we've finished our enquiries, and I'm grateful to you ladies for looking after them; it's thanks to your efforts they've survived. I didn't think they would. Sabina, I'll let you know when the babies' mothers can come, but it should be in the next day or two. Now, thank you all for your time, and I'll bid you good day."

CHAPTER 50

Within weeks of her marriage, Annie found she was vomiting every morning, and, remembering how she had been when expecting Selina, she knew the cause. For the first few days, Robert was concerned about her, but when she always felt better during the day, particularly when she ate, Annie assured him that she was not ill but pregnant. They were both delighted but decided to keep it to themselves for the time being. She was getting used to living at the Manor House now and was more comfortable since her previous workmates had joined the staff in the West Wing. She knew they had only her best interests at heart and felt she was amongst friends. Sarah and Aunty Margery had become regular visitors, and Annie was fond of them. Both ladies were helping Annie pick up tips about behaving and feeling like a lady. They didn't criticise her when she got something wrong but told her how it should be done, and she was grateful to them.

Each week, she entertained Sabina, Betsey, and Matilda and enjoyed ringing the bell and ordering tea and cakes. They all laughed together about how their station in life had changed. The two babies Sabina had cared for had been reunited with their grateful mothers. She missed them, but not the sleepless nights, and was glad she now had time to spend with her eldest daughter. Charlotte's daughter, Doris, was now seven months old. She was still small for her age and not yet sitting independently, but she was growing stronger every day. For the first few weeks, it was difficult to get any response from her at all, but she was beginning to come out of her shell and show her personality. The first time Charlotte heard her chuckle, she thought her heart would burst with happiness and began to believe that the little girl would eventually recover from her awful ordeal. Martha, the child that Eveline and Charlie had adopted, was also improving. It was not known how old she was, for she was so weak and emaciated when they found her that even Doctor Luckett was unable to say with any certainty. He thought she was probably about five months old, and like Doris, there was no response from her for several weeks. However, she was growing stronger, and recently, they had managed to get one or two smiles from her, which was heartening. Both babies were nearly weaned off the morphine, needing only a drop or two in their bottles at night to soothe them.

Annie had recently asked Aunty Margery to join the ladies for their weekly get-together, and despite their different backgrounds, the five women got on extraordinarily well. The visits had done Matilda a world of good, for since losing her husband, Ben, and son, Harry, she had found it difficult to take any interest in life. Knowing that Selina was not her granddaughter made her all the more grateful that Annie was keeping her in her life.

Aunty Margery visited Peter Webber regularly. They enjoyed each other's company and loved to discuss his paintings. He gave Margery advice on how she could improve her techniques, and she commissioned him to paint a seascape for her. The painting now hung in her drawing room and was her pride and joy. She insisted on paying him, and he was astounded at how much she gave him. He protested that he was happy to give her the painting because he enjoyed her company, but she would have none of it. Each time she entertained guests at her mansion, the picture was admired, and Peter now had commissions for three more. Sabina also still visited Peter and was thrilled at how his painting career had taken off.

"It's all thanks to you, Sabina. When I think about what my life was like before you came to see me that day and how it is now, I can't believe the change. I'm truly a different man. I used to dread waking up to another boring day, but now I'm so busy the hours fly by. I can never thank you enough."

With Christmas not far away, Annie asked Robert if she could invite the whole family for lunch on Christmas Day.

"Yes, I'd like that. Who are you thinking of inviting?"

Annie put her arms around him from behind his chair and kissed his neck. "That's the thing. Do you mind how many people I invite?"

"Oh dear, I know when you're trying to get around me for something. How many are you thinking of?"

"I want to invite all the family, but I've counted them, and it would be forty-three people. Would that be all right?"

"Goodness me. How do you get to that number?"

"Well, we're so happy now, and I want to share it with everyone. I've never got on with my Uncle George, but even he seems to be improving, and I was so glad to hear that he doesn't sell that awful Godfrey's Cordial in his shop. Perhaps he's not too bad, so I'd like to ask him, Mary Ann, and the two babies, as well as my cousins Theresa, Francis, and Harriet. I've always got on all right with them. Then, if no one objects, I think it's time to include Sarah and Bentley. It's time everyone put the past behind them, and this could be just the occasion to make it happen."

"I've no problem with any of it, but just make sure Sabina and Betsey don't mind. Who else?"

"Uncle Fred and Charlotte, Charlie and Aunty Evie, and all their children. Then there's Mum, Liza, and my brothers and sisters. I thought we could ask Charlie's brother, Alfred Chugg, his nephew, Jimmy, and Sam. Do you know, I don't even know his surname?"

"Is that it?"

"No, not quite. They aren't family, but I'd like to ask Matilda, Francis, and Jacob Rudd. For a long time, they all thought Selina was Harry's child, and they still treat her like she is. Do you know what your parents will do for Christmas?"

"I've not seen much of them, but I know father's not been well. They don't socialise much anymore or travel. Why? You're not thinking of asking them, are you? They won't come."

"No, I don't want them here, but I'd like to ask Aunty Margery and Sarah. I don't want to make things any more difficult than they already are, though."

"I would imagine that if Mama and Papa can't travel to London, then perhaps Victoria and Frank will come here with the children. We could ask Aunty Margery and Sarah and leave them to decide if they want to come. I think I know where they would rather be. Seating all those people for a Christmas dinner will be a challenge, but we managed it for the wedding, so it should be all right. I'll leave you to break the news to Maisie and Mrs Potts, though."

"Yes, it will be a lot of work for them, and I'd be willing to help." She held up her hands to stop Robert from protesting. "I know, I know, I can't do that, now I'm the lady of the house, but perhaps we could get in a few extra people to help, and we must make it up to them somehow. They serve us well."

"Of course, they do; they all adore you, and so do I; now come here and kiss me, now that you've wound me around your little finger yet again."

"I thought it would be an ideal time to announce our news. Doctor Luckett says everything is fine, and the baby will be born towards the end of June. Oh, sorry, there are two more people we need to ask."

"Who now?"

"Arthur and Peter Webber. Arthur and Mum are spending a lot of time together, and I think your Aunty Margery has fallen for Peter Webber."

"Never, she's far too old for all that. She must be over seventy."

"Well, maybe not romantically, but they have become fond of each other, and I know they'll enjoy spending time together."

"Very well, then. It should be a wonderful Christmas, but there is one condition."

"What's that?"

"I'm busy on the estate with Jack, and that's what I prefer to do, so I'd like to leave all the arrangements to you. Is that all right?"

"Yes, of course. I want to do it."

Annie wasted no time in making preparations for her Christmas party. Having consulted Aunty Margery and Sarah, she had some invitations printed. "It's how you should handle these things, my dear, and it's all a learning curve for you. One day, and before too long, no doubt, you'll be entertaining the gentry, and you must know how to do things properly." Annie couldn't see that happening any time soon, for she and Robert had not received one invitation anywhere the entire time they had been married. However, this did not trouble either of them. Once the invitations were printed, she delivered them herself, and they were greeted with delight. Her Uncle George's mouth almost dropped open, but he recovered his dignity quickly.

"Why, Annie, this is so kind of you; are you sure you want us there? I've not always treated you and your family as I should." He looked sheepish. "I'm sorry; I'm a silly, stuck-up old fool sometimes, but I'm happy things have worked out so fortuitously for you and your family. Tom would be so proud of you."

"Thank you, Uncle George, and yes, I want you to be there at Christmas. There is just one thing I would ask." He looked at her quizzically. "Please be nice to William's children. I know you don't like the fact they're half Chinese, but they can't help it, and they're William's children. If you aren't nice, I think Aunty Eveline or your mother will slap you."

"Yes, fair enough, and I think you're right, they will."

"Thank you. Mrs Potts will be in to see you soon to place a big food order. I must go now because Christmas is only a few days away, and the time seems to be slipping away fast."

CHAPTER 51

Carol singing was a tradition in Hartford that went back to the olden days. Some of the melodies were unique to the village, for they had never been written down, and the next generation learnt them by listening to their elders. For several nights leading up to Christmas, the villagers would all pile onto a cart or two and travel miles to the surrounding villages, singing their carols and collecting money for the workhouse children. Quite often, they would travel and sing all night long, often not getting home until the early hours, when they would grab a couple of hours of sleep and set off for another full day's work.

Each outlying farm that they visited would supply them with refreshments. It was often bitterly cold travelling around during the wintry nights, and they were glad of a chance to warm themselves by the fire and enjoy some food and drink.

It was late on Christmas Eve when Robert and Annie heard the carol singers outside. They opened the door and listened to the crowd sing a couple of carols and then invited them in. John Cutcliffe had always been a good singer, and even the strait-laced Noeleen could not object to him being out all night singing carols for charity. However, as he passed Annie and Robert on the way into the house, they both gasped. His hair had been virtually all cut off, and one eyebrow was missing. Seeing their surprise, several of the villagers started to laugh.

"What's happened to John?"

"Ssh, he doesn't know." Sam Symons tried to keep a straight face. "I don't know what Noeleen will say when she sees him."

"How does he not know?"

"We've been out singing since late afternoon, and, of course, everywhere we go, we get given a drink of something. He's had one too many, and he fell asleep at the last place. A couple of the lads gave him a haircut and shaved off one eyebrow for a lark. I don't know how he slept through it, the way everyone was laughing."

"I thought he'd given up the drink?"

"He has, but his willpower deserted him tonight, and he's had several. Of course, now he doesn't normally drink; it's had more effect than usual."

"Oh dear, I must stop him having any more. He'd better not be hungover for Christmas Day tomorrow."

"It's too late for that, ma'am; best let him enjoy himself while he can. I wouldn't like to be in his shoes when Noeleen gets her hands on him."

On Christmas morning, the West Wing looked amazing. A huge Christmas tree stood in the hall, adorned with shiny glass baubles and little candles. Boughs of mistletoe, holly, and ivy were hung around the walls, and in the dining room, the same long tables used for the wedding had been assembled and were covered with snowy white tablecloths. The crockery and cutlery, supplied by Aunty Margery, gleamed in the late winter sun, and in the centre of each table stood an ornate arrangement of blooms from the hothouses.

Robert put his arm around Annie as they both surveyed her handiwork. "It looks amazing. You have done a wonderful job, Annie. You should be proud of yourself."

"I've had a lot of help from Sarah and Aunty Margery. I don't know what I would have done without them these last few months. I wish Selina had stayed here with us last night so I could give her some presents this morning, but she didn't want to, and it's no good making her."

"It's understandable that she'd miss the other children because that's what she's always known, but she's getting better about coming here now, isn't she? She stayed the night recently, and I'm sure as she gets older, she'll want to come more. I suspect when she has a new baby brother or sister, she'll be quite keen to come here."

"Yes, I expect you're right. I hope she doesn't get jealous of the new baby. We must make a big fuss of her when it arrives."

"More than usual, you mean?"

"Oh, I know I spoil her, but I'm so glad I can. Listen, I think I can hear our guests coming. The Carters always were a noisy lot."

All the guests arrived at more or less the same time, and for a while, it was chaos in the West Wing as they were all served with tankards of ale, or a glass of wine, and some nibbles. Eventually, the gong sounded for lunch, and everyone took their seats. The meal, prepared by Maisie and Mrs Potts, was outstanding, for they had gone to a lot of trouble. With oxtail soup and freshly baked bread rolls to start, followed by a roasted goose and all the trimmings, many guests were full before pudding was even mentioned. Robert banged on the table with his spoon.

"Can I have your attention, please, everyone? I hope you've all enjoyed your meal, and I don't see how you could not have done, as it was delicious. I've asked Maisie and Mrs Potts to join us for a few minutes to thank them for their tremendous efforts. Can we hear it, please, for Maisie and Mrs Potts?"

Everyone cheered and toasted the cook and the housekeeper, who had both become red in the face and escaped as soon as they could.

"Now, you'll all be relieved to hear I'm not going to make a long speech, but I do have a couple of things to say. First, I'd like to thank Annie for organising all of this today, and I think you'll agree that she looks every inch a lady."

There were loud cheers. "Before we raise our glasses to Annie, we do have one other bit of good news to tell you, and that is we are expecting our first child in June. So, can I ask you to raise your glasses to Annie and our new baby?"

Everyone in the room rose and toasted Annie and Robert's announcement. When the noise had settled down again, Robert continued.

"Thank you. Now, I hope you all have room for a pudding because Maisie and Mrs Potts have made several. Thank you."

Arthur Webber stood up. "Would you mind if I also say a few words, sir?"

"No, of course not, Arthur. Please do."

"Thank you. Ladies and gentlemen, I don't think you will be surprised to hear that Sabina and I have become close over the last few months. She probably saved my father's life, not to mention that of two babies, and you all know what a wonderful person she is, so you don't need me to tell you. Anyway, I'm delighted to announce that she has agreed to become my wife. So, can I ask you to raise your glasses to Sabina? Thank you." Amidst loud cheers, everyone congratulated the happy couple.

When the meal was finished, the guests left the tables so they could be cleared away to make room for dancing, and this gave folk a chance to circulate and chat with each other. Sabina and Arthur were talking to Annie and Robert when Aunty Margery joined them.

"Do you mind if I join you?"

"No, of course not, Aunty Margery; did you enjoy the meal?"

"It was simply magnificent, my dear. If I weren't so fond of you both, I would offer your cook and housekeeper a big rise in salary to come and work for me."

"Oh no, please don't. I don't know what I would do without them."

"Now, there is something I must ask, for it's been troubling me since the double wedding. Who is the old man talking to Charlie and Eveline? Over there, look."

"Oh, that's Sam. I think I told you once before he used to be a tramp, but he lives at Hollyford Farm now."

"Do you think you could introduce me to him, please, Annie?"

"Yes, of course, but may I ask why?"

"I keep thinking I know him, but I can't place him, and it's plaguing me. What's his surname?"

"I'm afraid I don't know. He's always just been Sam. I'll call him over, and you can ask him."

Robert went to fetch the old man. "Sam, can I introduce you to my Aunty Margery? She seems to think she knows you."

"I'm pleased to meet you, ma'am."

"Hello, Sam. May I ask what your surname is, please? I'm sure I know you from somewhere, but I can't think where."

Sam's toothy smile grew even wider. "No, you don't know me, ma'am, but I know why you think you do. My surname is Fellwood, ma'am. In fact, I am your nephew." The shock on everyone's faces made Sam burst out laughing. "My father was your elder brother, Thomas. He was next in line to Joshua, Charles' father. As you know, there were many children in the family, and I believe you were the youngest, so there was a big age gap." Aunty Margery nodded. "Thomas fell in love with a gypsy girl called Jane when they were only teenagers, and she gave birth to a baby boy. I was that baby. Naturally, Thomas was told never to see her again, and the gypsies were forced to move on, but instead of doing as he was told, Thomas ran away with Jane and never returned. He married Jane before I was born because he wanted me to have the name Fellwood. Unfortunately, he was killed in an accident when I was only two, and my mother brought me up alone. I travelled with the gypsies for years until my mother passed away, and since then, I've fended for myself."

He reached into his pocket and drew out a gold locket. "You may remember my father from this photograph. My father gave my mother this locket, and she treasured it all her life. There's a picture of him on one side and my mother on the other. No matter how hungry I've been over the years, I've never been tempted to part with it." He passed the locket to Margery, and slowly, she nodded her head.

"My mother always told me that I was the spitting image of my father. I can't tell you what it has meant to me to eat at a table in the Manor House."

"Oh, Sam."

With tears in her eyes, Aunty Margery hugged the old man.

AUTHOR'S NOTE

I hope you enjoyed reading this book as much as I enjoyed writing it. If you believe this book is worth sharing, please consider posting a review on Amazon or Goodreads

An honest review is the highest compliment you can pay to any author and is much appreciated.

You can find me on Facebook or Twitter. If you would like to find out more about me and my books and keep up to date with new releases; please visit https://marciaclayton.co.uk/ to join my mailing list.

Thank you.

Marcia

About The Author

Marcia Clayton writes historical fiction with a sprinkling of romance and mystery in a heart-warming family saga that stretches from the Regency period through to Victorian times.

A farmer's daughter, Marcia was born in North Devon, a rural and picturesque area in the far South West of England. When she left school at sixteen, Marcia worked in a bank for several years until she married her husband, Bryan, and then stayed at home for a few years to care for her three sons, Stuart, Paul and David.

As the children grew older, Marcia enrolled on a secretarial course which led to an administrative post at the local college. There, she seized the opportunity to obtain more qualifications, including two Management Diplomas and two A levels, one in History and the other in English Language and Literature. Marcia progressed through various jobs at the college and, when working as a Transport Project Co-ordinator, was invited to 10 Downing Street to meet Tony Blair, the then Prime Minister. Marcia later worked for the local authority as the Education Transport Manager for Devon County Council and remained there for nine years until her retirement.

Now a grandmother, Marcia enjoys spending time with her family and friends. She's a keen researcher of family history, and this hobby inspired some of the characters in her books. A keen gardener, Marcia grows many of her own vegetables. She is also an avid reader and enjoys historical fiction, romance, and crime books.

Marcia has written six books in the historical family saga, "The Hartford Manor Series". You can read her free short story, "Amelia", a spin-off tale from the first book, "The Mazzard Tree". Amelia, a little orphan girl of 4, is abandoned in Victorian London with her brothers, Joseph and Matthew. To find out what happens to her, download the story here: https://marciaclayton.co.uk/amelia-free-download/ In addition to writing books, Marcia produces blogs to share with her readers in a monthly newsletter. If you would like to join Marcia's mailing list, you can subscribe here: https://marciaclayton.co.uk/

If you enjoyed *The Angel Maker* you might like to read the other books in The Hartford Manor Series:

Betsey

The prequel to the much-loved Hartford Manor Series

1820 North Devon, England

Betsey, a sadly neglected child, is shouldering responsibilities far beyond her years. As she does her best to care for her little brother, Norman, she is befriended by Gypsy Freda, an old woman whose family is camped nearby. Freda's granddaughter, Jane, is also fond of the little girl and is concerned about her.

Thomas, the second son of Lord Fellwood, happens across the gypsy camp and becomes besotted with Jane. However, Jasper Morris, the local miller, also has designs on the young gypsy, and inevitably, the two men do not see eye to eye.

Betsey is drawn into their rivalry for the attention of the beautiful young woman, and she finds herself promising to keep a dangerous secret for many years to come.

The Mazzard Tree

Book One in The Hartford Manor Series

1880 North Devon, England

Annie Carter is a farm labourer's daughter, and life is a continual struggle for survival. When her father dies of consumption, her mother, Sabina, is left with seven hungry mouths to feed and another child on the way. To save them from the workhouse or starvation, Annie steals vegetables from the Manor House garden, risking jail or transportation. Unknown to her, she is watched by Robert, the wealthy heir to the Hartford Estate, but far from turning her in, he befriends her.

Despite their different social backgrounds, Annie and Robert develop feelings they know can have no future. Harry Rudd, the village blacksmith, has long admired Annie, and when he proposes, her mother urges her to accept. She reminds Annie that as a kitchen maid, she will never be allowed to marry Robert. Harry is a good man, and Annie is fond of him. Her head knows what she should do, but will her heart listen?

Set against the harsh background of the rough, class-divided society of Victorian England, this heart-warming and captivating novel portrays a young woman who uses her determination and willpower to defy the circumstances of her birth in her search for happiness.

The Rabbit's Foot

Book Three in The Hartford Manor Series

1885 North Devon, England

Mr Edward Snell was more than a little curious when Robert Fellwood, the heir to Hartford Manor, and his elderly aunt, Lady Margery, begged an audience on a Saturday morning. However, being such valued clients, the solicitor was happy to oblige. As his clerk showed the visitors in, he was intrigued to see them followed by an old man who, though respectably dressed, had something of a vagrant about him. The crisp suit in which he was attired could not disguise his weather-beaten face or his missing teeth.

Robert introduced his Uncle Sam and explained he had come to claim his inheritance. The solicitor was old enough to remember the extensive search for Thomas Fellwood when his father, Ephraim, died in 1840. However, that was some forty-five years ago, and the young man had never been found. Yet, here was Sam, who claimed to be Thomas Fellwood's son and even more surprising was the fact that the Fellwood family appeared to have accepted him as such.

"The Rabbit's Foot" is an intriguing and compelling novel with many unexpected twists and turns. Set in the small seaside village of Hartford, it tells the tale of how an old man, who has spent his life with barely a penny to his name, suddenly finds himself rich beyond his wildest dreams. However, there is only one thing that Sam Fellwood truly wants, and that is to be reunited with his son, Marrok, whom he abandoned at the age of five. Will Sam find the happiness that has eluded him for so many lonely years?

Millie's Escape

Book Four in The Hartford Manor Series

1885 North Devon, England

It is winter in the small Devon village of Brampford Speke, and a typhoid epidemic has claimed many victims. Millie, aged fifteen, is doing her best to nurse her mother and grandmother as well as look after Jonathan, her five-year-old brother. One morning, Millie is horrified to find that her mother, Rosemary, has passed away during the night and is terrified the same fate may befall her granny, Emily.

When Emily's neighbours inform her that Sir Edgar Grantley has also perished from the deadly disease, the old woman is distraught, for the kindly gentleman has been their benefactor for many years, much to the disgust of his wife, Lilliana. Emily is well aware that Sir Edgar's generosity has long been a bone of contention between him and his spouse, and she is certain Lady Grantley will evict them from their cottage at the first opportunity.

As she racks her brain for a solution, Emily remembers her father came from Hartford, a seaside village in North Devon and had relatives there. Desperate and too weak to travel, she insists Millie and Jonathan leave home and make their way to Hartford before the embittered woman can cause trouble for them. There, she tells them, they must throw themselves on the mercy of their family and hope they will offer them a home.

With Emily promising to follow them as soon as possible, the two youngsters reluctantly set off on their fifty-mile journey on foot and in the harshest of weather conditions. Emily warns them to be cautious, for she suspects Lady Grantley may well pursue them to seek revenge for a situation that has existed between the two families for many years.

A Woman Scorned

Book Five in The Hartford Manor Series

1886 North Devon, England

Lady Lilliana Grantley has been seriously ill with typhoid, a disease that recently claimed her husband Edgar's life and that of his long-time lover, Rosemary Gibbs. Now recovering at last, the lady wastes no tears on her husband but is determined to wreak revenge on his two illegitimate children.

Embarrassed for years by his affair with Rosemary, a childhood sweetheart living nearby, she has falsely accused Sir Edgar's daughter, Millicent, of the theft of a precious brooch and wants to see her jailed or hung.

Fortunately for Millie and her little brother, Jonathan, their granny, Emily, insisted they leave home as soon as she heard of Sir Edgar's death, for she knew his widow would seek revenge. The old lady was soon proved right, and Lady Lilliana, furious the two youngsters were nowhere to be found, evicted the old woman despite the fact she, too, was dangerously ill.

After a long and hazardous journey to North Devon, Millie and Jonathan were united with some long-lost family members who made them welcome and gave them a home. However, aware that Lady Lilliana has put a price on Millie's head, they know they are not yet out of danger. Despite this, they are determined to find their granny, Emily, who seems to have disappeared.

Aided by her long-time lover, Sir Clive Robinson, Lady Lilliana is determined to find Millie and Jonnie and get them out of her life once and for all, but how far will the embittered woman go?

www.ingramcontent.com/pod-product-compliance
Lightning Source LLC
Chambersburg PA
CBHW020722310726
48979CB00004B/1021

* 9 7 8 1 8 3 8 3 2 5 9 5 4 *